N

O

A Nor

The Marvelous Orange Tree

A Novel of the Civil War

Betsy L. Howell

Rainforest
Press

Rainforest Press
P.O. Box 659
Port Townsend, WA 98368

ISBN:
13-978-0-9792716-4-9

Cover and interior design by Betsy L. Howell
Cover photograph by Betsy L. Howell

If I was only a man!
I dont know a woman here who does not groan over her
misfortune in being clothed in petticoats;
why cant we fight as well as the men?

—Sarah Morgan,
May 1862

CONTENTS

ACKNOWLEDGMENTS

This story would not have come together without the tremendous support and guidance from my partner Barbara Sjoholm. Over the ten years it has taken me to complete, she never stopped believing in the importance of the work and in bringing to light the lives of the characters we both came to know and admire. Thank you, my dear, from the bottom of my heart.

Likewise, many people read early versions of *The Marvelous Orange Tree* and generously gave of their time to do so. For their enthusiasm and helpful comments, I thank Sylvia Grisez, Carrie Phillips, Kyle Noble, Trish McKenney, Sue Olson, Kristina Wilkening, and Jeff Giambrone. My gratitude abounds for your willingness to read long drafts where ideas were still being formulated and the writing was still being polished; much thanks indeed!

Additionally, I want to thank all of the men from the 7th Wisconsin Civil War Reenacting Company, and most especially John Leyde, Gary Strombo, and Glen Allison. A woman soldier Civil War reenactor is not much more common than a real woman soldier from the period; thank you all for the warm welcome into the ranks, and for your impressive devotion to keeping history alive.

PART ONE

ONE

May 22, 1863, Vicksburg, Mississippi

"BIDDLE!"

In the instant that Robert Taylor yelled for his friend, a flying piece of shell took off the head of the man next to him. Everyone in the company dropped to the ground. The head rolled down the hill, navigating the bumps and dips of the land like any old ball. Taylor watched the gruesome site, then looked up. Private Lewis Crane's body still stood, a fountain of blood spurting from his neck, while round, red drops the size of coins splattered everyone nearby. Then a rapid series of whistling minie balls thudded into Crane, felling him instantly. Taylor covered his face, sure he would be hit as well. The Confederate soldiers above them had every advantage: fortified works at the top of a steep hill, an unobstructed view of their attackers, and all the time in the world to pick off the Northern boys on their suicide mission. There was no reason to think there wouldn't soon be many more heads bouncing into the ravine.

Yet, after some minutes, Taylor raised his head again. He still couldn't see his friend, Joseph Biddle, a big hulk of a man not easily missed unless you were enveloped in smoke and dust and dozens of other men dressed exactly alike.

"Biddle!" he yelled again, fruitlessly.

But then he saw him. Biddle was headed for the bottom of the slope, more recognizable now without the hat he'd lost sometime during the battle. He crawled in a zigzag manner like a bug that has just found itself in a fire. In the ravine they'd left only twenty minutes before, there was a labyrinth of fallen trees, tangles of newly cut sweetgums, magnolias, and cottonwoods. The Confederates had created this nightmare, adding to an already miserable chaos of thick canebrakes and deep gullies, making it virtually impossible for the Federal forces to move through. The same mess, however, would provide more cover than the open hillside.

Taylor started crawling himself. A sudden blast next to him eliminated what little hearing he'd had left. The effect was strangely comforting; he'd already heard enough screaming and crying to last a lifetime, from soldiers who would never leave this hillside, and from dying horses, their big bodies heaving and pouring out bloodied strings of intestines. When Taylor at last reached Biddle, he grabbed his friend's foot, yanking him flat onto the ground. Then he crawled on top of him, navigating toward the top of the six-foot length of Joseph Biddle. Taylor put his mouth up to Joseph's ear. Without being able to hear himself, he shouted at his friend to stop.

"Ya can't run Biddle!" he yelled. "Ya just can't!"

"I can't stay neither, Taylor," his friend shouted back.

"Yes, you can! It'll be all right, I'll be here with you!"

Corporal William Mohrmann from Company A suddenly popped up next to them. All around, men and squads had fragmented into hundreds of little groups, no longer the crisp, organized companies, regiments, and divisions they'd once been.

"You boys get back to the goddamn line!" Mohrmann shouted. "Ya can't kill anyone sitting back here in the bushes!"

The "line," however perfect it may have once been, no longer could be found with any certainty. Bodies lay all over the hillside.

Everyone seemed in charge of his own fate, and Joseph Biddle was not the only soldier heading away from the fighting. The corporal's stern words provided little incentive for Biddle to rejoin the fight, so Taylor just held onto him. They'd both lost their muskets, yet it wouldn't be difficult to find others. For Taylor's part, he was just as frightened as any man out here, but this is what they had trained for and there was some relief in being in the fight as opposed to just anticipating it. He knew he could do it and that he would do it. Death might be waiting just around the corner, but he could use his remaining minutes to take a few Confederates with him.

Eventually Taylor and Biddle moved. They found two muskets and got off a few shots before the fire from above became so severe that they dared not move. A soldier next to Taylor began digging furiously, his hands working like the paddle feet of a mole. Several feet away, Corporal Mohrmann was face up on the ground looking at the sky. By this time, only Brigadier General Thomas Ransom was standing. He urged his soldiers on even as the bullets fell thick and fast around him. A few brave souls followed his commands, but were cut down in short order. The regiment was trapped; they were not going back down to the ravine, and they weren't getting any closer to the Confederate works either. Only one end seemed possible. Strangely, Taylor felt nothing, no last thoughts, no emotions, certainly no regrets.

As he waited for the end, he suddenly noticed a few trees and bushes not completely obliterated from the effects of battle. The little copse lay just twenty feet away and must have been left standing by the Southern farmers who may have found a spring and decided the site was too wet to plow. The shot and shell from the fighting had severed some of the trees, but they still stood a few feet and would provide some protection. The Confederates must have had the same thought. Just as Taylor was about to shout to Biddle to head for the copse, the Southern soldiers poured a murderous fire into it. The stubby trees and bushes vanished in explosions of smoke and dirt. When the air finally cleared, Taylor thought he must be seeing things. Out of the mess, a white ball flew toward him. His first estimation of the thing was another shell now ricocheting his way. When he wasn't hit and it kept coming, he decided it was another head. Finally, as the thing's movement turned clearly into a scamper, he realized it was a cottontail running right at him. The little animal flew into Robert Taylor's chest, clawed around on his coat, and quickly disappeared into the opening where two buttons had popped off. When Taylor peered inside, he saw the rabbit laying perfectly still, its sharp claws pressed into his stomach like little hooks.

*

Capturing Vicksburg, Mississippi, had been the Federal Army's goal ever since Robert Taylor and Joseph Biddle had joined the 72nd Illinois Infantry, Company F. The nine hundred men of the regiment marched through snow, slept in the rain, rode the cars, navigated the swamps, and floated the Mississippi River, all in pursuit of this singular purpose. Finally, after eight months of moving farther and farther into the enemy's land, they stood at the city's back door. But what a door it was! The Federals stretched across bayous and hills in a curve that spanned more than ten miles, the boys in blue vastly outnumbering those in gray. They also had more artillery and more supplies, yet none of it seemed to matter. The thing that did matter was that Ulysses Grant's army was at the bottom of a long slope and John Pemberton's Southerners were at the top. To the west of these lines stood the fortress city.

The first attempt to dislodge the Confederates had taken place on May 19, a few days after the Federal Army finally arrived at Vicksburg. The men had been tested through five severe fights, from Port Gibson on the Mississippi to the Big Black River just east of the city, but they were still ready for another. After a mostly sleepless night, part of General Thomas Ransom's brigade had stood on a thin spine of land that provided little room to deploy and stretched out over a morass of canebrakes below. The Federal soldiers could see across the valley to the Confederate line, all a straight shot away if one was a bird. Yet, they weren't birds, and they would have to navigate the canebrakes, the slope, and finally the works themselves, all while enduring cannon and musket fire. Taylor and Biddle had stood that morning looking out at the Confederate works.

"Ain't no way we can take that," Taylor told his friend.

"I know. Expect we'll just keep 'em closed off till they give?"

"Nope. We've come this far and the boys are wanting to finish 'em off and the general's not going to disappoint them. Problem is we can't do it."

He was right. They failed that afternoon and three days later the situation wasn't any better. Taylor and Joseph Biddle and the other men of Ransom's brigade remained frozen on the hillside. A shell hit a soldier lying not ten feet from Robert Taylor. The man's body shot up several feet into the air. His musket cartridges began exploding on his belt, which caused his clothes to catch fire. Men closest to the man threw dirt at him to douse the flames. Taylor reached one hand inside his coat and felt the rabbit. *We'll probably be next, little cottontail.*

Suddenly, the order came to fall back to the ravine. Taylor and Biddle joined the wave of receding blue that was the 72nd and 95th Illinois regiments. Taylor kept one arm tight against his body to secure the rabbit; in his other he carried the musket. They had all barely taken twenty steps before the Confederate line exploded with gunfire.

*

That night, on the ridge above the ravine, Taylor couldn't sleep. Every time he closed his eyes, some terrible image from the day's events filled his mind. Every time it seemed like there might be a sliver of quiet, the Federal guns started up again. The rabbit had finally left him after he'd nudged it into a bramble patch. It hadn't wanted to go at first, but eventually jumped away with only the briefest look backward.

A new moon rose behind the regiment's camp on the Jackson Road. The air had cooled but was not cold. Snores filled the night around him from the boys who were able to sleep. The soldiers lay in the makeshift camp, twitching, coughing, and getting up to relieve themselves, much as they had all done for the past year, but with one important difference: there were now at least one hundred fewer of them. Some were missing and some had been taken to the hospital, while others remained on the far hillside, dead or near dead. Though it had done little good, Taylor had stuffed torn bits of handkerchief into his ears to block out their cries. How anyone could sleep through such sounds was beyond him.

Sometime after midnight, Joseph Biddle walked over and sat down. Taylor could hear him scratching the whiskers on his face. Taylor had never met anyone with a faster growing beard. Biddle could shave in the morning and by nightfall have shadows across his face. He was a handsome boy, with clear skin, bottomless black eyes, and thin lips. Biddle's smile though was his best asset, at once mischievous but also sincere, raised higher on one corner of his mouth and giving him the look of one who knows more than he ought. Taylor realized it had been days since he'd seen his friend smile.

During a break in the artillery fire, Biddle cleared his throat. "Thanks," he said.

"For what?"

There was a pause. "For helping me today. I ain't no coward, Taylor."

"I know you ain't."

"It's just...well..."

"Hey, it don't matter, all right? Besides, you wasn't the only one."

"Yeah." After a moment, Biddle asked, "You think we'll fight again tomorrow?"

"No." Taylor lay back on his blanket. "But I don't know for sure."

There were, in fact, no more charges. The next morning, the regiment commenced building fortifications. Company F was detailed back down into the ravine to gather lengths of cane, which would be made into fascines, great bundles of sticks. Wild grape vines hanging from the cottonwood and sweetgum trees were used along with the cane to make gabions, baskets filled with rocks and dirt. The piles of gabions and fascines grew so tall along the Federal line that soon a man could stand and be hidden from the Confederates' view. Still, whistling minie balls flew all around them all day long. Likewise, the Federal cannons never ceased their barrage. The sound seeped into a man's body, the reverberations becoming physical rather than simply auditory. In the rare moments when the noise ceased briefly, the quiet felt almost painful.

Taylor worked hard, cutting the cane and packing it and the vines back up the slope to the men putting the bundles together. As the day heated up, he discovered a small spring buried in the vegetation. The water was remarkably clear and free of the blood and bile that had saturated other parts of the hillside. As he stared at the spring, a small bird the size of a fist, with an upturned tail and a white line through its eye, landed next to him. The bird turned its head this way and that; it chirped once. Then it bent over to drink.

"You seen that cottontail, little bird?" Taylor asked it. The bird stopped drinking and shook itself, which Taylor took for a no. After the bird flew off, Taylor noticed where the long fingers of a coon had sunk into the wetness around the spring. The animals kept on with their lives even while men fought and died.

Two days later, Taylor returned to the little spring at midday and ate his dinner without enthusiasm. The bodies on the far hillside were now beginning to bloat and turn black in the intense, southern heat. A smell unlike anything anyone had ever experienced before had begun to permeate everything: clothes, food, hair. Men had taken to wrapping their mouths and noses with pieces of cloth, giving all the look of thieves but doing little good in the end. Rumors circulated that General Grant would not request a flag of truce to bury the dead and rescue the as-yet living. Upon hearing this the night before, Joseph Biddle had said the man must be a hard-hearted son-of-a-bitch to do nothing while his soldiers rotted. Robert Taylor said nothing to that. This was war; hard hearts were all that survived.

The gathering of cane and vines continued. One afternoon, Corporal Wallace Herrick told Taylor to help the others build sap rollers. Taylor found Biddle and Christmas Morgan, another private in Company F, stuffing cotton and dirt into the six-foot long bundles. The sap rollers, designed to stop bullets, were to be pushed along the ground in front of the men as they dug trenches and worked like moles, slowly moving up the slope ever closer to the Confederate works. As Taylor set to work, Christmas threw an armful of cotton into the bundle.

"'Bout time you showed up, Taylor," he said. "Where you been? Writing a letter to your girl?"

"Fuck you, Morgan. At least I ain't been back here hiding behind Biddle."

Christmas snorted. "I'm hiding behind whatever I can and I don't mind. But Biddle? He's gotten too skinny lately. I'll go with this." He picked up a large clump of cotton and held it up around his face, like St. Nicholas.

"Stop calling me "skinny," said Biddle, shoving the other man.

Taylor asked if they'd heard anything about the soldiers out on the hillside.

Christmas shrugged. "Only that Grant don't wanna look weak asking for a truce."

"That ain't right," said Biddle.

"No, but ain't too many things right with this business."

Just then, another round of cannon fire started up. Despite the cacophony, Christmas Morgan continued to talk, at least his lips were moving, and Joseph Biddle continued nodding as if he could hear him. Taylor thought this incredibly odd, but then Christmas was an odd one. His given name was Christopher, but after his birth on the same day as the Savior's, one of his six older sisters had nicknamed him "Christmas" and it had stuck. He was a pale fellow, with blond, almost white, hair and a laugh that sounded like a pig had gotten stuck in the mud. Christmas grated on Taylor's nerves at times, he talked too much and had a hot temper, but he also was good at gathering information and therefore an important person to know.

Finally, on the third day after the last charge, Confederate General John Pemberton asked for a cease-fire. Grant agreed and the truce was set for 6 p.m. Details were organized among the companies to help recover the dead. Despite volunteering for the effort, Taylor thought it the worst work he'd ever done. The bodies no longer looked human; the smell made the still-living soldiers hold their breaths so long some nearly passed out. Taylor tried to tell himself it was just another job, like collecting firewood or cleaning up the camp.

Later that evening, he sat in front of the tent he shared with Biddle. The journal he'd carried with him since joining up lay unopened on his lap. The moon was now half full. It cast shadows like big, thick worms around the camp, as well as on the far side where the Confederate campfires could be seen. The ravine itself remained in a deep darkness.

"You going to sleep, Taylor?" Biddle asked from inside the tent.

"Can't sleep."

After a few minutes, Biddle sighed and got up himself. "You writing in your journal?" he asked, even though he could plainly see Taylor had no candle lit.

"Nah, I ain't doing nothing but sitting."

"Sitting and listening to this fucking barrage."

"Yep."

"You'd think they'd stop for the night at least."

"You'd think," Taylor agreed. "At least there are a few pauses here and there."

Biddle grabbed his haversack from inside the tent. After another round of mortar went off, he placed a plug of tobacco in Taylor's hand. "Here's something to make you feel better!"

Surprised, Taylor bit off a chunk of the plug. "Thanks, old man."

"Looks like we're gonna be here awhile," said Biddle, his mouth full.

"Looks like."

TWO

BEHIND THE 72ND ILLINOIS' CAMP in Glass Bayou, there were no sinks. For one thing, the rolling hummocky ground wasn't ideal for digging long trenches. For another, there had been other priorities for work details. Consequently, everywhere one looked the woods were filled with soldiers dropping their drawers. One morning, Taylor sat drinking his coffee and watching Bean, their mess cook, fry up several pieces of salt pork. Joseph Biddle walked up complaining about the lack of privacy to do one's business.

"Ya oughta get up earlier, Biddle," Taylor said, taking a sip of coffee. "There are all kinds of places to go when it's still dark."

"I s'pose. Seems like we get up early enough already."

Taylor shrugged. "Suit yourself."

"What's for breakfast?" Biddle asked, changing the subject and pouring his own cup of coffee.

"Same thing as we have every day, private," said Bean, who called everyone "private" as if he himself were some other rank. "Why you always ask me?"

"'Cause one of these days you're gonna say we're having flapjacks and syrup and fried eggs and thick slices of ham and bread with butter and jam. Then I'm gonna be happy I asked."

"We all will be, private," said Bean, nodding, "but for now you're having tack fried in grease and sow belly. Best I can do."

Not for the first time did Taylor feel great appreciation for their cook. They might have been eating tack fried in grease and sow belly, but it was the best tack fried in grease and sow belly in camp. Bean was not your typical sort of cook. Taylor had only ever met one man taller and skinnier than Bean, and their cook's physical traits led people to believe he didn't eat, or even enjoy food much, both notions of which were quite untrue. Bean's real name was Archibald Shottenkerk, but he said he preferred a name that a person didn't have to take a second breath to speak, and when he grew two feet the year he turned twelve, "Bean" seemed a logical choice. Back in Cairo, Illinois, when the regiment was just learning how to be a regiment, Bean had volunteered to be the mess cook for the squad, a group that included Taylor, Biddle, Christmas, and a young man from Chicago by the name of Kit Johnson. In addition to having the skill to create masterpieces out of almost nothing, Bean also regularly received great care packages from his wife, a woman he claimed was not much of a cook herself but whom he loved dearly.

The breakfast was nearly over when Christmas came trotting up. "Sorry, boys," he said, taking off his hat and sitting down. "Any left for me?"

Bean grabbed the frying pan where the last two pieces of hardtack sat hardening in the grease. "Where you been?" he asked, scooping the food onto Christmas' plate.

The other man smiled beneath his rosy cheeks. "Just getting some supplies." He reached into a pocket and pulled out a large bag, setting it on the flat rock Bean used for cooking. "Help yourself," he added, his mouth full. "There's plenty more where that came from."

Kit said he'd told his mother he wouldn't drink, smoke, or curse while he was away, but neither Bean nor Biddle had made such promises. They each grabbed a plug from the bag.

Taylor looked at Christmas. "Where you get all this, Morgan? The sutler ain't got here yet."

Christmas looked as pleased as a rooster with a whole flock of hens. "From them," he said, arching a thumb backward.

"Who?"

"Them! Over there!" When Taylor still looked puzzled, Christmas set his plate down. "The Secesh, of course! They got so much tobacco, they ain't hardly know what to do with it. What they ain't got though is food. I swapped 'em hardtack for plugs." He chuckled. "'Course that ain't the best deal for them, but that's the way it goes."

"You got it from the Secesh?" Taylor repeated. "When was that exactly? As they were about to blow your fucking head off?"

Christmas laughed. "A course not! I done it during the cease-fire when everyone was doing it. All up and down the line, trading, chatting, talking 'bout the battle. Hell, I even seen a couple of Yanks and Rebs playing cards. Didn't ya notice?"

Taylor stared at him. "No, I didn't. I was too busy burying our dead, remember? The ones that sat out in the sun for three days. Didn't ya notice?"

"It wasn't the Southrons fault the boys lay out there for three days, Taylor. You can blame that on our own wonderful general." Christmas shrugged. "Anyway, them boys is just like you and me."

"They ain't nothing like me," Taylor said, his eyes as small as pins.

Christmas opened his mouth to reply, but Biddle had grabbed a plug and handed it to Taylor. "Here, take this and don't worry none about it."

Taylor pushed his friend's arm away. "I ain't taking nothing from them Southrons. You boys go on if it don't bother you none, but me, I come down here to kill the bastards, not trade trifles with them."

Kit Johnson glanced nervously around the group before standing to leave. Biddle picked up the dropped plug and put it in his pocket.

"They ain't so bad, Taylor," said Christmas. "I seen 'em and I've talked with 'em. They think they're doing right, just like we think we're doing right. You don't have to feel bad about it."

Taylor stood up too. "You have no idea what I think, Morgan, so don't tell me I shouldn't feel bad."

*

Day after day, the siege continued. The Confederates never let their muskets cool, but for the most part didn't use their artillery much. By contrast, the Federals' big guns rarely stopped. The noise was not to be believed, and yet it was the most real part of any given moment. The only slight respite came when the regiments were rotated back from the line for a day of rest.

Everyone suffered, a fact Robert Taylor could see clearly in the faces of the men around him. Yet, the toll seemed particularly hard on Kit Johnson, the young man, really just a boy, in their squad. Taylor guessed Kit was no more than 15, with a sharp nose and chin, small hands, powder-blue eyes, and a gut that protruded slightly like a baby's. Kit had been one of the last soldiers to sign on in Chicago. He'd arrived at Camp Douglas south of the city, loaded down with all the clothes and leathers he'd been issued from the quartermaster, as well as a pie his mother had given him. Taylor had watched him managing all this then winked at Biddle, whom he'd just met.

"Where's your umbrella?" he asked the boy.

"Umbrella?" Kit looked puzzled. "Do they give you an umbrella?"

"'Course they do, soldier!" smiled Taylor. "It rains a lot in the South, don't ya know? Now, get on back there and ask the quartermaster for your umbrella!"

After Kit returned red-faced and empty-handed, Taylor apologized, but it was some weeks before the boy would speak to him. Truthfully, no one thought Kit would make it. He seemed to have a knack for always doing the wrong thing. If a full pot of coffee had just been removed from the fire, Kit knocked it over; if the lid had been removed from a stewpot, Kit kicked dirt into it. He'd trip over his own feet and colored more than anyone Taylor had ever met, and the men took to calling him "Jonah" on account of his ill luck. Yet, everyone liked him. Kit was like a younger brother; you could tease him and yell at him, but you also wanted to protect and defend him. Kit tried very hard and nothing mattered so much when it came to being a soldier.

The Federal trenchlines slowly crisscrossed the hillside, moving ever closer to the Confederate works. Above the trenches, cut vegetation and dirt had been piled, along with "head logs," making the trenches relatively safe. Working on the breastworks could be monotonous unless soldiers found a diversion. One day, Christmas Morgan placed his hat on the end of his bayonet. Then he poked the hat up above the head log. Cracks filled the air as the hat drew the Confederate sharpshooters' fire. This seemed so funny to some that more started doing it. Bets were taken on how many shots any particular hat might sustain. After a few days, Christmas had eight holes in his hat.

"Look at that!" he shouted. "What a waste of ammunition!"

"Looks to me more like a waste of a good hat," Kit said tiredly to Taylor.

"You got that right." Taylor scooped another shovelful of dirt. "You doing okay, Jonah?" The boy looked as if he'd aged five years in the last five months.

"Sure," said Kit, unconvincingly. "You?"

"Same."

The days stretched into June and the temperature climbed to over a hundred degrees. Men vanished from the ranks due to heat exhaustion, dehydration, or illness. Insects, including mosquitos, wood ticks and chiggers, chewed furiously on everyone. The chiggers were the worst. They were too small to see and would bore beneath a man's skin and cause itching so severe that Taylor had watched soldiers reduced nearly to tears for the incessant scratching. He himself had had to remove himself to the woods on several occasions. In private, he could strip down and scratch the worst areas, sometimes until his skin bled.

In addition to bugs, the men found spiders and lizards on their blankets, and snakes just about everywhere. One morning, Taylor lifted the lid on the coffee pot and discovered a small lizard with stripes and a blue tail inside. Dew covered the grasses and a light layer of fog rose from the ravine, so the animal didn't move when Taylor plucked it from the pot. He set it behind a log where he knew the sun would soon fall.

The men worked and ate and slept and the routine didn't vary. After sundown each evening, all firing ceased briefly for supper, and it was now common to see blue and gray coming together. The enemies, quite willing to kill each other during the day, exchanged notes and goods and news at night. Laughter could be heard as well as singing. Christmas Morgan continued trading with the Confederates. Soon he had a large stash of tobacco and generously shared with everyone, but Taylor still refused the offering. He simply couldn't understand this cavorting with the enemy.

"I just can't figure it," he said to Biddle one evening as the other man sat writing a letter. "If they're no-good, rotten traitors in the daylight, then they're still the same at night. What's Christmas thinking?"

Biddle shrugged. "Same as most. What he can get for hisself. Besides, not everyone hates Rebs as much as you, Taylor."

"I s'pose." He pitched a rock at a small piece of wood he'd set up on a log. "But it's a damn funny business shooting at a man one minute and handing him a box of crackers the next. And them rascals would just as soon kill us as look at us. Why should we help 'em while they're doing it?"

"Hmm." Biddle held up a lime-green leaf in one hand. He studied it a moment, then placed the five-pointed object beneath his paper and rubbed his pencil back and forth over the top, creating an impression of the leaf.

"You writing to Katherine?" Taylor asked.

"Yep."

Katherine was Biddle's younger sister and he wrote to her every week. He would take out her likeness each time and set it nearby while composing his letters. Taylor picked up the likeness now. Katherine had the same olive skin and dark, smiling eyes as her brother. Her hair was pulled back and piled atop her head with a wide bow pinned near one ear. She wore a fine chain around her neck where a locket in the shape of a heart dangled. She wasn't exactly smiling but neither was she stern. In fact, she looked very nice.

Biddle glanced up from the leaf. "You think she's pretty?" he asked.

Taylor set the likeness back. "I s'pose."

His friend laughed. "You don't fool me none! You do think she's pretty!"

Taylor tried to think of something complimentary. "She has nice skin." Biddle laughed again. "Hey, she's your sister after all, old man. I wouldn't say nothing about your sister."

"I know you wouldn't. You're difficult sometimes, Taylor, but I know you got your soft side."

The evening grew darker. Biddle lit a candle and stuck it in the ring of his bayonet. The cannons suddenly fell silent along this part of the line, though firing continued to the north. The air, unable it seemed to make room for any attempted silence, quickly filled with the howling of the dogs. Vicksburg's canines ran in packs like wolves, up to a dozen likely by the varied voices. Some were high-pitched, others low and throaty, but all offered up their anguish at the activities of men and didn't stop to give those same men a break. It was one of the worst sounds Taylor had ever heard. The night before, to no avail, he had wrapped his frock coat about his ears to drown out the dogs' miserable complaints.

"How's your pa doing?" Biddle asked.

"Fine, I expect. Ain't heard nothing for a while."

"The money you sending home helping with his business?"

"Some. Probably not enough." Taylor paused. "Pa's got a lot of debts."

Biddle nodded. "I'm sorry, Taylor."

"What for? Ain't your fault."

"You gonna write in your journal?" Biddle asked, changing the subject and pointing his pencil at the unopened book on Taylor's lap.

"Nah."

Biddle shook his head. "You're funny, old man."

"How so?"

"You're always sitting around with that book in your hands, but I don't ever see you writing in it."

"Well, maybe I write in it when you ain't around. It ain't like we're always together."

"Maybe, but we're together a fair bit. I'm just beginning to wonder if you got some secrets in there."

"Like what kind of secrets would I have?"

"I dunno. Maybe you're a spy or something and the journal is where you keep all your notes. But if you kept it hidden, we'd know something was funny, so you bring it out in the open, in plain sight, as if there was no secret at all." Biddle shrugged. "Or maybe it's something else you don't want no one to know about. My ma always said everyone's got something they keep to theirselves."

Taylor put the journal back in his haversack.

Biddle smiled his crooked, little grin. "I'm sorry, old man, I didn't mean nothing." He handed Taylor a sheet of paper and an envelope. "Here, write your pa. It'll take your mind off things."

"Naw, I just writ him. I'll write again after we take Vicksburg."

"Well, why don't you write your girl then?"

"Fuck you, Biddle." Still, Taylor kept the paper. "S'pose I could write your sister though. Tell her what a lousy wretch you are."

"Aw, she already knows that! But Katie loves getting letters. She'd write you back too!"

Taylor lit his own candle and began a letter to Katherine Biddle. At first, he couldn't think of much to say, so he simply introduced himself and wrote a few things about her brother. It was clear by the letters Biddle received and sent that the two were thicker than a pair of bandits. Sometimes Taylor had felt a bit jealous of his friend. He didn't have anyone that wrote to him like that, but on the other hand, he also didn't want anyone loving him that much. What if he got killed, or worse? The loved one would suffer too much. They would suffer too much and they would suffer forever.

But writing to his friend's sister carried no risk. He didn't know her and it was something to do while the dogs howled. To Taylor's surprise, he found many topics to share: Bean's cooking, Kit's bungles, the lizards on their blankets, the morning mist in the ravine, a little gray mouse Taylor had found one morning building a nest inside his knapsack. The mouse had had big, dark eyes like small chocolates and had raced out when he turned over the flap. The nest of short lengths of grass also contained several seeds, a silver button, and one penny. After Taylor finished describing the nest, he looked over the letter. Apart from what he'd written about Biddle, it was, without a doubt, a most ridiculous transmission; a mouse's nest? Still, he sealed the envelope and put it in his haversack. For one blessed moment as he crawled into the tent, there wasn't a sound anywhere. Taylor closed his eyes. Perhaps he could fall asleep before the dogs, or the cannons, started up again.

*

On June 20, the regiment was called out in line of battle at four in the morning. Immediately, the most terrific barrage of Federal artillery began. Louder than anything heard so far, it continued without interruption for six hours. By five a.m., Robert Taylor's head throbbed as if someone was pounding on his skull with a hammer. Kit Johnson, pale and shaky from the shattering concussions, threw up several times. Bean's long face grew longer as the morning wore on, and the expression of every man hosted a sickly shade of yellow. The soldiers remained standing in their line as best as they could, under arms and ready to move forward should an opportunity arise to penetrate the Confederate works.

Such an opportunity never presented itself, however, and by midday, orders arrived to cease firing. In the strange silence that followed, everyone sat behind the line stunned. That night, the regiment found hundreds of dead blackbirds in the forest behind their camp, blasted out of their roosts by the noise.

All returned to more or less normal the next day. A warty toad had crawled into Taylor's pack during the night, hopping out under protest with one crackly croak. An owl, the first they'd heard since arriving, trilled its airy song even as the morning became lighter. While the company drank coffee, small birds scuffled in the bushes; the regiment resumed its regular duties in the trenches.

The days slipped away, one after the next, and on July 1, the Federal Army exploded a mine near the Confederate line. The explosion destroyed a large portion of the enemy's works, as well as seven enemy soldiers, yet the assault ultimately accomplished little. It was hotter than anyone had ever experienced in Illinois. The bugs increased in numbers and ferocity; water ran low. Christmas Morgan came back from his trading missions saying the Rebels were literally starving across the way. They'd been eating less than half rations for weeks and sickness was rampant. Likewise, Vicksburg's citizenry, more wraiths than people at this point, suffered from living in caves dug into the belly of Vicksburg's hills with nothing to eat besides rats and scrawny mules.

On the night of July 3rd, Taylor had nearly fallen asleep when Biddle crawled in the tent.

"The boys say if the Secesh don't surrender by July 4," he said, "then we'll commence with another assault."

Taylor turned over on his back. "I 'spect that's true."

"A lot more will be killed before it's done."

"Also true."

"I tell ya, Taylor, I hope it don't happen. I hope them bastards surrender."

"Me too."

As it happened, the next day the Confederates hung out a flag of truce and Generals Grant and Pemberton met to discuss terms. This time, the cease-fire was not broken by gay conversation, card games, or trading. Instead, it seemed as if every man in the hills of Vicksburg held his breath. The next day, July 4 and the anniversary of American independence, General John Pemberton of the Confederate Army surrendered to General Ulysses Grant's Federal forces.

THREE

LIKE KIT JOHNSON, Joseph Biddle was a Chicago boy. He lived with his parents and sister south of the city where his family managed their blacksmith business The war had been good for George Biddle, whose establishment sat four blocks from the newly constructed Camp Douglas. Annabelle Biddle kept their home and a small garden, and also found time to volunteer in the suffrage movement. She wanted her children to know something of the world, so Joseph and Katherine often found themselves in town, attending plays and listening to speakers on many topics. A few years before the war, McVicker's Theatre had been built on Madison Street, and it turned out the very best in legitimate theatre, as well as minstrel shows and opera. Biddle told the boys he'd seen so much Shakespeare that he figured he could write a play just as well as that old Englishman. The most impressive event he'd ever attended, however, was the Republican National Convention in May 1860.

"Pa and Ma are Lincoln folk through and through," he'd said one morning at breakfast during their training in Cairo, Illinois. "When the convention came to Chicago, we all went and I hadn't ever seen anything like it! Thousands of people in the streets, all the homes on Michigan Avenue lit up, every hotel full and even billiards rooms turned into makeshift lodging. Pa couldn't believe it either. He'd been in the city since the 1830s when it wasn't even a city, just an army post and fur trading station. Back then, wolves prowled the streets, which were really more just paths, and in the winter everyone lived inside the fort for protection" But Chicago had grown like the prairie grass since then, Biddle added. Railroads, a new machine called a telegraph, and steamships had all turned the wilderness into a civilization.

When the doors opened to the Wigwam, the hall built on Lake Street specifically for the convention, the crowds rushed forward in great anticipation. For three days, Biddle and his family lived in that building, going home only late at night for a few hours of sleep before returning in the morning. George Biddle worried that William Seward would get the nomination, and for a time it looked very much like that might happen, but in the end Lincoln took it. When the results were announced, the Wigwam trembled from the clapping and stomping of feet. Someone even fired a cannon from the roof.

"When the war came," Biddle continued, "of course, I was going to join and fight for Mr. Lincoln. But then I broke my leg right after Sumter and it took nigh on six months to heal. By the fall, Pa's assistants at the shop had left to join, so I stayed to help him. Every day we'd see the regiments at Camp Douglas. Finally, I could wait no more!"

The worst part about leaving, he'd said, was saying good-bye to his younger sister, Katherine. Once, many years before, she'd come close to dying, had lain with scarlet fever for several days. It had been the worst time of his life.

"I never left her bedside," Biddle told his friends. "Just sat there reading and praying, day in and day out. Part of me just couldn't believe that God would be so cruel as to take her, but of course, no one knows His ways, do they? Katie pulled through though and you ain't never seen a happier boy."

Robert Taylor liked hearing Biddle talk about Chicago and his family. He could easily imagine all of it, especially Biddle's happiness when his sister's fever broke and she began to recover.

Yes, it was a good thing to have someone that you loved that much. As long as you were also prepared for the eventuality of losing them.

*

Shortly after ten a.m. on July 4, 1863, the Union flag waved high above the Confederate works. Owing to their bravery in storming one of the Rebel forts, the 45th Illinois had been selected to lead the column entering the city; the 72nd Illinois would come next. It took substantial work getting the many regiments organized on the narrow Jackson Road, but when they at last commenced marching, the soldiers soon found themselves within the enemy lines.

Long rows of stacked arms bordered the road. The Confederate soldiers stared at the Federals blankly or looked away. Their eyes carried the smoky expressions of defeat, exhaustion, and fear, yet their faces remained strangely expressionless. For a long way, as the column bumped along, the only sounds came from the shuffle of boots and the plinking noisess of canteens, bayonets, and tin cups.

"How are ya, Yank?" one butternut-clad soldier asked Robert Taylor. The man's clothes hung on him like sacks and his cheeks were two dark hollows beneath red, watery eyes.

Taylor nodded. "Fine, Reb, how are you?"

The man nodded back. "Hungry. Ya got anything to eat?"

By this time, the column had stopped. Taylor found two loose crackers in his haversack and handed them to the man.

"Much obliged, Yank."

The temperature climbed as the march resumed. A few men dropped out of line from the heat. As the Federal Army left the battlefield and entered the city, the residents emerged from the caves where they'd been living for the past two months. Children looked at the men from behind their mothers' skirts; stooped over, old men wore the same nothing expressions as the younger versions of themselves on the line. Nearly every building had suffered in the bombardment. Some structures lay in piles of rubble, while others had fared better with only roofs or windows missing. The ground was covered in shell fragments and other debris.

Two hours after leaving their own lines, the Federal regiments arrived at the Vicksburg Courthouse. An impressive building set atop a high, broad swath of open ground on Cherry Street, it looked out over the equally impressive Mississippi River. Romanesque columns guarded the north and west entrances, while a cupola sat atop the third floor. Stretching out from this cupola now hung the American flag. Respectful of their foes' defeat up until this point, the men could restrain themselves no longer. Cheers quickly erupted everywhere. As if to answer, the flag began waving as a welcome breeze enveloped them all. One of the regimental bands finished playing *Yankee Doodle* and began the national anthem, *Hail Columbia*.

After stacking arms, many of the Federal soldiers went inside the courthouse. As Taylor and the others stood inside the building's dark interior, a group of drunken officers began climbing the iron staircase. They carried a captured signal flag and sang the *Star Spangled Banner*. When they got to the top, one intoxicated man bent over.

"Look at these steps, boys!" the officer shouted. "Baker Iron Company, Ohio! They're made in the NORTH! These impudent bastards thought they could whip the United States when they can't even make their own staircases!"

In the back of the court room, Taylor and the others found a staircase that led to the attic and then another one that carried them to the cupola. Several soldiers had already arrived at the viewpoint. Vicksburg and all they had been fighting for the past many months unfolded before them like a painting.

To the west the Mississippi River rolled by not two hundred feet below the courthouse; to the east lay the trenches and earthworks of battle, bare ground devoid of nearly all vegetation and strangely resembling a tunnel network of rodents. In between stood the city, with its wounded buildings, haunted-looking inhabitants, and broken-topped trees. By now, hundreds of residents had also gathered around the courthouse. Taylor had never seen so many miserable-looking people, but he cared little. He felt happy for the first time in so long he couldn't remember, and he would enjoy this day to the fullest.

Back outside the building, Biddle grabbed Taylor. "We done it, old man!" he shouted. "We done it and we didn't get killed doing it! Have I ever felt so good? I don't think so!"

Taylor hugged his friend back. "Too bad one a them men with the photographic wagons ain't here. We need our likeness taken here at the courthouse!"

"That would be good," Biddle agreed. He looked around then, his gaze falling on the base of one of the courthouse's columns where a roseate-colored slab stretched out like a small bench. "I know what we'll do, Taylor! We'll carve our names in this here slab. Then everyone will know that we were here!"

He took out a small knife and Taylor did the same. Christmas soon joined them, all three carving their initials into the slab. It wasn't so easy, and the marks looked more like scratches than proper letters. Taylor was almost finished with the "T" to follow his "R" when he suddenly thought of all the 72nd men who had been killed during the charges or died after. None of these men were sharing in the victory, though they had given the most of any of them. As Taylor realized his T actually looked more like a "7," he decided to start carving a "2" next to it. He had just enough time to finish three more large letters "I L L" before the regiment reformed. Soon, they were all marching back to the Confederate works where they would spend the night guarding their prisoners.

*

The regiment enjoyed one week of victory in Vicksburg before being ordered downriver to a town called Natchez. They left at 4 a.m. on board the steamer *Lancaster No. 4* and as the sun rose higher and the mists above the river lifted, the ship descended further and further down the Mississippi. To everyone's surprise, they found a lush, bountiful countryside, with trees growing to the water's edge that hadn't been broken by cannon fire. Plantations above the river bluffs glistened white, surrounded by blooming magnolia trees, as well as many orange, fig, peach and pear trees, all heavy with fruit. Moss hung from cypress and pine trees; ivory clouds, as thick and curly as the coats of sheep, filled the sky. As *Lancaster No. 4* paddled along, only a few of the region's inhabitants appeared onshore. There was no firing of guns, no sharpshooters hidden in trees, no cannons pointed down at the slow-moving steamship. Eden, someone called the land. The occupation of Natchez occurred without incident.

The next day, the 72nd Illinois crossed over to the Louisiana shore and began confiscating all the horses, mules, cattle, arms, and ammunition they could find. Both Natchez and Vidalia, Louisiana, had been important points for shipping materials east and west across the Confederacy. At one plantation, the regiment pressed nearly fifty horses into the service of the United States. The mare Taylor took was a fine animal, with a silky, dark red coat, and a small white star on her forehead. He suddenly felt a tremendous longing for home and his old mule and dog.

For the most part, every plantation looked immaculate, with grounds so tidy the grass might have been trimmed with a pair of scissors. Walking paths created from broken sea shells encircled rose gardens and bubbling fountains. Vines hung thick above archways and arbors. At one magnificent mansion, the owner raced out with a gun to meet the regiment. While he argued and shouted at the officers, the men, helped considerably by the plantation slaves, gathered dozens of bags of fruit, several tubs of butter, various containers of milk and eggs, and a choir of squawking chickens. The man's face grew as purple as an aster. He shouted at the Northern soldiers while one of his daughters walked over to where Taylor sat on the mare. She had thick, black hair piled high on her head and a small mole on one cheek. Her mouth formed a faint smile. She petted the mare, which obviously recognized her. Suddenly, she gathered a large breath of air and spit. The big glob landed right in the center of Taylor's frock coat. Her smile grew wider before the girl turned and returned to the house with her father.

"That bitch needs to be taught a lesson," said Christmas as they rode away. "A little time on her back with a real man would curb her fire."

"Somehow I doubt that," replied Taylor, wiping the spittle off with his handkerchief.

By the end of the day, the regiment had confiscated 500 mules, 500 muskets, 200 horses, thousands of Texan cattle, and five wagon loads of ammunition. In addition to the animals and supplies, the regiment swelled in size with the attachment of several thousand slaves who were "going to freedom." Men, women, and children had gathered all they owned into wagons of all shapes and sizes. They sang and danced and when the major told them the regiment had nothing for them and couldn't provide them protection they said they didn't care. One old, wizened woman walked up and addressed the major directly.

"I's nigh on eighty years, suh, and ah been waiting for this day nigh on eighty years. So, ah don't care none if ah ain't got nuthin' to eat, and ah don't care none if ah die tomorra. Cause I is a free woman NOW! From this day on, ah be living on my very own salvation!"

Taylor, Biddle, and Bean rode on the outside of the mass of people. One young slave woman, her short hair braided into tight plaits, approached Taylor and fell into step beside the mare. She had high cheekbones and blue-brown eyes and was wearing a ragged, gray skirt and blouse. Her muscled arms, like coils of rope, swung by her side. They had gone about a mile when the woman reached into a bag hanging from her shoulder. She brought out a boiled egg and a biscuit and after staring at Taylor a good while, handed him the food. Then she vanished back into the crowd.

"Goddamn, Taylor," said Bean, "you do attract the ladies dontchya?"

"Ain't something I want, Bean."

"Don't matter if you do. They still like you."

"I'd hardly say spitting on a fella constitutes 'like.' And this gal, who knows? She's had hard times."

Bean nodded. "That's the truth."

The regiment camped that night along the road in a forest broken up with meadows and a large lake. Taylor had just gotten the fire going when he heard the flapping of several herons above them. The birds landed in the enormous cottonwoods growing around the lake and only a few minutes later they all took off again. A white-headed eagle had appeared out of nowhere, sending the group into flight with a tremendous amount of squawking. The eagle grabbed one of the herons and the two birds tumbled toward the earth, a great tangle of wings and necks and legs. The unfortunate heron feebly protested as its captor disappeared with it across the lake. The event had taken place in less than ten seconds.

Taylor turned back to his fire just in time to see Kit Johnson's leg about to burn up. "Jesus, Jonah, get back! You're about to catch it!"

"What?" The younger boy was as pale as a cloud as he stared at the sky where the eagle and heron had vanished.

"The fire, old man, the fire!" Taylor shouted again. At last Kit understood and leapt back with a yelp.

All felt pleased with the day's work. The capture of so many supplies and ammunition would severely hinder the Confederacy and the liberation of so many slaves could not help but make a man feel good. The camping ground was a good one, and there was plenty of food to be found. When the others left to gather more fruit and firewood, Taylor began making biscuits to go with Bean's supper. He didn't have any yeast, so the biscuits wouldn't rise much but they'd still taste good. After spooning several globs of batter into a pot and returning it to the fire, he lit a cigar and leaned back against a log.

Christmas returned first and had just sat down when the slave woman from earlier appeared.

"This for you, suh," she said, handing Taylor a basket. "We all seen what you done and we awful grateful. Truthfully, can't hardly believe you're down here, but like I said, we mighty glad."

Taylor was only part way to his feet, the basket barely in his grasp, before she had gone again.

Bean returned at that moment after finding a flat rock to add to his kitchen. "What's this?" he asked, looking at the basket.

Christmas snorted. "It's a present from one of Taylor's women."

"Shut it, Morgan," said Taylor. He and Bean looked inside the basket and found a ham.

Bean nodded. "Good work, private. This'll go well in my stew."

"Really, Taylor, I don't know what the gals see in you," continued Christmas.

"They don't see nothing, believe me."

"Sure they do, only I can't figure out what. You ain't that pretty."

Taylor laughed. "Prettier than you at least."

Christmas grabbed Taylor's right leg and flipped him on the ground. As Taylor landed with a thud, he rolled to the side, bringing his knees up to avoid the fire, then half-stood and jumped on Christmas' back. The Louisiana dust mushroomed around them as the two wrestled.

"Hey!" Bean yelled at them. "You're getting dirt on the food!"

"Now, whaddya say, Morgan?" asked Taylor, after he'd pinned the other man down.

"You bastard!"

"I'm prettier than you, ain't I?"

"No." Taylor pushed him farther into the ground. "All right, all right! You is…a little prettier." Taylor let him go.

Christmas sat back up and brushed the dust off his coat. "Bastard."

"Pretty boy." They both laughed.

Bean, however, wasn't amused. "I'd say the both of ya's are equally ugly and you come purt near to ruining this fine ham."

After Biddle returned with his haversack full of figs and nectarines, they stuffed themselves with the lobscouse Bean had prepared, fresh fruit for dessert, and several cups of coffee. As the soldiers ate, they listened to the slaves singing.

Steal away, steal away!
Steal away to Jesus!
Steal away, steal away home!
I ain't got long to stay here!

My Lord calls me!
He calls me by the thunder!
The trumpet sounds in my soul!
I ain't got long to stay here!

Steal away, steal away!
Steal away to Jesus!
Steal away, steal away home!
I ain't got long to stay here!

Everyone told stories that evening, sharing different things they'd seen throughout the day, or snatches of conversation they'd heard. The Negroes of course were the most interesting topic and all wondered what would happen to them. The string of wagons and animals and goods that accompanied the newly freed slaves stretched along the Mississippi as far as the eye could see. Somebody was going to have to take charge of the situation, and nobody from Company F had any idea who that would be. Christmas crossed his arms and said he hoped it wasn't going to be them. Everyone nodded in agreement.

As the fire started to fade, Kit stood up. A sudden rustling in the bushes made him jump and his plate and spoon fell onto Bean's head.

"Hey!" shouted the cook.

"Sorry, Bean."

"Why you so jumpy, Jonah? Ain't no Rebs down here."

"Aw, he's just worried one a them big birds is gonna eat him for dinner!" laughed Christmas.

"I ain't neither," protested Kit.

"I think I'd be more worried about owls," offered Biddle, who'd heard the story about the eagle taking the heron.

"That's right," agreed Taylor.

"What? Why's that?" asked Kit, looking around worriedly.

"Why's that!" shouted Biddle, as if even a baby should know this. "Because, dear boy, you don't never hear an owl flying up; at least eagles flap and chitter and make all kinds of noise. But owls, they're as silent as a thought, and before you know it, smack! One has its claws around your head."

"But owls ain't that big, Biddle."

"They are in the South. Everything's bigger down here. Anyways, they ain't trying to carry you off, they just like pecking at your head. I heard tell of one that even got into a man's brain!"

As Kit's mouth fell open, Taylor chimed in. "I wouldn't worry none about it, Jonah. Owls are easy to kill. All ya got to do if ya see one is just start walking around it. See, they can turn their head all the way around, but they ain't very smart and don't know that. They just keep watching you and turning their head and pretty soon it pops right off!"

Kit thought about this a moment, then threw a pine cone at Taylor. "You're giving me taffy!" he shouted.

Despite feeling exhausted, Taylor couldn't sleep that night. He tossed and turned next to Biddle, then opened his eyes to look out at the stars. "Hey, Biddle, you awake?"

"No," came the muffled reply.

"I can't sleep."

"Well, why you bothering me about it?"

"I don't know." Taylor yawned. "Today was another good day, wasn't it?"

Biddle rolled onto his back. "Yep. 'Cept for that woman spitting on you."

"Yeah, that wasn't so good. The bitch."

"She was pretty though."

"Ya think?"

"Sure. Tall like she was with that pale, soft skin. Didya see how long her fingers were? I'll bet she plays the piano and sings and does all kinds of stuff a real lady does. Probably speaks French too. All smart ladies know French."

Taylor laughed. "Who cares about speaking French? A lotta good that would do a person here."

"I dunno. It's kinda nice to listen to. Katie's been taking French lessons for a few years now. I used to love just sitting and listening to her talk. Didn't have one idea what she was saying but it didn't matter 'cause it was nice just to listen to." Biddle yawned. "Yep, that's the kind of woman I'd like to marry."

"What, a French one?"

"Nah, just someone refined. One that knows a lot of things and plays music and would sing to me at night and maybe had traveled to other countries. Not just some simple girl from the country, but a real lady!"

"And what would someone like that see in you?"

"Nothing probably." He laughed. "I'm a nice fella though!"

"Are you telling me, Biddle, that you could love one of these Southern women?"

"Sure, why not?"

Taylor raised up on one elbow. "Why not? *Why not?* They're the goddamned enemy, that's why not!"

"The women ain't, Taylor. It's the men started this war, not the women. Women don't fight, it ain't in 'em. They're too good. Also, they don't think about complicated things like men do."

Taylor snorted. "You don't know what you're talking about, Biddle! I'll bet that woman from this afternoon thinks a lot of complicated things. And women can be pretty angry too. I've seen it."

"Aw, I don't think that woman was so angry. I think she just liked you." He reached over and pinched Taylor on the arm. "You being so pretty and all!"

Taylor pushed his arm away. "That ain't true, but even if it was, that's a pretty funny way to show liking someone."

"Well, that's women for ya." Biddle rolled back on his side.

"Thing of it is, Taylor, a fella can't help who he falls in love with, it just happens. He'll be going along one day, happy as a lark, and then, with no warning at all, it happens: he's in love. Knows it clear as he knows his own name. Maybe it scares him half to death too for she might not be the right one, but there's no undoing it."

Taylor thought about this. "Don't think that's gonna happen to me, Biddle."

"Well, don't come telling me about it if it does."

*

For the next three months, the regiment remained in Natchez. Occasionally, the men would move into the countryside to confiscate stores of cotton, but mostly their work consisted of guard and picket duty around the town. Mail began to arrive regularly, and all spent time writing letters. When their pay came, Taylor penned a brief note to his pa and sent most of the money home, keeping only a small bit back to play bluff and buy cigars.

The weather alternated between warm showers and sunny, clear, blue skies, but it wasn't as hot as Vicksburg. The duty was good, and with such a bountiful countryside, Bean continued to make great meals that included fare like fig sauce, apple cobbler, and sweet potato pie. In sum, everyone hoped upon hope that the regiment would remain in Natchez. Yet such was not to be. On October eleventh, just as the cottonwoods and sweetgums and tulip trees were all beginning to turn fiery shades of gold and orange, the men boarded the flag steamship, *E.H. Fairchild.* Two days later, the 72nd Illinois arrived back in Vicksburg. They bivouacked that night on the Mississippi River levee.

FOUR

MR. TAYLOR,

Thank you very much for your kind letter, which has lately arrived. My brother has written often of you so I feel as if we are already acquainted. The war stretches on interminably! I miss Joseph terribly and pray daily for his safe return. Now I shall pray for yours as well.

Summer has returned to Chicago and with it unbearable heat. The temperature recently topped 105 degrees, a record even for Chicago. Nothing moved that day, including our old gray cat, which remained more a puddle of fur than anything. I remain indoors as much as possible, reading and preparing packages and writing letters. In addition to my brother, we have three cousins and two good friends who have joined for the war.

With this tremendous heat, I feel great concern for the prisoners at Camp Douglas. The grounds there, very near to our home, provide little shade and of course, there is no chance for the men to go to the lake and bathe. My mother and I visit them and we have been most appalled at the men's condition. Many are quite sickly and the food provided is not sufficient by half. Recently, a relief committee has formed and Mother and I have joined. We help raise money to buy clothing and medicine and food and then deliver it to the camp.

Otherwise, I, along with my mother, volunteer for the reform newspaper, New Covenant. The Pastor Livermore and his wife Mary began the paper some years ago and its focus is abolition and temperance. Mother wishes they would also take up the issue of women's suffrage, however Mrs. Livermore feels *that abolition must be the focus, along with the care of our soldiers. Of course, Mother doesn't disagree, yet there are many kinds of bondage. Women have been subjected to so many restrictions for far too long. How can a country be totally free when some are kept from expressing their voice?*

Does your family reside in Chicago, Mr. Taylor? If so, you must tell me where they live. I shall visit your mother and we can share in the pain of having loved ones so far away. Do you have siblings? What is your father's situation? Given how highly my brother speaks of you, I should like to know more about his good friend.

Please take care of yourself and my dear Joseph. He is all to me. I do not doubt the need for this war, yet I worry every day.

With most sincere good wishes,
Katherine Biddle

*

By October 1863, Vicksburg had fully "turned blue," as the citizens referred to the transformation of their city. Many private homes had been taken over by the Federal Army and the city streets bustled with government wagons and hundreds of soldiers. Workmen had removed most of the piles of battle rubble and continued making repairs on the structures that were salvageable. Across the street from the courthouse, the jail overflowed with Vicksburg residents who had been arrested on sound charges (according to the Federal Army) or nothing so much as a disapproving look (according to the citizenry). These "looks" frequently came in response to the thousands of freed slaves that had traveled to Vicksburg from the countryside. A Freedmen's Camp had been established ten miles outside the city, which helped deal with the influx, yet the strange new situation remained: Negroes wandering the streets like any other person, Negro children attending schools, Negroes carry guns and acting as guards. For many white Southerners, all of whom had been forced to take the oath of allegiance to the United States or leave, this last had simply been too much. Leaving was all that was left to them, and they did so without a backward glance.

The 72nd Illinois established its camp at the east end of Clay

Street on the outskirts of Vicksburg near the battlefield. Daily life consisted of morning parade and guard or fatigue duty in the afternoon. When not on duty, the men wrote letters home, played games, or went into town. One afternoon in early November after dinner, Taylor left camp and walked along Clay Street toward the river. Fallen leaves lay crisp and curled and gathered into small piles from the wind. The days had grown cool, the grasses staying heavy with dew long past the morning hours. Two robins scratched around in a pothole as Taylor walked by; a thin cat watched the birds from behind a barrel. Taylor stopped. He found a chunk of salt pork in his haversack and tossed it at the cat. The animal snatched it quickly and disappeared.

On Washington Street, just north of Clay, was the establishment of Titcomb & Woodruff, "Headquarters of the Army and Navy, Wholesale & Retail Dealers." A business that seemed to have experienced little of the war's economic stifling, Titcomb & Woodruff bulged with goods. Books, photograph albums, gold pens, fine paper, pocket knives, meerschaums, and every kind of musical instrument filled the shelves. The place was packed with soldiers buying items for themselves or their sweethearts, or just milling about looking. A thin, pale man, mostly bald with sharp features and a crinkled ear scurried back and forth behind the counter. Taylor looked at the books while the man waited on his customers. After the store had emptied of people, he approached the counter.

"I need some notepaper and envelopes," said Taylor, "and I'd like to look at one of these meerschaums."

The man nodded. His brow glistened and he had the look of a very happy businessman. He pulled a key ring from his pocket and opened the glass cabinet separating them. "Which one do you like?"

Taylor chose a pipe that was simple but smart-looking with a smooth white bowl. He'd made an easy $25 the night before playing bluff and had decided to treat himself with the pipe and a bag of tobacco.

As the shopkeeper wrapped up Taylor's purchases, the man chatted about the weather. "Thank the Lord for the cooler days, eh? We gets 'em hot down here, but truth to tell, I ain't never seen a summer so hot and dry as this one. And I lived in Vicksburg my whole life! I mean, I walked to the shop just this morning and I seen ducks bathing themselves in pools of dust! You ever see such a thing? Ducks bathing in dust?"

Taylor didn't answer. Out of habit, he didn't like this man, but it wasn't just because he was a southerner. The shopkeeper clearly was working both sides of the conflict for his own gain, and that somehow seemed worse than being a simple traitor. Taylor paid him and quickly left. He could buy goods from such a scalawag but he didn't have to listen to the man's simpering conversation.

After putting the purchases into his haversack, Taylor walked two doors south on Washington Street until he came to Sam's Saloon. The unwashed windows and sign hanging above the door at an angle made the place seem deserted, yet loud voices and a whirly organ playing *Camptown Races* belied any such abandonment. Inside, Taylor ordered a whiskey and stood at the bar while his eyes adjusted to the dim interior. A few businessmen sat at tables, while soldiers clustered in small groups. A group had gathered at the organ where a red-haired woman with an enormous hat sat playing. After finishing *Camptown Races* to great applause, she began *Turchin's Got Your Mule*.

> *A planter came to camp one day,*
> *His niggers for to find;*
> *His mules had also gone astray,*
> *And stock of every kind.*
> *The planter tried to get them back,*
> *And then was made a fool,*
> *For every one he met in camp*
> *Cried, "Mister, here's your mule!"*

> *Go back, go back, go back, old scamp,*

And don't be made a fool;
Your niggers they are all in camp,
And Turchin's got your mule!

"Another one, sir?" the barkeeper asked.

Taylor nodded. Why not? It was early in the day, but he was off duty and felt deserving. The man brought him the drink and also commented on the weather. After a bit, Taylor put some tobacco in his new pipe, then slid a quarter dollar tip toward the barkeeper. This generosity nudged some of the tiredness from the man's face, and he gave Taylor a hearty, "Thank ya, suh!"

Taylor next walked toward the levee. Along this part of the Mississippi, the river had created an off-channel backwater in the shape of a quarter moon. The water here had grown warm over the summer and become an ideal place for bathing. Not surprisingly, Taylor found Biddle and Christmas paddling around like a couple of ducks.

"Hey, Taylor!" Biddle shouted, standing up in the shallows, "get on in here! Water's great!"

"Nah, I can't swim!" He sat down in the sand, puffing on his pipe.

"Hey!" yelled Christmas. "Get your ass on in here!"

"I can't swim, I tell you! Besides, they're gators and snakes in there!"

"Suit yourself!"

As Taylor watched the boys, he continued smoking and felt the easiest he'd been in some months. Not that everything was perfect. Despite sending most of his pay home and despite the fact that his pa had rented out their farm for more than a year now, the family's debts continued to mount. They both feared greatly losing their land, yet there was nothing to do but keep on, Taylor where he was and his pa back home.

"You don't know what you're missing, old man!" said Biddle, plopping himself, naked as a jaybird, next to Taylor.

"Probably not. But I got me this new pipe, a pouch of very fine tobacco, and I'm purt near as happy as a boy can be."

Biddle looked at him. "Yeah, I can see you are." He lay back in the sand. "I'm pretty happy too. I ain't felt so clean since I don't know when." Biddle cupped his hands around his eyes and looked at his friend. "'Cause of that, I ain't so sure I want to sleep with you if you ain't gonna bathe too!"

Taylor nodded. "You don't need to worry none, Biddle, 'cause I already had a bath. Just this morning in fact."

"What? Where?"

"One a them boarding houses on Cherry Street. Got me a bath, a shave, and a haircut, all for just $3. I sat in the tub for an hour this morning and didn't move a muscle except when the pretty gal came in with more hot water." He smiled. "Then I moved a few muscles."

Biddle laughed. "You bastard."

By order of President Lincoln, the last Thursday in November had been set aside as a national day of thanksgiving. The men were given extra rations and by great, good fortune, both Biddle and Bean also received packages from home. Biddle's contained pickles, onions, two cans of condensed milk, and several potatoes, while Bean's wife had sent him coffee, cheese, a cake, and several sacks of spices. Bean whooped when he saw the cake. He turned it over and showed everyone a hole in the bottom. Inside, a small bottle of whiskey had been wedged. The boys had a fine meal for the holiday and all agreed they were most thankful.

Vicksburg's first significant snowfall occurred on December first. Taylor woke up that morning half frozen and started a fire long before light. Later that day, he and Biddle walked out of town to a cornfield and gathered three bags of fodder. With the new snow, the tracks of deer and coons and wolves could be seen all along the Jackson Road. The country was so quiet that Taylor could barely remember the days of endless cannon fire. Back in their tent, they arranged the fodder and left it to dry. Later that night, they spread one wool blanket over the corn leaves, then covered themselves with the other as well as their two great coats which they'd buttoned together. That night, Biddle and Taylor slept spoon fashion, as snug as two kittens in a chimney corner.

*

In early December the regiment began constructing winter quarters. They cut down several small trees, notched each one, then stacked them together to form walls four feet tall. Next they collected bricks from an abandoned house and built fireplaces. Finally, came a framework of light rafters above the walls over which they arranged their tents. With mud, they chinked up the gaps in the walls. Though the structures could become smoky inside, the warmth more than compensated, especially when the temperature hovered near zero.

One evening, the clouds rolled in and the air turned warmer. After supper, the men sat outside their quarters, talking and eating Bean's stew. After the meal, Christmas suggested a game of chuck-a-luck and retrieved his cup from his haversack. The others quickly joined in, but Taylor at first sat out. He didn't generally play chuck-a-luck because unless you had your own dice, there was no way to rig the game. However, because you simply bet on what numbers would turn up when the dice were rolled, it was also an easy game to lose. Taylor had been winning so much lately at bluff that he needed to lose a little just to make the boys less suspicious. For this reason, he eventually decided to join in, letting his luck run the uncertain way of any man, up and down like the river winds.

They'd all been playing about an hour when three soldiers from Company C walked up. None of the three seemed too steady on their feet, and one in particular, Private Henry Beesley, weaved from side to side.

"Hey, whatchya all doin'?" Beesley asked slowly, crossing his arms then uncrossing them. "Ya got room for us in this game?" He looked more closely at the seated men, his gaze focusing last on Taylor, which triggered a clap of his hands. "Hey, Taylor! I didn't see you there!" He turned to his friends. "You being so small and all." The friends laughed. "Ya mind if we join your game, Taylor?"

Taylor, in fact, minded quite a lot. He hadn't had one pleasant interaction with Henry Beesley since they'd all joined up at Camp Douglas. For some reason, Beesley had taken against him from their first meeting and never missed an opportunity to call him a pretty boy or "Shorty," usually behind Taylor's back. For Taylor's part, he had many complaints against this soldier. He seemed to work as little as possible and tried to get others to do things for him. He also was terribly vain; Beesley had recently growing a mustache that Taylor thought looked like a giant worm but which was obviously a point of pride for the man.

"We don't want no trouble, Beesley," Christmas said.

"Ain't got no trouble to give. We're just wantin' to play with you fellas."

"Uh-huh."

"Well, sit down then before you fall down," said Taylor. "If y'all got money, then you're welcome to play." The others looked at him. "It's all right boys. Me and Henry are just fine. Ain't we, Henry?"

Beesley attempted a clumsy bow, then fell onto the ground. "That's right, *Robert*," he managed, struggling to sit up. "We are…just…fine."

It took the three some minutes to find their money. No one said much and very soon Kit left saying he was tired.

"G'night then, little boy," shouted Beesley. "Now the real men can get down to it. Right, Taylor?"

"Why don't you just leave it, Beesley?" said Christmas.

"Ah, Morgan, I don't mean nothin,' you know that."

"As a matter of fact, I don't know that. You always seem to be looking for a fight. Why is that exactly?"

There was no answer and Bean continued rolling the dice. Several rolls later and after Henry Beesley had lost most of his money, he turned and accused Bean of cheating. The cook calmly told him he could go find another game if he wasn't happy.

"You sons-a-bitches!" Beesley suddenly shouted. "I know y'all got it in for me. And I know that bastard," he pointed at Taylor, "is cheating right now."

"Yeah, I'm cheating all right," sighed Taylor. "And that's why I been losing so much money."

The others laughed and Beesley's face grew mottled. "You little fucker, Taylor! I've had it with you thinking you're better than everyone else. You ain't so different, ya know. You ain't that smart and you ain't that brave. You're just like the rest of us—"

"Get outta here, Beesley."

"You get—"

Taylor stood up then and grabbed Beesley by the collar, pulling him to his feet. He dragged him away from the others, and it all happened so fast that Henry hardly knew what had happened.

"You listen to me, Henry Beesley," Taylor said in a low voice. "I'm sick of taking your guff. You want a fight, I'll give you a proper, goddamn fight right now. Is that what you want?" Beesley didn't answer and in the shadowy light that reached them from the fire, Taylor thought the man was smiling. Yet, in the next moment, he simply slumped to the ground, the whiskey finally catching up with him. Taylor looked down. "Ah, Jesus."

His friends had scrambled away, so Biddle and Christmas helped Taylor carry Beesley back to his tent. Taylor was so annoyed that he didn't feel inclined to leave things there. After the others had gone to sleep, he got out his razor and went back to a still unconscious Henry Beesley. In just a few minutes, he had shaved off the man's bushy eyebrows and one-half of his caterpillar-like mustache. Taylor knew this would make things worse, but he still felt terribly pleased.

*

The incident with Henry Beesley put Taylor in an ill temper. In the ensuing weeks, the two mostly stayed clear of each other, but Beesley, having been forced to shave off the rest of his mustache, turned dark red every time they met. Taylor slept lightly and watched his back. He also talked little, smoking his new pipe and leaving his unopened journal on his lap for long stretches at a time. A week after the fight, Biddle grew tired of Taylor's sulking. You're about as much fun as a man headed for the priesthood, he told him.

"True," Taylor agreed, "but there ain't nothing to be done about it."

"Oh, yes, there is. You need a woman."

Taylor snorted. "That's for sure what I don't need."

"Yes, you do," insisted Biddle. "Some time with the fairer sex would soften up them hard edges. Be good for you."

"I don't think so, Biddle."

"Besides, it would stop the boys from talking."

"Talking about what?"

"You. Why you don't never talk about girls. Why you ain't interested in the catalogs Christmas gets, or them cards and pictures of naked ladies he orders."

Taylor waved his hand. "Maybe I just prefer the real thing."

"Then why don't you wanna go to the bawdy house?"

Taylor shrugged. Biddle waited for an answer, but when one didn't come he continued working on a carving he was making for his sister.

"Christmas tells of a house of nigra women down on Mulberry Street near the river," Biddle said after a few minutes. "We could go there sometime."

"Nah."

"Why not?"

"I don't know. I ain't got no money, I guess."

"You're a goddamn humbug, Taylor! You got more money than any of us!"

"I send it home."

"You don't send it all home. Besides, the girls are only a dollar at this place."

"I don't care if they're free, Biddle, I ain't going."

"Goddamnit, Taylor, you're a lousy friend."

"I know. Why don't you go with Christmas? Sounds like he knows the place. Then you can tell me about it after." But Biddle didn't want to go with Christmas. "Why not?"

"Because," he said, his cheeks turning pink, "you're my best friend. If you ain't going, I ain't going either."

"Hey, you're gonna make me cry."

"C'mon, old man, it could be fun. And maybe we get there and don't even stay, we just see what it's like."

Taylor emptied his pipe then filled it anew. He sat thinking. "All right, you son-of-a-bitch. I'll go. But don't be surprised if I just sit outside and wait for you."

Biddle laughed. "That's fair enough even if it don't make a lick of sense."

*

Liza's Place, the house of nigra woman and fair prices, sat on Mulberry Street a half block south of another more expensive establishment called the Cadillac. Christmas had been to both and said he preferred Liza's and not just because of the price. The women were more spirited, he claimed, and the place just as clean. Liza, a woman in her forties, had come to Vicksburg years before from Louisiana and begun her business with little money and almost no staff. Christmas said the girls had told him that Liza was smart, fair, and a great protector. She had allies in high places and was afraid of no man. Christmas had seen her a few times and confessed to feeling intimidated. This piqued Taylor's interest more than anything. He'd never seen Christmas intimidated before, and certainly not by a woman.

The opportunity to visit Liza's didn't come until the first days of spring. Taylor's courage began failing him on the evening of his and Biddle's intended visit. He had never paid for a woman before. What if he did something wrong? Or said something wrong? As they approached Liza's Place Taylor's stomach tightened. Two women sat outside on the porch railing.

"You boys lost?" one of the women asked, smiling. She was very tall, appeared to be about 30-years-old, and wore an array of jewelry, including several bracelets and a long necklace made of seashells.

"No, ma'am," said Biddle, his voice too loud. "We're looking for—uh, that is, we want to—I mean—" Suddenly, he stopped.

The second woman giggled. She wore little jewelry, in addition to little clothing, and looked to be much younger than her companion. After sizing up Biddle and Taylor, the first woman slowly removed a thin cigarette from a square tin and lit it.

"We know what y'all want, young man," she said, kindly. "And we're happy to help you spend your hard-earned money." She turned. "Ain't we, Sadie?"

Another giggle. "'Spect so, Esther. I'll take the shorter one. It looks like he could use a friend."

"Ain't no one taking anyone yet," said Esther, sliding off the railing, "until Miss Liza meets them."

The two women escorted Biddle and Taylor inside. The darkness closed around them and Taylor felt like he was suffocating. As his eyes adjusted, he found the large parlor nicer than expected, with chairs and couches around the edges and tables and chairs filling the middle. Candles hung between paintings of landscapes on the walls and a glass cabinet housed several porcelain dolls. While Esther went to fetch their boss, they sat down and waited. Sadie perched on a table, swinging her legs back and forth and looking down at them like a cat. After five minutes, Taylor wanted to leave. But then a voice spoke behind them.

"Well, well. Who've we got here?"

Both he and Biddle jumped to their feet and turned around. Before them stood a woman, tall like Esther, but with lighter skin and hair hung in braids down below her shoulders. She wore a splash of colors with red and blue beads woven into her hair, a gown of the same shades, and long fingernails painted tulip pink. High cheekbones, a prominent chin, and large, knowing eyes completed what Taylor agreed was a very intimidating presence indeed.

"We don't know they's names, Miss Liza," giggled Sadie.

"I see." Miss Liza poured herself a drink, then looked at them for a long minute. "You boys got names?"

"Yes, ma'am," crackled Biddle. "I'm Joseph and this here's Robert."

Miss Liza nodded then shook both their hands and said it was nice to meet them. She continued to stare and Taylor felt sweat trickling down his back. It might have been his imagination, but he had the distinct impression she looked at him the longest. The room remained very quiet. Taylor hoped fervently that Miss Liza might eject them on the grounds that they obviously didn't know what they were doing. Instead, however, she said nothing, slowly sipping her drink and apparently thinking. Finally, she spoke.

"Well, gentlemen, I am Miss Liza and you are very welcome here. As you can see," she waved an arm about the room, "business is a bit slow tonight. We've been open for hours and there's not a wet towel in the house!" Taylor felt sick.

"Yes, ma'am," said Biddle, rocking forward on his toes. "We come to fix that!"

"Yes," she replied, smiling. "I can see that you have."

"I think maybe I'll just step—" Taylor began.

"The girls cost a dollar," continued Miss Liza, "and you get one hour. As many times as you can manage, but no more than an hour. We don't tolerate drunkenness, rude behavior, stealing, or bad language. This is a reputable business after all!"

Biddle began digging in his pocket for money, while Taylor stood frozen. Miss Liza finished her drink and walked over to him. She suddenly stood less than a foot away, her breath a sweet smell that made him feel dizzy. If Taylor thought he couldn't be more surprised by what was happening, he was wrong. In the next moment, Miss Liza had put her hand between his legs. She rubbed him and didn't seem the least bit surprised.

"Not bad," she said, approvingly, "but I'll bet you can do better than that."

Without another word, she led him out of the room.

FIVE

TAYLOR sat in a large red chair by a glowing fire. The spring evening was cool but Liza had left a window in her private room partly open. The smells of jasmine and magnolia blossoms filled the space making Taylor feel slightly more relaxed. Liza asked him if he wanted a drink. He began to shake his head then changed his mind. After bringing him the drink, she sat down with her own in a nearby chair. She didn't seem inclined toward idle talk and he, of course, couldn't think of one thing to say. As the minutes stretched on Taylor felt more and more uncertain, but the whiskey helped.

"How long have you been in Vicksburg, Robert?" Liza finally asked. "I'm sorry, you don't mind if I call you Robert, do you?"

He managed a weak smile. "I don't mind. Though nobody ever calls me Robert."

She looked amused. "No, I imagine not."

He said he'd been in the city since the siege the previous spring. And how had he come to be in the infantry? she wondered next. What did his family think? Did he feel he was doing the right thing, joining for the war, or was the whole thing more of a lark?

Taylor looked at the amber liquid in his glass. "I never do anything as a lark." Then he looked back at Liza, who smiled at him but didn't say anything. "Do you always ask so many questions?"

"Only if I'm interested. But you're right. You didn't come here to talk."

"I didn't come here for anything."

"Oh?" She finished her drink then walked over and knelt down in front of him. "I think you most certainly came here for something. Maybe something you don't even know."

Taylor felt his insides going soft. Liza took his drink and set it on the table. Then she moved her hand down to his crotch and began rubbing him, slowly at first, then faster, then slow again. The effect of being touched like this made his entire body heat up; Taylor could feel his face growing red. Liza saw this too. She unbuttoned his frock coat, which helped, but when she moved her hands over his torso and then unbuttoned his trousers, he felt even more on fire.

"I don't do this very often," she whispered, reaching inside his pants.

"You don't have to do it now," he said, hoarsely.

"Don't you want me to?"

"I—I don't know."

But Liza seemed to know. And twenty minutes later, so did Taylor. He couldn't quite believe it, but he was awfully glad he'd agreed to go with Biddle to the bawdy house.

*

In early May, the regiment received orders for an expedition north of Vicksburg up the Yazoo River. The enemy was apparently on the move with ideas toward retaking the river city. The men laughed at this. As Lieutenant Richard Pomeroy read the marching orders, one soldier shouted that his mother and sisters would have a better chance of getting past the Federals. Pomeroy, a fiery Irishman with a quick temper and flashing green eyes, nodded seriously.

"Get them guns cleaned and oiled and get your food cooked. Five o'clock means feet are moving at five. Any man not ready will answer to me. Dismissed!"

That evening, Biddle left the campfire after being told

Lieutenant Pomeroy wanted to see him. Bean and Taylor sat playing cribbage, while Christmas was showing an uncomfortable Kit his latest catalog order. The set of naked women pictures entitled, "Mermaids Wearing Only Mist and Foam" had Kit turning every shade of red, and Christmas whistling like some kind of spring bird.

"You doing that, Morgan," said Bean, "means I can't concentrate on my counting." This was only met with another whistle.

After a half-hour, Biddle returned and sat down by the fire with a heavy plop. "That was strange," he said.

"What?" asked Taylor, who had just laid down his cards and was moving his pegs forward.

"Pomeroy."

"What about him?"

"When I got to his tent, he wasn't there but I could hear him talking with Lieutenant Mohrmann of Company A just on the other side. I didn't mean to listen but couldn't help hearing."

"And?"

"Pomeroy was telling Mohrmann, 'Take this book, Mohrmann. You've borrowed it often enough and I should like you to have it. I know I'm not coming back from this raid, and I'm giving away my things.'"

"He's not coming back?" asked Kit. "What does that mean?"

Biddle shrugged. "I'm sure I don't know. Neither did Mohrmann seems. He said, 'Very well, Dick, and when you want to read it, I will lend it to you.' That really set the lieutenant off. He shouted back, 'I shall not want to read this or any other book!' Then he stomped over to where I was standing like a damn fool in front of his tent. I thought I'd get it for sure, but all he did was look at me queerly. Then he handed me this." Biddle pulled a small knife out of his pocket. "He said he knew I liked to whittle."

The knife had silver blades inside a pearl handle and it was so small and delicate that it looked like something belonging to a girl. Pomeroy had told Biddle that holding the knife up to the light illuminated an image inside the translucent handle: a young woman kneeling beneath an inscription of The Lord's Prayer. Christmas held the knife up toward the sinking sun, but it was too dark to see much.

"That is strange," he said, handing the knife back to Biddle.

"Which part?" asked Bean, shuffling the cards. "You ask me, Pomeroy's a funny one. Touchy as a wildcat and just about as unpredictable."

Taylor agreed. "Rebs don't have much fight in 'em, boys. Besides, nobody knows the future, not even officers."

The next morning, the 72nd Illinois, along with the 11th and 124th regiments, marched northeast out of Vicksburg. The roads grew so dusty it was hard to believe it had been raining only a few days before. They encamped that night at a place called Bear Creek. All felt somber at seeing the ravaged landscape: homes burned and abandoned, skeletal livestock wandering listlessly around the ruins, lonely graves and weedy gardens. That night, the men tended to blistered and swollen feet. Taylor limped into the woods to do his business and found a pile of boards and logs that had once been a cabin. The demise of this structure could not be blamed on the war for it was much older; only the chimney remained, a teetering column of mossy bricks. After doing what he'd come to do, Taylor sat with his boots off and smoked a cigar. It was a few minutes later that he saw them. Hundreds by his estimation and appearing as if out of nowhere. They blackened a part of the sky above the line of trees, gathered slowly into a swirling funnel, and then, quite suddenly, began dropping from view into the chimney. They were the swifts, little, dark birds he'd seen many times back home doing the very same thing, occupying vacant homes or old, hollow trees for the night. He continued smoking until the last bird had disappeared. Then he put on his boots and returned to camp.

The next day, the regiments continued the march. Dust enveloped them and water became scarce. Two exhausting days later, they reached a village called Benton and were ordered to "double-quick" to the front. After another mile, the 72nd was sent forward through a dense wood with two companies leading the way as skirmishers. Lieutenant Pomeroy took command of Companies A and F. As one of the skirmishers, Taylor found himself drenched in sweat and afraid in a way he hadn't been in a long time. Biddle too looked pale as they advanced. Shells and shot passed overhead, tree tops and branches splintered and fell to the ground with tremendous thuds, and all the while the ear-splitting cries of the minie balls filled the air around them. As Taylor now recalled only too well, there were so many things happening at once that it was hard to know where to look or what exactly he was seeing. Yet, in the midst of it all, the noise and the shouting and the smoke, one thing stood out: the lieutenant going down.

Up ahead of them a shell had exploded above Pomeroy's head and he went flying headlong into the vegetation. By the time Biddle and Taylor reached him, another officer had arrived and wrapped a handkerchief around Pomeroy's bleeding leg. Using Biddle's frock coat as a stretcher, they carried Pomeroy back to a small building that had once been a farm office. The lieutenant looked pale, but insisted he was fine and kept encouraging the boys to leave him and go back to the fight. While waiting for the surgeon, two orderlies at the makeshift hospital gave Pomeroy morphine. Taylor and the others left, but instead of going back they lingered outside the tent. Just to make sure the surgeon came, just to make sure Pomeroy would be all right. When the surgeon arrived, all breathed a sigh of relief.

Yet, a few hours later, after the Confederates had finally skedaddled, word came that Pomeroy had died. The men of Company F ran back to the hospital. They arrived just as the surgeon emerged from the building. He shook his head.

"I'm sorry, boys. His knee was ruined, the leg needed to come off, but in the middle of the procedure his heart just stopped." The surgeon then left to attend to several wounded men who'd remained outside.

"Jesus," said Christmas.

"It can't be," whispered Kit, his eyes filling with tears.

The others said nothing. Bean walked a few paces away rubbing his temples, while Biddle absently took Pomeroy's knife from his pocket and looked at it with a pasty expression. Oddly, Taylor didn't feel the least bit surprised. That's what had happened to him during the months he'd been a soldier: nothing really surprised him anymore. He supposed this was a good thing, though it also made him feel sad.

"Well, that's that," said Christmas, clearing his throat. "Pomeroy knew he wasn't coming back and this is how it happened. Let's give him a good burial, boys, and that'll be the end of it."

Biddle nodded. "Must be an undertaker in this town. That or we build a coffin."

Benton wasn't very big and the few businesses along the main street appeared deserted. Behind Henderson's Embalming and Funeral Services they found a coffin and carried it back to the hospital. The orderlies had scrubbed Pomeroy's face and combed his hair, but he still looked disheveled and like himself and not the least bit ready for the grave. This seemed even more true when the men found they'd grabbed a coffin that was too small.

"Jesus Christ!" shouted Christmas. "He don't fit!"

"Guess we gotta go back and get a different one," said Bean, his voice shaking.

"But this was the biggest they had!"

The back of Taylor's head ached. Pomeroy's legs were sticking out of the coffin as if he had just propped them up on a log and was taking a nap under a tree. While all stood around arguing about what to do, Kit walked over to the surgeon's wagon. After a few minutes, he returned with an axe.

"What are you doing?" asked Christmas.

Kit headed for Pomeroy with a determined look. "I'm cutting off his goddamn legs."

"*What?*"

"He don't fit, but I'll make him fit."

With that, Kit raised the axe above his head and brought the blade swiftly down on the top of Pomeroy's knee. The angle was slightly off for a direct hit, but there still came a sharp, cracking sound. With surprising speed, Kit raised the axe again. Biddle, the first to recover from this disturbing solution to the problem, grabbed the boy around the waist and lifted him and the axe away from their officer. Bean then grabbed the axe, while Taylor stood there shaking. The expression on Kit's face, devoid of all emotion, filled him with a terrible fear. As Biddle set him down, Kit's legs collapsed from under him and he hit the ground like a raggedy doll. The jolt must have stunned him. Color began returning to his face, his eyes widening as if he was just awakening from a dream.

"What's the matter with you, Johnson?" yelled Christmas.

"Just leave him," said Biddle in a quiet voice. "He ain't right."

Taylor couldn't stop shaking. Everything they'd just watched was disturbing, but seeing a man, even a dead one, do nothing while another man tried to cut off his legs seemed the worst. Plus, they still had the original problem. While Kit sat dazed, the others searched for more tools and then began taking apart the coffin. With a few stray pieces of wood and some nails, they cobbled together an extension to the pine box. It looked uneven and there were several openings, but Pomeroy fit and that was all that mattered. They carried him to the Benton cemetery and began digging.

That evening, Lieutenant Mohrmann, who'd heard Pomeroy had been shot, came by to see how he was doing. The officer turned as pale as a peach when the men told him, "We're sorry, sir. The lieutenant is dead and buried."

*

A few weeks after the regiment returned from the Yazoo Pass expedition, Taylor finally had a chance to see Liza again. After that first visit and before the regiment had left, he'd managed one other trip to the bawdy house and found her just as receptive. Taylor had noticed Liza didn't talk much about herself, but on this third encounter he found her surprisingly talkative. She told him that she was forty-one and that she'd started her business for two important reasons: one, it made good money, almost without exception even when the economy was flagging, and two, she enjoyed sex. She knew any number of madams for whom the latter wasn't true, but Liza had always considered this odd; why get into the business if not to enjoy the product now and then? Liza had opened her establishment in the early 1850s with two friends she'd convinced to come north with her from New Orleans. She kept prices low, made sure her girls were clean, and her discretion was known throughout the region. Liza's grew and now she employed several women as well as a few men to manage the building and the grounds. The Cadillac, she told Taylor, might do more business overall, but she had faithful customers that returned year after year.

"In addition, of course," she added, "to new ones like yourself." They were sitting up in her bed, Liza smoking one of her thin cigarettes and Taylor enjoying the strange, yet wonderful, pleasure of being with her.

"Is your family still in New Orleans?" he asked.

"Some are." She looked at him for a moment before continuing. "My daddy's an attorney and a white man. He's also married to a white woman, and they're prominent in society there. Mama worked for them until she started carrying me and Daddy found an excuse to dismiss her and set her up in another part of town. Mama was one of the few, free women in New Orleans back then, but that didn't mean she had many doors of opportunity opened for her. Still, she was fortunate and so was I. My daddy's a good man at bottom and he got her set up with her own business. I saw as a young girl that a woman could run a business as well as any man. Mama's smart and so am I. It's fortunate too that Daddy's other children, he's got five, haven't amounted to a lick between them. He could see his bastard was the smartest in the group and he took care of me and Mama best he could."

"Did he give you the money to start this place?"

Liza laughed. "He loaned me some money, yes, though he thinks I work in dressmaking. But I was never much for sewing and couldn't stand to sit all day with a bunch of material piled on my lap. I'm too interested in people for that kind of isolation. Besides, a house of pleasure earns far more than a dressmaking shop ever could." She smoked. "That isn't to say it's been easy. We live in a man's world, as you well know, Robert, and I doubt that will ever change. But if you're a smart woman, and lucky, then you can do all right. At least I have."

Taylor nodded. When Liza offered him one of her cigarettes, he accepted it and smoked while thinking about what she'd said. It was all true of course, especially the part about the world they lived in belonging to men. Not that he ever thought much about it though. The world was what it was. The challenge for every person, in his opinion, was simply surviving, and that didn't come easy for either men or women.

The more important question to him at this moment was what did someone as beautiful, smart, and interesting as Liza see in someone like him? As if reading his mind, she reached over and began rubbing his thigh.

"Men like dark women," she said, "because we're different. They think what they desire and hope for is so unusual, but it isn't. Everyone likes to have something that, well, surprises them."

Taylor put his hand over hers. "I find it hard to believe that I surprise you much."

"You underestimate yourself, my dear. Don't you think I enjoy this?"

"Seems like you do."

Taylor wanted to kiss her, but Liza had told him that first night that she never kissed customers. Kissing was for love and this was business. He accepted this as he accepted everything she told him. Besides, the only off limits place seemed to be her mouth; she let him roam freely over every other part of her body.

"What do the others think?" she asked him, twining her fingers through his.

"About what?"

"About us."

He shrugged. "They give me a hard time."

"I assume you give the same back."

"Best I can." Taylor thought. "The boys, though they don't like to admit it, are in awe of you. They can't figure what you see in me, but I believe our association has helped my reputation." He smiled.

Liza touched his lips with her fingertips. "You have a nice smile, Robert. I wish you shared it more."

"Ain't usually a lot to smile about." Liza smiled too and put out her cigarette. Taylor moved on top of her then, and she in turn began moving beneath him. He nuzzled her neck and whispered, "The boys think I must be in love with you. They say, "Taylor never wanted to go to the ladies before, and now he can't stay away from one of them.""

Liza moved her mouth closer to his. "You're not in love, are you, Robert?" she asked. "For you mustn't be in love, you know."

"No," he said, kissing the corner of her mouth, "I'm not in love."

*

The next two months passed quietly in Vicksburg. Spring gave way to summer, and the bugs and reptiles returned as if they'd never been away. Taylor found the little blue lizard in the coffee pot again; small, green snakes could be seen curled up on the new sweetgum leaves. A chorus of birdsong woke the men each morning just before light appeared in the sky, and they didn't mind being awake during the only cool part of the day. Everyone's skin broke out in rashes from the humidity. Bathing in the Mississippi helped, but when a soldier was dragged underwater by an alligator, the river banks grew deserted.

That June, the occupied city began to have a newspaper again. In anticipation of the country's impending anniversary, the now Federally managed *Daily Herald* encouraged Vicksburg's citizens to celebrate the "glorious old fourth." The paper advertised American flags for sale and a town-wide celebration was planned with balls and lavish spreads for some of the Union-leaning residents. Additionally, the military was organizing the installment of a white, marble monument at the spot where the interview between

Generals Grant and Pemberton had taken place the previous year. The excitement grew among officers, but for the men life carried on much as it had been. They were glad for the peace, but sometimes it was too quiet.

Liza told Robert that she too planned a big celebration. She had much to be grateful for, business had never been so good, and she wanted to show her appreciation. Liza could afford to be generous. She could afford a great array of food and drink and even music. Of course, he would come, wouldn't he? Taylor had nodded enthusiastically for he liked pleasing her, but inside he felt dull. Despite the routine of his days, or maybe because of it, Taylor felt the press of other worries. Even when he was with Liza, even sometimes during sex, his mind wandered.

First there was Kit, who had barely spoken since their return from the Yazoo. The boy ate little and could not be roused with any amount of good-natured teasing. He had also grown very careful and made sure to never drop anything or stumble over anybody. On the one hand, this was a good change; on the other, it was not the Kit they all had known for nearly two years. The second problem for Taylor was guilt. Seeing Liza so much, as well as buying her gifts, which he'd begun doing occasionally, had meant he had less money to send home. Taylor had joined for the war in part so that he could help his pa; now to be far away and not helping seemed ridiculous. So he tried not to think about Liza and to go into town less frequently, but he never really managed it. Maybe he was in love after all.

The night of the big event, Taylor went to Liza's with Bean, Biddle, and Christmas. Though the Federal Army had done its best, the July Fourth celebration hadn't made much of an impression on Vicksburg's residents. Apart from Federal soldiers and officers in blue, the streets were largely empty. However, Liza's was packed. While the others immediately went off with their girls, Taylor accepted a drink from a young woman and slipped outside. The evening was still beastly warm despite the late hour and inside seemed a good ten degrees hotter still. Taylor was sipping a second drink when Liza found him.

"Are you having a good time, Robert?" she asked, kissing him on the cheek. Liza wore an off the shoulder gray and blue satin gown with layers of lace above her bosom and long, white gloves covering her hands. She'd piled her braids atop her head and Taylor couldn't take his eyes off her. He kissed her back.

"There's only one thing I'd rather be doing," he whispered.

She laughed. "Later, my friend."

They stayed outside, talking and drinking. Despite the somber feel of the town, the streets offered up all manner of noise: a pistol being fired, then another, two cats in an altercation, Vicksburg's dogs howling and telling the world they still had troubles. As the drink softened Taylor, he wished desperately to be locked away with Liza in her room. She agreed, but said she felt it necessary to remain the hostess while so many guests were present. He must have looked very sorry, for she suddenly laughed. Liza then set both their drinks on a table and led him down the porch stairs to the alley. Not ten feet away was the entrance to a small storage area. Boxes had been stacked around the door. Next to the door, the shadows quickly engulfed them.

Liza pulled him close. "I haven't ever done with anyone like I do with you, Robert." Then she kissed him, full on the lips, her mouth open, her tongue searching. After all they'd done together and the many ways she made him feel, this one kiss took his breath away more than all the rest. He kissed her back, tasted the sherry she'd drunk and the almond cake he'd seen her eating. He rubbed one hand over the lace that covered her sweet, dark skin. How he would ever get to all of her with the gown in the way and standing up in the dark doorway he had no idea. Clothes and the strange place didn't bother Liza however. She stepped back briefly to unbutton his frock coat. Then she moved to his trousers.

*

Later, on Mulberry Street, Taylor still felt flushed and thick in the head. He pulled a bottle of whiskey from his haversack and took a good, long drink. In the next moment, Biddle appeared beside him.

"Goddamn, Taylor," he said. "I feel about as fine as a man can feel."

"You look fine too." He handed his friend the bottle. "Are you in love?"

"Nah, not this time. But that don't mean I ain't having a very good time."

Neither wanted to go back to camp, so they turned south on Mulberry, then took a right on Lee Street and headed west toward the river. After skidding down the bank to the Mississippi's edge, they heard two watery plops. The foraging beavers swam gracefully away while measured wingbeats indicated the departure of a heron as well. Taylor and Biddle sat down, taking turns at the flask.

"Hey Biddle," Taylor said after awhile.

"Hmm?"

"You think Kit's gonna be all right?"

"I hope so. But truth to tell, I ain't sure."

"He's a queer little fellow, ain't he?"

"Yeah, but…"

"What?"

"Well, it's pretty queer what happened with Pomeroy too." Biddle thought. "My mama were here she'd say a boy like Kit has got too much on his mind. She'd say it's unhealthy for a person to keep so much to hisself."

"Works hard though," mused Taylor. "And he ain't no coward. It's more just like he ain't your typical soldier." He found a rock and threw it into the water, changing the subject. "You hear from your sister?"

"Yep, a week back."

"How is she?"

"Ah, Katie's well." Taylor could hear the happiness in Biddle's voice. "She's been working with our mother at Camp Douglas, tending the prisoners there. She bakes, sews, and writes letters for the men."

Taylor thought about this. "That bother you?" he asked.

"Nah, I don't think so. They can be prisoners, and in the wrong too, but they don't have to be treated badly."

"True. What else did Katie write?"

"Says she's been working in the city for Mrs. Livermore, and pretty much has no time for anything else. I asked her if she had a beau yet, but she says she don't have time for any man." Biddle tossed a rock too. "Kinda makes me glad, I s'pose, but…"

"What?"

"Well, it seems like she *should* be getting married. She's almost twenty-two after all. But she told me in one letter that she wasn't interested in finding a fella." He paused. "That seem queer to you, Taylor?"

"Not really."

"But shouldn't she be getting married?"

"Not if she don't want to."

"But shouldn't she be wanting to?"

"Not if she likes how things are. Maybe she likes what she's doing."

"The war won't go on forever."

"Seems like it's trying."

Biddle continued, "She can't be tending soldiers forever. I dunno, maybe I just don't like her spending time with all them men."

"But you just said it was a good thing."

"I know, but still, I know what they're like."

"Like you, you mean?" Taylor laughed.

"Yeah, 'cept worse since they're Secesh."

"Aw, I wouldn't worry about it, Biddle," said Taylor, taking a drink. "Katie seems like a smart girl. She'll figure out what she wants. Then maybe she'll find herself some nice fella, a clerk maybe who does numbers and such and agrees that women should have the vote, and then she'll settle down with him. After they get married, you'll end up with a whole passel of nieces and nephews."

Biddle thought about this. "A clerk? For Katie?"

"Who knows? Didn't you tell me that a fella can't help who he falls in love with? I 'spect it's the same for women."

60

"Yeah, maybe. I don't know if it's exactly the same though."

They sat then, listening to horn blasts from ships and voices carrying over from the other shore. Little triangles of light from the lamps of nearby ships dropped near them.

After a few minutes, Biddle asked Taylor if he had any sisters. He didn't. Brothers? No. "I mean, you ain't never mentioned anybody."

"Ain't nobody but me and my pa," Taylor said, more sharply than he'd intended.

"Taylor—"

"I don't wanna talk about kin, Biddle"

"All right, but can I tell you something?"

"Depends."

"It's just that, well, you know I'm your friend, right? If you wanna tell me anything, you can. I mean, I won't tell nobody."

"Like what would I tell?"

"Like about the troubles at home. With your pa's debts and such. I know having debts ain't easy. My uncle got hisself in a bad way with gambling once—"

"Pa ain't in debt from gambling," said Taylor, "and the debts ain't his fault. It's just, well, it's just what happens sometimes." He sighed. "Look, Biddle, you're my very best friend, all right? Ain't nobody I like better or trust more than you, and that's the truth. So, if you care about me the same, you won't ask no questions."

"But—"

"Do you care the same?"

"A course I do."

"Good." Taylor finished the last of the whiskey, then began taking off his coat. "Let's go swimming!"

"But I thought you couldn't swim!"

"I can't. I'll just wade in the shallows."

"What about the gators?"

"They sleep at night. Come on!"

After standing up, Taylor determined he was considerably more messed up from the whiskey than he thought. Consequently, it took him much more time to get out of his clothes than Biddle, who was already whooping in the water. As they cooled off and splashed each other, another ship went by. The triangles of light returned to the sand and willows above Taylor and Biddle, then slowly began sliding down the banks toward them. The light fell upon their faces and arms briefly before the southern night enfolded them once again.

SIX

As THE SUMMER HEAT gave way once again to autumn's chilly grasp, a rumor circulated that the 72nd Illinois would soon be leaving Vicksburg. Most of the soldiers didn't pay much attention. There was so much scuttlebutt every day, from increases in pay to the arrival of better rations to even one great story about President Lincoln coming to Vicksburg, that it wasn't really worth trying to determine what might be true. If any of these things actually happened, the men would know it soon enough.

One afternoon, Taylor and Kit had inspection of company streets. It was a simple task, they had only to walk up and down each line of tents and make note of all infractions. Unattended campfires, untidy quarters, or rubbish scattered about would be reported to the corporal of the guard. It was easy duty and for that reason Taylor didn't mind. It did, however, put him in other parts of the camp, places where he could run into Henry Beesley or other soldiers who might be suspicious of him.

They walked along, making the inspection and feeling glad to note few problems. Kit didn't say much until after they'd finished and were walking back to their own street. "You think this war'll go on much longer, Taylor?" he asked.

"No idea." Taylor smiled. "Why, you thinking of getting married or something?"

Kit colored. "No, I ain't thinking of that. It's just, well…"

"What?"

"Aw, nothing." Kit hadn't spoken so many words in weeks and Taylor didn't want him to stop now.

"Come on, Kit, what is it? I don't mean to hassle you."

"That's all right, I don't mind you teasing. It's just, well, I feel done, Robert, I truly do. I'm so tired, I barely know the day. It ain't been easy these two years."

"I know it ain't."

"The other thing is…" Kit looked away.

"What?"

"It's just hard, Taylor."

"What is?"

"Pretending, that's all. Pretending that I'm something I'm not."

Taylor stopped. "Whaddya mean?"

"I ain't no kind of soldier, Robert. No kind of good one leastwise."

"You ain't a bad soldier, Kit. You never run from a fight. And you don't never shirk your duty. That's all that really matters."

But Kit didn't seem to be listening. "My mama would say I shouldn't be here."

"But she sent you off."

"Nah, she didn't. She don't even know I joined up. Instead, she thinks I run off to the circus. Y'see," the boy's face turned a pasty color. ""Kit" ain't even my real name."

For a moment, Taylor didn't say anything. Then he started walking again. "Maybe you best not say anymore."

"I wanna go home, Taylor."

"Well, you can't go home. None of us can go home. Besides, you want the boys thinking you're a coward?"

"I don't care what they think."

"You will. Anyhow, it'd be worse than that. You know what happens to deserters."

"I know."

"So, stop thinking about it. Near as I can tell we're gonna be here in Vicksburg for the duration. Just patrolling streets and throwing looters in jail. Not much danger in that."

Kit's eyes filled with tears. "I see his face everywhere."

"What? Whose?"

"Lieutenant Pomeroy's. I worry, Taylor. I worry till I'm sick thinking..." his voice turned into a whisper. "Thinking maybe we buried him and he wasn't really dead!"

"Oh, Kit."

"Coulda happened, couldn't it?"

"No, it couldn't! How long did we work digging that damn grave, huh? Three or four hours as I recall. Pomeroy had turned cold as a stone by the time we set him in there. You saw him, Kit! There weren't no life in him. Maybe we got some real worries, but that sure in the hell ain't one of 'em!" Taylor's voice had grown louder.

"You think I'm crazy."

Taylor sighed. "I don't think you're crazy. You just—" He remembered Biddle's words. "—you just think too much. But you don't have nothing to fret about, all right? Pomeroy is gone. We're all sorry about that but it's a war and people die in a war, that's just the way it is. It ain't strange either that you feel tired; we all do. I could go home right now, I would do it in a fast minute, but that ain't likely to happen, so I just don't think about it. And you shouldn't think about it either. Instead, when you start fretting, I want you to come find me. I'll help you, all right?" Kit nodded. "Say it. Say you promise you will always come to me."

"I promise."

"Good." Taylor put an arm around the boy. "We've got to take care of each other. We're all we've got."

*

Taylor's words must have done some good. Several days later, Kit purchased a harmonica and began teaching himself to play. He didn't seem to have much of an ear for music, but all agreed it was good to see him doing something besides sitting and thinking. Meanwhile, Christmas and Bean worked on repairs to their quarters, finding more bricks for the chimney and sealing up the walls; they had no illusions that they wouldn't be spending another winter in Vicksburg. Taylor, for his part, spent most of his free time either with Liza or writing letters. He'd found a good correspondent in Katherine Biddle and enjoyed describing for her even the most ordinary of events.

As the days grew shorter and continued in their monotony, the only one who didn't seem quite himself was Joseph Biddle. He'd begun spending more time alone and didn't join in the conversations at mealtimes. In their tent at night, Taylor could hear his friend not sleeping. Whenever he asked what was wrong however, he got the same reply: nothing.

One evening in early October, Biddle appeared at their tent where Taylor lay on his blanket smoking his pipe. He was looking at some cards Christmas had given him, trying to figure out why photographs of naked, fat women were so appealing.

"I thought you didn't like those."

Taylor shrugged. "They're all right. Mostly I don't get why Christmas finds 'em so interesting." He looked up.

Biddle shook his head. "No, I imagine not."

Taylor put the cards away. "You feel all right?" he asked his friend.

"Sure. Why wouldn't I?"

"I dunno. You just been acting kinda different lately." When Biddle didn't say anything, Taylor continued. "You sore at me?"

A pause. "No. I ain't sore."

"Well, what is it then? I ain't never seen you so quiet."

Biddle changed the subject. "You know what you'll do after the war, Taylor?"

"No idea. Why?"

"I dunno. Just wondering. Thinking about when we might get to go home, I s'pose."

Taylor nodded. "You and Kit seems."

"You think we'll see more fighting?"

Taylor lay back on his blanket and put an arm over his eyes. "I don't know, Biddle. I try not to think too much about the future."

"How can you not think about the future?"

"Easy, I just tell myself I'm not thinking about it, and I don't. Whatever it turns out to be, it'll be less disappointing if I ain't counting on anything."

"Yeah, I s'pose that's best." Biddle changed the subject again. "Kit seems better."

"Yeah. He'll be all right."

"He said he talked to you. He said you told him we all gotta take care of each other."

"That's so."

Biddle sighed. "We all got secrets, don't we?"

Taylor opened his eyes. "What?"

"Kit, me, you. We all got stuff we don't share, don't we?"

"Sure, we do. Though maybe they ain't secrets so much as just stuff that never gets said." He sat up. "What's bothering you, Biddle? You worried about something? You can tell me you know, whatever it is."

"Thanks, Taylor. You are a good friend. Best I've ever had, in fact."

"But?"

Biddle smiled tiredly. "No buts. You're a good friend. And I just wish this war was over."

Taylor nodded. "Me too."

*

The orders arrived during the last week of October: the regiment was heading to Georgia. They would join Major-General William Sherman's army and move through that state toward the ocean. After breaking down their quarters and packing up tents and other gear, Taylor and Biddle went into town. They found a Mr. J.W. Young at his photographic studio and got their likeness taken. The man sat them side by side on a couch with their hats off and legs crossed. Taylor thought his friend looked very handsome. Biddle's beard was full and he'd just gotten his hair trimmed. Taylor had also gotten a haircut and was clean-shaven and tidy, but he appeared a little like a scarecrow next to Biddle. Still, both felt pleased. They bought small frames and Biddle headed to the post office to mail his home. Taylor continued along Washington Street, stopping at Titcomb & Woodruff to buy a few items for their journey.

The store was empty except for a large, silver tabby cat sitting on the counter. As Taylor scratched the cat's ears, he could feel its throaty purrs in his fingers. The business, by all indications, seemed to continue in its prosperity: more goods filled shelves from floor to ceiling, the feeling of the place one of unqualified success. Taylor liked stores, liked the atmosphere of people coming and going, of a community built around a central meeting place. If he thought about the future, which he didn't, he might want to own a mercantile, just a small one that he could manage by himself. He was fully absorbed in this though when the owner of Titcomb & Woodruff appeared. The man smiled at Taylor, then saw the cat on the counter.

"Git, ya beast!" he shouted, waving a cloth. The feline merely looked at the man and yawned, after which the man picked the animal up and put it on the floor. The cat walked away, unimpressed. "He's a rascal, that one, but the best mouser I ever had."

Taylor nodded. After requesting cigars and a few hard candies, he realized how much he would miss Vicksburg. In spite of the terrible way in which he'd been introduced to the city, the battles and the siege, and later the boredom, heat, and bugs, Taylor knew he'd never encounter another place quite like this.

"I hear you boys are leaving," the store owner said as he wrapped up the goods.

Taylor looked at the cat sitting on the floor washing its paw. "That's so."

"I 'spect you know most of us ain't got much use for Yankees around here," the man continued. "But y'all that's been here this year have been all right. Ya was always polite and ya didn't steal nothing. We appreciate that."

Taylor handed him the money. "I 'spect you appreciate the business more than anything."

The man colored slightly. He thought a moment. "It ain't been an easy time, that's the truth. Maybe ya ain't never had to make hard decisions, young man, but some day ya will. Anyways, I wish ya luck and pray this war is over soon."

He reached out his hand. Taylor looked at the man then shook his hand quickly before leaving.

Taylor's next stop was Mrs. Jeffers' Millinery & Fancy Goods where he purchased a headdress of green silk ribbon and purple daisies. In spite of Liza's insistence that he not bring her more presents, he nonetheless detected pleasure in her eyes at his offerings. Besides, this was it. He would not see her ever again, and he selfishly wanted to be remembered, even if just for a few months.

Liza's place seemed quiet when he arrived. Of course, it was mid-afternoon which might have been part of the reason. Taylor found Liza in the parlor talking with Sadie and another girl. She finished with them and came over to him.

"I didn't expect you today," she said, smiling.

"We're leaving tomorrow."

"Oh." She looked out the window.

Taylor took her hand. "Do you have time for me now?"

Liza did have time, and she led him away to her room. Taylor thought her mind on other things however as they slipped into the bed, yet she also didn't seem to hold back as they came together for the last time. An hour went by, then another. Taylor knew he needed to return to camp, but felt loathe to leave. He would never have this again, not with Liza or any other woman. As he lay next to her, stroking her bosom, he felt great appreciation for this woman he couldn't have imagined knowing even one short year ago.

At last, Liza turned his way. "I will miss you, my dear."

"I will miss you too."

She placed her hand on Taylor's, stopping his caresses. "I also am quite worried for you. You've survived so far, but who knows what is coming?" She moved her hand to his cheek. "I think you should go home before it's too late."

Taylor looked at her surprised. "I can't go home."

"This isn't something you have to do, Robert."

He thought. "Yes, it is. Besides, I'm not afraid of dying."

"There are worse things than dying, my friend."

"I know." Taylor rolled onto his back and looked up at the ceiling. "You know, I would have never met you but for the war. I would have never known such wonderful things but for our time together." He sighed. "I would not have ever imagined one blessed good thing could come from something that has taken away so much, but..." he rolled onto his side and placed both hands flat beneath his head, "...it has."

Liza smiled and kissed him. "You are the dearest. A fact that makes it all the harder for me to see you go."

Taylor nodded. "I will worry about you as well."

Liza laughed. "I think you should save your concern for yourself. I have taken care of myself for a very long time, and there are very few people I've ever met, men or women, who truly scare me."

"Have there been *any*?" asked Taylor, his eyes teasing.

After a moment's thought, Liza said, "None that are still living." She reached for her cigarette case on the bed table and lit two of the thin smokes. After handing one to Taylor, she added, "I'm not sure you and I are really as different as you think, my dear, and I'm not so sure that the war was the only way our paths would have crossed."

"Indeed?" He smoked and thought she must be having him on. If not for the war, he'd be back on the farm in Illinois and she'd be in Vicksburg, worlds so far apart that they might as well be on different planets.

She nodded, then said, as if reading his mind, "You might think you'd want nothing more than to stay on your family's farm, but I suspect you want much more than that. I believe you're the kind of

person who wants to see more, know more, do more. As I have."
She gave a slight shrug. "I simply pray this business ends soon so
all that may happen for you."

He nodded, uncomfortable. Liza had assessed him in ways that
were not inaccurate, but he didn't care to discuss the past or future.
"Did you ever think of removing to the north?" he asked, changing
the subject.

"Oh, yes. And I believe I will still get there one day, perhaps
when the war is over. Perhaps I shall come visit you."

"I would like that."

Liza stared at him through the smoke of her cigarette. "You
know, I believe you would. Well, who knows what the future shall
hold? I myself try not to think much beyond the current week."

"So, there's one way we are similar," he smiled.

"One *more* way," she corrected.

"Yes," Taylor nodded. "One more way."

"In any case, it may very well be wise to leave the South
sometime soon. The war is lost, of course, but the trouble shall not
soon be over. At least not for the Negroes."

Taylor considered asking her what she meant by this, but then
felt certain he already knew. "I expect you're right," he nodded,
"though it seems we've all been through enough already."

"That's true. We must hope for the best."

He put out the cigarette. "I will write to you."

"Good." Liza didn't add that she would as well, but Taylor was
certain this was so, and he felt awful glad about it.

*

Vicksburg Daily Herald, November 1, 1864
The 72nd Illinois Infantry

The departure of this gallant regiment on Sunday afternoon, on
the Continental, for a "place in the picture" at the front, was an
impressive and affecting scene. An immense concourse of citizens
and of their fellow soldiers gathered on the levee to see them off.
The Post Band delivered a thrilling musical adieu, and every
evidence of respect and good will was paid them.

The 72nd has been doing provost guard duty in this city for a number of months past, and both officers and men, by their kind, courteous and soldierly deportment, have won the respect and esteem of the citizens of the post. Many of them were endeared by the tenderest ties of friendship to those they were leaving behind; and many a brave solider whose cheek had never blanched in battle felt his eyes overflowing as he wrung, perhaps for the last time, the hand of some friend or comrade.

Capt. Curtis, the able and efficient Provost Marshal of this post, who is himself a member of this gallant regiment, paid his last respects to the boys by a present of something refreshing, which was pledged with full hearts and fond hopes of future happy meetings when war's rude voice should be heard no more. The scene of departments will long be remembered by those who participated in its regrets, its hopes and its fears.

SEVEN

AFTER A WEEK of travel on the Mississippi River, the steamer *Continental* pulled up to the wharf in Cairo, Illinois. In August 1862, the regiment had spent two weeks in this town, the best part of which had been leaving. Cairo sat on a narrow peninsula between the confluence of the Ohio and Mississippi Rivers, and despite the presence of numerous buildings, was more swamp than civilization. It had perpetually soggy ground, a bold rat population, mosquitos and mud, and humidity that made a man feel like he could never get dry.

As all looked down sadly at the dock, Bean remained cheerful. "Cheer up, boys. It ain't like we're staying. Soon we'll be on the cars headed home to vote."

This had been the rumor and it was confirmed when the regiment gathered off the ship to receive orders. Each man would be going home to vote in the upcoming presidential election, a duty considered vital if the North wanted to win the war. If the former Union general, Democrat George McClellan, was elected instead of Republican Abraham Lincoln, he would undo everything the soldiers had worked and died for these past three and a half years. McClellan said he would commence peace talks with the South at any cost, and all believed the dissolution of the Union would follow. Taylor, like all the rest, wanted desperately to cast his vote for Lincoln. Unlike the others, he didn't want to go home.

However, two days later the regiment was still in a camp just outside of Cairo. With near-constant rain, the mud came up to the men's knees as they marched back into town one afternoon for what they believed to involve boarding of the cars for home. Instead, however, they received four months' pay. Then they were ordered back to camp. With the election now just two days away, hope faded that anyone would arrive home in time to vote. The boggy camp, a thoroughly depressing scene, prompted Taylor and Biddle to request passes back into Cairo; at least there were businesses there that might provide some distraction. Unfortunately, owing to it being Sunday, most stores along Commercial Avenue were closed. The rain slid off the soldiers' rubber ponchos as they walked past H.H. Canlee & Co. Grocers, Koehler's Gunshop, and the post office. A few doors farther, however, a billiards hall was open and Taylor and Biddle gratefully got out of the rain and ordered two glasses of beer.

The man behind the counter squinted at them. "Now, you boys know we ain't s'posed to sell liquor on Sundays."

Biddle looked around at the few customers standing in small groups or playing billiards. "Well, just give us whatever these others are having." He then placed a half-dollar on the counter. "I spect you ain't got a problem taking money on a Sunday."

The man snickered and filled two glasses. As he handed one to Taylor, he smiled showing a mouth full of spaces and bad teeth. "You're a pretty boy, ain't ya?"

Taylor was about to reply when Biddle hustled him to a table. "Just leave it Taylor. It ain't worth it."

"This town gives me the willies."

"Yeah, me too. But we'll be home soon." He took a sip. "That'll be nice. Seeing my folks and Katie, sleeping in my own bed. What about it, Taylor? Won't that be nice?"

"Yeah, it'll be great. If it happens, that is."

Biddle opened his mouth to protest, but then didn't bother; they both knew better than to get their hopes up. As his friend's expression grew more somber, Taylor asked what he'd heard of late from Katie. Biddle's face lit up thinking of his sister, as Taylor knew it would.

She was well, said Biddle, still taking care of the Confederate prisoners and assisting their mother on the issue of women's suffrage. Mrs. Biddle had decided she wasn't waiting for the end of the war to deal with the subjugation of women. Unfortunately, Katie wrote, they seemed largely alone in this respect. Even the most ardent activists in Chicago had set aside the needs of their gender for those of their country since no one it seemed wanted to hear about the unfair plight of women while thousands of soldiers were dying every month on the battlefield. While Mrs. Biddle wrote articles, Katie read up on the topic. She'd spent many nights, she said, with the words of Lucretia Mott and Elizabeth Stanton, two women who'd been leading the movement since the 1840s. Newspapers describing the 1848 Seneca Falls Convention and its signature document, the *Declaration of Sentiments*, outlined the methods by which men in the United States had established dominion over women. Laws, created without women's input, did not permit any female to own property, vote, earn wages, or accumulate wealth.

Biddle finished his beer, then removed the letter from his pocket. "Here, Taylor," he said, handing it to his friend, "you can read it if you like while I get us two more glasses."

Taylor scanned parts of the letter, much of which he had already read in the missives she'd sent to him. However, Katie had not shared as much with Taylor regarding her continued self-education on women's suffrage and her increasing passion for the cause as she had with her brother. In order to better understand her own reasons for supporting the movement, she had recently been studying the writings of those fervently opposed to women's rights, including those of woman named Kate Gannet.

Miss Gannet believes that the biological differences between men and women naturally dictate that each should occupy distinct spheres; God did not create us equal, therefore how can any human law make us equal? She says that a woman's role is to create a home and nurture, while a man's role is to provide and protect. Men are more intelligent when it comes to politics and business, women have greater aptitude for raising children and working at moral reform and education. There is more power and prestige to be held, Miss Gannet believes, by striving diligently in these areas and leaving the other to men.

I confess, Brother, I do not agree. You know as well as I that Father's business would have failed long ago if not for Mother. All these years she has done the books and kept track of the money, the debts and the profit. No one can draw or shrink a rod of iron like our father, but I shudder to think of our fate if he had done the other. And that is just one example. The true fact, I believe, is that women are already doing the work that men do and are paid for. It's just that they do so in secret, like Mother. No one ever asks any questions, they simply make assumptions based on what they believe they know. In some ways this is fine. In other ways, it is intolerable.

Biddle returned with the glasses of beer and Taylor handed him the letter saying his friend was lucky to have such a sister. They finished their drinks, then headed back to camp before it became too dark. Much to their disappointment, they found all the tents broken down and packed away on the ship. Word had arrived that the Confederate Army of Tennessee was heading for Nashville. The 72nd Illinois, along with several other regiments, would be headed there to meet them.

*

Guards posted on the deck of the steamer *Fairplay* scanned the shore for Rebels while the ship made its way cautiously up the Ohio River and then the Cumberland toward Nashville. The soldiers huddled inside the cabin while outside lashing winter winds blew the rain and sleet horizontal. In Nashville, the regiment disembarked *Fairplay* and began marching along the Lebanon Pike. They were headed to a camping ground established north of the state's capitol building. Built upon the highest piece of land in the area, the impressive structure with Romanesque columns and a tower that stretched over 200 feet into the sky had been in Federal hands since early 1862. To the east, north, and west lay the Cumberland River, its gentle, wide bend enfolding the city; to the south a series of hills poked up from the earth.

In camp, the men organized streets and erected tents. While Biddle and Christmas went off to collect firewood, Taylor and Kit began helping Bean prepare supper. Taylor took the opportunity to ask how the younger boy was doing.

Kit shrugged. "Fine, I 'spect. Things ain't really changed much since Vicksburg, but I'm all right." He looked down at the pile of plates and bowls he was unpacking. "Truth to tell, Robert, I'm a bit ashamed. Kinda sorry I told you about wanting to go home."

Taylor waved his arm. "Don't be! Everybody wants to go home."

"I know. It's just, well, much as I feel give out, I don't *really* want to go home. Leastwise, not before the thing is finished."

"I know. And you ain't going home before the thing is finished. We'll see it through, and then," he leaned over and blew on the reluctant fire, "think how fine it will be to return home."

Kit nodded. "Thanks, Robert. You're a good man."

Owing to several hungover soldiers the following morning, the regiment was not allowed transport on the cars. The officers said they wanted to "take some of the liquor out of the men," so the column began the forty-two miles south to Columbia on foot. The Confederate Army was moving north from Atlanta, and the Federals wanted to meet them before they arrived at Nashville. After more than a year of garrison duty in Vicksburg, the men's feet were as tender as those of babes. It also didn't help that the Columbia Pike had been constructed of large, sharp stones. After only a few miles, soldiers began dropping out of the ranks. Taylor held out as long as he could, but at midday he too left the column. Behind an abandoned farmhouse, he sat down and searched his knapsack for another pair of socks. Then he closed his eyes. Just a brief rest was all he wanted, but even that was not to be. A sudden noise instantly brought him around, his musket at the ready and his heart pounding. Taylor had just cocked the weapon when a mama coon and four little ones emerged through a broken window. The family ambled into a nearby copse of trees, giving him not even one glance. Taylor hurriedly put on his socks and boots and caught up to the regiment.

The next day, the 72nd Illinois arrived in Franklin, Tennessee, a small village still some miles north of Columbia. Just before noon, they crossed over the Harpeth River and continued south along the pike into the center of town. Homes of brick lined the way; large, old sweetgum and cottonwood trees stood regally in front of each residence. At the public square, several streets came together where the courthouse and other businesses had been constructed. Between the arriving soldiers and dozens of townspeople, the square was packed. The residents of Franklin stared at the men as if they'd never seen a Northern soldier in their lives. Taylor couldn't figure this. Franklin had been occupied as long as Nashville, a fact which had allowed the people to enjoy relative peace these past few years. Yet, this good fortune didn't translate into friendly feelings; the people here looked just as sullen as those in Vicksburg.

As the regiment awaited orders, Taylor noticed a young woman standing near the Courthouse. She appeared to be about twenty years of age and was very pretty with soft features and golden hair that had been braided and arranged neatly on top of her head. She stood next to an older man, her father presumably, and a tall Negro man with whom she was conversing. Taylor didn't know why she caught his eye. It was odd, but something about her seemed familiar. Maybe she just reminded him of someone at home. Or maybe he just liked looking at her pretty face. When she caught him looking at her however, he regretted his staring. As the regiment began marching, the woman kept her eyes on Taylor and he felt himself coloring. In the next moment, he stepped into a large hole, tripped and fell spread-eagle in the dirt. Several soldiers hooted. Taylor didn't look at the woman again and felt immensely relieved when the column was well away from Franklin's center. They didn't travel much farther before making camp south of the town on land owned by a man named Carter.

The next day the regiment arrived in Columbia. They crossed the bridge over the Duck River and began improving the stone defenses of Fork Mizner just west of Columbia. Several details searched the town for any material they could add to the walls, including stoves, fence posts, and clapboards. Each day there was less daylight but more rain. The mud grew deeper, the temperature dropped. While the men moved heavy loads of material, skirmishing began with the first Confederates sent out ahead of their army. The shooting rattled everyone and all slept lightly, if they slept at all.

As they worked, Taylor realized that besides military horses and mules, he hadn't seen one animal anywhere. No livestock, no birds, not even a rat! True it was winter, but this absence still gave him a bad feeling. He mentioned it to the boys.

"Ain't no good when even the animals leave a town," Christmas agreed. Everyone else nodded somberly.

When the Confederate Army arrived in force and flanked Fort Mizner and the Federals were forced back into the town, the Northern soldiers grew even more nervous. Downstream of the bridge, they crossed the Duck River, now a thick soup the color of chocolate. Branches and even entire trees floated past them. Swift pockets of water sent several men swimming. On the north side, the regiments settled in for the night, but a few hours later were ordered back across the river. After laying on their arms there for another few hours, they were told to cross once more to the north side. No one got any sleep.

The morning of November 29th dawned clear and cold. The men sat bleary-eyed around a smoldering fire.

"Goddamn, boys," said Christmas, his teeth chattering. "I'd give about anything to be back in Vicksburg."

The regiment worked on fortifications north of the river, while Confederates could be seen growing in number to the south. Skirmishing continued hour after hour. At noon, a soldier passed by leading a mule packing a long, wooden box. The man was a sharpshooter, his target Confederate officers. One of the lieutenants called his attention to a rider sitting on a white horse above the river. The man then unloaded his weapon, a nearly 4-foot long Sharp's rifle that he'd affixed with a telescope. After a few moments to sight his target, the rifle's report sliced through the air. The officer slumped to the ground while the white horse, startled, jumped to the side, then trotted away.

Later that day, the men were told that the Confederate Army wanted to move toward Nashville and not stay and fight in Columbia. Consequently, the Federal Army would be doing so as well. Details from Companies D and K piled wood at the base of the Duck River Bridge and, with the addition of generous amounts of black powder, set off a conflagration above the waterway. Feeling relieved but also very aware that a number of Rebels had already crossed the river, the Federal column began heading north. That night, the men once again traveled on the Columbia Pike, the land around them silent and dark.

EIGHT

ROBERT TAYLOR didn't know what time it was or where they were. At some point during the night, the regiment had left the Columbia Pike. For what seemed like hours, they'd been marching over uneven ground to the east. Skirmishing continued as the hours passed. It was like being blind while men shot at you. Taylor's stomach ached, the sourness of fear residing in his throat and mouth that no amount of spitting relieved. He was also exhausted but couldn't imagine going to sleep.

Somewhere just south of a village called Spring Hill, dozens of campfires suddenly appeared. The 72nd Illinois led a column of five regiments and had just scattered a group of Confederate pickets when every man immediately dropped to the ground. Dark shapes moved around the fires and a slight breeze blew from the east. The wind carried the sounds of Confederate voices and wooden canteens banging against muskets. Time slowed so much that Taylor felt he must be dreaming. Why was the enemy not attacking? They had to know they were there. Not only must the pickets have conveyed this to their command, but behind the regiments hunkered on the ground moved the Federal Army wagon train, several hundred conveyances strong. The creaking wheels and the heavy thuds of cannons and supplies lumbering over the pike were very audible in the cold night air. Perhaps there were far fewer Confederates than what appeared in the distorted light of the campfires. The thought made Taylor breathe easier for a time. Then he considered the arrival of morning. If they didn't move soon, they were going to be caught in a bad way at first light.

At last, the order came to fall back to the pike. With dangling tin cups and frying pans stowed among clothing in knapsacks, the Federal men moved silently, daring not to speak or even to breathe. When they finally reached Spring Hill, they found their voices again.

"Good-bye Andersonville," said Christmas, referring to the notorious southern prison.

"We got lucky," agreed Bean, his voice crackling in the frosty air.

The Columbia Pike was a mess. Between the men and the equipment, the army traveled at a snail's pace. While stopped waiting for the long train to begin moving again, exhausted soldiers fell on the ground, instantly asleep. There was little talking and no time to stop and eat. As streaks of pink finally appeared in the eastern sky, the column topped a hill. Down the other side, they approached the town of Franklin once again. By 9 a.m. the regiments had arrived at the Carter farmhouse where they'd encamped just a short two weeks before. Here the Federal Army stopped and began spreading out east to west from the pike. The regiments filled in the spaces between the farm's cotton gin, smokehouse, and other buildings. The 72nd Illinois was placed one hundred yards southwest of the family's house.

The men drew rations, including one allowance of whiskey. As the quartermaster poured the liquor, Taylor and Biddle looked at each other.

"This don't bode well," said Biddle.

"No, it don't."

They began building fortifications. They dug pits and piled material above the pits. They dismantled the cotton gin and used the planks and timbers to form a barricade. Next they cut down a grove of locust trees, which became an abatis in front of the breastworks. The men worked fast and furious. Despite the cool temperature, they doffed frock coats and rolled up their shirt sleeves. All the while rumors abounded. General Hood of the Confederate Army outnumbered them greatly, or he had only a few regiments. The Federals would defend Franklin, or they would retreat to Nashville. There was even a theory that Hood was dead, and that's why they'd been able to sneak past the Confederates the previous night.

By noon, the works were completed. Taylor collapsed into the pit he'd dug earlier and was asleep before he knew it. Two hours later he awoke. At first, he had no idea where he was. Then he saw Biddle sitting above him smoking a cigar.

"What's happening?" he coughed, his voice nearly gone.

Biddle stared across the valley. "At the moment very little."

"The others?"

"Kit and Bean are sleeping. Christmas, I ain't sure."

Taylor crawled out of the pit and sat next to his friend. He felt too groggy to say or think much, so he just sat. Men were milling about, clusters of officers could be seen, but the day now seemed to have little ambition to it, a fact for which Taylor was quite relieved. The sudden caw of a raven behind them made him turn around. The big black bird was perched in a cottonwood tree. Taylor rummaged in his haversack. He liked ravens. While some considered them sneaky and prone to thievery, he felt them only to be smart and self-preserving. A raven wouldn't be here, Taylor thought, if it believed anything bad was about to happen. After locating a piece of bread, Taylor tossed it over. The raven swooped down, grabbed the bit, and flew away.

"You ever think about going west, Biddle?" Taylor suddenly asked.

"What? Going west? That's a funny question. Nah, can't say as I have."

"Why not?"

"I dunno. Guess I wouldn't want to leave my family."

"Yeah," Taylor nodded, "that makes sense. Still, sometimes it sounds kinda good to me. Maybe we could go together if you wanted. Get some land somewhere, maybe buy a store. Travel further north if we felt like an adventure."

Biddle looked at him. "I thought you didn't think about the future."

"I don't. Or, not much leastwise. Guess I'm just so tired, I'll think about anything that ain't this. Don't know how I'm gonna march to Nashville tonight."

"We ain't marching to Nashville tonight."

"What?"

"Look." Biddle pointed across the valley. "Them Southern bastards have started coming through the gap."

The Franklin valley was golden bright from the setting sun. There was little on the plain to block the view, and only a few scattered shrubs that sat like popped buttons, various small copses of trees, and three homes adjacent the pike provided any contrast to the mustard color grasses. Far across however, in the little notch that they themselves had just passed through from Spring Hill that morning, hundreds of Confederate soldiers now poured. There were flags and shiny weapons and even a smattering of music. In the space of a few minutes everything seemed to have changed. Taylor didn't like this one bit. He turned toward his friend. That's when he noticed Biddle holding various items in his hands.

"I know it's all some to carry, Taylor," Biddle said quietly, "but I'd appreciate it if you took care of these things for me. Kept 'em safe. Then when it's all over, write to Katie. Tell her what happened. Tell her," he placed Pomeroy's knife, their likeness, and a packet of letters in Taylor's lap, "well, tell her everything."

"What the hell are you talking about?"

"Don't argue with me, Taylor, I know what I'm about."

Taylor handed the items back. "You don't know nothing, my friend. Them bastards ain't gonna attack across two miles of open ground. And with us dug in like we are? It'd be damn foolish."

"Foolish or not, they're still gonna do it. Don't forget, we did the same in Vicksburg. We did it then, and they're gonna do it now.

I'll wager they're hopping mad right now after we snuck past 'em last night. 'Course, it won't accomplish nothing, same as then, but it's still gonna happen.

"Thing is, Taylor," Biddle took a deep breath, "I got a bad feeling this time. Can't explain it and maybe I'm wrong, but in case I ain't..." He passed his things over again. "Please, just do this for me. If I'm wrong, you can give it all back after. Fair enough?"

Taylor wanted to say that no, it wasn't fair at all, Biddle was asking too much of him. They had all asked too much of him. He didn't want to care for his friend's stuff because he knew just what that meant. And Taylor was tired. Tired of carrying other people's things, tired of giving to the war, tired of being the last one left.

"Biddle—"

"You're my best friend, Taylor. Really, I ain't never known anyone like you. It's, well, funny, I guess. Me and you, meeting like we have. I don't regret it, not one bit. And I want you to know I understand. All right? I understand and it's fine. You'll always be my best friend."

Taylor sat quietly. Then he put Biddle's things in his haversack. They barely fit with his own letters and journal, but he said he would do as Biddle asked. "You're my best friend too," he added, gruffly.

Biddle smiled. "You don't have to sound so happy about it."

"Well, I ain't happy about this, Biddle, I ain't happy at all."

Just then shouting erupted around them. Bean, Christmas, and Kit appeared and began talking all at once. The Rebs had started across the valley, they said excitedly. They were in for it now, they said, and the 72nd was forming up. Taylor and Biddle stood up. The battle line on the far hillside looked as tight as anything they'd seen. The bands now could be clearly heard, the flags flapping with great enthusiasm, and the skirmishers commencing their march. The Federal soldiers rushed into their lines. They loaded their weapons and checked their ammunition. They watched the far side of the valley, and they waited. Taylor looked at his watch. It was exactly 3:00 p.m.

*

Taylor never saw Christmas, Bean, or Kit again. After the Confederates swarmed the Federal works, he lost sight of everyone except Biddle. For a brief moment, Henry Beesley was next to him until his face was blown away and Taylor was pushed to the ground from the blast. The rush of feet and legs around him was so terrific that it took several minutes to get standing again. He had never seen such chaos. During the Vicksburg charges, the enemy was always well away from the Federal soldiers, deadly but distinctly separate. Not so at Franklin. These Southern soldiers, whatever else one might say about them, were the bravest Taylor had ever seen. They came on like wolves. They howled and they ran. They loaded their weapons, firing on the move. They took no notice of fallen comrades. They were coming into the Federal line and there was no stopping them. This, Taylor thought in the last moments when he could afford a thought, was their land and they would never give it over. He had known this for certain when he saw the Federal soldiers running. Some fool of an officer had positioned two brigades out in front of the main Federal line to check the Rebels and, to say the very least, it hadn't worked. After only feeble resistance, the Northern men were running full bore for the safety of the main line. Taylor and every other man behind the works watched in horror, helpless. By the time, their comrades reached them, so, too, had the Confederates.

The first man Taylor shot was 15 feet away from him coming over the top of the earthen barrier. The blow to the chest sent the rebel back down the other side. Taylor loaded again. Another soldier in gray with no hat or coat began sliding down the embankment. Taylor fired into the man's throat. He reloaded again. He fired again. Over and over, the same. Reload, fire, reload, fire. The musket grew so hot, the flesh on his hands burned as he pushed the cartridges and powder down the bore. With each passing moment, there was more enemy to kill and less time to reload. Taylor felt smashed between moving, falling, and thrusting bodies; at times he didn't know who was who, but more often there was no time to even consider what that uncertainty meant.

The smoke was so thick he could barely see, the noise deafening. The ramrod was still in his musket when he had to fire the weapon at a wild-looking Confederate whose face was drenched in blood and who had his musket pointed right at Taylor's face. The ramrod sailed into the man's heart like an arrow. This solved one problem but created another. Without the long piece of steel, Taylor couldn't reload his gun. No matter; he ran over and yanked the ramrod out of the man. Good as new.

No more thinking. No more light. The winter darkness had fallen like a curtain, broken only by bursts of flames from muskets and cannon shot. The crush of bodies wouldn't abate and Taylor had no time now for reloading. He used his bayonet like a knife, into the back of one man, the leg of another. Taylor swung his gun, the stock smashing against the side of a soldier's head. Then, he heard a crack on his own temple. He fell to his knees, ears ringing, spots blinking in front of his eyes. A large dark shape appeared in front of him, knocking him backward. The man was now on top of him; Taylor's ribs were breaking. Hands slipped around his throat. He clawed at the hands but they were locked firm. No air, tongue getting bigger, large fingers pushing him into the earth. Several musket shots suddenly illuminated the rebel soldier who was killing him. Then the face was gone. Warm liquid showered over Taylor as the man fell away and the hands released their grip. Taylor heaved in great gulps of air. More hands then, grabbing and dragging him. Biddle.

They stopped. Biddle wiped off Taylor's face with one sleeve, then put his mouth up against his ear. "Are you all right?" he asked.

Taylor nodded but the blood on his face wasn't all from the man Biddle had just killed. He felt the cut, from his temple down to his jaw. Could feel the blood, his own, leaking out of him. His breath came in quick, short gasps. His chest was on fire. One ear was completely quiet, mercifully so, for the screams of animals and men were nothing he wanted to hear, yet they still came through the other ear.

"Stay here," shouted Biddle, handing Taylor the pistol.

He half-stood then and turned around to move back toward the line. Biddle hadn't gone five steps when several muskets went off behind them. Night turned into day and Biddle fell to the ground. Taylor screamed and emptied the pistol over his head behind him. He screamed and screamed. The noise poured into his brain like a river. He began crawling amidst the roar of the battle, sloshing over ground now sodden with the sticky blood of men. When Taylor reached Biddle's rumpled form, he turned him over.

Touching Biddle's face with his hands, he felt the soft, full beard, the curly hair that tumbled back from his face. As his friend had just done with him, he put his mouth down by his friend's ear and shouted above the din if he was all right. No answer. He asked again in the other ear. Nothing. Taylor shook him hard. This wasn't supposed to happen. It, simply, was *not* supposed to happen.

Taylor waded back into the fight with his fists swinging. His body didn't hurt at all now. It seemed to vibrate, and hum, like a machine that is working very hard. Another burst of light illuminated the air around him. Taylor saw a musket not being used. He grabbed the weapon, swinging the stock and breaking a man's head in the process. He swung again. Another man's shoulder popped out of place and he fell to the ground screaming. Swing, hit, swing, hit. At some point Taylor tripped over an officer and landed on the man's sword. He quickly substituted the saber for the musket and thrust it into the belly of a soldier who wouldn't leave him alone. He now swung the sword at the necks and faces of the gray men. One man swiped his knife at Taylor's chest. The blade cut through Taylor's coat but he didn't feel anything. Taylor answered the Reb's ineffective attack with a stab in the man's belly.

*

Some years later, Taylor would be asked about the Battle of Franklin. He would be interviewed by journalists or questioned by family about what had happened during those tremendous five hours of fighting. Every time the curious came seeking, he had no idea what to say. It wasn't just that words felt inadequate to describe the battle; it was also that he simply didn't remember much. There were fragments, an image here or there, a sound, a smell, but he never felt fully able to connect one event to the next, a situation which didn't lend itself to great storytelling. In the early years after the way he made attempts to explain the fragments, but eventually stopped trying. His friend Kendall, another veteran, had chosen to never speak about the war to anybody who hadn't been there, and Taylor thought this a reasonable strategy. After all, the battle had seemed more dream than real, and dreams were better held in private than displayed publicly.

*

At some point, the fight became all there was; there had been nothing before and there would be nothing after. Biddle was dead, and so likely were the others. Yet, Taylor had no time to consider this. For all he knew, he might be dead too and that this was what being dead was: fighting, and more fighting.

Still, at some point, a deep, burning sensation gripped Taylor's leg. He knew he'd been shot, but when he looked down, he saw the strangest sight. A large, black wolf had grabbed ahold of him. Its sharp, yellow teeth held fast to his leg, its eyes glowing wildly in the light of the gunfire. Taylor didn't feel the wolf was trying to harm him. Instead, it seemed to be helping him, dragging him away, to safety, to a quiet place. The pain took his breath away however. Then he felt liquid running down his chest. Taylor was falling. The din of battle suddenly grew quieter; his vision blurrier. It was all fine though. Maybe now, finally, this was the real act of dying, a circumstance for which he wasn't sorry. He welcomed it in fact. He would be with Biddle. He would see the others too. In that moment such a feeling of peace enveloped him that he happily let go of the life he'd always known. The last thing Taylor remembered was spinning downward, endlessly it seemed, into the pit he'd helped dig that afternoon.

PART TWO

ONE

October 6, 1858, Toulon, Illinois

THE LOW, THROATY GROWL broke the nighttime silence. The animal in front of me was big, cornered, and by all indications very unhappy. I hadn't meant to create this circumstance. I'd only been checking this last rabbit trap and then planned to head home. The morning was not far off and as it was I was going to catch it for being out all night. Consequently, I'd been hurrying and not paying attention to the signs: the tracks I must have missed along the path, the lack of squeals from a caught rabbit, and the wild, musky animal smell that now filled my senses. A new moon provided little light in the bottoms of Spoon River, so of course I carried a lantern. I'd grown up in this country, knew every trail and bramble patch, as well as every kind of sound, and very little in the bottoms surprised me. Yet, I'd had no inkling of the panther's presence until she spoke.

I lifted the lantern higher. It looked like the cat had helped herself to my rabbit. She kept herself mostly hidden in the thick undergrowth of the pawpaws and red-bud bushes. The dry sound of an angry hiss sent chills through my body. I started backing up. More hissing. I moved faster and tripped on a tree root. The lamp flew out of my hands and broke apart. Darkness engulfed me. As I lay on my back, the wind knocked out of me, the most extraordinary thing happened.

The panther leapt right over me!

Her long form flew silently through the air above me, never-ending it seemed, from the tip of her nose to the end of her long tail. Yet, only seconds passed during the flight before the cat landed on the other side of my head. Her sour smell, mixed with the blood of the rabbit, rained down on me like a fine mist. I knew she had immediately started running at top speed away from me, yet there was not a sound to be heard. People in the Spoon River bottoms called this animal a Ghost Cat, or sometimes a Devil Cat. Few ever saw a panther, and the cat's perfect silence created fear among humans. For my part, I didn't feel afraid. In fact, when I finally stood up and collected the broken lantern and the three rabbits I'd caught earlier, I wondered if it had all been a dream. Yet, the tracks were plainly visible in the early morning light. The distance between where her back legs had left the ground to jump over me and where her front ones touched back to earth were fifteen of my own steps! Of course, no one would believe this story, and I wouldn't be inclined to tell them anyway. They'd want to set their own traps. They'd want to kill the panther. They'd say they must to make the bottoms safe again. The truth was the land wouldn't be more safe without her, so this encounter would remain our secret, the cat's and mine.

*

Back home, I skinned the rabbits, then hung them up in the spring house. The sun was above the eastern horizon when I entered our family's kitchen. My father sat in his rocker, drinking coffee and reading the newspaper.

"Morning, Papa."

He looked up. "Morning, Jennie."

I poured myself a cup of coffee and sat down. The heat from the fire felt good to my chilled body and I sipped the warm drink gratefully. Papa continued reading, his dark, curly hair, like a spring bush gone wild with new growth, his spectacles slightly askew across his nose. We didn't often have a newspaper, so this was a treat for my father. We'd been in town the day before, where he'd bought the paper, and we'd be returning today as well. I listened for my mother and brothers, but the house was quiet.

"Sleep well?" Papa suddenly asked, dropping the paper into his lap.

"Papa, you know I was down in the bottoms!"

He nodded. "I do know that. And so does your mother."

I winced. "Is she upset?"

"She don't like you staying out all night by yourself, Jennie. She worries. She'd feel better if your brothers were with you."

"Aw, Papa, you know they don't like to! Besides I can take care of myself."

"I know. And I ain't saying *I'm* worried, but your mother is different and you're going to have to answer to her this morning. You said you'd check the traps then be back before too late. Instead, you stayed out all night." Papa opened his paper again. "That just don't do with your mama, Jen."

"I'm sorry, Papa. Guess I just forgot myself."

My father grunted, but I knew he wasn't mad. I couldn't remember a time when he'd ever been mad at me. Besides, today was the day when his old friend, who he hadn't seen in more than twenty-five years, was to speak in town. We all looked forward to another afternoon of fun and festivities in Toulon. As I took another sip of coffee, my mother's voice filled the kitchen.

"Eliza Jane, you are in big trouble this morning!"

Mama set her basket of eggs on the table and folded her arms. Her cold stare made me feel more nervous than when I'd met the panther. Mama was still pretty for an older woman, with little gray to her long, copper hair and few lines in her face. She had warm almond eyes and a smile that transformed her into the very essence of goodness, but if she wasn't happy, everyone knew it. Unfortunately for me, she didn't look happy right now. "What do you mean staying out all night, young lady?"

"I'm sorry, Mama, truly. But I just couldn't come back. It was too beautiful, the sky, the stars, the—"

"You are getting too old, Eliza Jane," she interrupted, "to be running around the country like a bandit. You're a young lady now, and young ladies don't do this kind of thing."

I looked down at my trousers, dotted with holes and several mud stains, and told her I hardly seemed like a lady.

Mama sighed. She turned toward my father and, once again, began telling him how my wildness was all his fault. It was a familiar lament and one I quite disliked. I hated hearing about how I needed to start acting and looking different just because I was now fourteen-years-old. The trouble had all begun the previous spring when I finished my last year of school. Mama said now I was done with studying, I could start thinking about more practical topics. First, she had given me *The American Frugal Housewife* by Lydia Maria Child, a popular guide on the economy of housekeeping. Second, she had insisted that I start wearing dresses more often, and, despite our family's lack of money, ordered two new ones from the catalog at Trickle's General Store. Finally, she'd begun insisting on me taking piano lessons and attending meetings at the Toulon Literary Society. These last I couldn't abide. Mrs. Bertha McRae, one of the town mothers and a woman who made no bones about hating me, was the only piano teacher in Toulon and a leader of the Society. Truly, I'd rather die than spend an afternoon with her.

It just wasn't fair. Mama's peculiar desire to stop her youngest child from doing what she'd always done, including hunting and fishing, didn't extend to my brothers. Gardiner and Jothan, who were now seventeen and nineteen, never heard any nonsense about having to wear nicer clothes, or go to meetings, or take music lessons. Far as I could tell, they got to go about their lives as they always had. I'd pointed this out once, but the truth of the injustice didn't change anything.

After Mama left the kitchen, I slumped in my chair like a wilted flower.

Papa couldn't help smiling. He poured us more coffee. "Ruby escaped again last night," he said, changing the subject. "She must have gone looking for you. Your brothers fetched her back though."

In spite of the morning's bleak exchange, I smiled. Ruby was my mule and a terrible rascal. Papa had bought her many years before and I'd known her as long as I'd known anyone. She had steel gray fur and similarly colored eyes beneath two eight-inch long ears. Even as a youngster, Ruby had a will of her own. She was an escape artist and could clear a six-foot fence as well as any deer. I couldn't count the number of times I'd had to bring her back from our neighbor's pastures, or even town, where she would go visiting her many animal and human friends.

"Thanks, Papa."

"Don't thank me. Thank the boys." He stretched, removing his spectacles and rubbing his eyes. "They're in the barn right now. We're leaving at ten today."

"What time is Mr. Lincoln speaking?"

"One, but I'd like to arrive early and find a good place to stand."

In the past, our small town of Toulon, Illinois, had hosted county fairs, a theatre company from Chicago, and a traveling circus, but no event had ever evoked such turnouts as the back-to-back speeches of Senator Stephen Douglas and the man who wished to unseat him in this year's election, Mr. Abraham Lincoln. Mr. Douglas had spoken the day before after arriving in an elegant carriage drawn by six white horses. An entourage of supporters accompanied him, cheering frequently as he spoke about his platform of popular sovereignty. Mr. Douglas told us that the people of each state and territory should be allowed to decide for themselves the direction of local government. He said that popular sovereignty should be applied to all issues, but the most pressing need for such an approach was around the topic of slavery. Mr. Douglas stated his firm belief that the Negro was not equal to the white man, and that the Declaration of Independence never intended to include Negroes in its proclamations about equality and liberty.

"What do you think Mr. Lincoln will say today?" I asked my father.

Papa thought. "Old Abe has very different ideas from Stephen Douglas. I'm sure he'll refute all of the man's claims and offer up his own assessment of a nation burdened by slavery." He stood up, smiling. "The speech should be just as lively as yesterday."

*

My father had first met Abraham Lincoln many years before when they were both soldiers during the Black Hawk War. It was the 1830s and Papa was just twenty when he'd traveled to a village called Beardstown on the Illinois River to join the state militia. The men drew weapons and supplies and soon they were marching across the Spoon River country, down into the Mississippi bottoms, and all the way north to the Rock River where the Indian chief Black Hawk was encamped. My brothers and I loved Papa's stories of the wild country then and the conflict that had brought white men and natives together in battle. Illinois had been a state only a few years and there weren't many settlements back then. The militia unit walked for days without seeing anyone. Tracks of prairie wolves and panthers could be seen, and occasionally the men would catch a glimpse of one of the wolves. In the spring, millions of pigeons filled the sky, turning the world dark for hours at a time. The 12-foot tall prairie grasses had to be navigated carefully for a man, even on a horse, might vanish by simply taking a wrong turn. In general, it was better to stick to the woodlands or waterways.

Papa was only in the militia for a month before his company was mustered out of service. While Mr. Lincoln reenlisted, my father said a month was plenty of time to know he didn't want to be a soldier. After gathering his things at Fort Johnson on the Illinois River, he caught a ride on a packet boat heading south. The wide, emerald waters glided through the prairie country where again he saw grasses that could not be believed. Having been raised in the growing town of Springfield and having spent many a day working in his father's tanning shop, Papa was in awe of the fertile land between the Mississippi and Illinois rivers. At the mouth of the Spoon River, my father jumped off the packet, then made his way overland to a dripping creek called Jug Run. Here, on a dozen acres and with the help of friends he met in Toulon, Papa built a home and a farm. Then he convinced my mother to join him from Springfield. Our house and barn and fields at Jug Run Creek were all I'd ever known. If I thought about it, they were pretty much all I ever wanted to know.

Papa hadn't seen his old friend in many years, but he'd followed Mr. Lincoln's political career through the Illinois House of Representatives and later the U.S. House. Since 1854, Mr. Lincoln had been trying to get into the Senate, but had met with only failure. Still, in June this year, he'd been chosen by the recently formed Republican Party as their senate candidate. Immediately frustrated by Stephen Douglas' well organized and better financed campaign, he began following his opponent across the state. After Douglas spoke in Chicago, Mr. Lincoln offered a rebuttal the next day from the very same spot. One week later, he spoke only a few hours after Douglas in Springfield. This effort allowed Mr. Lincoln to always have the concluding speech, but it wasn't perfect. The pro-Douglas newspapers ridiculed him. They suggested he might also speak at one of the circuses or menageries traveling through Illinois. To counter such mockery, the pro-Lincoln paper, the *Daily Press and Tribune*, proposed that the two men should canvass the state together. Mr. Lincoln immediately issued a formal challenge to do this very thing. Stephen Douglas, reluctantly it seemed, had accepted.

*

As we sat in our wagon later that morning waiting for Mr. Lincoln to arrive, you'd have thought we'd come to the county fair. Jugglers and card readers and people dressed in every kind of costume walked up and down the East Road. A man with a cat on his shoulder claimed he could communicate with animals and began holding conversations with the horses and a small dog that couldn't stop barking. If you had money there were many things to buy: baked goods, candied apples, Dr. Christie's Ague Balsam, and plugs of tobacco. One man with sharp, pointed ears and an oily face had knives and pistols "for a fair price."

There was even a magician who called himself Owl. He approached our wagon and my father gave him a quarter whereupon he performed several conjures. My dog, Sam, barked nervously at the man, but my brothers and I clapped loudly as he made the very coin he'd just received vanish and then reappear from the bottom of his sleeve. An egg also disappeared after he'd placed it beneath a kerchief. Seconds later, he retrieved it from behind my ear! Owl wore a black frock coat with a top hat and a flaming red scarf around his neck. A long braid down his back was tied at the end by a small red ribbon. He was tall and thin except for a slight belly and had a soft, unbearded face and round, dark eyes. Indeed, he looked very much like an owl. When loud cheering suddenly erupted around us indicating Mr. Lincoln's arrival, the magician vanished back into the crowd so quickly that I had the strangest feeling I might have just imagined him.

Despite the morning's dew, a knee-high band of dust accompanied the long procession of Toulon-ites leading Mr. Lincoln's carriage. Young boys and girls, a fife and drum troupe, and a banner reading "FREE SOIL, FREE LABOR, FREE MEN," made up the parade. On a grand float being pulled by a six-horse team were several girls from town, each dressed up like one of the thirty-two states in the Union. Behind this float came a single rider wearing midnight black. Letters across the front of her dress read simply, "Kansas."

At long last, we saw Jeff Cooley, the tavern keeper, driving his span of sorrels. Two passengers occupied the carriage seat. The first was Thomas Henderson, one of Toulon's lawyers and now an Illinois senator. The second, a thin individual who sat a full head taller than Mr. Henderson, was the man himself. Abraham Lincoln bowed left and right while waving to the crowd. I could see little of his face, cast as it was in shadows beneath his hat, but what was visible seemed big: the disc-like ears that protruded beneath patches of tousled hair, the thick nose and long face, and the smooth jaw and chin that seemed as wide as a newly plowed field. Mr. Lincoln was unusual looking, but I instantly liked him. As the carriage neared my family's wagon, the crowd noise increased and you would have thought the president himself had arrived. The hoots and hollers were so loud that I only barely heard my father say, "I'll be! Old Abe hasn't changed a bit!"

TWO

MR. LINCOLN began to speak just as the autumn rain started to fall.

"Ladies and Gentlemen of Toulon," he addressed us. "Yesterday you heard Judge Douglas discuss several points to which I will now offer contrasting positions. I will begin with one against his statement that the Declaration of Independence never intended to include Negroes in the term "men." He called it slander to even suppose that the framers so meant such inclusion. Furthermore, Judge Douglas declared it impossible that Mr. Jefferson would have applied such language to the Negro race and yet still maintained a portion of that race in slavery!

"I, however, believe that the entire records of the world from the date of the Declaration of Independence up to within three years ago may be searched in vain for one single assertion that the Negro was not included in the term "men" within that hallowed document. I will remind the Judge that even while Mr. Jefferson kept slaves, he also said that he trembled for his country when he remembered that God was just."

Scattered applause erupted along with shouts of "Good, good!" and "Hit him again!"

"Now, I must also attend to Judge Douglas' claims," Mr. Lincoln continued, "that I make speeches of one sort for the people of the North and of another for those in the South. He obviously believes that I do not understand my speeches will be put into print. Ladies and Gentleman, I know that all reading men might read them and I have not believed—nor do I today believe—that there is any conflict in them." A woman yelled, "Hurray for Lincoln!" and another, "They're all good speeches!" before he added, "The Judge believes that if we do not confess the inequality between the Negro and white races that we must necessarily make wives of them." Raucous laughter. "Now, I will say that I have always made a distinction between the races, that inasmuch as there is a physical inequality between black and white that the blacks must remain inferior, however I have also always maintained that the right to life, liberty, and the pursuit of happiness belong to all men.

"If you will accommodate me, I would now reiterate what I told the Illinois Republican Party in June in Springfield, that the foment concerning the issue of slavery in this country shall not cease until a crisis has been reached and passed. It cannot be otherwise. Even as we enter the fifth year of a policy designed to put an end to slavery agitation, the agitation has only increased. I will also repeat what I told the good gentlemen who bestowed upon me the party nomination for senator, that it is my firm believe that a country so divided, a nation so at odds with itself, cannot stand. The government of this country cannot endure permanently half slave and half free. I do not know that the country will be dissolved, nor do I know that it will fall. I only know that it shall cease to be divided. Either the opponents of slavery will stop its spread or the advocates will push it forward until it shall be lawful in all states, present and those to come."

After the loudest applause yet, Mr. Lincoln began a discussion on the Compromise of 1850 and the debate surrounding new territories entering the Union as free or slave. For an hour and a half, he confronted Judge Douglas' declaration that any community that wants slavery can have it, a truism if one believes there is no wrong in the institution, but a falsehood if one doesn't.

"I believe that slavery is wrong," he concluded. "And as such, believe in the prevention of the enlargement of that wrong while looking to a future time of there being an end to that wrong. In these two days, Judge Douglas has expressed his opinion on this topic, as have I. It is now to you people, and other such citizens, to consider these opinions, look through them, turn them over, and arrive at your own conclusion regarding the future of new territories being slave or free. Will it do to overlook the one and only danger that has ever threatened the perpetuity of the Union? Will it do to overlook the one and only danger that has ever threatened our liberty in this country? I say that it will not and therefore shall be incumbent upon you to decide your answer before entering upon this policy of acquisition."

Mr. Lincoln then paused briefly, looking out over the silent crowd. "Thank you, Ladies and Gentlemen. Having said what I wished, I will now retire."

The applause and shouting thundered for many minutes.

*

When Mr. Lincoln saw my father, his serious countenance broke into a broad smile. The crush of people around Mr. Lincoln was thick, but somehow Papa cut a path. They embraced and then Papa's friend told Mama how glad he was to make her acquaintance. He shook hands with my brothers and bowed to me. I stood with my head tilted back; Mr. Lincoln was even taller close up! His clothes didn't fit at all well, the sleeves of his coat stopping above his wrists and the pants hanging high like unattached stovepipes. Only the tall hat seemed the proper size for his long, angular face. Mama nudged me to stop staring while she complimented Mr. Lincoln on a fine speech.

"Your words had a profound effect on all here today, sir," she said.

"Thank you, Madame," he returned. "It is my deep pleasure to speak to such a learned group of people." He turned to Papa. "You have a beautiful family, Graham. Life appears to be treating you well."

My father beamed. "That it is."

Mr. Lincoln then invited us later to the Virginia House, a hotel in town owned by Mr. Cooley. The Republicans were hosting a meal and he insisted that we should be his guests. After a few minutes, Mr. Lincoln was whisked away by a group of Toulon's businessmen, and my family and I were left to occupy ourselves until the gathering.

The rain hadn't dampened anyone's spirits. Despite the mud and cold, the town streets remained full of people, some eating barbecue chicken and ice cream, others just watching the goings-on. While my family joined a crowd watching a tightrope walker doing backward somersaults, I noticed Rosetta Trickle, the wife of my father's friend Washington, heading toward us like a strong wind. Mrs. Trickle's red, white, and blue dress, and her hat of many similarly colored birds' feathers, made her the very picture of patriotism. She was pulling her dog Fancy, who yipped at every step, on a leash. Washington Trickle trailed behind carrying two folding chairs.

"Oh, Julia!" Rosetta shouted, stopping briefly to catch her breath. "You and Graham and the children must come quickly! You will not believe it!"

My brothers and I grinned at each other. Mrs. Trickle was always talking about something that "could not be believed." Her husband saw us smiling and smiled back. Then he set up the two chairs in the middle of street. Washington sat in one, while Fancy took the other.

"Goodness, Rosetta, what is it?" asked my mother.

"Well! It's that magician! That's what it is!" Mrs. Trickled clapped her hands and Fancy barked. "Have you seen him?"

"Just briefly," Mama said, "while waiting for Mr. Lincoln to arrive."

"He found an egg behind my ear!" I shouted, only because Mrs. Trickle was shouting.

"And made my quarter disappear," Papa added.

"But then it came back," my brother Gardiner offered.

"Not to me, it didn't," said Papa, laughing.

Mrs. Trickle looked at us like she'd never seen us before. "Well!" she repeated, this time putting her hands on her hips. "Coins and eggs are one thing. Any half-wit can make those disappear. It happens all the time at the store. What I just saw was truly unbelievable!" We waited and she lowered her voice. "A glass of wine tossed into the air and then, poof! Completely gone, right in front of my eyes!" Fancy barked then danced in the chair on her back legs, apparently to confirm what her mistress had observed.

"Indeed?" Mama looked skeptical, but Mrs. Trickle was already herding us toward a ring of spectators gathered around the magician. The man called Owl was holding a flapping dove in his hand. He smiled at the people applauding. The bird, solid white except for a dark patch on its throat, seemed pleased too. It turned its head this way and that, much like a queen surveying her subjects. Owl then removed a black cloth from inside his coat. In the next moment, he had covered the dove. Suddenly, he jerked on the cloth. The bird was gone!

"See! See!" yelled Mrs. Trickle, jumping up and down. "I told you!"

Owl tucked the cloth back into his coat, then took a bow. "Now, for my next trick—" he began, but suddenly his expression became puzzled. His eyes turned upward, toward his hat. Very slowly, he lifted the hat off his head. There was the dove!

My mouth fell open. We all stared at Owl, who now let the dove walk around his head. He did more amazing conjures, and I felt sure that I must do nothing else with my life now but figure out how he had gotten the dove into his hat.

After the magic show my family sat for our likeness with a man who had a photographic wagon. Except for when we went to church, we never were so dressed up: my brothers in their black suits and derby hats, me in my new brown muslin dress with the scattered blue flowers that Mama had recently bought for me, Papa in his top hat and frock coat, and Mama in her maroon calico that went perfectly with her copper-colored hair. After the likeness was done, we all stared at it for some minutes. Though I found it startling to see us there as if we were a make-believe family from a fairy tale, I also thought we looked very fine. My brothers looked especially handsome; Jothan, now nineteen with dark, curly hair like Papa's and the beginnings of a mustache, and Gardiner, two years younger and taller with straight, blond hair and glasses.

At last we went to the Virginia House. A sizeable crowd filled the dining room. Mr. Cooley showed us to seats near Mr. Lincoln at the head of a long table and as we sat Papa's friend finished a story about a soldier, a broken wagon, and a rather contrary mule. Everyone laughed heartily at the tale's conclusion. Then Mr. Lincoln looked at me.

"Young Jennie Edwards," he said, his voice smiling, "did your father ever tell you that I was a military hero?"

I looked at Papa, who winked. "No, sir."

"Yes, miss, it's true. During the Blackhawk War, I fought and I bled too. Not from any Indians, mind you. Just a great number of bloodthirsty mosquitos!"

Everyone laughed again. I smiled too, but felt surprised. This funny man hardly seemed like the serious one who had spoken to us for nearly two hours in the rain on the grievous wrongs of slavery. Yet Mr. Lincoln told stories all evening as we ate Mrs. Cooley's roasted veal, boiled potatoes, and braised carrots. These tales were all funny, though every now and then I caught a glimpse of the other Mr. Lincoln, the serious, self-made man Papa had described as one of the most ambitious individuals he'd ever known. After the meal and just as I was wishing that he lived in Toulon, Mr. Lincoln pulled out a jackknife and turned again to me.

"Young Jennie, I bet you can't guess how I came to have this knife?"

"No, sir," I said, smiling.

"Well, it was back in the days when I was riding the circuit. I was accosted one afternoon in the cars by a stranger, who said to me, "Excuse me, sir, but I have an article in my possession which belongs to you." Considerably astonished, I asked him, "How could that be?" He then reached into his pocket and pulled out this knife. Then, do you know what he said?"

I shook my head.

"He said, "This knife was given to me with the injunction that I was to keep it until I found a man uglier than myself. I have carried it from that time to this. I believe, however, sir, that you are now fairly entitled to your property.""

The room erupted in laughter and hoots. My brothers and I giggled too until we saw Mama staring at us and shaking her head. But she wore a small grin too.

After the dishes had been cleared away, someone asked Mr. Lincoln about his debate with Mr. Douglas the next day in Galesburg. Soon, the talk was once again on politics. To my surprise, my brother Gardiner spoke up.

"Sir, do you really believe that the country will divide over the issue of slavery?"

Mr. Lincoln pushed back his chair and draped one long leg over the other. "I'm afraid it already has, son. Now, the question is, "Will there be a war over that division?" As to that, I cannot say. The situation for this country will change as it must. My worst fear is that the issue cannot be resolved peaceably; my greatest hope, of course, is that it can."

"I hope there is not a war, sir," said Jothan, "but if there is, I would fight to remove slavery from the country."

"Jothan!"

"I would fight too, Mama," Gardiner agreed.

"Me too," I added. Gardiner looked at me.

"You can't fight, Jen. You're a girl."

"I can too!"

"No, you can't!"

"Yes, I can, Gardiner Edwards, and you can't stop me!" My youngest brother's cheeks turned pink and a few people laughed.

"That's enough, all of you," said Mama, her voice rising. "No one is going anywhere, least of all to a war." She turned to Mr. Lincoln. "I pray, sir, that your worst fear will not come to pass."

"Indeed, Mrs. Edwards," he nodded, very much the sober man

in the rain again. "I am trusting that as well."

*

That night, I listened to my brothers talking in their room. The inside walls of our house were not so thick and years ago I had used my jackknife to pop out a knot in the green ash panel between my room and theirs. With my ear up against the hole, I could hear them perfectly. Jothan was saying he'd never heard someone as smart as Mr. Lincoln. Gardiner agreed and said he'd written down everything he could remember from the speech into his journal.

"I think he's much smarter than Mr. Douglas," Gardiner added.

"Maybe he is, but maybe we only think Mr. Lincoln is smarter because we agree with him. Mr. Douglas said some smart things too and also got a lot of cheers."

"True, but Pa believes Mr. Lincoln is right and will be voting for him."

Predictably, they also talked about the girls they'd seen in town. Jothan mentioned one in particular several times, Marie Parker. My brother's interest in Marie was old news, though I had done my best to ignore it. Marie and her parents had moved to Toulon five years before when her father, Caleb Parker, had transferred his law practice from Springfield. Marie was an only child and I suppose it would have been nice for me to be friendly to her, but I didn't really associate that much with any of the girls in town. For my money, girls were too boring and did mostly boring things, and Marie was no different. She played the piano and helped Miss Fowler at the school and spent a lot of time reading. I supposed she was pretty enough however. Marie had strawberry-colored hair that hung in ringlets about her face and deep blue eyes and very white teeth that almost gleamed when she smiled. Marie also had the most beautiful dresses owing to her father being a lawyer. Everything about her seemed to impress boys and girls alike, yet, she couldn't throw a ball to save her life. Or catch a fish, or, to my mind, do anything very useful.

After the boys stopped talking, I crawled back in bed and looked out the window. Outside, Jug Run Creek flowed east across our land to the Spoon River. The creek had little water this time of year and the sycamores and cottonwoods along its bank were black, spidery beings without their leaves. I felt wonderfully tired after our day in town and my adventures the previous night. Before I knew it I was fast asleep, dreaming of rabbits in hats and magicians dressed in red.

*

A few days after Mr. Lincoln's visit, I rode into town. Mama had given me a list for Mr. Trickle and though it was a sharply cold morning, Ruby seemed glad for the outing. She frisked and trotted and blew out deep, frosty breaths. Sam was also delighted. He sat between my legs and yipped happily. The more he yipped, the more Ruby snorted. Finally, I had to tell them both to settle down or we'd never get to the store. Sam had come to us as a pup eight years before and had immediately become best friends with Ruby. He was a shepherd mix and the smallest of the litter. The man giving the pups away hadn't put much stock in him, but I knew he was the best of the lot. Sam liked to howl more than bark, and when the prairie wolves were singing, he'd join right in. He was a hard worker too, took care of all our animals and made sure everyone made it back to the barn each night. Sometimes, he'd herd just for fun too. Many was the evening when I'd see him, for no reason at all, chasing Ruby, or being chased.

It looked like life had gone back to normal in Toulon. The streets were quieter and all the paper had been cleaned up, and the biggest crowd once again could be found at Trickle's General Store. Trickle's had everything anyone might ever need. Boots, gloves, hatchets, pistols, cloth and dress patterns, hats and bonnets, and of course every staple, including coffee, pickles, and molasses. There were toys for the children and books for the readers. If it happened that Trickle's didn't have what was needed, Washington could order it. With the recent extension of the railroad to the nearby town of Kewanee, goods from Chicago could be had in only a few days. Washington liked to tell customers that the ordered item would be at his store before they returned home.

Rosetta and Washington lived on the second floor of the store and rented out the other rooms in the building. In recent months, Rosetta had said she wanted a real house with a real garden. I for one wondered when she'd have time to tend flowers. She was a member of nearly every club in town, including the Toulon Literary Society, the Relief Society, the Ladies' Hospitality Association, and the Children's Musical Betterment Program. She also delivered purchases to members of the community who were housebound. All this, of course, while helping her husband manage the store. Though Toulon supported many businesses, Trickle's was a favorite. Washington's stories and Rosetta's gossip came free of charge, and a sitting area in the back around the stove, with an ever-full coffee pot, hosted customers and loiterers alike.

As I entered the store, a large group of ladies flowed out. They all greeted me except for Mrs. Bertha McRae, who was busy coaxing her two funny goats behind her. Upon seeing me, she gave a quick scowl and said, "Come along Teddy! Come along Tommy!" I was never sure what had made Mrs. McRae dislike me so much, but my wearing trousers and not doing things that most girls did likely had something to do with it.

Washington was standing in front of the counter staring after Mrs. McRae and her pets. His moon face and bald head were slightly flushed. The pencils and rolled-up pieces of paper that he kept in his wiry, fluffy beard, seemed askew.

"Hello, Mr. Trickle," I said. "Busy morning?"

Washington nodded. "Very! It's been as packed as a sardine can in here! Then on top of all the people, we got goats running around too. One of 'em just tried to eat my broom!"

"Yes, sir," I smiled. "Mrs. McRae's goats are very important to her. I think they're kind of like her children."

"I suppose. A bit queer though, don't you think?"

I shrugged. Everything about Mrs. McRae seemed queer to me, but it was better I didn't say that out loud.

Washington smiled for he knew me too well. "Well, anyway, you didn't come here to talk about goats. Your ma got a list for me?"

While Washington began filling Mama's order, I looked through the books to see if there were any on magic. Trickle's seemed to have every kind of novel and instructional booklet, but not a one that might explain how a rabbit could vanish beneath a piece of cloth. This was disappointing, but I could see if there were any in the catalog. I had just picked up *White Jacket* by Herman Melville when a voice spoke behind me.

"That's a good book," the voice said, "though painful in its depiction of cruelty."

I turned around, startled. My mouth fell open to find the magician behind me.

"I—uh—was looking for something else," I said, returning the book to the shelf. "I wanted to find—" I stopped. Suddenly, the dove Owl had had with him the other day appeared on his shoulder.

"A book on magic?" he finished for me.

I stared at the dove, then nodded slowly. "How did you know?"

He smiled. "A lucky guess. Do you want to be a magician?"

"I don't know. Maybe. Mostly I just want to know how you— that is, how *she*"—I pointed at the dove—"got from under the cloth into your hat."

Owl nodded thoughtfully, and the bird seemed to as well. He asked me if I'd like to hold her. On the back of my hand, her claws immediately gripped my skin. After pecking a couple of times at me, she walked up my coat and onto my shoulder. There she nestled into my neck and began a soft cooing. I stood very still.

The magician chuckled "You can relax," he said. "Julia is used to all manner of transport."

The bird tickled my ear with gentle pecks. "Julia is my mother's name too," I said, startled a second time.

Owl smiled again. "Well, isn't that a coincidence." He then asked my name and if I'd like to have coffee with him around Mr. Trickle's stove.

"Can I keep holding the dove?" I asked.

"Oh yes, but you must call her "Julia." She prefers people use her name."

The fire felt good after the long, cold ride into town. I sipped my coffee and waved to Ben Carter, the owner of Carter's Saloon and the Waxwing Theatre, who also sat enjoying a hot drink. I could see that Mr. Carter, like many others in town, was glad Toulon had returned to its quiet self. Though the Douglas and Lincoln speeches had been good for business, there'd also been a lot of drinking and fighting.

I tried to think of something to say. Owl however just drank his coffee, closing his eyes at one point as if he was having a rest. I couldn't completely see the dove but had the sense that it was resting too.

"What's your real name?" I finally asked.

He opened his eyes. "Owl is my real name."

"You mean your mother *named* you Owl?"

"Yes. She began calling me "Owl" when I was a little boy. I liked being out at night so much that she said she may as well just call me her little owl. The name stuck."

"I like being out at night too," I said. "But you must have had a different name when you were born?"

He thought. "Maybe, but I don't remember it." He poured us more coffee. "Why do you want to know about the magic trick?" he changed the subject.

"Just curious, I guess. It seemed impossible."

Owl nodded. "It's a serious responsibility to know how magic is done. Magicians only reveal their secrets to other magicians who take the oath of secrecy."

"What's that?"

"A vow never to reveal how conjures are accomplished. You see, Jennie," he set his cup down, "magic is all about illusion. Making possible what seems impossible. The joy of it is not in knowing, but rather not knowing. Once the trick is revealed, there's no more mystery."

I thought about this. "I don't know if I agree, sir. I think I'd be very happy to know how the trick is done and I'd still appreciate the mystery."

At that moment, Ben Carter walked up, tipping his hat. "Hello, Jennie."

"Hello, Mr. Carter."

"I don't believe I'm acquainted with your friend," he said, extending a hand toward Owl. "Benjamin Carter, sir."

"And I am Owl," the magician stood, taking the hand.

"I know you, sir. You gave a fine performance last week. A man came into my saloon and broke several glasses trying to figure out how you tossed the wine into the air and made it vanish."

Owl frowned. "I do apologize, Mr. Carter."

Ben Carter waved his hand. "Do not trouble yourself. There are many reasons for broken glass in my establishment, and magic is one of the better ones. In fact, I was hoping to invite you to the theatre I own here in town for a full evening of illusion."

Owl liked the idea though at present he had several engagements awaiting him in Chicago and other towns. The men discussed arranging something for the following spring, which I thought perfect. The months between now and then would give me time to learn more. I liked Owl but I didn't believe him that knowing the trick took away the joy. It had to be better to know than not know.

We finished our coffee and I returned Julia to her master. After collecting Mama's goods from Mr. Trickle, we left the store. Owl walked with me over to Ruby and Sam, both dozing in the autumn sun. Upon hearing my voice, Ruby opened her eyes. She thrust her ears forward like two trumpets then sniffed both Owl and Julia. My mule then let the dove hop onto her back.

"Ruby is friends with everyone," I said.

"So is Julia."

"I don't mind," I said, "that you won't tell me how she got into your hat. I'll figure it out though."

Owl smiled, then reached into his coat and handed me a small booklet, *Being a Card Sharp & Other Pertinent Information Related to*

Coins. In his other hand, a silver dollar suddenly appeared. "Buy yourself some cards, Jennie," he said, handing me the coin. "You might as well begin learning how to do tricks yourself." He put the dove back on his shoulder. "I am glad to have met you," he added, extending his hand.

"I am glad to have met you, sir."

"Good luck with your magic!" Owl called over his shoulder as he walked away. "And just remember one very important thing: Never, ever look surprised when the impossible happens!"

THREE

MR. LINCOLN didn't win. Despite Papa's vote and despite winning the popular vote, he still would not be going to Washington City. In 1858, senators were chosen by the legislature and those voters casting ballots would not be doing so directly for either candidate. A few weeks after the election, Papa received a letter from his friend. Mr. Lincoln thanked him for his own letter of consolation, but declared Papa need not bother himself with words of encouragement for "the next time."

"I fear I am quite dead politically," he penned, "and shall not trouble myself further with such pursuits." Then, "All will be well. We shall have fun again." The "fun" to be had was not elaborated upon until the post script, presumably written some days later after the feelings of melancholy had passed. "Perhaps all is not lost," Mr. Lincoln finished. "I am neither dead nor dying. Another occasion may present itself."

The Illinois winter bore down heavily upon the prairie. By November, every hardwood tree in the land stood declothed of its vegetative jacket. By December, the last of the fall crops had to be harvested or remain in the frozen ground. The snow fell hour after hour and the drifts grew well above a person's head. The swallows, vultures, and fish hawks had long since moved south. Only the white-headed eagles, a few hawks, and smaller birds, such as towhees and meadowlarks, remained on the ivory landscape.

Papa cut down a small cedar tree for the Christmas holiday. We decorated it with strings of dried mulberries, loops cut from colored paper, and branches of holly. For two days, Mama and I baked many desserts, and in the evenings Papa played his guitar and Jothan his fiddle and we all sang *Drive the Cold Winter Away* and other holiday tunes. I was learning to play the harmonica, but our family choir sounded better if I just stuck to singing. I loved these winter months. Our home along Jug Run Creek was warm and cozy and in addition to singing, we also spent many hours reading, telling stories, and playing games. On the days when the snow did stop and the sun appeared, my brothers and I went into the bottoms. We'd use the wooden shoes Papa had made for us for walking atop the snow, looking for the tracks of the many animals that remained out of sight most of the year.

The winter had barely begun when my oldest brother Jothan started spending less time at home. This was odd given the time of year, but he told our parents that he had decided to become a lawyer and Caleb Parker had agreed to take him on as an apprentice. Jothan talked about being affected by meeting Mr. Lincoln. He told us he wanted to do something worthwhile and figured the law would be the best place in which to help the less fortunate. Both Mama and Papa were pleased and agreed to his staying in town more. For my part, I had doubts about this selflessness. Jothan still talked about Marie a lot, so I knew his true reasons for wanting to be at the Parker home. Meanwhile our friend, Adam, who was Gardiner's age and lived in town, had told me that Marie was taking French lessons with his older sister. This news confirmed my assessment of her. There couldn't be anything more useless than learning French unless you were planning on living in France, and who would plan that? Yes, Marie was boring and given to silly pursuits and Jothan's infatuation could simply not be explained.

*

Three months into the new year, Papa brought home a package

from the post office. It was for me, a book from Owl entitled *The Expositor* by William Frederick Pinchbeck. A note fell out as I opened it.

My dear Jennie Edwards,

Please accept this book with my compliments and encouragement for your interest in magic. Perhaps the next time we meet, you shall perform some conjures for me!

Your obedient servant,

Owl

"I told him I was interested in magic," I said, staring at the book. I opened it up and started reading, but Mama interrupted.

"Magic isn't going to get your chores done, young lady. You can read your book later."

That night I stayed up very late. Mr. Pinchbeck described how to turn eggs into pancakes, how to break a watch into pieces and then put it right again, and how to make the ace of hearts in a deck of cards become the ace of clubs. Yet, the most astonishing idea of all was teaching a pig to understand cards.

Take a pig, wrote Mr. Pinchbeck, *seven or eight weeks old, let him have free access to the interior part of your house, until he shall become in some measure domesticated. When familiar, you may enter upon his instruction.*

He then explained how to gain the pig's trust and how to encourage him, through reward and reprimand, to pick up cards in his mouth. The pig could be made to select certain cards using a signal understood by magician and pig, by breathing or snuffling through your nose in a certain way. He made it sound so easy! While I agreed that pigs seemed very smart, they also didn't seem given to foolish activity. Still, Mr. Pinchbeck was adamant.

Of all other quadrupeds, the Pig in my opinion is the most sapient, though writers on Natural History say to the contrary, giving preference to the Elephant. I am convinced that the race of Swine claim a greater share of instinct than belongs to the Dog or the Horse.

I finally fell asleep wondering how I could convince my mother to let me bring a pig into the house.

*

A couple of weeks later, I stood in Trickle's General Store looking in the catalog for more books on magic. I had learned most of Mr. Pinchbeck's conjures (minus the Learned Pig trick since Mama had said absolutely not to letting any swine in the house), so had need of more instruction. The 1859 catalog had all manner of farm machinery available, as well as fabric, kitchenware, and toys. Yet, there was nothing about magic. As I read the dishonest claim on the catalog cover that, "Everything you need is within these pages," Mrs. Bertha McRae walked up. Her expression turned as sharp as a split rock as she took in my trousers, blouse, and straw hat. She stared at the vulture feather I'd stuck into my hat before her green, cat eyes narrowed.

"Hello, Eliza Jane."

"Hello, Mrs. McRae."

"How is your mother?" One couldn't say that Mrs. McRae wasn't cordial. She was simply icy at the same time.

"She is well, thank you." When the woman didn't say anymore, I looked away from those piercing eyes to the friendly ones of her goats. Tommy and Teddy were stiffing and licking my trousers. They were little miniature goats of some kind and rather adorable. Tommy jumped onto one of Mr. Trickle's barrels. He stood there alert like a sailor perched atop a ship's rigging. "How are Tommy and Teddy?" I asked.

"They are fine, thank you. Teddy had a cough due to the cold, but he is over that now."

"That's good." I put out my palm so they could lick it. "Do you ever think about getting a nanny?"

"No," she said quickly. "My boys are very devoted to each other. I don't believe they'd welcome another."

I doubted this. Most male animals very much welcomed the company of females. "Well, if you changed your mind, you could look in here," I said, opening up the catalog. "This is supposed to have everything a person needs, but," I turned a few pages, "I don't know if that's true."

Mrs. McRae stared at me. "You think I'm odd, don't you, Eliza Jane?"

My face grew warm. "Of course not."

"Oh, yes, you do. I can see it in your eyes." She picked up Tommy and put him back on the floor. "Well, I can assure you, I have no interest in what you think."

"Yes, ma'am."

After she'd gone, my stomach began to hurt. For as long as I could remember, things had been this way with McRae and I never could figure why she didn't like me. Mama had always insisted I be extra polite to the older woman, yet it didn't seem to matter. I'd just closed the catalog when another voice spoke.

"Hello Jennie."

I turned around, startled. "Oh. Hi, Marie."

She smiled. "Were you just talking with Mrs. McRae? I didn't know you were friends."

"We aren't. In fact, she hates me."

To my surprise, Marie laughed, a not entirely unpleasant sound. "I doubt that!"

"No, it's true. I think maybe she doesn't like the way I dress, or the way I talk…something."

Marie stopped smiling and looked at me carefully. My cheeks grew warm again under this new scrutiny.

"Well, I think you look just fine," she said, thoughtfully. "It's true Mrs. McRae is a bit queer, but I don't think she hates anyone. She's been giving me piano lessons for a year now. Never says an unkind word about anyone and likely doesn't think them either."

The mention of the piano lessons reminded me of how boring Marie was. I nodded and tried to move away, but then she asked what I was buying.

"Just some things for my mother. Also, I was looking for a book on magic."

"Magic! Really? I love magic! Do you know any conjures?"

I shrugged. "A few. I'm still learning."

"Well, I'd love to see them some time. When I was in New York City with my aunt and uncle last summer, I saw a magician. He did the most amazing tricks! Legerdemain, mentalism, illusions. He even sawed a woman in two!"

"Sawed a woman in two!" I squinted at her. "How did he do that?"

"I have no idea, but the woman was fine after." Marie then touched my arm, leaning in closer. "It was nothing though compared to when he vanished into thin air!"

"Vanished!" I fairly shouted, sure now she was making fun of me.

"It's true," Marie smiled happily. "He vanished right off the stage. Of course, that wasn't all. He reappeared too."

"Where?"

"On the balcony."

"That's impossible."

"I know." Marie thought. "Listen, Jennie, do you want to come over for tea this afternoon? I can tell you more about the show, and you can show me a conjure or two."

I stared at her and suddenly felt very odd. My stomach still hurt, but in a completely different way. It was getting late and I should get home, having promised Mama I'd help her bake pies. Still, I accepted Marie's invitation. One cup of tea wouldn't take long.

*

"Marie's nice," I told my brother later that evening. We were in the barn feeding the animals and Jothan suddenly looked at me as if I'd just sprouted horns.

"Whaddya mean?" he asked. "I thought you didn't like her."

"I never said that."

"You didn't have to."

"Well, anyway, she's nice. We had tea today. That's why I was late." I started brushing Ruby, who tried to nibble my braid. "Marie knows a lot of things." Jothan nodded, getting that dreamy look I was now familiar with. "Have you kissed her yet?" I asked.

"Jennie!"

"Well, have you?"

"That's none of your business!"

I smiled, seriously doubting if Jothan had even held Marie's hand given he was so shy. She and I had talked about magic for an hour and I did a couple of easy tricks with coins and cards, to which she seemed delighted. Marie didn't mention Jothan until I was leaving, but it was apparent how much she liked my brother. On the ride home, I decided this might not be such a bad thing after all.

Gardiner came in from feeding the pigs. I didn't hear him, and the next thing I knew he had dumped an armload of fluffy snow on me. I shook off the snow, threw down the comb, and tackled him. We rolled back and forth in the snow, mud, and hay. Gardiner and I wrestled frequently, and though he was taller and stronger, I often won our matches because I was faster. Now, however, he hadn't been surprised. I held my own for awhile, but soon I was flattened on the barn floor. With the promise of buying him some candy next time we were in town, I was released. I knew Gardiner wouldn't bother actually collecting; he didn't really care that much about winning.

As we walked back to the house, a half-moon brightened the snowy fields. Jothan wanted to hear more about my conversation with Marie.

"We didn't talk about you, big brother," I teased him. "We talked about magic."

"Magic? Truly?"

"Yep. She told me about seeing a magician in New York City and I did some conjures for her." In the moonlight, I could see Jothan's disappointment. I laughed. "Oh, Jothan, of course Marie talked about you too!"

"Did she? What did she say?"

"Truthfully?" He nodded. "She said you were the nicest boy she'd ever met. That you were kind and you made her laugh. She likes being with you."

Gardiner chuckled. "That don't sound like the brother I know!"

I nodded. "That's what I said!"

Jothan looked so happy hearing these words from Marie that he didn't mind us making fun. In fact, he started dancing and picked me up and threw me over his shoulder. As he turned us both in circles, Gardiner clapped his hands and sang *Camptown Races*. We all laughed and after Jothan put me down, I staggered all around the yard, dizzy. We had a snowball fight then and I felt happy too. I had two great brothers, a new friend in Marie, and with her encouragement, I had decided for sure that I would become a magician.

*

I worked all spring and into the summer mastering many simple conjures. These involved coins or cards, eggs or dice. My family didn't seem to tire of being my audience, and Mama only occasionally protested at my use of our food supply. Sam, however, was more suspicious. After I'd pulled an egg from behind his ear, he barked in alarm and refused to come near me for several hours.

In his letters, Owl said the most important task for a magician was to practice; every success was born on the wings of confidence. "You are in charge," he wrote. "What the audience sees and what they believe is completely of your making. They are all hypnotized in a fashion, directed mentally by your words, and visually by your actions. Like a string a cat will follow, their eyes are led only where you lead them. They will think they have never looked away from your hands, but indeed they have, if only for a second, and they have never even noticed their distraction. It is a great responsibility, that of holding their experience in your hands, but it is also the most wondrous of joys!"

The time arrived at last for Owl's return to Toulon. The morning of his arrival, Papa and I sat drinking coffee by the fire. I could barely contain my excitement and was talking my father's ear off. That's when Mama appeared suddenly. I tried to hide my cup and act normal. After kissing my father, she turned to me.

"Really, Eliza Jane, you think I don't know about you having coffee with your father in the mornings?"

Fortunately, she was smiling, and when Papa laughed, I breathed easier. "So, you don't mind?"

"Of course, I mind," she said, pouring a cup for herself as Papa went outside. "Coffee's not good for you. But you're also fifteen now. Old enough to make your own decisions." She smiled again. "Or some of them anyway."

Mama sat down in the rocker and motioned for me to sit on the floor in front of her. She undid my braid and began brushing my hair. I closed my eyes. As we listened to a pair of swallow parents tending their nest outside the kitchen window, Mama hummed. Finally, she asked about my "magician friend."

"His name is Owl, Mama."

"That must not be his real name, Jennie."

"He says it is." Then I added, "Owl wrote that he's bringing his assistant, Carmen, with him."

"Oh?"

"I was wondering, Mama, if we could invite them to supper? After the show?"

My mother didn't say anything. I'd overheard her telling Papa recently that she wasn't sure about my friendship with Owl. She wondered why he'd be interested in such a young girl like me. Papa had dismissed her concerns, saying Mr. Carter said the man seemed like an upstanding fellow. Then Mama said she wished I wasn't so friendly to people and instead more shy like other girls. I didn't understand their conversation, but now I worried her concern would stifle her curiosity.

"I think that would be fine, Jennie," she said at last. Mama tied the braid and kissed the top of my head. "I do wonder after all. I've never met a magician!"

FOUR

JULIA THE DOVE stood on Owl's shoulder as he stepped down
from the stage. My friend looked exactly the same except for one
thing: he now had a long beard. At the bottom of the beard, as
with his hair, he'd tied a red ribbon. Owl immediately waved.

"Jennie, my girl!" As he gave me a hug, Julia hopped onto my
shoulder. "Of course, she remembers you!" he clapped. "Indeed, I
believe she's been thinking of you the whole ride." I smiled, glad to
feel the dove pecking delicately at my hair. Owl turned to the
woman exiting the stage after him. "May I present Carmen, my
very beautiful assistant. My dear, this is Jennie Edwards."

Owl had not written much about Carmen except to say that
she'd been with him for some time and was the inspiration for
much of his magic. She was taller than Owl by a couple of inches
and her skin was very dark like a Negro's but her hair was straight
and piled high on her head like a white woman. While her jaw was
square like a man's, everything else about her, the soft nose and full
lips, the smile, so unmistakably female, took my breath away. After
kissing both my cheeks, Carmen laughed.

"It is such a pleasure to finally meet you, Jennie." Her voice had
a slight accent to it.

"And I, you, ma'am"

She laughed again. "Please, call me Carmen. Owl has spoken so much of you, I feel that we are already friends."

"Of course. Carmen. Yes, thank you."

I took them to the Virginia House where they'd be staying and then escorted Owl to the theatre. Benjamin Carter's Waxwing sat in the block north of the courthouse and across Washington Street from the bank, shoe shop, and Stockner's Hotel. The theatre had once been a hotel until Toulon's sheriff had determined more was being offered than just room and board. After the establishment was shut down, the building went up for auction and Mr. Carter bought it for his theatrical pursuits. Over the years, the Waxwing had hosted a traveling Shakespeare Company and productions of popular melodramas such as *Uncle Tom's Cabin* and *The Flying Dutchman*. But it had never had a magic show before. Owl's presentation was the talk of the town.

That evening, after my family and I arrived and found our seats, I returned to the door to help hand out programs. The Trickles came with Mrs. Trickle carrying Fancy and Washington snorting about how crowded it was.

"Have you ever seen a magic show, Jennie?" he asked.

"No, sir. Only those few conjures Owl did when Mr. Lincoln came."

He looked around. "From the look of this place, no one in town has either. Any seats left?"

Mrs. McRae arrived next with her husband, Council, a quiet, kind man whose connection to his unpleasant wife couldn't have puzzled me more. Following them came the Parkers. Marie looked elegant in a red and black gown and red silk bonnet. I had worn one of the new dresses Mama had recently bought me, but it still didn't come close to the loveliness of Marie's. To my surprise, she hugged me and said she hoped we could talk after the show. I said that would be nice.

It was warm inside the Waxwing and people stood fanning themselves and chatting. Everyone was catching up on news and gossip, but once the lights dimmed, all took their seats. After the hall quieted, Owl appeared on stage. The show had begun!

From the beginning, the audience loved him. Owl was warm, funny, and very, very good. Coins, cards, and balls all appeared and vanished, his movements smooth and perfect and utterly mystifying. He had told me that he never did the same trick for the same audience, yet Mrs. Trickle couldn't have been happier when he presented the vanishing wine glass trick. All eyes were upon him and Carmen as well. With her height and grace, she looked much like a queen on stage, and I found myself looking at her as much as at Owl.

One conjure began with a black box sitting on a table. Owl turned it on its side and twirled it upside down to reveal its emptiness. After proving to us that the box held nothing, he placed a lid on top.

"Ladies and Gentlemen, you see before you a very empty box. I am sure you find this, as I do, a most uninteresting object!" With that, he waved his wand back and forth, parting the air above the box. Then he removed the lid. Two white objects appeared at the rim. The ears and front paws of a rabbit! The little animal punched the air with its feet as Owl lifted him out, then upon being placed on the table, it stood on its hind legs. The crowd roared. Far from being frightened, the rabbit seemed to love the attention. It hopped all around the table. Owl introduced him as Oscar, the magical rabbit, and the applause continued.

The last conjure before the intermission involved a large bowl, a pitcher, and a black piece of cloth. Carmen set all these on the table in front of Owl. Without a word, he lifted the pitcher high and poured the water into the bowl. It splashed all over, dousing the table and Owl's long coat. He poured and poured until it seemed the bowl couldn't hold any more. Then he stretched the black cloth across the top of the vessel. After he'd lifted the bowl into the air, Carmen stepped forward to remove the tray. Owl walked toward us, while all of us watched the bowl that was still dripping water.

"Ladies and Gentlemen," Owl boomed, "my good friend Jennie Edwards tells me it has not rained here in a fortnight. I know well that summertime on the prairie is when water should be treasured and not..." he lifted the bowl higher, "...tossed away!" Then, to everyone's shock, Owl threw the bowl into the air.

The people in the front row immediately turned away, but the anticipated drenching never came. There was no water, and even stranger, there was no bowl! The only thing that fell upon the stage was the black cloth. A stunned silence in the Waxwing quickly turned to thunderous applause. Owl and Carmen took several bows, then disappeared behind the curtain.

During the intermission my brothers, father and our friends stood outside concocting theories as to how the magician had done his tricks. I listened, amused. None of their ideas came even close to the truth. I didn't know all the answers either, but I did know the men were going about their deductions in the wrong way. Owl had impressed upon me, in our brief correspondence, that with magic, you had to start your analysis from a different point in the story. For example, the men tried to explain how the bowl had vanished *after* Owl lifted it into the air. But what I knew was that he had never carried the bowl in the first place. It *seemed* as if he had. He'd *acted* as if he had. But somewhere along the way, the bowl had gone somewhere else. Owl had written to me, "You must believe what your mind would like you not to believe. This is so simple, yet it's the thing most people cannot do. If your mind says, "That's impossible!" you must consider that it is. And if your eye is following the movement of an object, consider that it might not really be there." Somehow the bowl had vanished after the water had been poured. Carmen had had a hand in its disappearance, of that I was sure. Interestingly, my father and the other men never considered that Owl's assistant might have something to do with the conjures.

In the second part of his show, Owl focused on mentalism. Many in the audience offered objects to Carmen while Owl, blindfolded and with his back to the crowd, named each one. The red ostrich plume in Marie's hat, a key from Washington Trickle, another man's watch, a sandalwood fan, and a lady's left-hand glove, all took no time to guess. Owl even knew a small collar collected from Mrs. McRae and belonging to one of her goats. This elicited a real smile from the old woman and I nearly fainted at the sight. She didn't look at all like herself, so transforming was the effect of the smile. Later, when I stood outside talking with my brothers and Marie and our friend Adam, I spied Mrs. McRae coming out of the theatre. She was still smiling, and I thought to myself that magic had indeed been done.

*

The light had just begun to fade from the long June day as my family and Carmen and Owl settled down to supper. It had taken a long time to leave the theatre owing to everyone wanting to meet Toulon's special guests. As Mama served bowls of venison stew, she asked Owl if he was from Chicago.

"No, Mrs. Edwards. Tennessee originally."

"Tennessee! You don't sound like you're from the South."

"No, ma'am. I've lived in a number of places and have always easily picked up the speech of the people wherever I've been. This can be a great advantage, especially if you don't want people to know where you're from."

"Why would you want that?" my brother Gardiner asked.

Owl thought. "Sometimes I've found that it's better if people don't know too much about me." He smiled. "More mysteries are better in my profession."

Jothan asked Owl what it was like to live in Chicago. The magician described a city full of contradiction, with wealth and poverty, good people and bad, tremendous culture as well as dark worlds and criminals. He described people living in homes resembling castles, while others had nothing and existed like animals along the banks of the Chicago River.

"It's a city for everyone," Owl concluded, "but also a place that all experience differently."

"It sounds complicated," said Gardiner.

"I think it sounds exciting," I said.

Owl chuckled. "There you are. You would both find very

different cities should you visit Chicago."

After supper, Papa and Owl smoked cigars and discussed the party nominations for next year's elections. Of great interest were the contenders for the ticket of the newly formed Republican Party. A man named William Seward, who many expected to win, had lately vanished on a months-long tour of Europe, while Salmon Chase, another possibility, was not making his presence known overmuch either. The only person who seemed to take the prospect seriously was Mr. Abraham Lincoln, and he had not yet actually declared himself a candidate. However, he had spoken several times on behalf of the other candidates. By this method he was making his own views known. Many in Chicago, Owl said, liked what they were hearing.

"However," he added, "even Mr. Lincoln proposes protecting slavery where it exists in the belief that it shall simply go away of its own accord." He shook his head. "As if it is no more than a houseguest who has stayed too long."

"Men will not give up that which has made them rich," Papa mused. "And for others, it may be more the familiarity of the thing than the money. It is easier to say we shall have no more of something, rather than take away what already is." Papa drew on his cigar. "Like many, I believe removing slavery from this country will not happen quietly. Perhaps not quickly either."

"Yes, I believe that too."

Owl then asked if I might do some magic tricks for him and Carmen. I hesitated, feeling shy. Gardiner, wanting to help, offered to let me read his mind.

"That will make for an awful short show," Jothan laughed.

I went to my room and got some of my props. To my surprise, my nervousness quickly passed. All my practicing had paid off and though my conjures weren't as smart or as smooth as Owl's, I still felt pleased. Later, as Papa and I drove Owl and Carmen back into town, my friend praised me.

"You have the talent and the confidence, Jennie, to be a fine magician. I do believe you delight in fooling people."

"Maybe, "I nodded, "though I hadn't thought of it like that."

Owl reached an arm back from the front seat of the wagon. "Here's a present, my dear. From me and Carmen."

Between the moonlight and the lamp on our wagon, I could see a small, narrow package wrapped in brown paper and red ribbon. I looked at Owl, then Carmen. She had not spoken much during the evening, but her elegant presence more than made up for the lack of words. Now she placed a hand on my arm.

"Open it, Jennie."

I took the box from Owl. Inside lay a wooden wand, marked at either end by brass tips. It was a delicate looking thing, very thin, but also fine with etching in the wood.

"People love wands," Owl said. "Use this to good effect and the audience will believe anything you do."

I waved it around in the air a few times. The brass tips gleamed in the moonlight; the wand felt as light as a feather. Directing my new prop over toward Owl and then toward my own head, I said, "I will now divine your real name, Owl the magician!" Everyone laughed.

"If you can do that, Jennie Edwards," he said, "then you deserve to know it!"

*

If most Americans wanted to focus only where slavery didn't yet exist, an event that October changed their minds. In Harper's Ferry, Virginia, a white man named John Brown attempted to take over a military arsenal, the weapons of which he planned to distribute to slaves who would then rise up in rebellion against their masters. The insurrection failed and several people, including some of John Brown's own sons, were killed. Order was restored, but the man's audacity shocked and frightened everyone. For two weeks while he awaited trial, people in Toulon spoke of little else. Some believed Brown divinely inspired; others thought him mad as a hatter. One thing all could agree on however was that he would hang. After his death in December, a note found in Brown's things was reprinted in the *Stark County News*:

I, John Brown, am now quite certain that the crimes of this guilty land will never be purged away but with Blood. I had as I now think vainly flattered myself that without very much bloodshed, it might be done.

In January came news that the Republican National Convention would be held the following May in Chicago. Many felt this to be a sign that Mr. Lincoln was indeed seeking the nomination. Papa, not surprisingly, felt delighted. He said that his old friend was surely the best candidate for keeping the country stitched together. Not everyone agreed. One Saturday morning around the stove at Trickle's, my brothers and I listened to the arguments.

"The man is known only in the West," declared Council McRae. "He could not possibly win enough votes in the East and certainly none of the Southern states will have anything to do with him. It's a waste of time to nominate him."

"Nonsense," said my father. "Lincoln has been stumping since August. He *is* well-known, and the people like what they hear. He is less of a radical than Seward or Chase and more of one than Edward Bates. They feel comfortable with his stance on slavery."

"More Northern people maybe. Southerners, however, are very uncomfortable. They want to move west and they want to take their slaves with them. Lincoln opposes this, so they will oppose Lincoln."

Washington Trickle agreed. "Even those who don't own slaves don't like too strong a government. They don't want to be told what to do. Or what not to do. And Council's right, he's not well-known in the East, having served only one term in Congress. People want someone with more experience."

"I'll take a man with smarts over experience any time."

If Papa was so sure, Council said he should wager on it. They bet one three-dollar coin, Papa to win if Lincoln got the nomination and Council if any of the others did. On the ride home that afternoon, I asked my father if Mr. Lincoln really had a chance.

""I think so, Jennie," he said, "but politics is a funny business.

Sometimes the most qualified man doesn't get the job for reasons having nothing to do with skill. I believe Abe is the smartest of the bunch, but Council and Washington may be right. He may not be well-known enough."

That, however, was soon to change. The following month, Mr. Lincoln traveled to New York to give a lecture at a recently established private college called Cooper Union. Still not having publicly declared his bid for the nomination, he nonetheless attracted 1,500 New Yorkers to the event. The *Stark County News* printed the address as well as notes from an observer who said that Mr. Lincoln, looking disheveled and out of place, became a man transfigured at the lectern. He told his audience that the answer to the question of whether slavery could be extended into the territories must be sought in the Constitution with the long-stilled voices of the men who had framed that document. He explained that of the thirty-nine signatories, twenty-three had left behind documentation of their voting for or against the prohibition of slavery in the territories. Of these, twenty-one had voted for the prohibition.

"The sum of the whole," Mr. Lincoln explained, "is that a clear majority certainly understood that no proper division of local from Federal authority, nor any part of the Constitution, forbade the Federal Government to control slavery in the Federal territories, while all the rest probably had the same understanding."

He next addressed the Southern people and their belief that "Black Republicans," as they had begun referring to the Republican Party, were no better than reptiles or outlaws. Republicanism, they claimed, was a sectional party, revolutionary and destructive, while Southerners were conservative. Mr. Lincoln asked the audience what was conservatism if not an adherence to the old and tried, something which they themselves seemed intent on ignoring as they rushed toward the ideas of secession, popular sovereignty, revival of the slave trade, and laws that would forbid Congress from prohibiting slavery in the territories

"Not one of all your various plans," he continued, "can show a precedent or an advocate in the century within which our Government originated. Consider, then, whether your claim of conservatism for yourselves, and your charge of destructiveness against us, are based on the most clear and stable foundations."

Mr. Lincoln discredited the South's claim that the Republicans stir up insurrections among the slaves and their citation of John Brown as an example. John Brown was no Republican, he said, nor were any Republicans implicated in the Harper's Ferry enterprise. Even those in the slaveholding states who acknowledged this truth still claimed that the Republican "doctrines and declarations necessarily lead to such results." To this assertion, he said simply, "We do not believe it. We know we hold to no doctrine, and make no declaration, which were not held to and made by 'our fathers who framed the Government under which we live.'" Still, he understood that the Southern people would not tolerate the election of a Republican president and therefore said to them, "In that supposed event, you say, you will destroy the Union; and then, you say, the great crime of having destroyed it will be upon us! That is cool. A highwayman holds a pistol to my ear, and mutters through his teeth, 'Stand and deliver, or I shall kill you, and then you will be a murderer!'"

Mr. Lincoln concluded his speech with a call for Republicans to do their part to make all parts of the country at peace with one another. He asked if the Southern states would even be satisfied were the territories unconditionally surrendered to the institution of slavery, then emphatically stated that they would not In fact, the desire for the extension of slavery was less the topic of the day than invasions and insurrections. They wish to be let alone, he said, but even more than that they wish the North to cease calling "slavery *wrong*, and join them in calling it *right*. They do not, of course, explicitly state this, but rather speak words such as "Let us alone, do nothing to us, and say what you please about slavery." But we do let them alone—have never disturbed them—so that, after all, it is what we say, which dissatisfies them.

"If slavery is right, all words, acts, laws, and constitutions against it, are themselves wrong, and should be silenced, and swept away. If it is right, we cannot justly object to its nationality—its universality; if it is wrong, they cannot justly insist upon its extension—its enlargement. All they ask, we could readily grant, if we thought slavery right; all we ask, they could as readily grant, if they thought it wrong. Their thinking it right, and our thinking it wrong, is the precise fact upon which depends the whole controversy.

"Wrong as we think slavery is, we can yet afford to let it alone where it is, because that much is due to the necessity arising from its actual presence in the nation; but can we, while our votes will prevent it, allow it to spread into the National Territories, and to overrun us here in these Free States? If our sense of duty forbids this, then let us stand by our duty, fearlessly and effectively. Let us be diverted by none of those sophistical contrivances wherewith we are so industriously plied and belabored—contrivances such as groping for some middle ground between the right and the wrong, vain as the search for a man who should be neither a living man nor a dead man—such as a policy of "don't care" on a question about which all true men do care. Neither let us be slandered from our duty by false accusations against us, nor frightened from it by menaces of destruction to the Government nor of dungeons to ourselves. Let us have faith that right makes might, and in that faith, let us, to the end, dare to do our duty as we understand it."

*

After I finished the article, I knew I had never read anything so smart in my life. As I sat at our kitchen table, Papa walked in. He saw the paper and clapped his hands, smiling.

"You've read the article, Jen. So you know!"

"Know what, Papa?"

"That I've just won three dollars!"

FIVE

THE YEAR OF 1860 unfolded in much the same manner as every
other year. Snow accumulated in great amounts on the prairie, and
when we thought we couldn't take the cold and ice and deep drifts
one minute longer, it all melted in a great rush. The banks of Jug
Run Creek vanished beneath the high water, carrying away the
leaves and branches that had accumulated during the fall and
winter. Flowers popped from the earth enthusiastically; the grasses
grew tall. Birds returned and baby animals were born and we were
all busy from before light until after dark. Somehow amidst the
busy spring and early summer, Jothan still had time to study the law
with Mr. Parker. And to see Marie, of course. She also began
coming to our house for supper. I could see now why Jothan loved
her; she was funny and smart and seemingly more pretty every day.
Mama told me that my brother had spoken of marriage, but was
too nervous to ask her. I didn't understand this; Marie clearly loved
him as well.

Toward the end of summer, I left our house one morning with
Ruby and Sam. The day was already warm with the heat beginning
to melt the jasmine and honeysuckle vines into a kind of breezy
syrup smell. We headed for the deep pool on Jug Run Creek where
my brothers had taught me to swim. Later, I planned to meet our
friend Adam to cut Indian grass for our mothers' basket making.

The path had begun to vanish under the reach of hazel tree branches and sassafras shrubs. Ruby snorted and nipped at the pawing limbs, while Sam yipped like a young pup. Songbirds fluttered in the bellies of the plants and a few jumpy sparrows took flight. The haunting sounds of the wood thrushes filled the air. It was a perfect summer day, with chores done and no need to travel to town. When we got to the creek, I found my brother Gardiner already there, his horse Spirit munching on grass nearby. He whooped happily and splashed like a duck. I quickly got out of my clothes and joined him in the cool water.

After we'd swum and had a water fight, we lay on the grass to dry. I saw Gardiner had his notebook with him. "You been drawing?" I asked, pointing to the journal.

He nodded. "I made a sketch of one of them thrushes. It was sitting in that mulberry bush yonder. Sat there for the longest time, singing its heart out. I don't know why it was so happy, but it sure was."

"Can I see?"

Gardiner's thrush looked similar to a robin, but with more spotting in front, a little fan of feathers below and in back of its eyes, and more tiny dots on its throat. The delicate legs stood on the mulberry branch with a few mulberries drawn in as well.

"This is real good, brother. Maybe you should sell your drawings."

He closed his book. "Nah, they ain't that good. I just like doing it is all."

The thrush returned to the mulberry. After a few minutes of grooming itself, the bird quickly cleaned its beak on the branch then flew away. Gardiner lay on his back and looked up at the sky.

"Jen, can I tell you something?"

"Sure."

"I been thinking how I might like to go out west someday."

"Out west! Where?"

"I dunno. Maybe the Yukon."

"Where's that?"

"Up north. Where there's snow all year. Big, white bears too. I read about them in *The Wide World of Animals*."

"Is that where the white owl lives that comes here in the winter?"

"Yep."

"Sounds pretty cold, Gardiner. You sure you'd like it?"

"I think so." He sat up and brushed the grass off his back. "Don't know for sure though. It'd be an adventure sure enough." He went on to describe a flat, treeless land where few white people lived and the natives survived by eating seals and whales. The summers were so short that plants grew only a couple of feet tall. Wolves and foxes, a big deer called a caribou, and a really strange-looking animal called a musk-ox lived in the Yukon. The more Gardiner talked, the more excited he became. I had never heard him mention going west before, but it seemed as if he'd been thinking about it for a long time.

I thought a minute. "Can I come too, Gardiner? I'd like to see big, white bears."

He nodded. "Yep. I was hoping you'd want to. Well, I better go. I told Papa I'd help him fix the plow." Gardiner stood up and started putting on his clothes. Then he looked around. "I hope Ruby ain't led Spirit off."

"She ain't. I told her to stay close and she always listens to what I say."

Gardiner laughed.

*

It wasn't hard to find Adam, even among the 8-foot tall grasses. Our friend was a whistler and the soft sounds of *I Ain't Got Time to Tarry* led me right to him. He shouted as I appeared in the grass forest.

"Jen!"

Adam lifted me off the ground in a big hug. I'd known him ever since I could remember and in some ways he was more like a third brother to me, yet things had changed between us in recent months. It had started last summer when we were both helping

Washington Trickle at the store. Moving boxes around the crowded back storeroom had somehow resulted in me thinking it would be fun to kiss him. We were alone, it was kind of dark, and I was curious. I'd been thinking about Jothan and Marie, and Adam was my best friend, so it seemed a fine thing to do. The whole thing surprised me, but not as much as it surprised him. Upon hearing my idea, Adam stared at me like I'd just laid an egg. Then he smiled. After that, whenever we went fishing or set traps, we'd do a little kissing too. It wasn't as if we were sweethearts though, just good friends who kissed sometimes. Adam had plans to become a sheriff and I wanted to be a magician and neither of us really had a desire for marriage. He'd told me once that his disinterest in this area alarmed his mother, but it couldn't be helped. "I might go out west to be a sheriff," he said once, "and then where would that leave my wife?" I pointed out his wife could go too, but he said he thought it might be too dangerous.

It didn't take us long to collect all the Indian grass we needed. Our harvest was barely noticeable as the remaining grasses towered tall, the golden flowers murmuring in the summer breeze. We also picked strawberries and black cherries and talked about the latest goings-on in town. Adam lived just a few blocks from Trickle's and could regularly be found around the stove drinking coffee. In addition to working for his father, he also hired himself out to do odd jobs and garden work for the widows and other spinster women in town. Extra money was the goal of these endeavors, but the result was also that Adam grew very popular in town. And very well-informed. He made me laugh with stories of tea parties, which he was inevitably invited to, funny pet cats that followed him around while he tidied yards, and even one polite offer of marriage, which, he figured, must have been a joke.

After securing our buckets of berries in the creek shallows, we sat down and ate a lunch of boiled eggs and biscuits. Adam's mother had also given him some gingerbread. Sam suddenly appeared, wiggling and carrying a stick and soaked to the tip of his nose. I threw the stick for him back into the pool.

"Jen?"

"Hmm?"

"The boys been talking about joining up if there's a war?"

I threw the stick again for Sam. "Some. When Mama's not around. Why?"

He shrugged. "There's a lot of talk at Trickle's about it. Most figure it's coming, it's just a question of when." He thought. "Pa went to Chicago last month. He met some men from Mississippi and they told him straight out that if Lincoln is elected, the Southern states will secede. A course, the North won't let 'em go, so that means war. I'll be joining too."

"What about becoming a sheriff?"

"That'll have to wait. I don't mind. All of us have to go."

I looked at Adam. Every summer, he grew his blond hair long and when he was younger this had the effect of making him look like a little girl. Now, however, with light stubble covering his face and a deeper voice and his height and strong, broad chest, he looked anything but feminine. Taking his hand, I leaned over and kissed him on the cheek.

"You're a good man, Adam Ward, but I hope it don't come to that."

"Thanks, Jen. Me too."

As we rode back, flounces of Indian grass and big bluestem waved above the high ground in between Jug Run Creek and Jack Creek, the next tributary to the north flowing into Spoon River. Hawks glided above us in slow circles, while deer bounded away as we grew nearer. Clouds like cotton were beginning to take up more room in the sky, indicating the approach of a great, prairie thunderstorm.

*

Stark County News, November 9, 1860

Victory!!
GLORIOUS TRIUMPH
OF

Republicanism & Freedom!
Honest Old Abe elected!!!
One hundred and sixty-five Electoral votes sure for Lincoln and
probably more when the returns
are complete

Let the world rejoice and be exceeding glad, for unto us
Is given an honest man for President!!

Up to this time we have only returns from the Northern States,
yet sufficient to show that the gallant Lincoln has the whole
electoral vote of those States, and enough to secure his election.
The Southern States, as near as we can judge from the meager
returns received from that quarter, will be nearly equally divided
between Bell and Breckinridge. We have not heard where Douglas'
States are.

Elsewhere in this paper, we give the official vote of Stark
County, and it will be seen that the Republicans have achieved a
glorious triumph. All honor to the true Republicans of Stark. They
have fought a good fight—they have contested every inch of
ground with a steady, but manly opposition. They have worked
early and late. They have worked earnestly and faithfully. We have
never been engaged in a canvass conducted with more spirit than
the Republicans of Stark County have displayed in this.

*

Jothan proposed to Marie on January 1, 1861. She immediately
accepted, then asked what had taken him so long. Planning began
for a wedding in late spring. The Parkers would host the ceremony
in their beautiful garden. In May, the rambler roses, trumpet vines,
columbine, and coneflower would all be bursting with life and
color. Though anxious to be a married man, Jothan didn't mind
waiting. The months would give him time to continue his studies
with Mr. Parker and prepare for the bar exam.

Everyone in my family was pleased, but no one so much as
Mama. She began spending evenings with Mrs. Parker to discuss

the arrangements. There was the music to think of, the food to organize, and of course Marie's wedding dress! I had never heard so much fuss over one garment. I began going to the barn or on walks before Mama returned, so as to avoid hearing about their plans. I was as glad as the next person Jothan and Marie were getting married, but there were other things in the world to discuss.

"You just don't like doing all the cooking while Ma's busy," Gardiner said one day as we cleaned out the barn.

"That's not true. Mostly I just miss her is all. She spends so much time with Mrs. Parker now."

"She'll settle down after a bit. Besides there can't be that much to do."

"That's what I thought!" After finishing our chores, my brother and I wrestled in some fresh hay. I won two of our three matches, though I suspected he gave me one of those victories.

As the winter cold continued, the talk of war heated up. The stove at Trickle's was crowded every time I went there, with men, and some women too, voicing their opinions. However, one particularly stormy day at the end of February, I arrived and found the place empty. A howling wind blowing the snow sideways had encouraged people to stay home. This was a wise move, I thought, as I stood half frozen at the door.

"Jennie Edwards!" shouted Washington Trickle, coming in from the back and carrying a load of wood. "You must be froze solid!"

"I am a bit, Mr. Trickle. Also, Ruby was a little wet so I put her in the storeroom. Hope you don't mind."

"I don't mind," he said, looking toward the door, "but she better not get into my sugar cubes again."

"No, sir, she won't," I said, confidently, then added, "I don't think."

Washington laughed then built up the fire in the stove, took off his hat and jacket, and sat down. "I can't believe you didn't get swallowed up in the snowstorm."

"I'd never get lost around here, Mr. Trickle, even in a

snowstorm. And even if *I* did, Ruby wouldn't. She's the smartest mule ever."

"Can't argue with you there." He sipped his coffee. "Hey, you wanna see something?"

Washington led me over to a corner of the room where a box sat covered by a piece of cloth. Pulling back the cloth revealed a large, brown tabby cat nursing four kittens. The thick, little blobs squirmed and suckled while the mama cat looked up and meowed. Washington rubbed the top of her head and she purred loudly.

"Where'd she come from?" I asked.

He shrugged. "Where do cats ever come from? I found her in the storeroom last week, so heavy with kittens she could barely move. I brought her inside and made her this box and she ain't hardly left it. 'Course, Fancy ain't too pleased, but then she don't come into the store much."

"What'll you do with all the kittens?"

"Give 'em away, I s'pose, keep some. We've been having a bit of a mouse problem." Washington replaced the cloth and we returned to the fire.

"I hope I got this much material," he said, after I'd handed him my list from Mama. "Julia must be making everyone's wedding clothes."

"Yes, sir, she's pretty excited. It's kind of all she talks about these days. I guess that's fine though; I'm happy too."

"When they getting married?"

"June first."

"Huh." Washington finished his coffee and reached for the pot. "I hope this business don't turn bad before then."

"What business?"

"The war business, of course. The *Chicago Tribune* just reported there are seven states gone now; Texas went last week. I don't know what'll happen when Lincoln is inaugurated in a few days. Southerners are a bunch of hotheads, but then any man can act foolish given enough encouragement."

"You think there'll be a war, Mr. Trickle?"

He thought. "Yeah, I expect I do. If not now, then soon. Slavery's a dying institution, but it ain't going to die quietly." Outside, the snow blew in a million different directions. The wind whistled down the stovepipe, sending small puffs of smoke into the room. Washington sipped his coffee, lost in thought. Finally, he looked up. "How old are you now, Jennie?"

"Seventeen."

He nodded. "You're probably too young then to remember what happened in Quincy some years back."

I didn't know a thing. "What happened?"

"Well, it had to do with a runaway slave."

Washington then told me about a man who had been captured and thrown in jail to await the arrival of his owner, who was coming up from St. Louis, a day's travel away. Word spread quickly through the underground about the Negro man's plight. That evening, three Quincy ladies arrived at the jailhouse with supper for the prisoner. The jailer let them in. After no more than an hour, the man had eaten, been blessed by the good ladies, and left alone to his fate. The next afternoon, the sheriff arrived with the slave's owner. Both men, however, found the Negro gone.

"Gone?"

"Gone!" Washington boomed. "Gone like my money when Mrs. Trickle goes to Kewanee! The only person in the cell was one a them old ladies who'd come the night before. She was dressed in the slave's clothes and sitting on the bed, happy as you please."

"But—"

"Don't ya see, Jen? Them gals had traded him out! They were all part of the underground and they'd planned the break the whole time. One of 'em had distracted the jailer, who never even noticed another one of 'em changing clothes." He chuckled. "Those gals had a lot of sand in 'em. People talked about the great escape for weeks."

"It must have been like a magic trick," I said, thinking how surprised the jailer must have been.

"Yep, just like a magic trick. Thing is, Jen, helping a runaway slave is serious business, even in a free state like Illinois. Slaves are considered property, not people, and stealing a person's property, well, that's a hangable offense."

"Did the ladies hang?"

"Nope. The jailer never said who they were. Too ashamed, I'm sure. I guess the reason I'm telling you all this is that people hate slavery and they don't care a damn about laws or punishment or anything else when it comes to helping even one slave. The laws are wrong and they'll do anything to make things right. Look at that Brown character. That's why there'll be a war."

After Washington left to help a customer who had made it through the snow, I thought about his story. There weren't any Negroes in Toulon, and though freemen passed through now and again, they didn't stay. Apart from Carmen, I had seen only one other dark-skinned person in my life. She was a person just like me, spending an afternoon at a theatre many years before.

Susan Richardson had been living in Galesburg, a city much bigger than Toulon, for more than a decade when my family went there one Saturday. Papa had wanted to purchase a cider press and Mama needed a new spinning wheel, but to make the day more fun for my brothers and me, we also went to a show. "Exhibition of Dissolving Views by aid of Magic Lantern, for Lovers of Science and Art," was playing at Dunn's Hall. The big room on the second floor of the bank building was packed with people by the time we arrived. My family and I found four seats in the back, with me sitting on Papa's lap. While waiting, I noticed a black woman sitting down below us in the front row. She was sandwiched between two large white women, and all three talked and laughed and acted as normal as any three women talking and laughing might. After the show began and we watched the moving picture shows provided by the magic lanterns, I forgot all about the black woman. On the ride home, however, Papa told us about her.

"Susan ran away with her three children and ended up in the Knoxville jail," he said. "A group of abolitionists bailed her out before her owner arrived and she went to work in town doing washing. One of her sons got a job on a nearby farm. Of course, the owner did eventually come around. Susan escaped again by disguising herself."

"How'd she do that, Pa?" Jothan asked.

"The woman she worked for gave her some different clothes and a veil and no one ever noticed."

"But what about her black skin? How could people not notice that?"

"Hats, gloves, the veil," said our mother. "People don't always see something if they're not looking for it. Or, maybe they did but didn't like to say anything."

"So she wouldn't be sent back into slavery?" said Gardiner.

"That's right."

"She's not disguised now though," my youngest brother added.

"No," said Papa. "Susan was given her freedom some time ago. She's been working and living in Galesburg ever since."

More people began arriving at Trickle's. The wind had stopped howling and the snow fell more quietly. Mrs. Trickle came in from the back to help her husband and waved at me. I should have been getting on home, but was now caught up in thoughts of Susan Richardson. What had her life been like before? What had it been like to be someone else's property, like any old cow or horse? What had it been like to be punished for simply having a black skin, while never being allowed to do what you wanted to do? And even if you could leave all that behind, as Susan Richardson had, would it truly be possible to live your life freely and the way you wanted to, especially if you were a woman? Of course, there had been women who had lived lives different from most: the writer Jane Austen never got married and lived a life devoted to what she loved; Susan Anthony also devoted all her time to the issue of suffrage; and in our very own town, there was Miss Fowler the schoolteacher, a very pretty woman, but one who was too smart for any man and seemed very happy to be alone and doing what she wanted. Yet, all of these women were white. The challenges would be many times greater for a Negro woman, though Carmen had obviously managed them somehow.

My mind spun with so many thoughts, but in the end, I couldn't really imagine any of it. Supposing a slave's life would be the same for me as imagining I was an Indian, or a man, or maybe even a mule, all silly notions for I would never be any of those things. The land Susan Richardson came from and the life she left behind were all very far away from Jug Run Creek. They were all very far away from the Illinois prairie and my own quiet life.

SIX

A MONTH and a half later, the first guns in the oft-predicted war between the states were fired. Fort Sumter, an island outpost in the bay at Charleston, South Carolina, had been the subject of controversy for weeks. The state wanted it occupied by forces under the new Southern Confederacy, a request that Washington City refused. In early April, President Lincoln informed the governor of an impending re-supply effort. Additional men, arms, and ammunition would not be included in the delivery as long as the ships were allowed to proceed without incident. The Southerners, in turn, refused this request. During the early morning of April 12th, Confederate guns opened fire on the fort. Through the hail of shells, the supply ships could not make their delivery, the small garrison occupying the structure could not respond in kind to the attack, and thirty-three hours after it had begun, the American flag above Fort Sumter came down.

President Lincoln immediately issued a proclamation calling 75,000 militiamen into service to put down the insurrection. The day after the announcement in the *Stark County News*, men gathered at the courthouse to sign up. Some were too young or too old, but most who wanted to join did so, including my brothers and Adam. Jothan and Gardiner returned to Jug Run Creek that evening with signed enlistment papers and huge grins. They said crowds of people had come from all over the county, and the Trickles had set up tables with pickles, crackers, peaches, and lemonade. Gardiner said it reminded him of the county fair.

"Except that you were there to sign up for a war," Mama said sternly as she set the table.

"It's not a war, Mama," he replied.

"Oh, is that so? What would you call men firing guns at each other then?"

"The enlistment is only for three months. The recruiter said that thousands had already signed up, way more people than even live in the South."

"It's true, Mama," Jothan agreed. "The man said it would probably be all over by July Fourth. We might not even see any real fighting."

Mama stared at my oldest brother. "And you! What does Marie have to say about all this? What, young man, *about the wedding?*"

Jothan began talking about Marie being proud of him and I went into the kitchen to get our supper of biscuits and stewed oysters. After the blessing, no one spoke until Jothan touched our mother's hand.

"Don't worry, Ma," he said. "Everything will be fine. We have to do this. What would people think if Gardiner and I didn't go? They'd think we didn't care, or that we were afraid. That would be the worst."

"Believe me," Mama snapped, "that would *not* be the worst."

"He's right, Julia," Papa said, quietly. "They have to go, but it's also true that this probably won't last long."

"You don't believe that, Graham!"

Our father shrugged. "Old Abe wouldn't have made the call for just three months if he thought it would be a greater affair. I think we shouldn't borrow worry."

Mama sighed. "I agree it's important, but there are plenty of others who can go instead. You're both too young!" She stabbed at her oysters.

After supper, Mama and I carried the dishes into the kitchen.

She asked about Ruby, who had a cut on her leg, and I said she was improved enough to go into town the following day.

"Why do you need to go into town?"

"I'm signing up too, Mama. Jothan and Gardiner can't go without me."

The color drained from my mother's face. "You are doing nothing of the kind, Eliza Jane."

"Mama—"

"I will lock you in this house, young lady, before I'll allow such a ridiculous thing!" She untied her apron and threw it on the table.

"That's not fair, Mama," I shouted, following her into the other room. "I can shoot and ride just as well as the boys!"

"I don't care if it's the least fair thing in the world, Eliza Jane, you are still not going anywhere. It's foolish enough what the men are doing; women at least are smarter than that."

"What's going on?" asked Papa.

"I'm going to sign up for the war," I said.

"*What?*"

"I'm signing up to go with Jothan and Gardiner," I repeated. My brothers looked as puzzled as my father. "Well, why shouldn't I?"

Papa stared at me. "Well, for one thing, you're a young lady and young ladies don't do such things."

"Maybe those that can't shoot and ride don't, but I can do everything the boys can do. I'd make just as good a soldier as them. Maybe even better."

"Now wait a minute—" said Jothan.

"I don't care if you're good enough to be a general!" said my mother. "There will be no more discussion about this." Mama looked at my father. "This is all your fault, Graham. You let her wear trousers and blouses and run around the bottoms like a wild creature. Of course, this would be the result."

"Don't worry, my dear, Jennie's fine. She's not going anywhere."

"Stop talking about me as if I'm not here!" I shouted. "I *am* going. Just see if I don't!"

I stomped out of the house. Sam came wiggling up to me outside and together we went to see Ruby, who had been confined to the paddock because of her leg. My mule and dog sniffed noses, then Ruby nuzzled me.

"You two are my only real friends," I said. "Of course, I don't want to leave you, but I care just as much as the boys. It's just not fair!"

Sam yipped in agreement and Ruby bobbed her head. I opened the gate and we walked down to the creek and sat down on a flat rock. I *could* go, I thought, and they couldn't stop me. I could disguise myself like Susan Richardson had done and no one would recognize me. What had Mama said? People didn't always see something if they weren't looking for it. In this case, people wouldn't be expecting a girl to join for the war. I'd wear some of Jothan's clothes and cut my hair and no one would ever know. How hard could it be?

"Hey, Jen."

I started. "Geez, Jothan, what're you doing sneaking up on me like that?"

He smiled. "I wasn't sneaking. You just weren't paying attention."

"Leave me alone."

"Are you all right?"

"I'm fine. Now leave me alone."

"*Jennie.*"

"It's not fair, Jothan. You know, I can do everything you and Gardiner can do. I should go too."

He sat on the ground next to me. "Why though? Other girls aren't wanting to go."

"I'm not like other girls. Why do *you* want to go?"

My brother looked toward the creek. Then he searched in the sand for a few, small flat rocks to skip across the water. "I guess 'cause it's the right thing to do."

"Well, I think it's the right thing too."

"I know you do. Look, Jen, I'll tell you something if you promise not to tell Mama. Truth is, I think you should come. Both me and Gardiner do. We'd like to have you with us. But there are also reasons I don't think that's a good idea and they don't have nothing to do with thinking you can't do it." He took a deep breath. "Thing is, Jen, I'd very much appreciate it if you would look after Marie while I'm gone. Just keep her company and make sure she doesn't feel too lonely. You both like each other." When I didn't say anything, he added, "You do like Marie, don't you?"

I sighed. "Of course, I like her, Jothan. She's great and you know how glad I am you're getting married." He beamed. "But she doesn't need me to look after her."

"I think she does. Marie frets and it would be a lot nicer for her if she had you around, to do things with, go places."

"Marie has lots of friends though."

"Not so many as you'd think. She's kind of shy truly. Jen, I'm not just saying this. I really would appreciate it if you took care of her while I'm gone. You'd be doing me a big favor."

I doubted the frailty of Marie as Jothan portrayed it, but I could hardly say no to my big brother. Especially since I did have doubts about how to do the other. Also, the boys would also only be gone three months. They'd be back before we knew it.

*

On April 25, 1861, my brothers and Adam, along with several others from town, were sworn in as privates with the 7th Illinois Infantry, Company B. From Springfield, they took the cars to a little town called Alton on the Mississippi River. There the men learned the manual of arms and bugle calls. They practiced moving as a company and as a regiment, doing wheels and skirmish formations and loading and firing their muskets. They did all these things, known generally as "drill," until they were exhausted. Then the next day they did them all over again.

In early June, the regiment traveled down the Mississippi River to the very tip of Illinois and a village called Cairo. Two weeks later they moved by foot up the Ohio River to another town called

Mound City. The days passed quietly, with nothing but drill and writing letters home to pass the time. Then toward the end of the month, Confederate soldiers were spotted on the Kentucky shore. A squad from Company B crossed the river and the Federal soldiers fanned out, weapons at the ready. They scoured the shore and uplands for the traitors. However, the "hostile forces" turned out to be only peaceable farmers with their unarmed herds of cattle. Adam wrote me that though the incident had been unremarkable, it had also made him feel like a real soldier.

I still didn't feel very good about my decision to stay, but my mother seemed immensely relieved that I no longer talked about going for the war. Plus, there was the promise I'd made to Jothan. Marie did seem glad for my company and it happened that we always had a lot to talk about. We'd drink tea, she might play the piano (she'd become very good over the years), or I might do some conjures. We met at Trickle's sometimes as well to have coffee, or attended readings together at the Toulon Literary Society.

One afternoon, I went to Marie's house with a bunch of bird's-foot violets. The delicate purple flowers bloomed early on the prairie and were easy to find when the grasses were still low. Marie set them in a vase on her piano and stepped back, smiling. Then she kissed me on the cheek.

"I was only doing what Jothan would do," I said, coloring.

Marie laughed. "I love your brother, Jennie, but I doubt he'd think of flowers. You're very sweet."

It was still early and cool, so we left her house and walked to Indian Creek. Marie and I discussed the boys' letters and agreed that all the marching and sitting around camp sounded pretty dull. Except for the false alarm with the cows in Kentucky, they had not even left Illinois. This was fine with Marie; she just wanted them all home safely. It was also fine with me, as I didn't want my brothers and Adam having too much fun without me.

The violets, as well as lupines and phlox, blanketed the ground near the water's edge. Only a few short weeks before there had been nothing here but the sharp, dried forms of fallen leaves. Now the earth breathed and exhales the swaying forms of the prairie's many early blue flowers. Warm breezes released the plants' earthy perfumes.

After we'd sat awhile, I asked Marie why she loved Jothan.

"Really, Jennie, what a question!" She finished making a braid of phlox stems and placed it on my leg then thought. "He's kind, funny, handsome. I don't know, why does anyone ever love someone? It's not always so easy to explain." She shrugged. "You must feel the same about Adam."

"Oh, I don't love Adam. I mean, he's my best friend, but that's different."

"Is it? I guess I just thought there was more between you two."

"He's a good boy, Adam," I agreed. "We have fun together. Who knows? Maybe after the war."

She nodded. "Yes, after the war."

*

In early July, I escorted Marie to the Independence Day celebration. Toulon had filled with people and even though we arrived before ten a.m., the square could barely be navigated for the crush of bodies. The tightrope walker from a few years back had returned. So had the man with the magic lantern from Galesburg we'd seen so long ago. There were jugglers and a mime and two clowns doing somersaults. Marie and I left our parents and went to see the magic lantern show before the picnic dinner commenced. As we sat inside the Waxwing Theatre waiting for the lights to dim, Marie leaned over and whispered, "You look very pretty today, Jennie."

I smiled. She had loaned me a dress for the celebration, a light indigo and peach-colored calico that she said brought out my blue eyes. My initial reluctance (there was nothing wrong with any of my own dresses) vanished after trying on the dress and feeling its softness slip over my skin like warm water.

I kissed Marie on the cheek. "All because of you."

"Thank you for being here with me, Jennie. It helps, you know, with Jothan being gone."

"I wouldn't want to be anywhere else."

In a few short weeks, Marie Parker had become my good friend. Though our time together was simple pleasure, the deeper bond helped us both when the letter arrived five days after the Fourth of July celebration and I had to tell Marie that Jothan, Gardiner, and Adam wouldn't be coming home just yet. They had reenlisted, this time for three years.

*

Before the longer term began, the boys were granted a short furlough. They all returned home and the wedding was on again. Mama looked like her old self as she and Mrs. Parker resumed their preparations. It was fortunate that they had already done so much. They needed only to get the invitations out, revisit the band and make sure they could come on short notice, and get the food organized. They also planned a short trip to Galesburg for the honeymoon. All went perfectly and even the weather cooperated. The wedding day in July arrived with sunshine and warmth but none of the white heat that usually accompanied the Illinois summer.

Jothan looked like a storybook prince in his new suit and Marie was the most beautiful girl in the world in a pale yellow, silk taffeta gown with orange blossoms braided into her hair. The dancing and singing lasted all day in the Parker's cool garden, after which the wedding party left for Galesburg. For the next two days, Gardiner and I were alone at Jug Run Creek. We did chores but also found plenty of time to swim, play townball, a new game now very popular, and take walks. Gardiner sketched hawks and butterflies and the skull of a fox he found; I showed him all my new magic tricks. In the evenings, we stayed up late with me asking him many questions about the war. Had he seen any Rebels yet? What were the officers like? Were the other boys nice? He told me so many stories I thought my ears would burst. He also let me try on his frock coat, which I wore happily despite the warmth.

Gardiner's stories about "doing his part" convinced me I'd certainly made the wrong choice. Being a soldier seemed like the best thing ever.

*

By autumn, the boys had traveled across the Ohio River from Cairo to Fort Holt, Kentucky. I followed their movements by studying a map I'd ordered, "Hazard's Official Railroad and Military Map of the Southern States." As the days turned colder and shorter, the regiment undertook to build houses for the winter. They cut down red cedar and green ash trees and made log walls for the tents. They chinked these walls with mud and installed their canvass shelters on top like little caps. After scouring the countryside for stones, they constructed chimneys. This work took many weeks and it wasn't until the middle of December that the companies moved into their new homes. After the houses were complete, the routine resumed. Gardiner wrote:

We drill and march most hours of the day, a necessary, but tedious, task. There have been moments when we thought our time had come to join the fight but they were only false alarms. Sometimes we have marched into a situation, only to find the 7th must remain behind and only listen to the sounds of battle. This is what occurred at the recent engagement at Belmont, Missouri. Perhaps Grant would not have been repulsed had the 7th been there!

Gardiner said that he never felt really bored because he filled the time not spent drilling with drawing and describing the landscape and the birds and other animals he saw. He enclosed in one letter a sketch of a duck known as a "baldpate." "They are all over down here," he wrote, "whistling and tipping upside down in the shallow lakes and ponds."

The duck had a dark stripe around its eye and dark tail feathers. Gardiner had also drawn the pond and its vegetation, including the strangest looking trees I'd ever seen. They grew in the water, he wrote, and had fat bases resembling onions. The roots did not go into the earth but rather rose up in the air, resembling very much a collection of wooden dolls. He had written alongside one, *A Bald Cypress Tree.*

For my part, I wrote every day to my brothers or Adam. I told them about the autumn harvest, patching the barn, and repairing fences. I described our lambs growing big over the summer and our rooster vanishing for a time, then reappearing five days later with several feathers missing. All the horses, plus Ruby and Sam, were fine, and so were Mama and Papa. Another book on magic had arrived from Owl, *The Magician's Own Book, or The Whole Art of Conjuring*, so I kept busy learning new conjures. The boys didn't have to worry about things at home, but that didn't mean we wouldn't like them to return as soon as possible.

Events in Toulon didn't seem particular exciting, but I wrote about them anyway. A young deer with a limp had wandered into town and started living behind Trickle's General Store. Mrs. McRae was seen less often with her funny goats causing some to suspect illness in the animals. Traveling shows continued to arrive at the Waxwing.

As the snow piled up, I saw less of Marie and spent a good part of each day in my room. I reread all the stories of Natty Bumpo and the wild country to the north, then finished *Uncle Tom's Cabin* and thought more about Susan Richardson from Galesburg. At Trickle's, I bought another book by Harriet Beecher Stowe called, *Dred, A Tale of the Great Dismal Swamp*. This story so discouraged me from every wanting to go to the South that I now felt less envious of my brothers. Another package also arrived from Owl. This time he sent a new booklet just published by a French magician named Jean Robert-Houdin. He said he was busy with many shows these days.

The city fairly bursts with the drumbeat of war and the presence of soldiers. Owing to this influx, Carmen and I have been offered a run of ten shows at McVicker's Theatre. I have been creating new conjures and I confess that the busy-ness pleases me muchly. Julia has been slowing down some, so we now have a new dove as part of the show, and Constance has taken readily to the stage.

Owl then suggested I might come for a visit sometime. He

wrote,

The distraction would do you good, Jennie. It is not an easy time for anyone with family members off to a war. You are, of course, most welcome here anytime.

Owl's letters always included descriptions of the fast-growing city and the many things to be seen and done there. In the ten years he'd been living in Chicago, it had grown from a town of 30,000 residents to over 100,000. Where only one railroad operated in 1850, by 1856, there were ten. Lodgings known as "luxury" hotels dotted the streets between the Chicago River and Lake Michigan and provided such amenities as French food, gas lights, and steam cars. It all seemed like a wonderland to me, more mythical than real, and a place I would very much like to see.

As it happened, after the holidays Marie told me that her father needed to go to Chicago for a case he was working on. She planned to accompany him and wondered if I'd like to go too. I said I would love to, but that I couldn't leave Mama. After the wedding and the boys' departure a second time, my mother had grown quiet again. It seemed to help that I was there; in the evenings we played cards and sewed and sometimes Mama would forget her worries and laugh and tease like she used to. Marie said she understood this of course.

A few days later, however, after telling my father about both Owl's and Marie's invitations, he surprised me.

"You should go, Jen. You might not get such a chance again."

We were cleaning stalls in the barn and Ruby had walked over to bother me for a carrot. I pushed her away but she wouldn't be dissuaded. "But what about Mama?" I asked as Ruby grabbed my braid.

"What about her?"

"She seems so sad with the boys gone."

Papa stopped raking. "Yes, that's true." He shook his head. "She's worried, Jen, that's all. Until your brothers are home safe, it will be that way. Meantime, you have to live your life too. I think you should go."

"I don't know."

After finishing, we left the barn and walked down toward the creek. The sky was clear, the first time in many days, and the night cold and my ears tingled beneath my hat. A rising moon lit the way, the snow crunching as we walked. At Jug Run Creek, frozen and silent, I looped my arm through Papa's and leaned in close to him.

"Are you worried too, Papa?" I asked.

He put his arm around me. "I want to tell you something, Jen, but you must promise me that you won't tell your mother I told you."

"Of course, Papa."

He took a deep breath. "Many years ago, before Jothan was born, we had another baby, a boy also and his name was Martin. He died, Jen, just after his third birthday, and we buried him in the Toulon Cemetery. Your mother was heartbroken. So was I for that matter. But it took her months to recover, and release from the pain didn't really happen until two years later when Jothan was born." He took a deep breath. "So you see, having lost one child, she is rightfully worried, and always has been worried, about losing another. I worry too, but it's different for Julia."

"Another baby?" I said, confused. "What happened?"

"There was an accident." I waited for more, but Papa didn't explain further. "Afterward, we tried to keep the little boy alive in our hearts, but after your brothers and then you were born, we didn't anymore. This seemed easier on both of us and, well, it didn't seem important for you to know. I'm not so sure that was right, but it's what we did. I hope you understand, Jennie. I'm only telling you so that you'll understand your mother's fears." He rubbed his beard. "It's hard being a parent. Even in the best of times, there is so much danger for a child. And now there is a war. I pray each night for the best."

I looked up at the sky. My thoughts were spinning. "What happened?" I asked again. "You said there was an accident."

"It doesn't matter, Jen," he said, his voice quavering. "It was an accident, a moment's inattention, a piece of bad luck, and just like all accidents that result in the most horrible of regrets." He turned toward me. "Please don't tell your mother I told you. And take Owl and Marie up on their offers. You going to Chicago may be good for your mother. When you come home, she will see that it's possible children can go away and that they can come back."

We walked back to the house. That night, the wind returned and howled outside like a demon unleashed. It seemed to me as if the blowing had something to do with the revelation of the family secret surrounding the baby Martin. After a sleepless night and strange dreams, I mentioned the next morning going to Chicago. Papa's face looked patchy as if he hadn't slept either, but Mama seemed fine, even chatty. And my father was right; at first my mother looked startled by my news, but then agreed it was a fine idea. Later that day, I rode Ruby into town and told Marie I'd be glad to accompany her to the big city.

SEVEN

ONE WEEK LATER, Marie and I stepped off the cars at the Illinois Central Railroad Station on the shores of Lake Michigan. In front of us rolled the Chicago River; to the east and south, a sea that stretched to the horizon.

"It's the ocean!" I cried.

Marie laughed. "No, it's not, silly! It's just the lake."

"Well, it looks like the ocean." The train's last half-mile had taken us out over the water on trestles built away from the land. When we stepped off the car, I was sure we'd fall in.

"Yes," she said, linking her arm through mine, "I expect it does."

Mr. Parker had gone ahead to collect our bags and hire a carriage. We would lodge the next three nights at the Sherman House, one of the luxury hotels Owl had written about and a place Marie's father knew well. After leaving the railway station, our carriage turned east on Lake Street and a forest of buildings closed in around us. Four stories, five, six, no structure seemed shorter than three, and they were filled with all manner of businesses, including banks, bakeries, millineries, sewing machine rooms, and printeries. Some buildings rested on long lengths of wood several feet above the ground. Mr. Parker, a soft-spoken man with red hair and a beard and inquisitive, blue eyes, explained that for the past several years the city had been lifting all the structures in order to install a sewer system. At present, the waste from businesses and homes went straight into the river and then the lake. Chicago's drinking water also came from Lake Michigan, so the result had been several disease outbreaks. A cholera epidemic in 1854 killing more than 3,000 people had propelled the city to take action.

"Two years ago," Mr. Parker continued, "the city raised an entire block off the ground. In only five days, they lifted the structures over four feet. When they finished, they let people walk beneath the buildings. It was amazing, truly!"

We left Lake Street and turned south onto Clark. Despite the January cold, people hurried along Chicago's thoroughfares, clustering in small knots at shop windows or at the base of stairs that led to the now raised buildings. The men wore stovepipe hats, high collars, and heavy, woolen frock coats; the women had winter coats as well and large bonnets. As the carriage slowed to ease around a wagon stuck in the mud, Mr. Parker asked his daughter her plans.

"We will visit Mrs. Allenton of course, then maybe do some shopping. Jennie also wants to see her friend the magician, and I would like to attend his show as well."

Her father nodded. "I have already asked Mr. Timmons to come to the Sherman House in the morning. He will see to you during our visit."

"Thank you, Father."

"Who's Mr. Timmons?" I asked.

"He's a man I hire sometimes," Mr. Parker replied, "to help me with research. He'll escort you two around the city."

"Do we need an escort?" Marie and her father smiled.

"This isn't Toulon, Jennie," said Mr. Parker.

The Sherman House stretched into the sky for six stories and covered most of a city block. Four big, rounded pillars guarded the entrance and reached above to the second floor where a balcony full of ladies watched the goings-on below. Businesses filled the bottom floor, including the establishment of Mr. Brewster, Hatter, and the bankers of Alexander & Co.

"The Sherman House has only just been finished," Marie said. She looked amused as I stared up at the building, gaping like a landed fish. "Come on, Jennie! We're here at last!"

Inside we ascended a smooth, marbled staircase that delivered us to the main lobby. Several corridors connected this reception area to the ladies' rooms: the ordinary, a reading hall, and a public parlor. On the far end, two wide, oak stairways led to the floors above. Many young, Negro men hurried every which way, carrying trays or baggage or stacks of towels and linens.

"They're the staff," Marie whispered. "Mr. Sherman hired them when he opened the hotel last year."

"But are they freemen? They can't be runaways, can they?"

"I don't know, honestly. Father says their hiring has caused no small amount of controversy. Some people in Chicago believe them to be stealing jobs from the whites, or at least lowering the wages of the work. They obviously earn less than a white boy would doing the same job."

"What does your father think?"

Marie shrugged. "He says they are hard workers. He also believes it proper they have real jobs. The abolition of slavery without subsequent work and opportunity would be like removing a man from a burning house only to put him into another with flames licking at the foundation. There must be places for Negroes in society that are not simply the trod earth beneath the boots of white men."

One of these young men stood at the iron mesh door of the steam car that was to take us up to our room on the fifth floor.

"Hey, Mista Parker," he said to Marie's father. "How you been, sir?"

"Very well, Daniel," Caleb Parker replied, extending his hand. "And yourself?"

"I be doing fine as well, sir."

Daniel had smooth skin, a strong, square jawline, and large eyes that acknowledged Marie and me but seemed careful not to stare.

He opened the iron door, and then a second door inside the first. After we were all inside, I asked him why there were two doors. He looked surprised.

"Don't rightly know, miss. I 'spect the men felt they needed both."

Daniel slid a lever up and with a jolt and a low hum we began moving. My stomach lurched a little, though the sensation of rising wasn't unpleasant. The car climbed slowly. Large numbers appeared on the wall behind the iron mesh doors: 2, 3, 4. When we reached 5, Daniel pulled the lever down.

"Here you be, Mista Parker."

"Thank you, Daniel."

The room Marie and I were to share had a large sitting area with several lamps, chairs with plump, red cushions, and a writing desk. Beyond, a bedroom was connected by a short hallway. As I took in the tall, heavy drapes around the window and the wallpaper and paintings, I barely heard Marie's father leave and say that he'd collect us later for supper. Being in such a grand room made me feel like another person. Soon, the biggest surprise of all presented itself: water coming out of the small sink in the bedroom. Marie showed me the knob that made the magic happen through pipes that extended all the way from the ground. After I played with the knob several times turning the water on and off, I told Marie I guessed we'd never have to leave our room. With running water and meals that could be delivered there'd be no need.

She laughed. "We are certainly not staying here the whole time! If you think this is amazing, just wait until I show you the city!"

Below us on Randolph Street, the horse cars moved on tracks next to the public square and courthouse. Evergreen trees grew around the building and one still wore the red paper chains and tinsel from the holiday celebration. I raised the sash on the window. A blast of cold air hit me, as well as a terrific smell. The odor was heavy and earthy and rotten and very similar to the air around the swamps back home.

Marie squealed. "Oh, Jennie, do close the window!"

"What's that smell?"

"The river, of course. Even in the winter, the smell can be frightful. Come here and let's unpack." When I continued looking out, she added, "Then I will tell you a secret."

I closed the window and carried my small trunk into the bedroom. Mama had loaned me her finest dress, which I hung next to Marie's many elegant ones.

"I brought plenty for both of us," she said.

"I can't always wear your clothes, Marie."

"Of course, you can. It's ridiculous I have so many." She turned around. "Help me with this so I can put on something fresh."

I began undoing the buttons on her dress. "What's your secret?"

Marie didn't answer. When she was out of her clothes, she turned around and I immediately saw the raised mound beneath her chemise.

"What—?"

"This is my secret, Jennie. Oh, you're so surprised, I love that! You look so much like your brother! And now I hope the baby looks like both of you. Here, feel it!" Marie placed my hand over the light material. Her body felt warm as she moved my hand over her stomach. When the baby suddenly moved, I jumped.

"It's okay!" she said, smiling. "He does that sometimes."

"He?"

"Oh, I'm sure the baby's a boy, though—" she paused. "Jothan hopes for a girl."

"Jothan knows?"

"Of course, he knows! I wrote him immediately after I knew for sure, but asked him not to tell anyone. I know I should have told you sooner, Jen. It's just, well, I wanted to make sure nothing happened. This being my first time and all."

Marie's cheeks had turned rosy and her eyes fairly danced. I put my hand back on her stomach and tried to imagine the little being inside. A little Marie or a little Jothan. *I have a secret too*, I thought. Mama also must have felt happy like this when she carried the little baby Martin so long ago. Then he'd been taken away. Babies dying never surprised anyone but as I felt Marie's kick, I prayed that something so awful wouldn't happen again.

"Jennie?" Marie's expression had grown uncertain. "You are glad, aren't you? I do so want you to be glad and you simply must be. We've already decided that if the baby *is* a girl, then we'll name her Eliza Jane, after you, and we couldn't possibly do that if you're not glad."

"After—?"

A sudden raucous outside diverted my attention. A great squawking of crows and pigeons and gulls had erupted, the shrieks readily coming into our room. If these birds were like those back home, one of them had just found some food and now all wanted to share in the bounty. After the noise died down, I turned back to Marie and pulled her into my arms.

"Of course, I'm glad," I said. "More glad than anything. It's just that, well, I'm surprised is all."

Marie hugged me back. "I know, Jen. I'm sorry I didn't share this sooner."

"I'm very happy, Marie. But—"

"What?"

"I'm not sure you should call her Eliza Jane. Maybe just 'Jennie' would be enough."

Marie laughed. Then she cupped my face in her hands and kissed me. "Jennie it is then."

*

That evening we ate in the Sherman House dining room, enjoying orange glazed chicken, cauliflower with cheese sauce, and roasted golden potatoes. Between the trip from Toulon and Marie's news and seeing the great city at last, I was famished. All the tables in the Sherman House dining hall were full; the waiters kept busy bringing tray after tray crowded with plates and bowls of food of all kinds. Bottles of wine sat on every table including ours. I'd never drunk wine at a restaurant before; for that matter, I'd never eaten in any restaurant apart from the Virginia House in Toulon.

Everything smelled fruity or savory and tasted so good I feared running out of food before running out of hunger. Marie and her father talked about all the changes they'd noticed from their last visit to the city. For my part, I wondered how I could have lived this long without visiting Chicago before now.

After finishing our meal, a waiter appeared and offered the evening's dessert selections. We all chose the same: tree cakes filled with crème. In what seemed like seconds the man had returned with three small plates forested by the confectionary pines. With the first bite, I thought my mouth might melt. I closed my eyes.

"Jennie?" Marie touched my arm. "Are you unwell?"

I opened my mouth to declare I was anything but unwell, then closed it quickly and swallowed. "I am far from unwell," I said. "In fact, I believe I'm in heaven." Marie and Mr. Parker laughed.

"You're the perfect traveling companion, Jennie," her father said, smiling. "We're very glad you came with us."

"Thank you, Mr. Parker. I am glad too."

The last part of the meal involved strong, dark cups of coffee. As we sipped our drinks, I asked Marie's father about the case he was working on.

Mr. Parker waved a hand. "I doubt you'd be very interested, my dear."

Marie nodded. "He's right, Jennie. Father's work is dreadfully dull, coping with the misbehavior of all those bad people. I shouldn't even like to think about it."

"But I'm interested in bad people. Besides, Jothan wants to be a lawyer too. I should know something about the profession."

Mr. Parker took a sip of coffee then leaned back in his chair. "A few weeks ago a prominent businessman was found dead in his home on upper Couch Street, only a few blocks from here. The neighbors heard several shots in the middle of the night and summoned the police. When they arrived, they found the grounds empty and dark. There also seemed to be no one inside the house. They searched every room. When they came to the library, the door was locked from the inside. The police broke a window in the garden to get in and that's when they found the man, shot several times in the back. He'd been murdered of course, but by whom? And where was the culprit? How did he escape?" Mr. Parker shook his head. "The library had only one door. There was only one window, and it was intact until the police broke it. Other secret passageways? None to be found so far. There was no one else in the house on this particular night. The servants, for reasons still unclear, had been dismissed by the man earlier that week, and his wife was in Springfield visiting relatives." He paused, sipping his coffee. "Truly, it seems like an almost impossible crime."

"Perhaps the man killed himself," I offered, "and to avoid the shame made it look like a murder."

"That's been considered. But he would have had to arrange some mechanism for shooting himself in the back, and no such mechanism has been found. Incidentally, there's been no murder weapon found either, not in the library or anywhere else in the house."

"The other possibility," I said, taking a sip of coffee, "is that maybe the murderer was still in the library when the police arrived. Maybe he was hidden and left only after the door had been opened and everyone else had gone."

Mr. Parker nodded. "Except that there was no place large enough for a man to hide. The library isn't very big and it was searched thoroughly."

Marie set her cup down heavily. "Could we please not discuss this anymore? Whatever the answer is, I'm sure you'll figure it out, Father, but honestly, there are other, nicer things to discuss."

"What if the murderer was a woman?" I asked, ignoring Marie. "Or a midget? Someone small enough to hide in an unlikely location. Maybe even a child?"

"Jennie!"

I shrugged. "All right, maybe that's too fantastic. I'm just trying to think about this differently. That's what Owl says you have to do when you're faced with something that seems unbelievable. He says that what looks impossible often turns out to be very simple and, of course, entirely possible. It's just a question of thinking in a different manner from how you're used to thinking." Marie was still staring at me as if I'd suggested *her* child could have been the murderer. Her father however nodded.

"Yes, I agree with you, Jennie," he said. "Yet, I still have no explanations, so I am glad there are others at work on this case, thinking "differently" as you say. My part is only to represent the man's wife who, despite not even being in Chicago during the crime, fears being implicated in her husband's death." He sighed. "Whatever the true circumstances, she is set to inherit an enormous amount of money."

*

The next morning, Mr. Parker's assistant, Oliver Timmons, collected Marie and me in the brougham and we headed north on Clark Street. The snow fell lightly, the clouds had sunk to just above the tallest buildings and we discussed the easiest of all conversation topics: the weather. Mr. Timmons said he couldn't remember a colder, snowier January in Chicago. From his pinched expression, he didn't appear too happy about the fact. He was a tall and long-limbed man with sandy hair and gray eyes. He looked younger than my parents but walked with a cane and a slight limp. As the brougham traveled over the frozen road, Mr. Timmons winced over each bump. I didn't even know him and already felt sorry for him. Marie asked after people they knew in common and he congratulated her on her marriage.

We continued north for many blocks after crossing over the Chicago River, then turned right on Huron Street. The tightness of the downtown's tunnel-like thoroughfares had vanished, and the streets grew wider to let in the sky. Large homes made of brick and stone lined either side of the road. Many places had fairy tale round towers and balconies on the roofs.

"I've always loved coming to visit the Allentons," Marie mused. "Their home is right on the lake and they have a splendid garden, which Mrs. Allenton tends personally."

"How do you know them?"

"When we still lived in Springfield, Father worked on a case for Mr. Allenton. They became friends and after the work was over, they invited us to visit them anytime. Their daughters were older than me but very kind and they became sort of like sisters. After the girls both removed to New York and we went to Toulon, we didn't see each other much, but I've always remained fond of them. For many summers, we took our holiday here and it was such fun! We'd go the theatre or the American music academy. I loved every minute, of course. Then I was always glad to return home to the quiet of the prairie too."

As Lake Michigan came into view, we turned into a winding drive bounded by boxwood shrubs. Inside the palatial home, a servant girl welcomed us into an entryway with a wide, swirling staircase and then to the sitting room to wait for her mistress. The room was easily as large as our entire house at Jug Run Creek. It was filled with chairs and sofas, tables and lamps, and large, dramatic paintings of seascapes and ships. As Marie showed Mr. Timmons and me the view of the garden, the door opened again.

"Marie!"

A big woman, tall as well as fat, shrieked happily and crossed the room with the speed of a rabbit. She wore several necklaces, rings on each finger, and had thick, white hair bundled atop her head like a cloud. After folding my sister-in-law into a hearty embrace, Mrs. Allenton kissed both her cheeks then stared at Marie as if she hadn't seen her in many years. "Oh, my dear, my dear! You have come at last and you are most welcome! It has been too long, simply too long! Please, please! Come sit! Mary will be bringing tea and scones shortly."

After we'd gotten settled, the old woman fanned herself. "I am so grateful you have come, my dear," she told Marie. "It is frightfully boring this time of year. The holiday parties are done, the theatre is dark most nights, and the girls are busy with their lives far away. And with my garden asleep like Persephone, I have little to do besides keep on top of the servants, which really, they hardly need after all these years."

"What about Mr. Allenton?" Marie asked, affecting a wind-blown look.

"Ha! Well, yes, of course, he *is* here." She lowered her voice, "But not here, if you know what I mean. Works all the time and leaves me to my own self mostly. Really, it's hardly like being married at all anymore.

"But listen to me, going on just like an old lady! And look at you! Prettier than ever, and a married woman too. Imagine! The girls and I were so disappointed when we couldn't come to the wedding."

"I was most sorry too, Mrs. Allenton. It was rather hurried owing to Jothan's short furlough."

"Yes, but I was still most sorry." Suddenly, she noticed the other two people with Marie. "But here's your new husband now!" she said, grabbing Mr. Timmons hand and pumping it generously.

"No, no, this isn't Jothan," said Marie, smiling. "He's still gone for the war. This is Mr. Timmons, Father's assistant."

"Oh, of course, how silly of me! The war is hardly over, is it, though it seems like it should be." She stopped shaking Mr. Timmons hand. "How are you, sir? Very good to meet you, of course."

"My pleasure, ma'am," said Mr. Timmons, tipping his head slightly.

"And who is this dear girl?" Mrs. Allenton turned toward me.

"May I present my husband's sister, Jennie Edwards." Marie winked at me. "My sister now as well."

"Delighted, dear girl, delighted!" I also experienced the vigorous handshake as well as kisses on both cheeks. Mrs. Allenton's bright mien, white hair, and exuberance all reminded me of Mrs. Santa Claus.

*

Mrs. Allenton had invited several of her friends over to see Marie and they soon began to arrive, shivering, snow-laden, and chattering like small birds. While our host whisked Marie around the room to see everyone, Mr. Timmons and I sat by the window overlooking the garden. The grounds were as splendid as Marie had indicated, with numerous paths, bushes and trees, and benches and gazebos surrounding the house. The snow had covered the gardens to where everything looked vaguely the same, all pillow-like and soft. After the tea and scones arrived and I'd had some of both, I gazed outside not sure what to say to Mr. Timmons who looked like he'd rather be anywhere else.

"Are you from Chicago?" I finally asked.

He nodded. "Lived here my whole life. Thought about leaving once but then wasn't sure where I would go."

"If I lived here, I don't think I'd ever leave." Mr. Timmons asked me if I'd been to the city before. "No, this is my first visit."

"What do you think so far, Miss Edwards?"

"Oh, it's thrilling! My family will not believe all that I have seen." Mr. Timmons nodded again, then took a handkerchief from his pocket. He wiped his forehead. "Are you unwell, Mr. Timmons?"

He shook his head. "No. Thank you for asking. I had an accident, nothing to do with the war I'm sorry to say, that has made walking and sitting difficult. Most unfortunate as that is mostly what a person does, walk or sit. In any case, there is some pain and it can leave me breathless at times." He colored. "Forgive me, I have said too much."

"No, you haven't. Of course, you should tell me. Otherwise, I will think you are simply pained at my company."

He smiled sadly. "You seem a nice young lady, Miss Edwards. I do not think I could be pained in your company."

"Thank you." I took a sip of tea, then asked, "May I ask how you're able to do work for Marie's father? That must involve a lot of sitting."

"It does, but Mr. Parker lets me keep an odd schedule. I work an hour or two, then take a break. After the break, I work again for a short while. It takes much longer to accomplish the same amount as a normal person, but it's the only way I can do it."

"And your wife doesn't mind? You being gone so much, I

mean?"

"Oh, I'm not married." He looked away. "Probably never will be."

"Why do you say that? Don't you want to be married?"

"I don't know. It would surely be nice but perhaps not fair to the lady. I get around so poorly."

"That's silly. You get around well enough and you seem like a nice man. That's more important than whether or not you can run a race. In fact, I know ladies back home who wished their husbands would stay put more."

Mr. Timmons smiled. "Yes, I do too." He changed the subject. "What about you, Miss Edwards? Do you plan on marrying soon?"

"Oh, no, I don't think so. I want to be a magician."

"A magician! That's an interesting idea."

"We are going to see my friend Owl tomorrow night at McVicker's Theatre. He's a great magician and has been teaching me."

"I have heard of him. The *Tribune* is very admiring of his show."

"Of course, you must come with us. You won't believe your eyes!"

"Thank you. I would like that."

I looked around for Marie and saw her far across the room in the center of a group of ladies. They were all laughing and smiling and I could see some pointing toward her stomach. She must have told them the good news. I turned back to Mr. Timmons.

"Tell me," I said, "why are you sorry you weren't injured in the war instead of what actually happened?"

He shifted slowly in his chair. "It is of no matter, truly."

"My brothers have both gone," I said. "I would have gone too, but my brother Jothan, Marie's husband, made me promise to stay home and take care of her. Though she hardly needs it, I promised I would. I know I'm just a girl, yet I still wished I'd gone."

Mr. Timmons didn't laugh at this and he didn't say I couldn't have gone because I was a girl. Instead, he looked out the window a long moment, his gray eyes growing darker.

"It's a terrible thing, Miss Edwards," he said, at last, "when the most important thing ever to happen is happening without you."

*

The next day, Mr. Timmons took Marie and me on a tour of the city. The snow continued to fall and the cold bore into us through our coats. Still, we carried on, riding the horse car, visiting the shops along Lake Street, and watching big chunks of ice bump around in the Illinois and Michigan canal. We laughed at how ridiculous it was to be out in such weather, especially as we stood on the shore of Lake Michigan and gazed out at the frozen expanse. Mr. Timmons wanted to show us a small structure that had been constructed 600 feet out into the lake. The city can no longer use water taken from the shore due to the river contamination, he explained, so they built pipes out to where the water was more pure. A tunnel of great design under the lake facilitated installing the pipes and it was considered a marvel of engineering.

"Even so," he said, "the intake remains too close. Heavy rains and flooding still send sewage far out into the lake.

Notwithstanding the water problems in Chicago, I deemed it a most wonderful city. As we returned to the Sherman House in the brougham, I thought about how people did big things here. They thought big, they built big, they didn't believe anything to be impossible. Lift a building into the air? Let's do it! Build a tunnel under a lake? We can do that too! Clearly, more than one magician lived in Chicago.

EIGHT

LATER THAT AFTERNOON, Marie teased me about Mr. Timmons. As we got dressed at the Sherman House for Owl's show, she asked pointed questions. What had we talked about at Mrs. Allenton's house? Did I think him handsome? Would I like to see him again? I gave vague answers for truly I had not thought so much about Mr. Timmons. He seemed a nice man, a bit old perhaps, but kindly.

"He is easy to talk to," I added when she kept looking at me.

"Hmm." She returned to brushing her hair.

"What?"

"Nothing."

"Marie!"

"I just think he seemed very taken with you, Jennie. He's always been so quiet and has never offered to take *me* on a tour of the city, but this trip, well, he seems a new man and it can only be because of you. True, he is a bit old, but that's not the worst thing. Just think, if you married him, you could live in Chicago!"

"Marry him! Really, Marie, I don't want to marry him. Whatever would put such an idea in your head?"

"Oh, I'm always thinking of who you might marry." She looked smug.

"Is that so?" I stared at her. "Have you thought of yourself then?"

"What?" Now Marie was puzzled.

"If I married anyone, Marie, it would be you." I crossed my arms. "Unfortunately, you're already married."

"Jennie Edwards, you're a very silly girl!" She winked at me. "But I do love you."

McVicker's Theatre, a three-story building on the horse car line on Madison Street, glowed in the frosty night. Many conveyances had already gathered by the time we arrived, the weather not deterring anyone from a show that the *Chicago Tribune* promised would "astound the masses." In the lobby, Marie and I, along with Mr. Parker and Mr. Timmons, edged our way through the crowd toward an open space. Suddenly, one voice among the many stood out.

"Marie!" shouted Mrs. Allenton, scampering over to us and pushing poorly anchored people out of the way. "And Caleb, darling! How good to see you!" She kissed father and daughter and then began fanning herself. Noticing Mr. Timmons and I, she gave us a hearty hello as well.

"It's good to see you as well, Ruth," said Mr. Parker. "You're looking very well."

"I am now, that's true! Oh, it is such a relief to be back in society! I had no idea, truly. So many people wanting to see conjures! I would have attended such a show before if I had known. And a man called Owl; what a queer name!"

"It's not his real name, Mrs. Allenton," said Marie.

The older woman looked taken aback. "It's not?"

"No, of course not. Is it, Jennie?"

I shrugged. "He says it is."

"Well, I've never heard of such a thing! A man named Owl and not named Owl at the same time!" Mrs. Allenton fanned herself more vigorously, saying she was now close to overheating. Unwinding the thick animal fur coiled about her neck seemed to help. This unfortunate piece of winter wear was quickly given to a large man standing a few feet away. Mr. Allenton had the same white mane as his wife and also wore many rings on his fingers. He seemed to be just as big a talker and upon turning away from the men he had been conversing with happily found more listeners in Mr. Parker and Mr. Timmons.

While we waited for the doors to open, a man approached us with a note for Miss Jennie Edwards.

My dearest Jennie,

Please forgive me not greeting you in person. The final moments before a show are always devoted to last minute preparation, but do know that I am VERY pleased that you have come tonight (thank you for your message!). Mr. Brandy, the deliverer of this note, will escort you and your party to front-row seats. After the show, you shall be my guests at a small gathering.

Your friend, Owl

Ahead of the many other theatre goers, we were taken through the big double doors to find our seats. Our group was half-way to the front when I noticed we lacked Mr. Timmons. He remained near the entrance walking slowly.

"The sloping floor is difficult for me," he said when I walked back.

"Would holding my arm help?"

He nodded. "Yes, thank you."

As the heavy black curtain rose, two young men, one on each side of the stage, began rolling two wide panels to the middle of the stage. The panel coming from the left crossed in front of the one coming from the right, and after continuing in their respective directions, Owl suddenly stood where they'd crossed! He waved and graciously bowed, and while the audience clapped, the assistants brought out a large box on a platform with four wheels. Owl opened two walls of the box to show it completely empty. Then he closed the doors. He walked around the box, spun it in a circle and finally opened one door a second time. This time though the box wasn't empty. Instead, Carmen stepped out to great cheering!

Owl looked the same to me, dressed all in black, with a red scarf around his neck and his hair and beard both tied with small red ribbons. Carmen looked as beautiful as I remembered her, elegant and tall and wearing a white gown that highlighted her olive skin. The gown had faint streaks of blue and seemed to glow in the theatre's lights.

Carmen exited the stage and another man appeared, dressed in a bright orange shirt and black vest. He worked with Owl to carry a thick, dark blanket onstage. The two of them held the blanket vertically between them and walked in a circle to show that nothing was attached to it. The assistant then stepped behind his end of the blanket and slowly began rolling himself up in it. Owl meanwhile kept hold of the other end. When the man was completely rolled up, Owl patted the blanket, then looked out at the audience.

"Well, Ladies and Gentlemen, what do you think?"

Silence ensued as Owl began pulling on a corner of the blanket, slowly unraveling the man inside. When he finished, however, it was Carmen who stepped out of the cocoon! I almost slipped out of my chair. She now wore a different gown of orange and black, clothing much in the style of the man who had disappeared. As we all sat there stunned, the theatre lights shone toward the back of the room. Everyone turned. There, near the back rows, stood the man now dressed in white and blue, just like Carmen's dress. Thunderous applause shook the floor of McVicker's Theatre.

*

After the show, Mr. Brandy escorted us to Owl's reception. Mrs. Allenton talked the whole way about how she planned to see every show of Owl's from now on, while her husband vowed over and over that he'd "figure out this magic business if it was the last thing he ever did."

"Jennie Edwards!" Owl swooped over to us. "At last you have come! And look at you! No longer a little girl, but a grown woman! I nearly didn't recognize you!"

Carmen quickly joined us and I introduced the Allenton's and Mr. Timmons. A waiter brought trays of drinks and we stood chatting, all praising Owl and Carmen while they graciously thanked us for coming. As more people arrived, Mr. and Mrs. Allenton splintered off to greet friends, while Mr. Parker decided to return to the Sherman House and Mr. Timmons said he also wished for an early evening. While Carmen escorted Marie away to meet some people, Owl took my hand.

"Come, Jennie, let's escape for a few minutes." He grabbed two glasses of champagne and we left the reception for a small room off one corner. Owl sat down in one chair and waved me into another.

"Sit, my dear, I want to hear how you are. What news of Toulon? How are your brothers? Where are they now?"

I told Owl about the boys being in winter quarters in Kentucky and not having been in any battles yet. "Though of course they greatly anticipate it."

"And your parents?"

Suddenly, I found myself telling Owl of the brother I had never known and about how much it had hurt my mother to lose her child.

"And your brothers don't know about this either?" he asked.

"No." I paused. "I feel angry with them, Owl. I don't mean to, but I do."

"Why?"

"For not telling us. For having a secret. For having *this* secret."

"Everyone has secrets, Jennie."

"I don't."

Owl thought. "You might someday."

"I doubt it."

He smiled. "You're young now and life seems simple. Things may happen later though that will be too painful to share. I hope not, but sometimes it happens."

"I would not keep something from someone that she should know."

"Telling a secret may be the right thing to do," Owl agreed. "Or it may not be. A good idea is to ask yourself how the other person might feel if you share something. If it will upset them, then maybe it's not the right thing. Your parents probably thought that would be the outcome if they told you and Jothan and Gardiner about your brother."

"Then why tell now?"

"Maybe your father thought knowing would help explain some things. Maybe he thought it would make *him* feel better. There can be many reasons for sharing a secret." Owl shrugged. "Maybe he told you for the same reasons you're telling me: to share something that hurts."

"Maybe we should talk about magic instead," I said, wishing suddenly that I hadn't said anything about my family. "I do have an idea about how you did that conjure with the blanket!"

He laughed. "Well, let's hear it!"

*

The next morning, Owl and Carmen, as well as Mr. Timmons, came to the Illinois Central Station to bid us farewell. I felt sorry to leave them and Chicago, but was also anxious to return home. Carmen handed me a gray feather.

"Julia dropped this and I thought you might like to have it." She hugged me. "I am sorry, Jennie, that we did not have more time to talk. You must come again and we'll make time for just the two of us."

"I would like that."

Owl wished me God speed and said he hoped I would return soon, while Mr. Timmons gave a slight bow, touching because it obviously was painful to do so.

"It has been a pleasure to make your acquaintance, Miss Edwards."

"And I yours, Mr. Timmons. Truly, though, you must call me Jennie."

He smiled. "May I write to you?"

"Of course, you may. And I will write you as well."

"That would be nice."

As the train pulled away from the lakeshore, Marie and her

father and I stood watching out the window as the buildings of Chicago grew smaller and smaller. Soon, the prairie became more of the view and we returned to our seats. Mr. Parker immediately opened his briefcase. When I asked him how his case was going, he shook his head.

"Not very well, I'm afraid. The police have no more clues to the mystery, and they still have no murder weapon or credible suspects. The investigation has not been carried out in the most efficient manner and unfortunately the more time that passes, the more the trail grows cold."

"I'm sorry, Mr. Parker."

"Thank you, Jennie." He looked out the window. "People are funny and the most complicated of creatures. I see this all the time in my work, yet it never fails to surprise me. I met with my client three times. We talked at length, for some hours. Unless she is an extraordinary actress, I will remain convinced that she did not want her husband dead."

*

It felt good to be home again. Mama and Papa wanted to hear all about Chicago and I happily related everything that had happened. Mama especially asked many questions, from how Carmen and Owl fared to what the Sherman House was like. Perhaps Papa had been right. That I left and came home safely may have brought her comfort that the same would transpire for my brothers. It was also probably true that my mother, like all of us, had grown used to their absence.

The Illinois spring began early in 1862. The snow melted only a few weeks after our return; the earliest blue and green grasses sprouting shortly after that. Papa and I began plowing the fields and fixing fences damaged by snow, while Mama planted and repaired the chicken house. With my brothers gone, there was much more work for all of us. This necessarily left little time to indulge in worry or fun.

During the last week of March, I visited Marie. I'd seen little of her since our trip, and with both Mr. Timmons and Owl writing

181

and asking me how Marie fared, I determined I should find out. I took the Parkers several trout I'd caught in the melting Spoon River. The fish smell caused Marie to wrinkle her nose, but Mrs. Parker seemed pleased.

"We'll have them for supper tonight," she said, happily. "Can you stay, Jennie?"

"No, ma'am, but thank you. Mama expects me home after I stop by Trickle's."

"Another time then."

Marie and I went to her room. The sun streamed in through the large windows and made everything warm and bright.

"Come lay down with me, Jennie," she said, stretching out on the bed. A fine layer of sweat covered her face. I took off my boots and lay beside her. After a moment, I began rubbing Marie's ballooned stomach.

"Oh, that feels so good. I swear I'm about to burst, Jen. I wish the baby would hurry up and come."

"Are you very afraid?"

"Some. But mostly I'll just be happy to see our baby. It will be like having Jothan home." She put her hand over mine. "I do miss him so."

"Me too. I miss them both."

"There's a letter from him on the bureau if you'd like to read it. It's only three weeks old."

"I can't read your mail, Marie!"

She waved a hand. "Of course, you can. Read it out loud; that will be nice for me."

Jothan wrote about missing home and Marie and his excitement around the arrival of their baby. He planned to request another furlough after *she* had arrived. Even better, perhaps the war would be over by then. They'd had some success, including a victory at Fort Donelson along the Cumberland River, after which the Confederates had retreated in terrible confusion. My brother wrote:

I almost felt sorry for them. To be defeated at such an ignoble cause must send a man's spirits lower than nearly anything. Yet, my sympathy did not last long. Two days after the fight, the 7th helped bury the dead. I confess this task, long after the excitement of battle had departed, left me cursing the Southerners for beginning this dreadful business. Too, I cursed them for shackling men and women, something that not even wild animals do to each other, and then I cursed them for making killers of us all. These people have made me see human beings at their worst. It was not a sight I welcomed. War is a mad machine, there is no doubt, yet I continue in the belief that our cause is just. All will be well.

Jothan had written this letter some days after Fort Donelson as the regiment traveled up the Tennessee River. He'd posted it from Clifton, the last village before their destination, a place called Pittsburg Landing.

I returned the letter to its envelope. "He writes more to you than he does to us."

"Does he?"

"Of the encounter at Fort Donelson, he said very little; Gardiner was the same. Mostly they write about camp life and funny things. Jothan told one story about a waking up in the middle of the night to see a raccoon rummaging in his knapsack. It ended up stealing his spoon! That's a funny thing to write when there's a war going on."

"I don't think they want to worry your mother."

"Are you worried?"

Marie thought. "I am proud of my husband. He is a man and he's doing what is right. What I feel isn't so important."

We continued to lie on the bed. I kept rubbing her stomach and after awhile she fell asleep. I crept away quietly, said good-bye to Mrs. Parker, and rode Ruby over to Trickle's General Store.

The only other customers included Mrs. McRae and Mr. Cooley, the owner of the Virginia House. They were talking with Mr. Trickle when I walked in. It had been many weeks since I'd seen any of them, yet Mrs. McRae still looked as if she'd seen too much of me lately.

"Eliza Jane, you are too old to still be wearing trousers. What does your mother think?"

"She doesn't think anything, Mrs. McRae, since it doesn't make a lick of sense to wear other than these when I'm working."

The woman's cat eyes narrowed. "You're saucy, Eliza Jane, always have been. I suppose you would even get a job if you could, eh? Work in some ridiculous place, like any old ridiculous man?"

"Yes, Mrs. McRae, I would. In fact, I'd be off to the war right now if I could."

"Oh, would you now?" She appeared delighted with this information. "A little soldier girl, is that right? Well, I think that's a charming idea. I imagine the men would think so too. You could do their washing and cooking for them."

"I wouldn't do anybody's washing and cooking."

"I think you would, Eliza Jane. War is no place for a woman." She turned to the others. "Isn't that right, Mr. Cooley? Mr. Trickle? Imagine! Eliza Jane wanting to be a soldier girl!"

Mr. Cooley looked confused, while Washington Trickle handed two spools of thread to Mrs. McRae and pulled a pencil out of his beard. "I imagine Jennie would make a good soldier," he said, adding up the woman's bill. "And who knows? Maybe if there were more women on the battlefield, there'd be less battling. Women are smarter than men after all."

"Really, Mr. Trickle," she said, gathering up her goods, "you do have the strangest ideas." Turning back to me, she added, "You just better be wearing a dress, Eliza Jane, the next time I see you at the Literary Society!"

With that, she was gone, the door banging loudly after her. After Mr. Cooley had purchased his cigars and left as well, I asked why Mrs. McRae seemed more grumpy than usual.

"Aw, she's just sad, I expect," said Washington. "Council said the other day that one of her goats died."

"Well, that's too bad, but she doesn't seem sad to me, just angry."

"Folks got all kinds of ways of being sad. Now, what brings you in today, Jennie?" I handed him Mama's list, then asked how his new store cat was doing.

"Cat!" he yelled. "Ain't no *cat!* Try *cats*! That old girl had them kittens, remember, and they all stayed. Five cats I got now! I'm about to start purring and meowing myself. Go back and see them. I kept 'em all so they could mouse, but they don't hardly move from the stove."

I poured a cup of coffee and sat down, petting the cats and reading the newspaper. After Washington finished the order, he joined me. I set the paper down.

"I think this battle they're predicting at Corinth, Mississippi, is near where Jothan and Gardiner are. Leastwise, where they were last time they wrote."

Washington nodded, sipping his coffee. "Seems things are heating up, for sure."

We continued drinking coffee and listening to the purring cats and the crackling fire. Then I asked, "Mr. Trickle, you got any secrets from Mrs. Trickle?"

"Eh-heh, now there's a question!"

"I been thinking about secrets lately."

"You mean like with your magic?"

"Nah, not like that. I'm thinking about things people keep from other people. Things they don't tell because it might make the other person worried or sad. Do you think that's right to do that, keep those kinds of secrets?"

"I expect it depends on a person's reasons, Jennie. If you want to protect the other person or just yourself. Why you asking this? Did something happen?"

"Did you know that I had another brother, Mr. Trickle?"

Washington Trickle's moon face turned the color of chalk. He didn't answer right away. "I do know that," he said at last. "I didn't know you did though."

"Papa told me a few weeks back."

"I see. And that's the secret you been wondering about." I nodded. "Your mama know you know?"

"No, sir."

"Good. My advice is don't never mention that little boy when your mama's around. I ain't never seen a woman hurt like she did after he died. Grieving didn't stop for Julia for nigh on three years, not until Jothan was born."

NINE

TWO WEEKS after the event, the *Stark County News* related everything about the great battle of "Pittsburg Landing," which had transpired in early April. The paper described great blunders by the exalted Union generals, as well as heroism from the ordinary soldiers. The article included quotes from Grant and Halleck and even the Southern commander, Beauregard, who sent a flag of truce to bury their dead, "I deem it prudent to retire and not renew the battle." Very importantly, the losses had been tallied at 1,500 killed and 3,500 wounded. The enemy's losses were much higher.

We all waited anxiously for letters from my brothers and Adam, but it wasn't until early May that one arrived from my friend. It was dated April 16th and written from the 7th Illinois' camp at Pittsburg Landing:

> *Dearest Jennie,*
> *I have begun this letter three times and each time have quit it. Me and the boys have been through some terrible days, Jen, real terrible.*

I suddenly had a funny feeling in my stomach and folded the letter back up. Mr. Griffin, Toulon's postmaster, asked me if anything was wrong.

"No, sir," I said. "I think I'll just save this for when I get home."

He smiled. "Right smart idea, Jennie."

I gathered up the other post for my parents, but instead of heading for Jug Run Creek, I went the opposite direction. On the banks of Indian Creek, I sat down and once again opened Adam's letter.

Some days have passed since the battle here. Since then there has been nothing but rain. Our camp is a mess, the mud is up to a man's knees, and there ain't no chance of getting dry. We been burying men and trying not to fall ill. But I should go back to the beginning.

On the morning of April 6th, we were making fires and cooking breakfast, all business as usual. Gardiner had left before light to finish drawing some night bird he'd found that was sleeping on a branch. I ain't never seen anyone draw so much as your brother, Jen. He liked the birds and critters most of all but had started sketching scenes in camp too. Anyhow, Jothan and me made coffee and were drinking it all right. It was Sunday and quiet.

Suddenly, we heard musket fire and men started running everywhere. Gardiner came rushing back and then we were in a line marching for a mile or more. This was it. We had us a fight and a good one it was. I hardly knew what I was about, there was so much smoke and noise but I kept loading my gun and firing, what a good soldier is supposed to do. We'd been in some messes before but nothing like this one.

We held 'em most of that first day. I felt a terrible blow at one point and knew I was hit. Funny thing though, the bullet smacked my canteen, blew it all apart but didn't hurt me none. That's when I thought all would be well. Toward evening though they pushed us back. Fires had started everywhere and men were down and it was just awful, Jen. About midnight the thunder and lightning began, rain coming down in buckets. It lived up to all my expectations of hell.

I hadn't seen your brothers for hours but then by some miracle I came across Jothan. He said that Gardiner was hurt. He showed me where G. had been since the afternoon and together we carried him to the steamboats where there was a hospital. A surgeon saw him and told us Gardiner was shot up pretty bad.

I stopped reading. What had been a mushy feeling in my stomach suddenly turned hard like a rock. In that moment, I knew. A little songbird breaking into song above me nearly caused me to jump out of my skin. Reading or not reading, it wouldn't make a difference now; I continued.

It was terrible crowded on that steamer but we found a quiet corner and we sat with Gardiner all night. He slept mostly. We tried to keep him comfortable, that was about all there was to do. Jothan looked sick and could barely speak. We were both exhausted.

Finally toward daylight, Gardiner awoke. At first he didn't say anything, then he asked about his journal. He said to please send it to you and to tell you and your folks that he wasn't afraid or sad, this was just the way things were. He said, "Tell Jennie I think she should go out west someday. I think she'd like that." That's what he said, Jen, and then he was gone. I wish there was more to write or something better to say but there ain't.

The next morning we carried Gardiner off the ship and planned to bury him but there wasn't no chance before the fighting started up again. We wrapped him up in a blanket and tucked him into some willows and headed into it again. The Rebs came on just as hard as before but we had more men and hit them hard too. Your brother and I stuck close together. We gave those bastards all we had. Then along in the afternoon, I saw Jothan fall. God, Jen, you don't know how hard it is to write this. He was gone instantly, shot right through the heart. Didn't suffer at least, the only good thing.

The fighting finally ended, and the next day the burying began. Several boys helped me arrange a place for your brothers. We laid them side by side, we did. But here's the important part, Jen, where the boys are buried. Some day we got to come back and get them. We got to come back here and bring them home.

Adam had drawn a map of the area. My brothers were buried west of Pittsburg Landing about a mile, passed a pond and two small buildings. After the second building, there was a small grove of trees and in the middle of the grove five trees grew together in a perfect row. Jothan and Gardiner were in between two of the trees.

Adam had gotten the lid to a cracker box and carved their names on it so there wouldn't be no mistaking who was below.

Notwithstanding it's in the South, the boys are in a fine place, Jen. We been working hard every day here but I've still gone back each afternoon to make sure all is well. Violets started coming up around them too, and wouldn't you know, one morning I saw that funny nightbird sleeping on a branch above the boys. I know I'll sound soft, but I think that bird knew they were there and had come to pay respects. I hadn't seen no animals since before the battle, yet now this bird was back. It made me feel a little better.

I'll write more as soon as I can. I'm sending Gardiner's notebook and both of their things separate but you should be getting them soon.

Your friend, Adam

*

All the rest of that day I felt in a dream. My head told me the letter was the truth (how could it be anything else?), yet my heart had doubts (such terrible news, *both* Jothan and Gardiner gone, could not be believed). For this and many other reasons, I didn't tell my parents about Adam's letter. When I couldn't eat my supper that evening, Mama asked if I was unwell.

"A little," I said, "I think I've caught a cold."

She nodded and suggested I go to bed early. I did so gratefully for I wasn't sure how long I could maintain this silence. Two days later, I declared myself well enough to go into town. I had to collect Adam's package before Mama or Papa did. Every day for a week found me riding Ruby to Toulon, making varied excuses for these many excursions. Finally, the package arrived. That night, I put Gardiner's journal beneath my pillow, vowing to never let it out of my possession. Many hours later, I finally fell asleep. In a ragged dream that morning, I thought I heard my brothers talking in their room.

Three weeks later, a letter arrived from the captain of Jothan and Gardiner's company. Papa read the letter and began to weep; Mama fainted and we had to carry her to her bed. When she awoke, she began wailing and couldn't stop. I went into town and fetched the doctor, who prescribed laudanum. For the next three days, she alternated between drug-induced sleep and hysteria. Papa and I began making sure one of us was always in the house with her, and while he was "on duty" one morning, I hurried to Marie's, sure, of course, that she had received a letter from the regiment as well.

My friend collapsed into my arms upon seeing me at the door. Mrs. Parker and I got Marie to the sofa and while the older woman went to fetch some tea I held Marie while she cried. She shook so hard that there was no possibility of holding a cup of tea, so Mrs. Parker set the tray on the table, squeezed her daughter's hand, then nodded to me with a look that indicated she would be in the other room. I could say nothing. I could barely think. The only thing I could do was hold Marie, in this moment, with nothing at all to offer her but an embrace.

She sobbed so much that eventually she sank into a sleep. I leaned back on the sofa and closed my eyes as well. When Marie awoke an hour later, my arm had fallen asleep from holding her. She moved only slightly and in a rough voice began speaking into my blouse.

"I'm sorry, Jen."

"Don't be sorry, Marie. We've just had the most awful news. You mustn't be sorry."

"Oh, Jennie, this can't really be true, can it? I mean, perhaps there's been some mistake? Maybe Jothan was captured instead. Maybe the captain confused him for someone else. I've read that this has happened in the East. The battlefields are such a mess, such a confusion..." She took a deep breath. "Do you think that's what might have happened? That there was a mistake somehow?"

I might have told Marie then about Adam's letter, but I didn't, I couldn't. I might have also given her some false hope because I would have done almost anything to make her feel better, but I didn't do that either. Instead, I just kissed the top of her head. "I don't think so, Marie. I'm pretty sure the captain wouldn't have written if he hadn't been sure."

She nodded slowly. "Yes, of course, you're right. I do wish you weren't though."

"So do I." I kissed her again. "Oh, so do I."

*

One morning, my mother got out of bed. I came in from outside to find my father having dozed off and Mama gathering up various books, including her Bible, and throwing everything into the fire. We gave her more laudanum and as the days passed, Papa spoke of a specialist in Galesburg. Yet, between all the work on the farm and watching Mama, there was no time to investigate this idea.

My trips to town included going to the post office and seeing Marie. It comforted both of us to be together. The baby was due any day now and I hoped to be there for its arrival. However, that was not to be. Washington Trickle paid a visit to Jug Run Creek one morning to say that another Jennie Edwards was now in the world, and that the birth had come quickly and relatively simply for Marie the previous night. Washington volunteered to stay with Mama while Papa and I went into town as fast as the team would take us.

Marie looked up and smiled. After giving Papa his first grandchild to hold, she hugged me. "I don't know what I'd do if I didn't have her," she whispered, tears sliding down her cheeks. "Because of the baby I must look forward now instead of back."

I nodded and looked at my father holding the little girl. Completely swaddled in a blanket, only the tiny head, barely larger than a melon, was visible. Jothan's big, chocolate eyes gazed back at us, causing my knees to shake and Papa's cheeks to become wet with tears. From Marie, she had was the upturned nose and perfect ears. Jennie, almost smiling, seemed to be studying my father closely, and I had the strangest feeling that she understood the sad circumstances into which she'd been born and was determined to make up for them.

"She looks like you, Jen," said Marie.

"Do you think so?"

Papa didn't feel comfortable being in Marie's bedroom, so after he'd held Jennie and kissed Marie and told her what a proud and happy grandfather she had made him, he joined Mr. and Mrs. Parker downstairs.

"Oh, yes," Marie said, after he'd gone. "But then you and Jothan look so much alike too." Marie leaned back on the pillows. "Father has started calling her "Jen-Jen" and Mother says simply, "Little Angel." The house already is a different place with her in it."

I stared at my namesake, then looked at Marie. "How are you?"

"Tired. So happy to finally see my daughter. So heartbroken that I will never see my husband again." She began to cry. "Honestly, Jen? These last weeks, one minute I feel myself, more or less; the next I seem to be disappearing. Part of me doesn't believe this could have happened..." her voice trailed off.

Soon, Marie was asleep and so was the baby. I kept holding Jennie and thought how a life goes out of the world, and a life comes into the world. It made sense, for all things have ends, yet such truth brought me no comfort. Surely, the end for Gardiner and Jothan was not supposed to have come so soon.

We all seemed in a strange landscape where belief and disbelief mixed and struggled for control. Jennie's arrival was a blessing; Mama's continuing decline a cause for increasing worry. Papa finally made time one day to go to Galesburg and talk to the specialist. The next afternoon, the doctor paid us a visit. He had warm, gray eyes and the reassuring presence of a preacher. He examined Mama, who was as docile as a lamb and wholly uninterested in his presence. Back in the kitchen, he asked Papa many questions. Had Mrs. Edwards suffered from melancholy before? Was there a history of it in the family? Had there been other trauma in her life? Papa, his voice breaking occasionally, answered the questions as best as he could. Then we both waited while the doctor wrote many notes. I poured us all coffee. When the man finally finished writing, he looked at us with a grave expression.

"I don't have very good news for you, Mr. Edwards. Your wife's condition appears quite serious. From what I can observe, and from what you have told me, I would diagnose her with nervous disease. This has been brought on by severe melancholy, a condition that appeared with the loss of your first child and has now been compounded by the deaths of your two sons in the war. It is not a surprising turn of events under the circumstances though people with nervous disease often are able to talk and recognize others, particularly family. At the moment, however, Mrs. Edwards does not seem capable of either.

"Sometimes the shock of a tragedy is too much for a mind," he continued, "and it simply shuts down entirely. I've also seen people experience amnesia for short periods of time. After they come out of these episodes, they don't remember anything, including where they were or what they've done. Others will somehow simply block off the memory of the one painful event and go about their lives in a remarkably normal fashion. I'm sorry, Mr. Edwards, but there are many things we don't know about these kinds of mental conditions. We do know that women, due to their delicate natures, are particularly prone, but I have occasionally seen nervous disease in men as well."

Papa looked as pale as a ghost. I cleared my throat. "I don't believe my mother is so delicate, sir. She's had a shock, we all have, but she will return to herself."

He looked at me, nodding. "I hope that is true, my dear, though I think it unlikely without treatment." He then suggested a rigorous program of various proven methods such as bleeding, hot and cold baths, and mercury. These could only be done in Galesburg and it would likely require Mama to be there some months. After the doctor left, I told my father that he couldn't possibly consider sending Mama away to Galesburg.

"I know, Jen," he sighed. "For one thing, we can't afford it."

"It's more than just the money, Papa! We can't send Mama away to people who don't know her. We can take care of her here. You'll see. She'll get better soon."

But Mama didn't get better. She didn't speak and she ate little. She'd allow herself to be moved from bed to chair and back again, and also to be bathed and taken to the outhouse, but she did nothing on her own. I told Marie and Mrs. Parker one afternoon that I felt like I now had my own baby to care for. Marie's mother suggested that bringing Jen-Jen to see her might help. I agreed, so the next afternoon they rode out. Mama didn't seem to recognize them. She never stirred from her bed though we all sat in her room and talked and held Jen-Jen and tried to act as if everything was normal.

One night in late May, I couldn't sleep and went down to the Spoon River. The sky was deep and dark, with stars bright and blinking, and I looked up at it for hours. Somewhere, in the far-off mists of the heavens, now lived my brothers. It seemed that this couldn't be so, and yet everything now, from Mama's condition to the emptiness in our home (so wholly different from the absence that comes about when people are simply away for a time), provided ample evidence that the very worst had indeed happened. That morning, my father had said he was going to figure out a way to get Mama to Galesburg, that we had no other choice. I had reluctantly agreed; it was all too apparent we couldn't go on like this. As the eastern sky began lightening, I determined that I must get a job. We needed money.

A few hours later, I gathered up Sam and Ruby and rode into town. Mr. Trickle looked surprised to see me.

"Jennie!" He squinted, looking me over. "Goodness, girl, you look exhausted. Go on to the stove and get some coffee. No one's there. I'll be along directly." After finishing up with a customer, he came back and sat down. "You know how sorry me and Mrs. Trickle are about the boys."

"I know," I said, my throat tightening. "Me and Papa are appreciative, well, of all you've done, Mr. Trickle. That is, all the food you and Mrs. Trickle been sending."

He nodded. "Jennie, you don't look so good."

"I know. I ain't sleeping too well and Mama is so sick. Thing is, Mr. Trickle, Papa wants to send her to Galesburg for treatment."

"I do know that."

"I don't much like it but it's about all we can do. We just can't take care of her ourselves. Problem is it's going to cost a lot of money." I took a deep breath. "I was wondering—"

"You'd like a job then."

"Yes, sir. I could work at night, maybe clean up, stock shelves, that way nobody'd see me. I know it ain't usual, a girl working in a store and all."

Washington snorted. "I don't care about that! I'd be happy for your help, but I don't want you working too much, Jen. You look as run down as an old pair of trousers." He took a piece of paper and pencil out of his beard and did some scribbling. "Let's say you work a couple of hours after closing every other day, and I'll pay a dollar a week. You can have supper with me and Mrs. Trickle and take some leftovers home to your ma and pa. That way, Graham won't have to worry about you not being there to make the meal."

"A dollar's too much. Half-dollar per week."

"It ain't too much at all!" he shouted. "Now those are my terms, take 'em or leave 'em."

"Thank you, Mr. Trickle, I really appreciate this."

His moon face turned more rosy. "Don't thank *me*! You're doing me a favor! You can help me keep track of all these cats!"

To my surprise, Papa didn't seem to mind this arrangement. Mrs. Parker, as well as Mrs. McRae and some other women in town, had started coming out to help with Mama, and though my mother didn't seem any more responsive, I felt sure their presence to be helpful. It was also good for me to be away. I started sleeping better and found great satisfaction in having a job. Washington would be there when I arrived and he'd give me a list of chores. I'd do these while he organized his books. Sometimes we took a break and had coffee. One night he offered me a cigar. He'd just received a box of some very nice ones and thought I may as well try it.

"Just don't tell Mrs. Trickle," he winked.

*

June became July and the prairie grasses began turning yellow. Mama was still at home, but Papa had nearly finished the arrangements to move her to Galesburg. Fortunately, paying for the treatment could be done in installments; the important thing, the doctor said, was to begin the work. I gave Papa everything I made from Mr. Trickle, but I began to wonder how I could make more money.

Some days, before starting my shift at Trickle's, I'd visit Marie and Jen-Jen. The little baby was growing like the summer wheat! She was a happy baby, smiling and gurgling and interested in everything. One afternoon, after she'd been put down for her nap, Marie lay down on the bed. I stretched out next to her. She started crying, so I held her close. After awhile, I kissed her forehead and stroked her hair.

"I don't know how, Marie, but I believe it will be all right. It doesn't seem so now, but it will be."

She nodded. "I know. It's just, I don't know, Jen, sometimes I just feel so frightened."

"Frightened? Why?"

Marie wiped her eyes. "I'm not sure I believe I'll ever see Jothan again. I'm not sure," she paused. "I'm not sure I believe in God anymore. How could I? There can't possibly be a god that would allow all this killing and hatred. Or a god that would have allowed slavery in the first place?" Marie took my hand. "What do you think, Jen?"

"I try not to think too much, Marie."

"You're all I have now, you know. You and Jen-Jen."

Marie moved her hand from my hand to my face. She stared at me a long while. Even as tired and as sad as she was, she was still so pretty and of course someday she would find another husband and that would probably make me sad but I would be glad for her too. I was just about to tell her this, but for some reason, I kissed her fingers instead. Her hands trembled and her tears fell anew. She watched me. She smelled of fresh soap. I kissed her fingers again. Marie closed her eyes. Then she opened them again, lifted her head, and kissed me on the lips. I kissed her back, pulling her closer. It seemed like we stayed like that, our mouths pressed together, for a long time, but perhaps it wasn't more than a few seconds. Just as quickly as we had come together, suddenly we were apart. Marie lay back again and told me how glad she was for our friendship.

For my part, I suddenly felt very queer. I couldn't speak and a fluttering in my stomach had moved to other parts of my body. I wondered if I'd eaten something bad, or if I was getting the ague. Now, Marie was talking again, but I barely heard anything she said. It was only later that I understood she had been telling me about an invitation that had arrived from Mrs. Allenton inviting her to come to Chicago for a few weeks, an invitation that she and her parents had talked over and agreed was a good idea. Consequently, Marie and Mrs. Parker and Jen-Jen would be leaving for the big city in only a few days.

TEN

ONE EVENING, Papa told me it was finally settled: Mama would go to Galesburg in two weeks' time. He also informed me he was planning to stay there with her.

"I'm sorry, Jennie," he said, shaking his head. "I'm going to rent out the farm for the rest of the season. There are two fellows that Washington knows who need work and I agreed they could have half the profits from the harvest if they'd stay here and take care of the place." Papa looked so tired and sad that I didn't chastise him for not even consulting me. He continued, "Washington knows the men from a long time and they're hard workers though not inclined to settling. Seasonal work seems to suit them fine. They're also too old for soldiering. We'll come back every few weeks to check on things."

Going to Galesburg, even to be near Mama, sounded awful to me. What would I do all day? Who would take care of Ruby and Sam? These men might be fine for the other animals but not my mule and dog.

"I understand, Papa."

"I don't know what else to do, Jen."

"I know."

A few days later, I sat in the back room at Trickle's reading the *Chicago Daily Tribune*. News from the city included repairs to the train tracks above Lake Michigan shifting all travel to a station on Johnson Street; pigs feeding on garbage in the streets becoming a problem; and the police wearing straw hats because of the heat. One particular article caught my eye: a new call for troops. Several states had begun the process of "diligent recruiting" and in Kankakee a $50 bounty was being paid to every man who enlisted before August 20th. This vast sum, along with the monthly pay of $13 meant a soldier could make over $200 in a year. This was far more than we ever earned on the farm. Working at Trickle's it would take me many years to make so much money.

"They need people, Mr. Trickle," I said, after Washington had come over and sat down. He looked at the article. "They need *men*, Jennie."

"I wanted to sign up a long time ago, when Gardiner and Jothan did. Now's my chance. I can make a lot of money too, all the money we're going to need for Mama's treatment."

Washington sighed. "I've known you since you were a wee thing, Jen. You ain't never been like the other girls and I've always liked that about you. But it's worried me too."

"I can take care of myself."

"You can't do this thing, Jennie."

"Maybe if I'd been there with them they wouldn't have got killed."

He snorted. "That's just silly! You would have been killed too. That's what war is all about: killing and dying! Your ma and pa need you with them."

"No, they don't. They need money. Mama's treatment is expensive and it's great you giving me a job but it's not enough. If I go, I can send money to Papa. That's what they need."

Washington's cheeks went pink. "You can't send money home because you won't be able to sign up! They'll never let you!"

I smiled. "Because I'm not a man? That's easily remedied, Mr. Trickle." His face turned redder. "You gotta promise me you won't tell anyone."

"I'll promise no such thing."

We argued until Mrs. Trickle called us for supper. Washington didn't say much during the meal, but after, as I was getting ready to leave, he asked me not to make him choose between loyalty to my father or loyalty to me.

"You can be loyal to us both," I told him. "You saw her, Washington. Her mind is gone. This is what I can do to help and I'm doing it. Please don't make it harder than it is."

"Oh, Jennie."

"I promise I'll be back before you know it. The war can't go on forever, right?"

"Seems like it's trying."

I got up on Ruby. "My mind is made up."

"Yes, I can see that."

"I would appreciate it if you would do one thing for me."

He sighed. "Anything, dear girl."

"It's a lot to ask, but could you take care of Ruby and Sam?"

*

I could argue with Washington and feel pretty confident I'd get my way in the end. The same would not be true with my father. With Papa, I would have to lie.

"Owl has offered me a job," I told him that evening, "helping with his shows in Chicago. He'll pay me two dollars and a half each week and I can stay with him and Carmen." My father started to protest. "Look, Papa, we need the money and I can help."

He thought. "Working for Washington is one thing, Jen. But going to Chicago? No, I don't like that at all."

"How are you expecting to pay for Mama's treatment?"

Suddenly, Papa looked like he might cry. "I don't know."

"This will help then. I'll be with Owl, Papa, and Carmen. You like them. Besides, I'm old enough to take care of myself."

My father looked at me a moment then walked outside. In the end, he never said I could go to Chicago, but he never said I couldn't either. On the appointed day, we packed a bag for Mama, got her dressed and then settled in the wagon. She watched the swallows flying around for a few minutes then wished me a good trip and that she hoped I'd write.

"I'll write every day," I said, kissing her on the cheek. Papa hugged me tightly. "I'll write every day," I whispered. "Don't worry, Papa."

Then they were gone, the wagon rolling up the hill away from Jug Run Creek. As it vanished over the rise, I felt like the last person on earth.

That evening, Ruby, Sam, and I went down to the river bottoms. The wood thrushes sang quietly in the growing coolness; the Indian grass and sassafras waved slightly in the evening breezes. While I sat on a rock ledge above Spoon River, Ruby nibbled at patches of grass and Sam sniffed around in the thick shrubs. After awhile, both my mule and pup settled down. We all watched the dragonflies buzzing about the rocks and the swallows flying above the river. Ruby and Sam had both dozed off when I suddenly saw the panther below us, down by the water. One moment there had been only clumps of willow, and in the next, the great, giant cat.

She looked upriver, then down. Minutes passed. She watched the swallows as well with an expression not unlike Washington Trickle's store cats observing sparrows. Yet, this was no store cat. With a tail stretching back into yesterday and paws as big as tea plates, I wondered if she was the same animal I had encountered in the night almost four years before.

I had only glanced away briefly to see if Ruby or Sam had noticed her, but when I looked again the panther was gone.

That night, I packed one of my dresses, my map of the war, Adam's last letter, Gardiner's journal, and a little money I'd kept from my wages. At the last moment, I also included our family likeness, the one taken on the day of Mr. Lincoln's visit, so long ago.

"We'll take good care of them," said Washington Trickle as I set Sam down outside of the storage building and tied Ruby up to the post. For once, my dog had been quiet the whole way into town. Ruby, too, didn't frisk about or dawdle. "They both know, sure, but they'll be fine." He coughed. "I am proud of you, Jennie. But if you don't come back, I won't be able to live with myself."

"I'll come back."

The next morning, I put on my dress and fixed my hair on top of my head and looked like a right proper lady. Washington shook his head. Mrs. Trickle worried about me traveling by myself.

"But I'm glad you're going to join Marie," she added. "She'll be needing her friend. And the change will do you good, Jennie. You've gotten so thin! Take care of yourself, dear girl."

"I will, Mrs. Trickle." When the stage pulled away for Kewanee, I waved heartily to the Trickle's. Washington had said he'd get the men he knew settled at Jug Run Creek and in spite of everything, I felt grateful. For the Trickle's, for the women in town who had helped us, even for Mrs. McRae, who seemed like a wholly different person in the midst of tragedy. She had sat with my mother for hours and even occasionally patted me on the shoulder. Still, my relief at leaving grew with each turn of the stage's wheel. Plenty of challenges remained, not the least of which would be telling Owl and Carmen my plans. There also was the problem, however small in a city of thousands, of possibly seeing Marie in Chicago. To avoid this last, I would have to change my appearance immediately.

*

After getting off the cars on Lake Michigan, I hailed a carriage and told the driver to take me to Water Street just north of the Chicago River. Even with the August heat, people and carriages and animals filled the streets. The noise blasted from every quarter, the smell from the river hung almost visible above the waterway, and every direction I looked showed more construction and industry. In spite of delays from the many conveyances all trying to get somewhere, we soon pulled up in front of the large establishment of C.H. McCormick & Bro. Reapers & Mowers.

"I'm meeting my husband," I told the driver as he looked around at the warehouses and factories, so different from the business district south of the river.

After he'd gone, I slipped around the side of the building and into a deserted alley. Quickly doffing the dress, hat, and shoes, I put on my trousers, blouse, and boots, and tucked my hair into one of Jothan's caps. For good measure, I rubbed some dirt on my cheeks. Returning to the reapers and mowers building, I walked inside. A man with a visor and a pencil in his mouth stared at some papers on his desk. Upon looking up, his expression turned sour.

"Ain't no work here, boy, so git!"

My smile only added to the man's scowl. "I'm not looking for work, sir. Just wanting to join up. For the war, you know."

Walking around to the front of the desk, he looked me over. "Gittin' the bounty, is ya? Well, I don't know as they need anyone so scrawny, but Calhoun Street is just south of the river. Keep heading down this road and a couple blocks past the horse car tracks you'll see the sign."

I thanked him and to test my disguise further, I stuck out my hand. He shook it. My hand was smaller than his but not noticeably so. The man's crankiness vanished altogether and he wished me well. Perhaps it was that I wanted to do my part for our country. Or, maybe I reminded him of someone. Whatever the reasons behind his change in demeanor, the important thing was that he saw before him a young man. Never in a hundred lifetimes would he stop to consider that I might be anyone else.

*

Owl stared at me. His pleasure at my surprise appearance gave way to confusion and then upset as I told him my plans. "You're doing *what?*"

"I know it seems fantastic."

"That's one word. Another is impossible. Or dangerous."

"Owl—"

"Does your father know you're here?"

"Yes."

"And he knows of your plans?"

I looked away. "He thinks I've come to work for you."

Owl shook his head. "This is no good, Jennie. Doing this won't bring your brothers back and you mightn't come back either. You must think about your family."

"I am thinking about my family."

"No, you're not. You're thinking only of yourself."

Suddenly, Carmen spoke up. "Owl is right, Jennie. It is not certain that the same fate won't befall you too. You know you are most welcome to stay here and live with us. There is work you could do and that money would help your family."

"I appreciate that, but I can make much more money going for a soldier."

Owl ran his fingers through his hair. Then he opened up his tobacco box and took out a cigar. He chewed on it for a minute. "I'll tell you my real name."

"What?"

"Look, Jennie, I would do anything for you, both Carmen and I would. I'll give you a job, give you money, even tell you my real name. Anything to get you to stay."

It was a silly notion, that the revelation of Owl's true name could make me change my mind about something so important. "Tell me and I'll consider it," I shrugged.

Owl stood up and went to his secretary. He wrote something on a piece of paper and handed it to me.

"This can't be your real name," I laughed. "It's too plain, it's nothing like you!"

Owl laughed too. "It's not always satisfying to know the truth, is it? Yet, whether you believe it or not, that *is* what my mother named me."

For the rest of that evening, we enjoyed a meal together and Owl showed me a few new conjures. The next morning he had left by the time I woke up. Carmen and I drank coffee together, enjoying the cool breezes coming in the kitchen window. We talked of topics besides the war, including their latest shows, the summer heat, and the city's latest plan to solve the problem of clean drinking water. This last involved building a tunnel under Lake Michigan for two miles. Carmen poured us more coffee, then she squeezed my hand.

"I think you're doing the right thing, Jennie."

"You do?"

She nodded. "Do not worry about Owl; he will come around. You have the courage for this, of that I have no doubt, and why shouldn't you go? There are so many things about women that men don't understand, and that is why Owl will never understand your desire." She thought. "I shall help you if you like. Owl has gone for a few days, to talk to a man in Indiana who is interested in engaging us for some shows. He has left you a note." She handed me a small envelope. "So, you will have no one to bother you about this. I can even cut your hair for you. I think that will be necessary."

Owl's note implored me not to go and added he was most sorry to have these previously arranged meetings that he must keep. He admired my courage but hoped I would come to my senses and that he would find me in Chicago upon his return. After I'd read the note, Carmen took it from me and placed it in the fire.

Later, we went into her room and she undid my braid. As she brushed out my hair, we talked a little but mostly we didn't. Then she began cutting. It took more than an hour before Carmen felt satisfied it looked short and tidy enough. I stared at the glass and a stranger stared back.

Carmen walked me south to the river from their place and again told me I was doing the right thing. "Remember what you've learned about magic, Jennie. People only see what they want to see. They believe only what they want to believe. You are now going be a magician in your real life. I pray God speed to you, dear girl."

I didn't know what to say as we embraced, but I thought I would never meet anyone quite like Carmen. Continuing south along Clark Street, I immediately noticed the effect of my new appearance. Few men looked my way and not a single lady. Only a street boy approached wondering if he could clean my boots, which I declined. When I arrived at the Sherman House, I stopped. It seemed so long ago that I had stayed here though it had been but just eight months. As I remembered all that had occurred since those wonderful few days with Marie, I very nearly missed noticing

Mr. Timmons. He was coming out of the hat shop beneath the hotel, carrying a box under one arm and his cane in the other. He hobbled down the steps, then began walking north. I crossed the street and walked right up to him.

"Beg pardon, sir?" He looked over. "Could you spare a dime, sir? A bit down on my luck."

Mr. Timmons nodded. He looked tired and rosy-cheeked from the heat. He might have paused for a second looking me over, but by and large he had no interest in me. Digging in one of his pockets, he found a coin, and flipped it my way. I thanked him then watched as he continued up the street. It was almost too easy.

At the recruiting office, I stood in line behind two boys. A man in a blue uniform sat behind a desk, his pumpkin face shiny with sweat. The boys finished signing their papers and I moved forward. A sign near the edge of the desk read, "Captain Christopher."

"Which branch?" he asked, chewing on his cigar and not looking up.

"What?"

"Infantry, artillery, or cav?"

"Uh…"

The man looked up. My confidence suddenly vanished. Captain Christopher surely had been signing up hundreds of recruits; he would notice that I didn't look like all the others. He would notice I didn't have a beard (or even the makings of a beard). He would see I had no Adam's apple and he would hear my higher-pitched voice. Maybe he'd even call the sheriff when he realized the deception.

"Got a horse?" He looked back down at the paper.

"No, sir. That is, not with me."

"Infantry then." He wrote something on the paper. "Put out your hands." After glancing at my hands, he made another note. "Now, open your mouth." He stood up, took a look in my mouth, and sat back down. He wrote a few more notes, then asked my name.

"What?"

"Your name!" He looked up a second time. "Jesus, boy! You do have a name, don't you?"

Name! I hadn't even thought of what to call myself. As I stood there like a fool, I was saved by a man appearing in the doorway and asking Captain Christopher a question. My mind raced furiously. I couldn't use my brother's names, that was unthinkable. I couldn't use Papa's either, or Adam's, or Mr. Trickle's. They were all using their names and it just wouldn't be right. I closed my eyes. To get this far and be stopped for want of a name!

The other man left and Captain Christopher looked at me again. He leaned back and relit his cigar, giving a slight sigh. "Look, I don't care much what name you use, I just gotta put one down. Now, what is it?"

I stared at his cigar and then I knew. Owl's real name was not being used by anyone, including Owl himself, and no one was going to care if I borrowed it now. I looked back at the captain.

"Taylor," I said. "My name is Robert Taylor."

PART THREE

ONE

December 1, 1864, Franklin, Tennessee

I COULDN'T MOVE. The bodies had wedged in tight around me.

Some were dead. Some, like me, lived, though barely.

The trench, meant to stop the other side, had thrown us together like ingredients in a stew.

I didn't know I was screaming until I stopped.

A brief moment of silence. Then moans, crying, sounds from men I'd only ever heard before on other battlefields. I screamed again.

I had to get out of the trench. Bodies shifted, but the dead would not make way. Bile rose in my throat. I threw up. Choked. Panicked. Such a feeling I'd not experienced, not even during the charges in Vicksburg. I was being buried alive.

I flailed my arms and crawled upward. Every last bit of strength I had went into hefting myself out of the trench. I ignored the dead men who willed me to stay. I dug my fingers into them to use as anchors; then I dug into the frozen earth. I was very nearly free when something yanked me backward. I lunged forward, then fell back again. My boot had gotten stuck. I looked down. The lace seemed to be wrapped around something. I pulled. Still stuck. I began to sob. Then I heard voices. Clear voices. Not rattles from the dead or near dead. I looked around.

People were walking around, bending over. They weren't soldiers. They looked like…women. I thought I must be dreaming. I went back to trying to get free. Nothing worked. I couldn't break the hold. After some minutes, I looked up again. A woman stood over me.

"Please," I coughed. "My boot…it's…stuck."

She knelt down. I turned on my side and she reached toward my boot. In the next instant, I could feel the weight of someone drop from me. I was free! I crawled a few feet more then looked back. It was hard to see much of the woman. A hood covered her head. My vision grew blurry.

"I have to go," I mumbled, just before the darkness closed around me.

*

Upon waking, I found myself in a wagon. Other soldiers also lay in the wagon. Around us stood three people: the woman who had helped me out of the trench, another dark-haired girl, and a very tall Negro man. They stared at the soldier, clearly dead, beside me. My rescuer, her hood pushed back now and her blond hair scattered about in an untidy braid, spoke to the Negro.

"Take this man," she said, pointing at me, "to the little house. Put him in the front room. Do the same with the others, finding places for them where you can. After, carry this one," she indicated the soldier who was dead, "up to the big house. Someone will come for him later."

The Negro nodded. "Yes, Miss Sarah."

Before I could protest, the black man had me in his arms. He carried me toward a small building and inside to one of the rooms. He set me on a bed and left without a word. A few minutes later, the blonde woman appeared. She looked me over, squinting in the darkened room.

"You're quite safe here," she said.

"Where am I?"

She took a deep breath. "My family's home. Outside of Franklin."

"Outside?"

"Yes."

"Who are you?"

"My name is Sarah. My father is James Hawkins." She looked at me more closely. "Your head is bleeding." She walked over to a table where there was a pile of cloths. When she returned to the bed and tried to put one on my head, I turned away.

"Don't."

"What?"

"Don't...help me. I know you...mean well," I paused, each word a tremendous effort, "but I don't need...your help." I took the cloth from her and placed it against my temple. In that moment, I felt the dried blood and swollen skin. Fresh blood dripped into my eye. I started shaking. The woman stood up again.

"Well, the doctor will be here soon," she said. "I believe that you may need *his* help."

*

As soon as she left, I lay back on the bed and fell asleep. When next I awoke, my head pounded and my leg felt like it was on fire. I tried to sit up. The effort sent shooting pains throughout my body. I gently turned onto my side. My body started shaking again and wouldn't stop. I kept as still as possible and eventually fell back asleep.

It was night when I came around a second time. Now, a lamp sat on the table and someone moved around the room. The person had started a fire. They'd also placed a blanket over me.

"How do you feel?" Sarah asked upon seeing I was awake.

"Bad."

"I'm not surprised."

"Are there others here? I thought I heard voices."

"Yes." She looked away. "I'm sorry. There was no doctor today. Tomorrow hopefully."

"I don't need a doctor."

Sarah's eyes grew wide. "You will die if you don't see a doctor."

*

The night air took my breath away. Fresh snow covered the ground, but the sky was clear. It had taken me a long time to get up, stand up without feeling dizzy, and make my way out of the little building full of wounded men. Sarah, for all of her pretty face and soft voice and apparent kindness, would not help me. She and her Negroes, I felt sure, had brought us all here only to kill us later. There would be no doctor, there would be no help. I had to escape now, tonight. If I didn't go now, there might be no other chance.

At a row of small houses, I stopped to catch my breath. A stick helped me walk, but the fiery pain in my leg kept me from moving fast. After a few minutes, I began again. That's when my foot kicked a can. Suddenly, a door to one of the houses opened. A woman with a lamp in her hand walked outside.

"Who go there?" she called.

I froze. In the next moment, the big Negro man from the morning appeared beside her. "Ain't nothin', Essie," he said, "but that old coon come around."

"That old coon don't kick cans, Pick. Somebody be out there and I be finding out who."

"You ain't finding out nothing. We got us enough trouble already. Come on back in now."

The woman protested but the man was insistent. Soon, the door closed. A minute later the cabin went dark.

I stumbled through the woods. Every dozen yards or so, I had to stop. My head spun and I fell more than I walked. Somehow, through everything, the battle and now this, I'd managed to keep hold of my haversack. Inside were Gardiner's journal, all my letters from home, and Biddle's things. The sack bulged, spinning me around as it got caught on branches and shrubs.

Eventually, I heard the sound of the river. It grew louder and I knew on the other side awaited the regiment. I turned to make my way down the slope toward the water, but a hole in the ground caught me unaware. As my bad leg sank into it, the searing pain made me crumple over unconscious.

When I awoke, the eastern sky had become a dull yellow. I tried to crawl toward it. Everything hurt and I couldn't seem to get enough air. The sun rose above the horizon; small winter birds began hopping about the bushes; a raven flapped overhead. When I heard a voice, I tried to lift my head. The voice sounded high-pitched, like Kit's! I waved my arm so he'd know where I was. When I opened my eyes, however, it wasn't Kit who stood before me.

"What are you doing?" Sarah asked, her question brittle in the cold air. "How did you get here?"

I had no strength to answer. Besides, everything now seemed confused. Hadn't Kit just been speaking? Where was I? What *was* I doing? Sarah dropped to her knees beside me.

"Why are you here?"

"I had to leave."

"What? Why?"

"I'm not a—a man."

The words sounded funny. Sarah, rightly, looked confused. The look cleared however and I could see she thought me delirious. I grabbed her arms. "I'm not a man," I whispered again. "And I mustn't see the doctor. He'll...send...me home."

Sarah stared as comprehension slowly replaced puzzlement. She closed her eyes. "We must return."

"No. If I—"

"Listen, we're wasting time!" she said, rising. "I won't tell anyone, all right? You'll be safe, and you simply can't stay out here."

"But the doctor will know."

Sarah shook her head. "I doubt the doctor is coming anyway, so you needn't worry."

She was stronger than she looked, and in little time Sarah had helped me up on her horse and we were heading back to the building I had worked so hard to escape. There were some soldiers stirring outside, but they paid us little notice. Once we were back in the room, Sarah lit a lamp and began looking me over more. There was my head, and my now swollen eye, at least one broken rib, and the leg that hurt like the devil. She washed everything as best she could and bandaged my head and leg.

"I think there may still be a bullet in your leg," she said. "Something will have to be done about that."

I closed my eyes. "Thank you."

"What's your name?"

It had been so long since anyone asked me this that I had to think for a minute. "Jennie," I said, finally. "My name is Jennie."

Sarah stood up. "Well, stay put this time, won't you, Jennie?"

"I don't know why you're helping me," I mumbled, drifting off to sleep.

"I'm sure," she said, walking toward the door, "I don't know either."

*

My brothers were talking in their bedroom, their voices carrying through the knot I'd popped out of the wall when I was a child. Gardiner mentioned seeing me; Jothan wanted another baby. It was the most ordinary of conversation and I grew bored. Why weren't they talking about more important things? Like, for example, why they hadn't come home? Or, what they were going to do to help Mama? Or, how about explaining why they'd gotten killed in the first place? I crawled, for I couldn't walk with all my wounds, over to the knot. I opened my mouth to ask these questions. Then a loud explosion stopped me.

I woke up.

The next moment, the door opened. It was Sarah. She carried a basket, which she set on the table. She began removing several pieces of linen from the basket and a plate with a biscuit and a jug of water.

"You're awake," she said, looking my way. I nodded. "Do you want some water?"

"Yes, thank you."

Sarah poured water from the jug into a glass and brought it to me. The winter sun had filled the room, so I saw her more clearly for the first time. She had pale blue eyes, an expansive forehead and high cheekbones. Her hair hung down in an untidy braid and she tossed it back before helping me drink. After a few sips, I lay back, wheezing.

"Riding your horse this morning hurt pretty bad," I said.

She looked at me. "That was two days ago." She rinsed the cloth in the washbasin. "You've been asleep this whole time."

"Oh."

Sarah looked at my leg. "You really must see a doctor."

"I can't do that. They'll know. And they'll send me home."

"That would be preferable to dying, I should think."

I shook my head. "No, I don't think so."

After Sarah left, I listened to the soldiers in the other rooms. The words were not clear, but they must have been in the same predicament as me. Only it wasn't the same predicament at all. After so many years of successfully making my way in the world of men, the masquerade was about to end. How I wished that it had done so on the battlefield. After Sarah returned from seeing the others, she moved a chair next to the bed and sat down.

"Look…Jennie. We must do something about your leg. It is infected and if you are to live, the bullet must come out." She paused. "It may be too late already, but we must try."

I stared at her, wavering in between who I had been and the person she now saw. "God, you really are very pretty."

"What?"

"The prettiest woman I've seen in a long time."

Sarah's expression grew tight. "Are you listening to what I'm saying?"

"You don't know me," I said, looking away. "Why should you care? You should have left me out there."

Her eyes grew wide. "What's the matter with you? I'm trying to help you."

"I told you I don't need your help."

"Oh, is that so? I'd say you rather do need my help." She took a deep breath. "But you're too stupid to see that. Maybe I *should* have left you out there. Especially since all you seem capable of is feeling sorry for yourself. There are others suffering too, you know. Some are much worse off in fact." She leaned toward me. "Since you've been a man this whole time, why don't you start acting like one?"

"Stop it! You don't know! You don't know what it was like!"

"I know enough. Too much, in fact." Sarah stood up. "My home right now is full of men, some of them dying at this very moment. I haven't slept in three days, we've almost no food, and there are no doctors, nobody period, to come out here and help. I'm willing to do what I can for you, though I have no earthly idea why, but if you refuse me one more time, I'll leave now and won't come back until we have to cart your body away." Sarah's cheeks had grown pink. "It's up to you."

I stared at her. It took a tremendous effort not to cry. "I don't know what you can do."

"The bullet must come out of your leg."

"Yes, but—"

"I will do it." With that, Sarah pulled a small knife from her dress pocket. After a moment, she took out a bottle of whiskey as well. Her voice shook. "I know it seems absurd, but I don't have any other ideas. Several men here have already died, Jennie, and with the same problem, a bullet in the leg."

I nodded. She was right, of course. "Well, then, I better have some of that," I said, pointing to the whiskey.

Sarah first cut away the bottom of my trouser leg. I was shocked to see my calf. It had swelled to double its normal size and was every shade of purple and red possible. It smelled none too good either. If the gangrene hadn't set in already, I would be surprised. I took another large sip of the drink. Sarah cleaned all around the wound. She next held the small knife she'd brought in the fire's flames, then let it cool. Finally, she found a small piece of wood and handed it to me. I put the wood in my mouth.

I nearly fainted from the pain. The small piece of wood kept me from screaming but I hadn't had enough whiskey, or waited long enough for its effects, to relieve the sensation of a knife digging into my body. A terrible smell poured out of the wound. Sarah mopped this up with a cloth, pressing on the leg to release more of the pus. I closed my eyes and heard Sarah take a ragged breath. Then she worked a finger into the opening she'd created. Flashes of light filled my vision. Tears streamed from my eyes. The only good thing to happen was that she was able to locate the bullet quickly. With a swift movement, her finger encircled it and popped it out onto the bed. I spit out the wood. After cleaning the wound again and bandaging it, Sarah sat back in the chair.

"We'll just have to see," she said. "I just don't know."

"You're very brave," I said, my teeth chattering.

Sarah wiped her eyes. "So are you." She reached over and uncurled my fingers from the bed frame.

*

That night I dreamed I was in Toulon. I went to Trickle's General Store, walked down to the banks of the Spoon River, sat with Marie in her home, and watched a show at the Waxwing Theatre. Dream realities impossible in the waking world unfolded easily: Jothan and Gardiner were alive and dead at the same time, animals spoke to me, rivers and streams flowed uphill. Also, it seemed I could fly! This made it possible for me to be at home as well as the war, and neither duty to family or country suffered.

Upon waking, I saw Sarah in the chair dozing. Outside, the snow fell in big, heavy flakes. I watched the snow and the woman, then returned to sleep. Soon, someone else came into my room. I couldn't open my eyes but heard them moving around and then sensed them trying to steal my haversack. I clung to it tightly. The person grabbed a log for the fire and tried to hit me over the head. Thrashing about, I evaded his murderous hands. Biddle! Kit! I yelled. As soon as my friends arrived, the thief/murderer ran away. Then I slept again, waking occasionally to see Biddle sitting on the edge of the bed. It was so good to see him! Where had he been this whole time, I wanted to ask, but was too tired.

*

In the morning, I heard a man's voice. He spoke Sarah's name. Then I heard someone moving around the room. I still couldn't open my eyes and now felt very afraid. The man might be from the regiment, and Sarah, of course, now knew everything. She would tell him, I was sure she would. Why had I ever trusted her? I tried to get up but someone's hand was on my arm.

"That boy all right?" the man asked.

A woman's voice said, "No, Pick, he isn't, but I've done what I could do."

"Your mama is worried, Miss Sarah. She come home this morning and no one knew where you were."

The next words were muffled. The voices frightened me. They would either reveal my magic trick, or they would just be done with it and finally murder me. Suddenly, someone spoke close to my ear.

"Jennie?"

I started to cry. "Go away! You're not my friend!"

"Jennie, it's Sarah. Remember? You were dreaming, that's all. Everything is fine."

I opened my one good eye slowly. The woman before me was no one I knew. "You're nice," I managed. "And pretty too."

She smiled faintly. "Thank you."

"I think you should post a guard," I added. "Someone is trying to steal my bag."

TWO

I FLEW back and forth several times between Toulon and where I seemed to be living now. It was tiring but I had to see Mama and Papa. I also had to make sure Sam and Ruby were all right. And Marie. I missed them all so much. I would have just stayed in Illinois, but it seemed the war needed me. Sometimes, as I flew, high above the land and the rivers and forests, I felt confused, who I was, where I should be. But then I would arrive at one location or another and all seemed well.

At some point, I stopped flying or seeing people or doing much of anything. A blissful nothingness enveloped me, and I stayed in that in between place for a long time. Then it too came to an end.

A soft ringing filled my ears. Everything in my vision moved like a bunch of puzzle pieces trying to pull themselves together. I blinked many times to clear the jumble.

"Jennie?" someone said. I nodded. After a moment, she asked, "Do you know who I am?"

"Yes," I coughed. "You're Sarah."

She looked relieved. "How do you feel?"

"I'm not sure. Tired. Sore. But all right, I think. I don't remember much."

"You've been delirious for some time."

"How long?"

"A week, I think, maybe less. I'm not sure. The time…" She stopped. "Well, I just don't know anymore."

"You look tired."

"Yes."

"Are the others still here?" She shrugged. "I have many questions."

Sarah gave a weak smile. "I have some too, but I think you better rest now."

"Will you come back?"

"Of course."

*

The days passed. I slept, and the fever lessened. Out the window of the small room I could see men who had died being carried away from the little building. Others walked around outside. They smoked or just stood, all bandaged on some part of their bodies. No one ever came in my room besides Sarah, the big man Pick, and another slave named Dora who brought food and water and firewood. On one occasion, another young white woman walked in without knocking. She set a bowl of stew on the table and stared at me, her arms crossed. When I started to say something, she left the room. Later, Sarah told me this was her younger sister Isabelle.

One night very late, I watched the snow falling. The flakes descended downward with several occasionally dashing this way or that from a winter puff of wind. I had the strangest feeling suddenly that maybe there had never been a war. How could there be a war when the snow fell so gently? A light tapping on the door broke into my thoughts. Sarah walked in.

"Jennie? I know it's late. Are you awake?"

"I'm awake."

She set a lamp on the table and looked at me. In her other hand she carried a small plate with a piece of cake on it.

"It's pumpkin bread," she said. "It's…well, it's Christmas Eve. Merry Christmas."

I sat up carefully, taking the plate. "Oh. I didn't realize. Merry Christmas."

She pulled the blanket back to look at my leg. In the days since the "surgery," my calf had shrunk back to nearly its regular size, the colors had faded, and the cut Sarah had made was closing up nicely. It seemed like a miracle; the only odd thing was that most of the calf felt numb to any touch, but in light of the pain I had felt, this didn't seem a bad thing.

"It's astonishing," she said, replacing the blanket. "Men are dying everywhere from wounds not nearly so severe. You are indeed fortunate."

"I'm fortunate you found me." When she didn't say anything, I added, "You're the nicest person I ever met."

"I'm sure that's not true."

"It is true. You've done all this. Thank you."

She shook her head. "Don't thank me, Jennie. I've only done what was right, and what everyone else in Franklin is doing. You're the one who has survived."

We sat in silence then, watching the snow. Sarah got up to add more wood to the fire. She didn't seem inclined to leave and I was glad. Her presence comforted me even if she seemed at times like someone from a dream. After eating the cake, I asked if this little building was her house. She shook her head.

"My grandparents built this place many years ago. It was where they lived while they built Ravenswood."

"Ravenswood?"

"My family's home. What they built when they first came to Tennessee." She paused, looking around. "I haven't spent so much time here in years as I have the last few weeks."

"Are they still alive, your grandparents?"

"No, and I'm glad of it," she said, quickly. "That is, I am glad they are not here to see what has happened. To our family, friends. To our land."

"Why—"

She stood up. "I should go."

"Please don't go. I mean, it's Christmas."

Tears suddenly fell down her cheeks. "I am glad you're better, Jennie. You must get home to your family, to your mother. I will help you if I can."

"You already have helped me."

She picked up the lamp. "Good night."

"Good night."

*

In early January, Sarah told me about the battle in Nashville. It had occurred in mid-December after both armies had left Franklin. After two days of fighting, the Southern army retreated south in a chaotic tangle of scattered regiments, broken equipment, and thousands of dispirited and wounded men. They roared through Franklin like a flooding river, followed closely by the Federal forces. It was mayhem once again for the little village as the Northerners took over the town a second time, rounding up any Confederates they could find and confiscating anything they felt they needed. I could tell Sarah wasn't telling me all she knew, but I didn't ask any questions. I knew what towns looked like after the blackness of war had overtaken them. I knew what men were capable of, and even worse, what masses of soldiers were capable of. I knew how you became another person when you became part of an army. How you sometimes weren't even like a person anymore, but more like one little part in a vast machine, the workings of which became more mysterious the longer the time went on.

For my own part, I began to worry how I was ever going to find the regiment again, and I still had no idea what had happened to Biddle or the others. I didn't know if they'd survived, or if they, too, were in someone's home in Franklin right now being cared for. For all I knew, Kit or Biddle or any of them might have been on the other side of the wall from me. I hadn't mentioned my friends to Sarah; part of me didn't want to know what had happened to them.

Some days later, the black woman Dora came to my room and

224

found me burning up with fever. She immediately fetched Sarah.

"You are warm," she agreed, feeling my forehead.

"I felt fine yesterday," I said, my teeth chattering.

She nodded. "Yes. Others are ill too. It's the winter ague."

Sarah returned that afternoon with broth and a bit of bread, but I could eat nothing. She bathed my face with cold cloths and kept the fire high even though I asked her not to. The days crept by. I slept but it was a difficult rest. Dreams of home and people there mixed with my soldier friends and Mississippi and the terrible, terrible things that I'd seen. One night I awoke and immediately start throwing up. Sarah was in the room. There was nothing in my stomach for this, so I wretched while she held the pot. After it was over, I lay back in the bed.

"This is it," I told her. "I can't do it anymore."

Sarah sat on the bed. "After all I've done for you? I think not." She attempted a smile.

I looked at her. "It seems like forever that I've been in this room."

"All the more reason then to get through this, so you can leave soon." Sarah paused. "If it makes you feel any better, it seems forever to me that you've been here."

I nodded. "That does make me feel better."

When the fever finally broke for good, I felt hollow and exhausted. I had no sense of the time and my memory was a cloud of impressions rather than specific events. One morning, I limped to the window and sat in the chair. Fresh snow had covered everything, even the path that extended from this building up a hill toward a much larger manor house. A raven hopped around, its feet sinking into the fluff. It probed in the snow with its long, thick bill, turning one way and then another to look for morsels. One of the bird's wings stuck out at a slightly odd angle; it had a patch of gray feathers behind its head. Suddenly, it noticed me. The bird hopped toward the building, then flapped upward onto a branch hanging close to the window. At least, it could still fly with the funny wing. The two of us were regarding each other when Sarah arrived.

"You're out of bed," she said.

"Yes, finally. I was just sitting here watching that raven."

Sarah walked over and looked out the window. "That's Gideon."

"Gideon?"

"Yes. He's, well, he's kind of a pet you might say. My grandfather began taking care of Gideon when the bird was young and had nearly been killed by a coyote. Papa fed him and talked to him and ever since the bird has been devoted to our family." She paused. "I've not seen Gideon for some days and had been wondering if was all right."

We watched the raven watching us, the bold eye, inquisitive and knowing, like a window into the animal's soul yet revealing little we humans could understand. I thought about the many times I'd gone ice fishing on the Spoon River. When I was with my brothers, the ravens always kept their distance, but when I was alone, they'd come right up to me. Of course, offering to share my lunch assured them of my good intentions.

"I like ravens," I said.

Sarah nodded. "They are interesting, aren't they? Before my grandfather passed, he and Gideon were very close and the bird followed him everywhere. Even stranger, he learned to imitate Papa. Once I was down here and heard someone calling my name. "Sarah! Sarah!" it said, and then, "Come home!" I didn't see anyone, but when I walked around the building, there was the raven." She stopped. "It seemed impossible, so I never told anyone. But there were other occasions too when I heard him talking."

"It doesn't seem impossible to me," I said, knowing that ravens were smarter than the average bird.

Suddenly, I felt exhausted. Sarah helped me back into the bed. She asked me if I wanted to have a bath. Pick would bring the washtub down and fill it with water if I did.

"I expect I rather need one, don't I?"

"I just thought it might feel good. Since you seem better."

"Yes, it would. Thank you."

Later, after Pick had brought and filled the tub, Sarah returned and handed me a pair of trousers and a white blouse.

"These are my brother's. I think they'll fit you. I've cleaned your coat as best I could, but I think your other clothes should be discarded."

I couldn't disagree. I'd been wearing the same trousers since shortly after the Vicksburg siege and the blouse, owing to its now threadbare look, revealed more of my body than was safe. Still, it was no small matter to wear a Confederate boy's clothes. Robert Taylor, in fact, would never have agreed to it. But Jennie Edwards had fewer choices. I gratefully accepted her offer.

It took some doing, from getting undressed to settling in the tub to getting back out again. Sarah helped me, providing assistance I wasn't entirely comfortable with but needed nonetheless. An hour later, when I collapsed back on the bed, clean and wearing fresh clothes, I felt better than I had in weeks.

∗

Several days later, Sarah appeared in my room with a Federal officer. I attempted to salute and get out of the bed at the same time.

"Sit, private," the man said, smiling. "You may be allowed this once to salute from your bed."

"Yes, sir." I looked at Sarah, who gave a nervous shrug.

The officer pulled the chair up to the bed and sat down. "I am Major William Casing," he said. "Sarah tells me you've had a time of it these past weeks."

"No more so than others, sir."

"Yes, well, there have been some lively times. I am sorry to not have seen you sooner."

"I'm sure you've had more important things to do, sir. Truthfully, if not for Sarah I would be quite dead and buried by now. Then there'd be no need to be sorry."

He nodded. The major, handsome with a mop of curly, blond

hair, bright blue eyes, and a thick mustache, looked thoughtful.

"Sarah and her family have helped many of our boys. Which regiment are you with?" I told him and he pursed his lips. "You were in the thick of it then."

"Yes, sir."

Major Casing related what he knew at present about the 72nd Illinois. After Nashville, the regiment had headed to Corinth, Mississippi, and then back downriver to Cairo. There'd been skirmishes here and there, but nothing so severe as the Tennessee battles. He scratched the stubble on his chin. "I'm not certain but believe they may be along the coast now." Major Casing stood up. "I must go. Get better, private, and we will see about getting you back to your regiment."

"Thank you, sir."

Sarah left with the major. I heard her taking him to see the other soldiers in the building. Then out of the window, I saw her walk him up to the big house. A little while later she returned.

"How did you do that?" she asked.

"Do what?"

"Make him believe that you're a boy?"

I shrugged. "I didn't do anything. I just let him believe what he assumes to be true."

"But I don't understand." Sarah looked out the window. "How could he not see?"

I thought. "It's kind of like a magic trick, I suppose."

"A magic trick?"

I nodded. "If someone does magic, say like making an object, or even a person, disappear, those things haven't *really* disappeared. It only *seems* like they have."

"What?" She looked confused. "But you aren't—I mean—you haven't disappeared."

"I think I have actually. In a way, that is."

Sarah shook her head. "I still don't understand."

"Sit down. I'll show you something." I reached into my haversack, took out my bandana, and slowly began stuffing the cloth into one fist. When I was done and had waited a few seconds, I opened my fist. The bandana was gone!

Sarah's mouth fell open. She reached toward my hand. "How did you do that?"

Extending my arm downward, a small, wooden cup fell out of my sleeve. Inside was the cloth. She still looked puzzled, so I explained and also showed her how I'd had the cup in my fist when I began stuffing the bandana away. Then when she wasn't looking, I'd slipped the cup inside my sleeve and presto, my hand was now empty.

"But I was watching your hand the whole time," she shook her head. "You couldn't have moved a cup from it to your sleeve."

I smiled. "You *thought* you were watching my hand the whole time. In fact, you weren't."

"What? Of course, I was. Besides, how do you know where I was looking?"

"I just do. That's how magic works. You don't even know you've been distracted, but you have. Afterward, your mind believes what your eyes *think* they've seen, but the truth is your eyes missed it all."

Sarah crossed her arms and sat back in the chair. "Are you a magician?"

I put the cup and bandana back in my haversack. "Yes. That is, I was learning to be one. Before the war, I mean. My friend, he's the magician. I'm just...well, I'm not sure what I am now."

"Tell me how this explains your passing for a man."

"Do you plan on turning me in?"

She looked surprised. "No."

"I'm not sure I can explain it any better than how I already have. People see what they want to see. They see what they already believe. So, with the conjure I just showed you, if you start out believing that my fist is empty, which is a perfectly normal thing to believe, then you'll always believe it was empty. It will never occur to you to think otherwise." I rubbed my face. "So, I have no beard, right?"

"Of course not."

I nodded. "Yet, no one thinks, "Oh, she might be a girl." They just think, "He hasn't begun to shave yet." Similarly, I can't just stand around somewhere relieving myself like the other boys, so I go off by myself to do such things. No one wonders, "Why doesn't he use the sinks like everyone else?" They just think, "He's rather shy." And on it goes. My feet are small." I shrugged. "He's got small feet. My hands? People don't even notice. Fortunately, I'm taller than most girls and have a small bosom, which wrapping has taken care of. Really, it's no more complicated than that. Most people don't imagine very much, and therefore, they don't see very much either."

Sarah nodded slowly. Then, coloring slightly, she asked, "What about your monthlies?"

"Ah, yes, those. They just stopped. A long time ago."

"Truly? How can that be?"

"I don't know. It's the one thing I don't understand. Who knows? Maybe it was just being around all those men."

Sarah thought for a minute. "I've never met anyone quite like you, Jennie. You're very clever."

I shook my head. "I don't know about that. I used to think I was clever."

"But not now?"

"No."

"Does your family know about this? Do they know where you are?"

"My father does. At least, he knew when I was in Vicksburg. My mother, well, she thinks I'm in Chicago being a magician."

Sarah considered this. "That's probably for the best. Sometimes it's better not to know too much."

"Yes," I said, not wanting to think about my mother, "I think so too."

THREE

I HAD TWO thick bundles of letters in my haversack. One was from Katherine Biddle to her brother, the letters he'd asked me to safeguard before the battle. The other was a packet of unopened missives from Marie. After reading the first letter she'd sent me, which had arrived in Kentucky some months after my departure from Chicago, I'd left the rest unread. That's not to say that I didn't write to my friend. In fact, she was the person I wrote to most. It was more that I just couldn't bear to read her sadness and loneliness on the page. I'd made my choice and I was determined. My success keeping my identity secret depended in part on me not succumbing to sentimentality.

Now, however, as I still recovered but felt well enough to become bored just lying in bed all day, I brought all the letters out. Perhaps it had to do with being around Sarah, another woman, or maybe it was just my exhaustion, but I began to allow myself the comfort of missing Marie. If I couldn't see her, at least I could hear her words, painful as they might be. I started from the beginning and the one letter I knew:

November 18, 1862
My dearest Jennie,
To say that I am shocked would not do justice to my feelings at the

moment. Mother and I have just returned from Chicago where we saw Owl one afternoon and he informed us that you'd gone for a soldier! Of course, we thought he was joking. Too soon, however, we saw he wasn't and we listened as he explained. Oh, Jennie, how could you? And why? Owl is most distressed, Mother is beside herself, and I am, as stated above, shocked and deeply worried. I still can barely believe it, though the other day I remembered that Jothan had told me long ago that you'd wanted to go with him and Gardiner when they'd left. Now, it seems, you have done it.

Oh, Jennie, I cry so much. For Jothan and Gardiner, for my baby who has no father, for the other Toulon boys whose names are printed every few months in the newspaper. And now I must worry over you as well. Please do come home! I simply could not bear to lose you too.

Marie

January 15, 1863
Dearest Jennie,

Your letter is my only comfort. I read it many times the other night. Then the next morning I went to Galesburg to see your father. I told Graham he must write to the colonel of your regiment and tell him who you really are. I said this was too dangerous what you had done, that it was wrong, and so forth, however, to my great surprise, he was not inclined to do so. He said that after you'd written and told him what you'd done, he knew there would be nothing to stop you. Your father said that should you be exposed and dismissed, you would only find another regiment. For now, at least, you are not in the thick of it and that is where he prefers you to stay. I was most unhappy with this position. I told Graham that if he would not write your colonel, then I would.

Jennie, your family needs you more than the war. Julia is improving, or, at least, not getting worse. She still speaks little though and is unbearably sad; what would it do to her to lose another child? I feel it selfish of you to do this, but your father has mixed feelings on that point. He says that he and your mother would not be able to stay in Galesburg without the money you have sent. I am sure this is true though will the contribution be worth the possible cost of losing you?

Please come home, Jen. If something happens to you, I don't know what I shall do.

232

All my love, Marie

I returned this letter to its envelope, wondering if I should go on. As expected, Marie's sadness pained me greatly. If I had read this when it first came, I might have returned home. If I had returned home, then there would have been no money to help Mama. Besides, what would I have done there? It had grown harder during the years away to remember my life before becoming a soldier. That time was filled with some people who no longer lived and problems that made no sense to me now.

The next letter had been written in the spring. Marie didn't mention any more about exposing me to the colonel. Instead, the bulk of this correspondence described my niece, now a lively one-year-old.

Jen-Jen is walking and into most everything. She is full of sand, that girl, wobbling after birds and butterflies in the garden and turning over every rock and piece of wood looking for animals. On one unusually warm day in February, she found a spotted salamander near Mother's pond in the garden. The funny creature must have emerged from its burrow due to the sunny day. We spent a long while looking at it then drew some pictures of its wonderful dark body and spots.

She is very precocious, Jennie. Many people tell me they're surprised she is not yet one and already walking so much, talking up a storm, and even drawing pictures that reflect the skill of a much older child. Of course, I am terribly proud. Jen Jen does seem unusually gifted and smart; she must have gotten that from your side of the family! Certainly she looks so much like Jothan, having inherited his dark, curly hair and bright, blue eyes. It is a blessing for it makes me feel he is not so far away.

Later that summer, Marie wrote of the great celebration in Toulon over the fall of Vicksburg. There were fireworks and a town picnic and all felt hopeful that the war would end soon. It seemed that only Marie, Mr. Trickle, and my father knew of my true whereabouts; everyone else believed me in Chicago, so there was no hopeful talk of "when Jennie would be home," a common sentiment for other Toulon soldiers.

Marie kept busy working for her father, doing bookkeeping and organizing his appointments and court dates. She also was helping Mrs. McRae to set up the fall meetings of the Toulon Literary Society. During the early weeks of summer, my mother had returned home.

Julia is much improved, Jennie, and I believe being at home will further her recovery. She is thin and looks much older, but she is talking again and appears interested in resuming her life. It is true that she never speaks of Gardiner and Jothan, but then many of us don't as their deaths are too painful to discuss. Along with your parents, Sam and Ruby are also returned to Jug Run Creek (they are well!). As you can imagine, there is much to do on the farm. The two men who were renting the land are now gone and in their place, your father has hired an ex-soldier, a man Washington Trickle met at the store and who also needed work. Amos is from New York and was serving with the 25th Infantry from that state when he lost an arm in battle and was made to return home. He apparently had little or no family to return home to, so decided to head west. Amos told your father that by the time he got to Toulon his money was gone. I met him only briefly, but he seems a nice man, a bit shy, but diligent in his efforts. Your father appreciates his help.

The next several letters mentioned Toulon gossip and the many goings-on about town, reminding me of the kind of news I had sent to my brothers once. I appreciated hearing about the ordinary events of everyday life: Washington Trickle's spoiling of Jen-Jen and her delight at his wild beard with "all the things in it"; Council McRae's fall from a ladder and Bertha's subsequent tiring of waiting on her husband during his recovery; the first snowfall in early October; new businesses starting up or shutting down; and finally, an interesting change taking place around the stove at Trickle's. It seemed that women now made up the majority of sitters and drinkers of coffee there. Marie wrote that this began with the ladies sewing circle needing a place to meet while work was being done on Mrs. McRae's parlor.

Mrs. Trickle suggested the back room at the store and all quickly agreed. The days were turning colder and the warm seats around the stove would be welcome. After the first meeting, the following morning several ladies returned to the store to do their shopping. First, however, they felt a cup of coffee would be nice. The couple of men sitting at the stove were surprised and not a little disquieted apparently. They spoke to Washington about it, but the women kept on sitting during the ensuing days, with the result that there's been no room for the men. I confess, Jennie, I'm rather enjoying this! I've sat at the stove a few times too. Of course, there had never been a rule before that women couldn't sit there. It just was assumed, by the men at least, to be an area reserved for them.

This amusing story contrasted sharply with what Marie told me next about our friend, Adam.

Adam is at present returned on a furlough. Elijah Ward fell and broke his leg and so Adam was able to secure the furlough for a few weeks to help his mother and sisters. Truthfully, Jen, he does not seem well. He is thin, his face has lines reminiscent of a much older man, and he is easily distracted. He also apologizes to me repeatedly for what happened at Pittsburg Landing, believing apparently that Jothan and Gardiner's deaths were his fault in some way. Of course, he desperately hoped to see you while home. When I told him where you'd gone, he could not believe it. It seems I have grown used to you being away, but for Adam it was too much. He is to leave in a couple of days and I fear for him; he seems oddly fragile.

Marie wrote more about working for her father and how much she loved it, the getting out and interacting with people, as well as the financial recordkeeping and managing of appointments. Once she had thought Caleb Parker's work painfully dull; now it seemed endlessly fascinating, and her job filled her days with a sense of purpose. She'd also accompanied her father recently to Chicago. There she'd worked with Oliver Timmons on library research and interviews and Marie wrote that she now saw why Jothan had been so interested in the law. "The framework is all there," she said, "for a just society, though of course it also is unavoidable that there will be imbalance, with means such as connections and money providing more support for some." While in the big city, Marie had also seen Owl and Carmen, who were well, and she and Mr. and Mrs. Allenton attended one of their shows. It was the best she'd seen yet, Marie wrote.

Too soon, I found myself opening the last letter from my friend. It was dated September 15, 1864, just a few weeks before we'd left Vicksburg.

Dearest Jennie,

The autumn days and cooler weather have found us at last, and I am not sorry! I can't remember a warmer summer…well, perhaps I can but not in recent memory. At all rates, I am glad to be able to sleep better and get through a day without feeling soaked in the wetness of my own sweat.

Still, any problem I have with the heat is at most an inconvenience, is it not? I must tell you, Jen, that Adam is now returned for good. The regiment had been near Florence, Alabama, and during severe fighting along the Tennessee River in early May, Adam was wounded in the leg. The doctors there had told him it was beyond saving. He protested greatly to an amputation. He said he'd rather die a man than live a cripple's life. The next thing he knew, however, he was waking up in a hospital with a bloody bandage and stump where his leg had once been. Mercifully, he remembered nothing of the operation.

After being discharged, Adam arrived here in late July on the cars from Chicago. He has crutches but doesn't use them so goes nowhere beyond his home. Sometimes, I have visited him in their garden. Adam does not talk much, but I attempt to make conversation enough for the both of us. If I bring Jen-Jen, she also supplies her own chatter. Mr. Trickle is at work ordering a wooden leg for him, a task not hard these days owing to the great demand. Still, I fear Adam's melancholy is stronger than a wooden leg can cure. He sees nothing left for himself in this life.

He asked once what I had heard from you, and I told him what I knew. Oh, Jennie, this insufferable war! It exacts its toll in lives lost, and then further chips away at the shadows of lives that remain. I fear being overcome by a bitterness that is so large; the only thing that keeps me anchored to hope, however small that hope may be, is that I must set an example of love for my daughter. Soon enough, she will learn how much suffering there is in this world. Until then, I want to help her feel strong so that she may withstand the worst, while praying the worst (apart from losing her father) never comes to my dear, sweet child.

I shall write more soon, my dear. You are ever in my thoughts. You will have noticed I sent no letter to your colonel. Thus, you must promise me you'll stay safe. Indeed, the other night I dreamed of your return, which left me glad the whole next day. I know we shall see each other again.

Your very dear friend, Marie

*

The day after reading Marie's letters, I felt desperate to leave Sarah's little cabin. I wasn't sure how long I'd been there, but it seemed like forever. My foot and ankle remained remarkably numb, however with the aid of a hefty stick I could walk slowly.

I made my way outside, then began down a path that headed toward the river. The bright, winter sun upon the snow made my eyes water but the cold winter air felt like a tonic. The effort of walking barely 50 feet made my legs shake. Through the leafless trees, I could see the river, its slow waters carefully inching along. Though I had wanted to make it to the banks, I opted for sitting on a log some distance away.

I took out Marie's letters again and had just begun rereading them when a shadow fell across my lap.

"What are you doing out here, Jennie?" asked Sarah, sounding much as she did the morning I'd tried escaping. "You're not well!"

I put the letters away. "Well enough, I should think."

"You look pale."

"That's because I've been inside for months."

Sarah sat down on the log next to me. "That's an exaggeration. It's only been a few weeks." I looked at her. "All right, almost three months. Still, I think you should rest."

"I am resting. I was a bit out of breath walking just this little way, but now I am fine. I must get stronger if I'm to return to my regiment."

She nodded, looking toward the river. "Yes, I suppose that's true."

As we sat, the staccato calls of a kingfisher carried up from the water. Then a bulky splash indicated the bird's attempt at a fish. I looked carefully toward the sound but we were too far away to see much. After a moment, I asked Sarah why she had done all she had done these last weeks.

"I mean, there are many Federal soldiers still here," I said. "You and your family have been taking care of us for months. It seems surprising."

"Because we are Southerners?"

"Well, yes, I suppose so."

"You'd think we should have been glad to leave you out in that field to die?" She shook her head. "That would be a terrible thing to do."

"And yet a lot of terrible things happen in a war."

She nodded, picking up a dried leaf and twirling it in her fingers. "My oldest brother was killed more than two years ago. It's been some months since I've heard from my other two brothers. I fear the worst and hope for the best. This is surely what other sisters, and mothers and daughters, in the north must also be fearing and hoping for." She paused. "I don't know, Jennie. Around every moment of every day, I feel bitterness so complete that if I gave into it, I should never be without it. But I mustn't of course. There are my sisters, my parents, friends, all of whom need me to be strong. Still, there are days…" Her voice trailed off.

I didn't say anything. It would be easier if she hated me.

Sarah looked at me. "You wish I hated you."

My face grew warm. "What makes you say that?"

"It's true, isn't it?"

"Are *you* a magician?"

"Hardly. It's not so surprising, is it? Strong opinions are more easily held when tremendous hate or anger support them. Can I ask you something?"

"Sure," I said, not at all sure that I wanted someone so smart asking me anything.

"Why are you here? That is, why did you do what you did, dress as a man, go for a soldier? Did you live as a man before the war?"

I coughed. "Now that's a thought! No, I didn't live as a man before. I suppose I'd like to think I left because it was the right thing to do. That it's not right to keep people in bondage, that all men deserve to be free, that I would not like that for myself, so why should another like it."

"You sound very noble and principled."

I colored again. Why did she have to be so calm? "Perhaps, but I only said I'd like to *think* that was the reason. The truth is that both my brothers also died at Pittsburg Landing." I shrugged. "After that, I couldn't bear to be at home any longer."

Sarah looked at me as if studying some strange animal she'd just come upon. At last, she said, "I admire you, Jennie. Part of me wishes that I'd done what you've done. Part of me wishes I was more like you. But yes, I also feel upset you're here. However, my father is a Northern sympathizer. Such a position has made our family pariahs in town but it has also stood us in good stead with Major Casing. We've been protected in some measure and able to live through the occupation in relative comfort. Yet, there's been a cost."

I nodded slowly. "You're right, of course, except for one thing."

"What's that?"

"You definitely shouldn't wish you were more like me. You may wish many things, but please don't wish that."

*

The next morning, as I sat on the bed and considered going out again, the big man Pick walked into my room. He set a plate of hoecake and a cup of grain coffee on the table.

"I seen you yesterday, boy. Seen you with Miss Sarah, sitting above the river."

I nodded. "Yes, that's so."

He breathed deeply. "Essie tell me she think Sarie like you. That you like her too."

I shook my head. "No, it's nothing like that. I mean, yes, she's very kind. But—"

"But I tell Essie," he continued, "that she crazy. Why would Sarie like the very devils that come and destroy her home? It make no sense t'all. But now, since I seen with my own eyes, I think maybe she be right." The man's cold stare grew colder.

"I don't think you have to worry," I said, my voice a bit higher than I liked.

He nodded. "No, I ain't got to worry 'cause I tell you right now that you even *think* about touching that girl, it even cross your mind one time, and I come find you. They hang any nigger, sure, that kill a Yankee soldier, but I do it all the same. You hear me?"

I swallowed. "I hear you."

"Good."

He left without another word. I sat there for a long while, my appetite quite gone. As the coffee grew cold, I tried to imagine what the man thought he was seeing.

FOUR

THAT NIGHT I awoke suddenly. It seemed there'd been a noise, but as I lay there I heard nothing more. I had nearly fallen asleep again when someone clearly shouted. Pulling on my trousers, I grabbed the walking stick and went out into the dogtrot. The snores of the other men could be heard, but otherwise all seemed normal. Then I heard the cry again.

The position of the moon in the sky cast a yellow glow on Ravenswood's grounds. Down the hill from the manor house stood many buildings, including barns, storerooms and springhouses, and many small cabins for the plantation's slaves. Before the war, it all must have been an impressive enterprise. Now the foundation for success, the people, seemed to mostly have gone.

More than one voice carried on the gentle breeze. I could see people standing at the entrance to the big house. I walked closer then dropped to the ground behind a hedge of roses.

"We got no truck with you, missus," a man with a gravelly tone was saying, "though we know y'all is Yankee lovers. Best just let us be if you don't want no trouble."

A woman laughed sarcastically. "I would say that since you are trespassing on my land, I already have trouble." The speaker wasn't Sarah or her sister, so I wondered if it was her mother, a person I had never seen. She continued, "If you and your men don't want your own trouble, I'd suggest you turn around now and leave immediately."

The man snorted. "Me and the fellas ain't looking for trouble. We just come on some hard times is all. We don't need much. Just three horses would be great, and whatever coins or silver you got laid up. Then we'll go. Won't bother you no more."

"You talk mighty polite, sir, but you are dumber than an ox if you think we still have any of those things. There is a war on, or perhaps you didn't know? Perhaps you've been too busy avoiding the fight to notice?"

One of the men laughed. "Shut up, Bushrod," said the leader. Then, "We ain't got time for this. Either you get us what we need, or we'll just start taking whatever strikes us." He paused. "Including maybe these pretty little girls you got there by your side."

At the mention of her daughters, Sarah's mother moved down the steps toward the men. Sarah and Isabelle next emerged more fully from the shadows. They walked slowly behind their mother wearing night coats and scarves and must have been sleeping when they first heard the intruders outside. When she wasn't but a few feet from the three men, the older woman raised one arm.

"I'm telling you one last time: leave now, sir."

"Or what? You'll hurt me with your little toy gun? That wouldn't drop a squirrel. 'Sides, you've only got a single shot. You can't kill all of us."

Sarah's mother spoke slowly. "That's true. But the fact is I don't have to kill all of you." She pulled back the hammer. "I just have to kill you."

Silence. The two followers started mumbling how it wasn't worth it and it was getting on toward morning and that they should just leave. His men's faltering gave the leader the excuse he needed to back away and not have the decision appear to be his. Additionally, noise from the slave cabins could now be heard.

"All right, we'll go," the man said. "For now. But we'll be back, missus. To see you and your daughters."

The other two had already headed apace back down the path that wound out to the pike, and now the leader left too. Isabelle put her face in her hands and started crying; Sarah went to her mother. Mrs. Hawkins didn't lower the gun until the three dark forms had vanished entirely.

"Do you think they'll return, Mother?" Sarah asked, her voice shaking.

"No. They wanted to steal if it was easy. But when it wasn't going to be easy, they were only too happy to give up."

"Would you have really killed that man?"

Her mother uncocked the pistol and lowered her arm. "I would have, Sarah. I would have, and I wouldn't have thought a thing about it."

*

The next morning, the slave woman Dora brought me breakfast. When I asked after Sarah, she said the mistress was sleeping late. After a moment, she offered that there had been a disturbance in the night that had kept everyone awake. I nodded. When she turned to leave, I stopped her.

"Dora?"

"Yes, suh?"

"Can I ask you a question?"

She nodded. "I expect you can ask."

"Why are you still here? I mean…you are free after all."

She looked surprised despite having a face that appeared well versed in not showing her true feelings. "Mama and Pick here," she said, simply. "So I stay too." She added, "For now."

"But why? I should think—"

"This is their home." Dora crossed her arms and I got the feeling she didn't consider Ravenswood *her* home. "Can I ask you something, suh?"

"Yes."

"Why *you* still here?"

"Oh." I looked away. "I suppose it's easier to stay than to

leave." Embarrassed, my voice dropped off. "I think I'm tired of leaving…"

Dora considered this. "You a funny boy. Mama and Pick worry that Miss Sarah like you. That something might start up."

"Yes," I said, feeling strange that they all had been talking about me. "Pick told me. They don't have to worry though."

Dora smiled. "That's good."

*

I started taking long walks along the river every day. I *should* have been gone already, but what I told Dora was the truth: it was easier to stay. I didn't want to go back to the war, and, desperate as I was to see Marie, going home didn't appeal either. The excuse that my leg and foot still didn't have complete feeling, and that the winter weather made travel difficult, seemed good enough to justify my continuing to take advantage of Sarah's kindness. Fortunately, too, the major hadn't returned to check on my progress.

One afternoon, I found Sarah sitting on a rock along the river bank. She was wearing a pale peach day dress beneath her cape and had removed her hat. Her hair hung down unbraided, and she appeared more relaxed than I'd seen her before. The day was bright with sun, and warm, and the snow had started melting in a few places. Jays and cardinals flew like shots through the trees; smaller birds scuffled among the fallen leaves. Spring would soon be here and the weather would improve. There soon would be no more excuses for me not to leave.

"You are walking much better," Sarah said, looking up and not altogether surprised, it seemed, to see me.

"Yes," I said, easing down gently on another rock next to her. "I am better, I think. Good enough to leave soon, I expect."

She didn't say anything. I told her then that I had observed everything with the men the other night. "You must tell Major Casing about this, Sarah, if you haven't already. He will send men to protect you. That is the Federal Army's job after all, to protect civilians."

"Yes," she nodded. "So they say."

I noticed Sarah held a piece of paper in her lap. When I asked what it was, she said it was a newspaper article from early in the war about a woman soldier. She had cut it out and kept it in a box these last two years.

"She was discovered and sent home immediately," Sarah explained, looking at the article. "I have read this every now and then and have often thought about this woman. "Did she join up again? I wondered. Was she successful? Is she still alive? Of course, I will never know the answers."

"Can I see?"

The article was from the *Nashville Daily Press*, dated January 21, 1862. It was a long story about a young woman who had arrived with her regiment in Tennessee's capital, ready to serve her country, but ultimately denied. The details of the exposure seemed less important to the authors of the article than the woman's motives, which they characterized alternately as unfathomable, debased, and romantic (she must have followed a lover off to war, mustn't she have?). The story concluded encouragingly with the woman's return to "appropriate dress" and a hope for recovery from the "ill" that had first propelled her to take such action.

"I am sorry she was treated that way," I said, handing the clipping back.

Sarah nodded. "Yes, I am too. Men seem to believe they know what women are thinking more than the women themselves. I have never understood this."

"No."

"There have been other articles since this one," she continued. "Especially early in the war, many women were making the attempt. If they were written about in the paper, it meant they were discovered. In most cases, the editors said little beyond ridiculing them."

Something in Sarah's tone struck me. "Did you think of going?" I asked.

"Of course. We all wanted to support our country, that is, my friends and I. But then...we didn't. I regret it now, truly." She put the article in her pocket then reached for my hand. "Jennie, I don't want you to go back. To the war, I mean." Tears filled her eyes. "It is lost, of course, for the South. People don't want to believe that, but it's true. I should think it will not be many more months. Please don't risk being killed at this late hour. For your sake and for your family's sake." She kept hold of my hand, looking at me.

"Truthfully?" I said, enjoying the feel of her hand in mine. "I don't want to go either, but I am a soldier, Sarah, or have been at all rates. If I am determined a deserter, they will shoot me if they find me."

"You won't be determined a deserter because you simply will go home. Away from here, away from the war. You may not like to, but if you put on a dress and return to your old life, you'll at least be safe. Please, Jennie, I don't want to see you hurt again." She looked out across the river. "The thing too is that Major Casing has been asking after the remaining soldiers here. I have put him off saying you were all still too weak. But I won't be able to do that for much longer."

"I see."

Sarah looked at me then pulled her hand away. "I barely know you, of course, but I suspect you won't do as I ask. And if that's the case, I will tell the major who you really are."

"You don't mean that."

"I assure you, I most certainly do mean it."

"But—"

"No, I could not live with myself if anything were to happen. This is how it must be."

"But the article?"

She didn't answer and instead stood up. "Walk back with me, Jennie."

I thought about Pick and his promise. "Maybe we shouldn't, Sarah. It might give people the wrong idea."

"About what?"

"Don't forget everyone else sees me as a man. They might think that," I colored, "well, that something is going on with us."

246

"But that's absurd!"

I had already guessed that Sarah wasn't the kind of person who cared at all for what people thought, and so my reluctance only inspired her determination. We walked upstream along a well-worn path, far from the eyes and ears of the plantation. At first, the conversation felt awkward, but then she asked me about my home. To my surprise, the stories of my old life tumbled out easily, even happily, and she only seemed more interested as I talked. I asked her, too, of her life before the war. She told me she had just graduated from the Tennessee Normal College that spring when the first shots were fired. She loved her studies, her teachers, everything about school. She had hoped to travel to France that summer and see one of her teachers, but everything changed after Fort Sumter. I told her she should go when it was all over, that she *must* go.

"Yes," she said, "I think so too."

At that moment, with her expression reflecting the ordinary dreams of a young woman and not the burden of war, Sarah looked most lovely indeed. If I had been a man, I would have kissed her right then. But I wasn't a man and for all that had brought us together, there was still more that separated us. So, I didn't do anything besides smile. Then we turned around and headed back.

*

That night, a knock on my door was followed by Sarah entering the room. A few snowflakes rested on her hood and the back of her cape.

"Hello, Jennie."

"Hello. You look cold."

"It is cold. Another storm is moving in. There are already a few inches of new snow." She sat down on the bed. "Sometimes I think this winter will never end."

"You don't have to think that. It already is ending. Just this evening, I saw two eagles playing in the sky. They only do that when they're about to start sitting on the nest, which is a sure sign of spring."

"That's true."

Sarah then pulled a small leather bag out of her pocket and changed the subject. "I am very worried, Jennie. I am worried that you are not going to get home."

"Of all the things to worry about, Sarah, I don't think you should spend time on that."

"I want you to have these," she said, opening up the bag. Several gold coins fell onto the bed.

"What is this?"

"Money I have been saving." She picked up one coin. "Before the war, I wrote some stories for the newspaper, as well as one magazine, and was paid for them. It's the only money I have ever earned. In those days, I had no need of it and so I just put it in this bag and tucked it away. By the time I had need, there was nothing to buy." Sarah gathered the coins up and returned them to the bag. "Take these, Jennie, with my blessing. Get yourself home."

"Oh, Sarah."

"Please don't argue with me."

"Why do you think I'd argue?" She smiled. "How is it these haven't been stolen?"

"I'll bet you can guess. Being a magician and all."

I thought. "I'd say they were either out in plain sight, and for that reason no one saw them. Or, they were simply hidden in a most unlikely spot, a place no one would ever think to look."

"The latter," she nodded. "I gave them to Essie and Pick and they've kept the money, as well as all our silver, under the floorboards in their cabin."

"You are very generous, Sarah. Truly, I owe you my life. But I can't take your money. As you said, the war will be over soon. You are going to need this."

"The war will be over soon, but there will still be nothing to buy. Besides, we will figure that out then. You need this now." She put the bag in my hand, closed my fingers around it, keeping her hand on mine. "This is what you will do, Jennie. First, take a steamship from Nashville to Cairo. I have a friend who can get you there, and we'll ride into town in the morning to meet him."

"In the morning? So soon?"

"From Cairo, there are the cars to Chicago, which you know well from having traveled them before. It will not take long and you will not have trouble booking passage." When I didn't say anything, her tone became stern. "Don't even think of telling me you're going back to your regiment."

"No, I'm not thinking of going back to the regiment." This was true; just that morning I had fully decided what I must do next. "It's only that..." I felt my face growing warm. "I don't really want to leave is all. I suppose I will miss you."

"Yes," she nodded, "I will miss you too." She sighed. "Oh, Jennie, you are the oddest girl. I confess at times you make me feel odd too."

We looked at each other. Sarah reached over and touched my cheek. I didn't think about it this time. I leaned forward and kissed her. At first, she didn't respond. But then she tentatively kissed me back. And then she pulled away. It was all over before I knew it.

"Oh, Sarah, I'm so sorry. I didn't mean to do that. Truly."

She put her arms around my waist. "Just hold me, Jennie."

FIVE

SARAH RETURNED to the cabin early the next morning. I had already packed my things and was sitting in the chair when she arrived. My stomach churned at the thought of leaving, but Sarah was right, I might miss my chance if I didn't go now. Yet, there was no war here, at least for the moment, and for the first time in more than two years I had felt like myself. When I walked out of the door, I'd return to being Robert Taylor, a person I felt less enthusiastic about now than the first time I'd met him.

We rode into town as the eastern sky began to change color. I wrapped my arms around Sarah's waist and leaned into her. A screech owl trilled from high in a tree. Far in the distance, a wolf howled. The fresh snow made everything lighter, brightening the darkened shapes of trees and rocks and the sky above. I hoped the ride would take more time, but too soon the outline of Franklin's buildings appeared. As we entered the town, even in the dim morning light, the truth of war presented itself once again.

Several buildings lay as pile of rubble, while others were only partially intact. Debris, bricks and rocks, and trash filled the streets. Crows and scrawny dogs vied for whatever morsels of food they could find, but there were no people to be seen, no sounds from carriages or riders or the busy, hopeful sounds of industry. The lack of activity didn't have to do only with the early hour. I'd seen this before in southern towns; with no economy and fewer people, there simply wasn't much to do.

Sarah took us to Rainey's Mercantile on the north end of the square. While I waited outside, she walked around to the back. Soon the front door opened. An older man holding a lamp shook my hand. He introduced himself as Mr. Rainey.

"Thank ya, son, and good luck to ya." Then he nodded to Sarah and left us.

"What did he mean by that?" I asked.

Sarah pushed me further from where the man still moved around in another room. "Shh! I told him that you are a Confederate soldier and that you were left here in town after the battle and now you need to get back to your regiment."

"Well, that's half true."

"Thank heavens it's too dark and Mr. Rainey's eyes none too good that he'd see the blue coat. Do you have the money I gave you?"

"Yes."

"Good. Here's this also." She placed a bag in my hands. "Some food for your journey."

"Sarah—"

"Unfortunately, there's no stage going to Nashville today. But Mr. Rainey's nephew, Cecil, can take you north. Cecil's a good man, I've known him all my life, and he's smart too, but the road between Franklin and Nashville is dangerous these days. Stay watchful, Jennie. Once you're headed downriver, you should be all right."

"I don't know what to say."

"Neither do I. Write to me. Let me know you are returned in one piece."

"I will. And you must write as well."

"I will." Sarah kissed me on the cheek. "Cecil will be out back. Wait for him there. Can you sound like you're from the South? If not, don't talk. On second thought, just don't talk period. It'll be safer that way."

"Sarah, I'll be fine. You don't have to worry."

"I shall worry nonetheless."

"You are a very good person." I wanted to tell her I was sorry for everything, that maybe if things were different we might have been friends. But such words amounted to little against all that had been done during four long years of war.

"Good-bye, Jennie."

"Good-bye, Sarah."

Then she was gone. I waited a moment and walked toward the back of the store. Mr. Rainey had vanished and there was no sign of anyone else either. I could hear Sarah's horse trotting back down the street. It didn't seem I had waited but five minutes when a wagon pulled up. A man of about forty with a worn hat, scraggly, red beard, and thick, sausage fingers, waved at me.

"Y'all going to Nashville, are ya?"

"Yes, suh," I said, adopting my best southern drawl.

"Well, climb on in then. Best to get going early these days."

*

After crossing the Harpeth River just north of the square, I asked Cecil to stop. He immediately looked worried.

"It's just I ain't actually going to Nashville," I said.

"What's that? But Sarah said you was."

"I know. And I am going there soon, but first I got to get to Pittsburg Landing." I eased out of the wagon.

"You ain't walking!"

"My brothers were killed there."

Cecil nodded. "I am sorry. But you still can't walk. It's a good hundred miles from here!" He eyed me carefully. "You don't seem in too good a shape neither."

"I expect I'll be fine."

"Hmm. Won't be easy. Country's full of Yankee soldiers and they stop everyone. Listen, I can take you as far south as Columbia if you want. I got an aunt lives there. You could stay with her and then travel on."

"You don't mind?"

He shrugged. "I'll help any friend of Sarah's."

This seemed curious given what she'd told me of her family's standing in town, but I didn't ask questions. "I'd be much obliged, but didn't you need to go to Nashville?"

He shrugged. "Sarah paid me to take you there, but if you want to go somewhere else it's not much to me."

Cecil turned the team around and we returned to Franklin. The town showed a little more life, with more people beginning their day. After turning south on the Columbia Pike, Cecil told me to get in the back of the wagon under a blanket.

"You never know," he said. "People might see that blue coat and get the wrong idea."

After we were well away from the center of town, I poked my head out to look around. A brick house appeared on our right. It looked familiar. The remains of another building to our left had collapsed in jagged pieces. A rumbling sound began in my ears. Soon, we were traveling through the heart of the battlefield. The remains of war lay scattered everywhere: tattered clothing, books, watches, packs. A canteen crumpled under the weight of Cecil's wagon. Atop the breastworks, a horse still lay, skewered and stiff. The carcasses of other animals were only partially covered by the snowfall. I shrunk back under the blanket.

By early afternoon we had reached Columbia. Cecil's Aunt Lou lived in Mt. Pleasant on the road to another town called Ashland. We called on her and I met a round, short woman with red hair like Cecil's, pink cheeks, and probing blue eyes. She looked at me with curiosity while Cecil explained that I knew Sarah. This made all the difference.

I lay down on a small bed Aunt Lou said was for guests and was asleep within minutes, waking up only briefly later for a supper of boiled potatoes and fried partridge. After the meal, Cecil and his aunt discussed family and friends and my eyes grew heavy again. The next thing I knew it was morning. Cecil had already left and Aunt Lou was handing me a cup of coffee.

"It ain't real," she said. "But I expect you're used to that."

"Yes, ma'am," I said, groggily, taking the cup.

"I collected a couple of eggs this morning from my old gals," she continued. "Them damn Yanks didn't get my chickens at least! You want one? Got more potatoes too."

"Yes, ma'am," I said again. "That's very kind."

My body ached so much from the ride in the wagon that I could barely stand up. I wondered if I still had Sarah's money. If I were Aunt Lou or Cecil, I wouldn't have hesitated to go through a stranger's things. Especially a stranger wearing a blue coat.

"Cecil tells me you're going to Pittsburg Landing," she said, setting the plate of food on the table.

I sat down. "That's so."

"I can take ya to Ashland if ya like."

"Ain't that a ways?"

"It's a piece. But I got a sister lives there, and she don't leave often, so I don't see her much. It'd be good to check on her."

Later that morning, after Aunt Lou had gotten a young boy to come over and watch the chickens, we left for Ashland. She chattered like a mockingbird the whole way. By noon I knew about most of her life, including a husband who had died young and two sons, one killed at Chattanooga and the other currently missing. Of course, she had never supported the war, a foolish endeavor as far as she could tell. As for the nigras, she'd never owned one and didn't see why they couldn't fend for themselves just like everyone else.

"Tried my best to keep my boys at home," she said. "Said they were too young, that others could go instead if it was that important. I wasn't gonna lose my boys on the whim of a bunch of fat men in South Carolina who didn't know their heads from their tails. But do you think them sons of mine would listen? No, they would not! Now, I got one dead and another probably dead." She looked at me unhappily. "But I 'spect you done the same to your ma, didn't you?"

"Yeah," I said, slowly. "I expect I did."

Aunt Lou softened. "Ain't nobody suffers during a war like a mama. At least you ain't dead."

"No," I said, shaking my head, "I ain't dead."

There wasn't much to Ashland but an old church, a mercantile with a sign that read, "SHUT," and a few houses.

"Don't know why Betty stays in this ghost town," said Aunt Lou, as she pulled the wagon up to one of the houses. "Ain't hardly nobody here anymore. But will she come live with me, like I ask her to over and over? No, I tell you, she will not!"

If Aunt Lou had the shape of a bird's egg, her sister Betty was the exact opposite. Tall and slim like a beanpole, she looked nothing like her sister except for the rosy cheeks and tendency to ask questions she already knew the answer to. After supper, I left the women and slowly walked around the town. Betty had given me some tobacco for my meerschaum and I smoked it gladly and felt pleased to have some time alone. But I found myself exhausted and unable to walk far. A few times during the afternoon, I thought the two women looked at me curiously, but whether they knew my secret or not I didn't know. Certainly the few people I saw in Ashland took little notice of me. Their thoughts had long ago turned inward, their hearts losing out to hopelessness. After a supper of boiled cabbage and a few withered turnips, I listened to Aunt Lou and Betty talking. No matter what the topic, they always returned to their lives before the war. Before the devastation. Before the Yanks had come and ruined everything.

*

Now that I was on my own, my progress slowed considerably. Getting to the next little town on my way to Pittsburg Landing took another five days. The closer I came to the river, the more Federal soldiers I saw. Betty had told me that they regularly scoured the hills for Confederates or any goods or weapons they might confiscate. I kept the roads in sight when I could, but generally traveled through the forests where I could remain hidden. At Savannah, a man with a flatboat said he'd take me across the Tennessee River. On the other side, I gave him one of Sarah's dollars. His eyes grew wide at the coin in his hand, but he didn't ask any questions.

As the man returned to the other side, I looked up at the bluffs above the river. After so long, I had finally arrived at the place Adam had written about in another lifetime. Somewhere up above those bluffs, my brothers rested in the ground. Somewhere close to where I now stood, my brother Gardiner had died on the hospital ship. It was hard to believe on this quiet afternoon that thousands of men had once filled the riverbanks and forests here, but I knew from my own experience that the worlds of war and peace could co-exist, in memory if nowhere else.

A wave of dizziness came over me. I sat down on a log and took out Gardiner's journal. Tucked in between the pages was Adam's map. I looked at the drawing for a long while, then stood and began walking. At the top of the bluffs, there was a track that continued west for a mile, past a small building and into a grove of sweetgum trees.

I quickly found the five trees lined up in a row. Then the crackerbox lid with my brothers' names etched on it. Everything from the past three years, from the first moment I'd read of their deaths, rushed back to me like a flood. I fainted dead away.

*

When I awoke the sky had darkened and the snow was falling. I felt ill and returned to the empty building I'd passed. Inside, I ate some potatoes I'd found a few days before and the evening passed slowly. What would I do now that I was here? An uneasy sleep followed with dreams I couldn't describe but which left me feeling hopelessly sad.

The next morning, fresh snow covered everything. A golden, winter sun brightened my mood and I returned to the marker. Small birds had been dancing above my brothers; a small roof of snow sat atop the crackerbox lid. I cleared away a spot in the snow and sat on my haversack. I had the strangest sense that I was simply waiting for the boys to return. The hours passed. Birds came and went. Piles of snow fell from the trees. A tree squirrel scampered by.

I returned to the building when it grew dark. I had no more food but also didn't feel hungry. I lay down. It was hours before I fell asleep, but mercifully there were no dreams. The next morning, the sun shone again and I readied myself to return to the sweetgum grove, though to what end I couldn't say. However, when I stepped out of the building, I encountered a man looking at my footprints in the snow. He seemed as startled to see me as I was to see him.

"Hey, young fella! Whatchya doing out here? Ya look purt near froze!"

"I expect I am."

"Well, what are you doing out here by yourself?" he asked again. The man had a scraggly beard and a cheek full of tobacco. He held a musket in one hand and three dead rabbits in the other. I looked at him.

"I don't know."

His eyes got bigger. "Well, ya might as well come along then and have some dinner. I live just yonder down by the meeting house. About to fix me some stew if that suits ya."

I nodded. "I'd appreciate that."

The man cast an occasional glance at me as we walked, but didn't say anything. As the track opened up into a meadow and a small house appeared, he waved an arm. "You probably don't know but there was a goodly battle here a couple years ago now."

"Yes, sir, I do know."

He shook his head. "Bad business that. Each winter I'm glad when the snow covers everything."

As we neared the house, I thought I must be seeing things. It looked like a wildcat sat on the porch. It was a huge animal, with a thick, spotted coat and long tufts atop its ears. Upon seeing us, it immediately leapt off the porch then stopped and looked back at us.

"Luther!" the man shouted. "I knew I'd find you waiting!"

He untied one of the rabbits and threw it toward the cat. It caught the rabbit in its mouth then scampered out of sight behind the house. It was then I noticed it only had three legs.

"Shot off during the battle," he explained. "After the armies left, I found Luther under the porch here. I can tell you I wasn't none too crazy about having a wildcat living with me, but then a man can get used to anybody if he has to. 'Sides, he's pretty good company; don't talk much and he don't snore neither."

Inside the cabin, the man threw the rabbits on a table and took off his coat. "Have a sit, young fella, and I'll get this going. There's a bit of coffee left on the stove. Real too! Got it from Yanks who traded it to me for some tobacco. Make yourself at home."

A table and two chairs, a narrow bed, and shelf of books made up the whole of the cabin's furniture. On the back wall hung several animal skins, including one of a large, black wolf.

"Don't normally kill those," he said, as I rubbed a finger over the soft fur. "But this was a young 'un without a pack and it had taken to bothering Luther. I couldn't have that after all I'd done caring for him."

I sat down in one of the chairs. "What's your name?"

"Theodore, but everyone calls me Teddy. You?"

"Robert."

The man wiped a hand across a trouser leg and stuck it out. "Good to meet ya, Robert."

"Likewise. Thanks for—" I stopped. For what? I suddenly felt confused and very tired. "For coming along, I guess."

Teddy laughed. "You're welcome, Robert. That's what I'm good at, I expect. Just coming along."

In no time at all, Teddy had skinned the rabbits and had squares of meat frying in a pot. To this he added some onions and a couple of potatoes. While the food cooked, he pottered about the kitchen and I sat looking out the window. When the food was ready, he scooped it up into two bowls.

"Don't get many visitors around here," he said, sitting down in the other chair. "Weeks can go by where I don't see no one."

I nodded, and then ate the stew like I'd never had a meal in my life. After a second bowl, I thanked him heartily. Teddy looked pleased. After finishing his bowl, he cleared off the table and suggested a smoke. With a full belly and the meerschaum with new tobacco, I felt more myself.

"I come to find my brothers," I said.

Teddy nodded. "I expected that. You know where they were?"

"Yep. Back by that shack where you found me."

He smoked. "I'm sorry, young Robert, truly."

"Thank you." Suddenly, my eyes began closing.

"Get some sleep, lad. Ya can lie down on the bed while I check my traps. I'll just be gone a few hours."

"I am obliged."

Teddy snorted. "I should be thanking you. I don't mind the dead in these hills, but it's nice to have someone else to talk to."

SIX

I DIDN'T WAKE UP until the next morning. Teddy wasn't in the cabin but there was a pot of coffee on the stove and a bowl of cold stew on the table. Every part of my body felt as heavy as a bag of stones. I ate and drank and soon Teddy returned.

"'Bout this time of year," he said, "the Yanks start appearing and it's good to know what they're up to." He poured a cup of coffee and sat down.

"They bother you?" I asked.

"Nah. I ain't a soldier and I made it clear I ain't for one side or the next, so they let me alone." I looked at him, puzzled. He shrugged. "Ain't nothing really. I just don't feel like raising a gun to no man. People here don't much care for that sentiment, but it puts me all right with the Yanks."

I nodded. "I understand."

That afternoon, I returned to my brothers' graves. After the food and rest, I felt better, though my mind still seemed queer. At times, I seemed to be waiting for the boys to return; at others, I knew they weren't coming back. At times, I was just a younger sister, in a plain brown dress with blue flowers. Then I'd look at my clothes and see the strange person I'd become, a woman dressed as a man with experiences I could share with no one.

The sweetgum grove wasn't so far from Teddy's, but when I

returned to his place, I was again exhausted. The wildcat was sitting on the porch again. It ran off when it saw me but didn't go far. We stared at each other a minute, then I went inside.

Teddy fed me a second supper.

"I ain't never known anyone who had a wildcat for a pet," I said.

"Ah, Luther ain't really a pet. It's more like we're just living under the same roof."

"He come in the house?"

"Has," Teddy said, chewing on a mouthful of stew. "When it gets real cold. Kinda like any old cat at times. But that don't happen often."

"That beats all."

After supper, we sat outside smoking. Teddy went back inside after a bit and returned carrying a bottle and two glasses. "I been saving this for a special occasion, and I guess your showing up is special enough." He poured out some of the amber liquid and handed me a glass. "I'm counting on the war being done soon, so we'll just consider this an early celebration."

I took a drink, expecting fire water but the whiskey was as smooth as old leather. "That's pretty good," I said.

Teddy smiled. "Ain't it?"

"I ain't gonna ask where you got it."

The smile grew. "Best not, Robert. Best not."

After a few more sips and I could feel myself relaxing, I said, "A long time ago I hoped to bring them home, but ain't no way that can happen."

"No."

"So I expect I should be getting back to the war."

Teddy didn't say anything. I suddenly felt like telling him who I really was. Teddy seemed a good man, better than most. Anybody who took care of a three-legged wildcat wouldn't care that I was really a girl. Fortunately, before I could make this admission, he poured us each another glass, then said, "You could do that. Or, you could just stay here a few days. Ya come all this way. Like I said, my opinion, the war's about done. Don't need to be one more death from it."

"Huh. A woman recently said the same thing to me."

"I expect a lot of folks are thinking the same. At all rates, you're welcome to stay here a bit. Ya can have the bed. I can sleep out here and I don't mind none. Usually too hot inside for me anyway."

"That's too much," I said, "though I appreciate the offer."

"All right then, you sleep out here. I got some blankets. It ain't bad now it's warming up."

"I don't wanna go back," I said, abruptly.

"No, 'course not."

"What'll I do here though?"

Teddy looked at me. "Ya come a long way, Robert. To see your brothers. This is where they are now. Spend some time in the hills. Talk to 'em. You ain't the first to come. You ain't gonna be the last."

"You think it'll help?"

"That I couldn't say. But I know for sure, it ain't gonna hurt."

*

Before I knew it, a week had passed. Then a second. I returned to the sweetgum grove many times, sitting on the ground and doing nothing. Teddy didn't ask me any questions about what I was doing and I never saw another person. One day though I didn't go. I stayed on Teddy's porch and looked across the meadow. Early blue flowers were starting to pop up where the snow had begun to melt, and birds were announcing the arrival of spring. Teddy's cabin faced east and the morning sun warmed everything. I sat so still just enjoying the quiet and warmth that I didn't even notice Luther creep up onto the porch. I didn't that is until a rodent appeared and he took off like a shot. Caught it too. Three-legged or not, he was still a cat and one of the best hunters around. To my surprise, Luther brought the rodent to me and set it at my feet. I smiled and thanked him, the sound of my voice sending him around the back of the cabin.

As the days grew longer, I helped Teddy with chores around his place. We checked his traps, made repairs to the cabin, and built a new smokehouse. At first, I felt so sore from this work that I could barely move at the end of each day, but slowly my body got stronger. It felt good to be doing something besides being a soldier.

As the middle of April arrived, the battlefield's snow blanket had mostly disappeared. Bullets and bayonets, packs and frying pans, coats and rubber ponchos and saddles and bridles, all reappeared to tell the story. There were skeletons too, of animals and men, clean and white with the passage of time. When I went to the sweetgum grove, I tried to follow paths with less debris, but often it couldn't be avoided. One day, I found a Remington pistol. It had seen better days but with some work could be made useful again. I tucked it into my pocket. Later that night, I showed Teddy and he got out some grease and we started cleaning it.

*

One day in early May, Teddy left to go to Corinth, the nearest town and a place he could trade his animal hides for goods. When he returned the next day he had a newspaper. The *Nashville Daily Press* was dated April 11, 1865. Next to the most ordinary of advertisements for photographic and ambrotype apparatus, appeared the most extraordinary headline:

GRANT!
GLORIOUS NEWS!
SURRENDER OF GEN LEE!
FULL PARTICULARS!
END OF THE REBELLION!

The paper had printed the correspondence between Generals Lee and Grant and the terms of the surrender of the Army of Northern Virginia. They were generous terms and they had been accepted on April 9. The war was over.

I looked at Teddy. He grabbed me and we embraced. When we pulled apart, I saw tears in his eyes. "It's gonna be okay now,

Robert. It's gonna be okay."

That night, the whiskey bottle came back out and we drank and ate fish that Teddy had caught and he told me about some of the places he'd been, including New Orleans, St. Louis, and even Florida. Now the war was over, he seemed more relaxed. He said he'd always been kind of a wanderer, not one for settling down. I said this seemed like a fine thing to be.

"It's got its advantages, Robert, and some disadvantages too. But that's my life. I settled here a few years ago, never really planning to stay."

"Why did you stay? I mean, after the war came and the battle?"

"Don't rightly know and that's the truth. I ain't got no family to speak of, a bit old for soldiering though they woulda taken me sure. But I had no intention of going, so this seemed as good a place as any to stay out of their sights. Then the battle come and I had to leave anyhow for a while. When I returned, I found Luther and a heap a dead men." He took a sip. "Ya know, I think I just felt so sad for the land. Ya know that church over in the next valley?" I nodded. "It's called Shilo, which means "Place of Peace." Couldn't have been further from the truth for those few days. Maybe I just stayed hoping the peace would return.

"I don't know, Robert. It ain't gonna be easy coming out of this. But the land is good. Your brothers will be all right here. I'll look after them."

I nodded. "You're a good man, Teddy."

He waved. "I'm glad we met, Robert."

"Me too."

"Truth to tell, I wouldn't mind ya staying on. We could build you a cabin and you're young enough you could find a wife and probably be pretty happy here."

I nodded. "That's true. But I got to be getting home. To my ma."

"Yep, I know you do. And that's good. She'll be wanting that. The steamships are starting to move now, so it's a good time to catch a ride on one. The newspaper said all men were allowed to return home without disturbance. Still, I'd keep my eyes open and…" he paused, "…maybe pretend you ain't from the South. You got that blue coat; just let 'em think you're a Yank. That is, if such don't stick in your craw too much."

*

The next day I left Teddy and returned to the sweetgum grove one last time. This time I made the effort to talk to my brothers. At first, the endeavor felt foolish. Yet it would be a long time, if ever, before I'd be back. Anything that needed saying had to be said now.

So I began. First there was Mama. It was true that Jothan and Gardiner getting themselves killed had made her go crazy, but I didn't need to make their spirits feel any worse. I said only that she'd gone away for a bit, and now was back. Second, Papa seemed all right though it was hard to know for sure because we'd both had to worry so much about Mama. And me, well, they wouldn't recognize their little sister, but I hoped they wouldn't mind too much what I'd done.

Very importantly, there was also Marie. Jothan might have wanted me to take care of his wife should anything happen to him, but I was pretty sure he wouldn't have approved of me falling in love with her. On this score, I kept my words mostly about his beautiful daughter and the last things I'd heard of Jen-Jen. Finally, I talked about Toulon and people in town, but soon I was tired of talking and just stopped.

I stood up and tidied the area around the marker. Then I found several large stones and set them at the base of the crackerbox lid. Violets had come up, so I collected a few and pressed them into Gardiner's journal. Two red-colored stones and a handful of dirt went into a little leather bag Teddy had given me.

There was nothing more to do. Part of me wished I was buried in the cold, ancient earth with my brothers, but since I wasn't I knew I had to go home. I had to return to the people who still lived, the people I still loved.

PART FOUR

ONE

May 5, 1865, Chicago, Illinois

IT TOOK ME three weeks to get to Chicago. From Pittsburg Landing, I found passage aboard the *U.S.S. Peosta*, a side-wheeled steamer that had been converted to a river gunboat. Initially, the regiment on board had thought me a deserter. I quickly explained about the battle at Franklin and how I'd been there recovering until just recently. I told them I had been returning to my own regiment when I got word of the war's end. The corporal lowered his musket.

"I'm sorry," he said. "It's just we can't be too careful these days. After President Lincoln's death and all."

"What?"

"You don't know?"

I shook my head. "Know what?"

The corporal then explained how our beloved president had been murdered by the traitors while watching a play at Ford's Theatre. How the killers had also tried to kill the Secretary of State, as well as a few others, but the death squad had only succeeded with Mr. Lincoln. He'd lain for some time insensible after the shooting and people had prayed for a miracle, but there was no miracle to be had. I sat by myself, numb, all the way down the Tennessee and Ohio rivers.

In Cairo, I used Sarah's money to purchase a ticket for the cars to Chicago. Unfortunately, the next trip would not occur for another week so I procured lodging and got a haircut and spent the warm days sitting on the point where the Ohio and Mississippi Rivers came together. Fort Defiance, where we'd all trained to become soldiers, still bustled with activity. My mind wandered back to those days, when I'd first met my friends, when the war was real but still far away too. Now my brothers as well as the others, Christmas, Bean, Biddle, and Kit, lay forever in the Tennessee ground. I couldn't imagine why I sat here and they didn't. That afternoon, I bought a bottle of whiskey and drank the better part of it. The next morning I felt so sick that I threw the rest of the drink into the river.

To keep myself occupied, I did odd jobs for the man who owned the hotel. He had three sons off to the war and hadn't heard from any of them in months. I made deliveries and stocked the shelves, swept and cleaned up. In the evenings, I walked around town before the light faded.

One night, I wrote Marie and my parents and told them I would be home soon.

On the morning of May 30th, I boarded the cars for Chicago. After finding my seat, I unbuttoned the top of my frock coat. The air inside the coach grew warmer as more people arrived. I closed my eyes. Finally the Illinois Central began moving forward. That's when I heard a tiny voice.

"You a soldier, Mister?"

I opened my eyes. A young boy of about seven sat across from me with his mother. He stared at me, hopeful but uncertain. The young woman, who clutched her son's hand, colored when I glanced at her.

"I'm sorry, sir," she said, then looked at the boy. "Don't bother the man, Billy." He continued staring.

"It's all right," I said. "I am a soldier. Or, at least, I was."

The boy's eyes grew bigger. "Were you in many battles?"

I nodded. "A few."

"Did you shoot some Rebs?"

"Billy! It's impolite to ask someone questions before you know them. You must leave this man in peace."

The little boy sat back, chastened. "Yes, Mama."

Billy was disappointed, but he didn't stay that way for long. As soon as his mother had dozed off a half hour later, he leaned toward me and whispered, "What was it like, Mister?"

*

That evening, the train moved slowly above the waters of Lake Michigan. Gulls chased each other then dropped heavily into the gentle waves like sacks of flour. Far from shore, a small house protruded above the surface. I didn't remember this structure from when Marie and I had stood with Mr. Timmons looking out at the lake that winter day so long ago.

"That's new," said Billy's mother, noticing my gaze. Her son now slept across her lap. "They began building it last year."

"What is it?"

"Something called an "intake crib." It's for collecting water for the city. Men are digging a tunnel under the lake between the crib and a pumping station on Chicago Avenue. When it's done, the tunnel will be two miles long."

"I see."

"Have you been to the city before?" she asked.

"Yes. Though it was a long time ago."

"You're returning home then?"

"That's right."

On the platform, I said good-bye to Billy and his mother and began walking west on Lake Street. The city seemed as busy as ever, with people and carriages filling the streets and noise filling the air. It felt too crowded at times, but also familiar and friendly. Unlike my last time in Chicago when, newly outfitted as a boy, no one had given me a second glance, now I found ladies smiling at me and gentlemen tipping their hats. One older woman stopped and asked where I'd been during the war. After I told her, she smiled and said my mother would be glad to see me home.

This attention soon grew tiring and I slipped into the dark interior of Cameron & Hays Bookseller and Publishers. Cool inside, the bookstore appeared empty. I looked at a few of the books realizing I didn't have a plan. Should I go to Owl's? Should I go to the Sherman House? Maybe I should have just bought a ticket to Kewanee and stayed at the train station. Suddenly, I began shaking. I felt afraid but of what I wasn't sure. As I walked back toward the door, I noticed the advertisement board.

The thought of Owl must have conjured him up.

The board had one announcement, and it was for my friend's show. A series of illusions, including the Floating Lady trick, was to be performed at McVicker's Theatre. Two nights only, May 29 and 30.

Tonight was the thirtieth. If I hurried, I might still be able to get a ticket.

*

The crush of bodies inside the theatre made the streets seem vacant by comparison. I paid for a ticket, one of the last the man told me, and made my way slowly through the lobby. Beautiful women in gowns of all colors drank glasses of champagne on the arms of men dressed in spotless frock coats and silk vests and ties. They were all very gay, laughing and smiling with not a care in the world. There was no war here, never had been. There were no other soldiers either. I bought a glass of champagne and drank it quietly in a corner.

Getting one of the last tickets relegated me to the very back row. As the lights dimmed, the crowd grew quiet. Nothing happened for a moment then a sharp crack filled the air and a poof of bluish smoke appeared on stage. Suddenly, there stood Owl bowing to great applause! He looked exactly the same to me except his hair appeared longer. In the next moment, two assistants wheeled a tall box onto the stage.

"Ladies and Gentlemen," Owl boomed, "tonight you have

come for an evening of magic, where your mind will not believe what your eyes witness. But of course, I cannot do this all alone. May I now introduce my very lovely partner, Carmen Bajoliere!" With that, Owl opened up the two doors of the tall box.

It was empty.

My friend looked puzzled, then embarrassed. He peered inside the box, underneath it, all around. He seemed genuinely vexed and when he called the assistants back onstage and had whispered words with them, I became uncomfortable. Owl had told me over and over that even with many hours of careful planning, something could still go wrong. Still, he'd never made a mistake before. Could this be the first time?

At last the assistants left. Owl thought a moment, then stepped into the box. Turning around, he shrugged heavily. Upon stepping back out, he closed the doors.

"Well, Ladies and Gentlemen, what do you think? Do you suppose that perhaps I have not been paying Carmen enough?" Many people laughed at this and one person shouted, "You haven't!" Owl nodded. He looked up and around. "Carmen, I agree with these people: you deserve more money. Beginning this evening, you shall have a raise. Please, now, come out for the show!" With that, he wheeled the box around again and waited. Soon a knock came from inside. Owl opened the doors.

There was Carmen. Though we'd all seen the inside of an empty box, now it released Owl's beautiful assistant, wearing a glittering gown of red, white, and blue. Applause and cheers shook the theatre.

For the next hour and a half, my friends dazzled us. I had always thought Owl a great magician, but in the years I'd been away he'd become a brilliant one. His illusions were better than ever, more surprising and more complex. His stories and jokes made the audience laugh and the people loved Carmen without question. Their act was a perfect combination of mystery, humor, and escape. Yet, his real genius lay rooted, not so much in his conjures, but in his genuine affection for the audience. He brought several people up onstage to assist him, always rewarding them with a prize, either cards or a magic handkerchief or some other prop that they unexpectedly found in their pockets. Owl made people feel at ease and he didn't mind looking the fool, though in the end of course he wasn't a fool once. Even if something had gone wrong, the audience would have loved him all the same.

The final conjure of the evening was the Floating Lady trick. As the curtain rose behind Owl, we could see two high stools with a plank stretched between them. Three steps had been placed in front of the plank. Carmen appeared and stepped up a to lie down on the long board. A black cloth on top of the plank was then used to wrap Carmen up like a mummy.

Owl, standing behind Carmen and facing us, stretched his arms out wide above her head and feet. In the next moment, the assistants appeared at each stool. Very slowly, one stool was moved away. Carmen, miraculously, remained horizontal. The second stool was moved. Now there was nothing holding Carmen in the air besides magic. The man next to me squirmed in his seat.

"That's impossible!" he whispered.

"It's impossible," I agreed.

One of the assistants produced a large hoop. Owl passed the hoop around Carmen, showing that there was no hidden support. The audience continued mute. Not until the stools were replaced and Owl had unwrapped Carmen and helped her down to the stage did the giant room explode in appreciation.

*

I left the theatre with the crowd, then circled around the building to the backstage entrance. I didn't have to wait long before a short, chubby man appeared in the door carrying a bulky bag. He exited and I slipped inside before the door closed. No one else seemed to be backstage. I stood for a few minutes uncertain. After such a performance, I doubted Owl and Carmen would have gone straight home, but where were they? Then I thought of the show I'd attended with Marie the first winter of the war. There'd been a reception in an upstairs room of the theatre; perhaps tonight was the same. I hurried back to the lobby, then up the winding staircase to the second floor. It took only a few minutes to find the very same room filled with people, all come to congratulate Owl and Carmen on their success.

A man at the entrance asked if he could help me.

I nodded, removing my hat. "I'm here to see Owl. We're old friends. I've only just arrived in town."

The man's eyes narrowed. "Do you have an invitation?"

"No. As I said, I've only just arrived."

"I'm sorry then. No invitation, no admittance."

"But—"

"This is a private party. We can't just let anyone come in saying they're friends of Owl's."

"But I'm not just anyone!"

"I'm sorry."

I stared at the man. "I'm sorry too," I said, "because I'm going to see my friend." I shoved him aside and walked past. This gatekeeper started shouting but a few seconds where he was too surprised to do anything else allowed me to slip into the crowd. I grabbed a glass of champagne from a passing waiter to look more like I belonged and searched the room for Owl and Carmen. At first, no one paid me much notice. Then the door guard appeared.

"You, sir!" he shouted, drawing everyone's eyes to him and then to me. "Stop right there!" As he approached me, he continued. "I think you've had a little too much to drink. You best leave now!"

The man grabbed one of my arms. I elbowed him in the stomach with my other. As he doubled over, I pushed him onto the ground and walked away. That's when two other men grabbed me. My glass of champagne hit the floor and shattered. Owl then appeared.

"What is happening, James?" he asked, helping the guard up.

"It's this cretin, sir," the man wheezed, flipping a thumb in my direction. "Say's he's come to see you, but he doesn't have an invitation!"

"I told you," I said, trying to shake off the grip of the other two men. "We're old friends. I just got into town!"

"And I told you that no one gets in without an invitation!" He looked at his boss proudly, but Owl's face had turned pale. He stared at me for many seconds. The more he stared, the more pale he grew.

"Thank you, James, it's all right." Owl said at last, then nodded at the men to let me go. "This is indeed an old friend of mine."

TWO

IF CHICAGO had been hovering on the brink of greatness before the war, it had since fully made the leap into its own bright future. During the four years of conflict, factories had been built, commercial ventures had sprouted like seedlings, and immigrants had poured in from the South, East, and Europe. In 1863, the First National Bank had been formed. By the time I returned, there were thirteen national banks in Chicago, more than existed in any other city in the country. This huge influx of money prompted the construction of new buildings above the earth and tunnels below. Several streets, including Clark, had been paved with wood blocks, a welcome improvement to combat the problem of mud and dust. Something called a Fire Alarm Telegraph now connected most parts of the city with the courthouse, providing rapid communication with different fire engine stations. Collection boxes for letters eliminated the need for those living a distance from the post office to actually visit the post office.

Such industry made the war seem almost a dream. In fact, the prisoners housed at Camp Douglas were now gone; the uncertainty of a strife that, for a time, had seemed without end, was also now gone. Abandoned homes and landscapes no longer connected by the serpentine tracks of the cars were unimaginable in Chicago. All was well here. Soon, all would be even better.

Owl and Carmen had moved from their rooms on Michigan to Clark Street north of the river. A rust-colored Italianate, two-story row house, their home sat high above the elm-lined road and was linked to the thoroughfare by a long series of steps. A large sitting area, dining room, and small kitchen comprised the downstairs; three bedrooms and an office for Owl filled the upstairs. The morning after their show, I awoke in the bedroom facing Clark Street and the rising sun.

At the reception, Owl had at first been too tongue-tied to speak. Carmen, however, had handled my arrival with such grace that I felt perhaps she had sensed my return. After the initial shock wore off and there'd been hugs and introductions all around, I had left my friends for the balcony and some fresh air. I needed a moment alone, but an old man followed me outside, tapping me on the shoulder and asking if he could shake my hand.

"Owl said you were with one of the Board of Trade regiments," he said.

I nodded. "That's so."

"You boys are a good bunch. I been keeping up with you. Know'd Joseph Stockton since he was just a young man, first come to the city."

"Yes, sir. Colonel Stockton is a good man."

"Us here know all about the Franklin fight and 72nd losses. Reckon you're mighty lucky to be alive, young man."

"Yes, sir, I expect that's so."

As he shook my hand a second time and turned to head back inside, I suddenly felt dizzy. The man's suit suddenly changed into a coat of blue and it looked like he now carried a musket as he walked away from me. I blinked my eyes, but the fact remained: the old man had turned into a Federal soldier. The cool, summer air around me became icy and I could see my breath. The man was now swallowed into the crowd, but it was no longer a crowd of party-goers. Soldiers in blue and gray uniforms mixed together. They chatted in low voices, one or two occasionally looking out at me. I turned around quickly and there, much to my relief were the

278

buildings of Chicago. I stayed looking out at the city for more than a half-hour. When I at last turned around again, the soldiers were gone.

Owl, Carmen, and I talked long into the night after returning to their home. Of course, they had believed me dead, not having had any letter from me for almost a year. I explained only briefly about Franklin and my time recuperating for I knew it would upset them to hear of the terrible battle.

"I suppose Marie and Mama and Papa also believed that too," I sighed, "but fortunately they now know I am returned."

"Do they?" asked Owl.

"I wrote to them after arriving in Cairo, two weeks ago now. They should have the letters by now."

"They will be so relieved, Jennie," said Carmen. "You will soon return to them, but you must stay a few days with us."

"I would like that."

The next morning, Owl was gone by the time I arose. Carmen said he had gone to attend to business and would not be back until supper. I took a bath, then enjoyed a late breakfast of fried eggs and potatoes, strawberry muffins, and several cups of strong coffee. Carmen and Owl's cook, a black woman named Temple, was delighted at my appetite and gratitude. She was from Louisiana, Carmen explained, and after Carmen's own mother had died some years before, Temple had taken over the roll. It had only been a year since Carmen had finally been able to bring Temple north.

"She arrived exhausted and fretful," Carmen said after the cook had returned to the kitchen. "Times aren't so good in New Orleans these days. But she was still happy. It's close to forty years I've know that woman, and I hadn't ever seen her looking so pleased as when she stepped off the cars that day."

Temple appeared again. "More eggs, suh?" she asked.

I nodded, handing her my plate. Watching her go, I whispered, "You didn't tell her?"

"Tell her what?"

"About me."

Carmen didn't answer until after Temple had come and gone for the second time. "No, Jennie, I didn't tell her." She took a small, thin cigarette from her case and lit it. "I don't know what I *would* tell her. You know, I blamed myself terribly after you had gone. For helping you; for encouraging you. I'd even cut your hair! When the war dragged on and every battle became worse than the previous one, I knew I had surely done a very bad thing."

"It was my own wish to go."

"I know, but I still could barely live with myself. I would never do such a thing again. I am so sorry, my dear."

"You must not worry, Carmen," I said, finishing the last of the breakfast and feeling full at last. "I have not died and now I am returned. Except for Jothan and Gardiner, things shall go back to how they were. Please don't be sorry." Carmen nodded, but still looked unhappy. I now noticed several streaks of gray in her long, dark hair, as well as lines around her eyes. I smiled. "You may offer me a cigarette and all will be even between us."

She returned the smile. "Not quite, but I am happy to do anything for you. Owl is too, you know."

We smoked in silence and drank more of Temple's coffee. At last I asked Carmen if she had any plans for the day. She shook her head. "Nothing important, why?"

"I need a favor."

"As I said, dear girl, anything."

"I wonder if you might buy me some new clothes."

"What kind of clothes?" When I told her, she looked surprised. "What? Are you teasing?"

I smoked. "Not in the least. I'd like a dress, maybe two, a hat, gloves, underclothes, everything. I think some green or gray colors might be nice, maybe a light blue, but I leave it up to your good taste. I can pay you back, of course. I haven't the money at the moment, but will in a few hours."

Carmen looked at me. "I thought you might be done with such items, Jen. I mean, after all this time, after everything that's happened."

I thought of the men on the cars from Cairo who had made their way to my seat to shake my hand. I remembered the little boy Billy asking about the battles, and the woman on Lake Street who had told me my mother would be glad to see me. Too, there was the man at the party the previous night. They all had questions I couldn't answer or praise I couldn't accept. Being a lady again would thankfully release me from having to respond to people wanting to know something that even I didn't know.

"No," I said, shaking my head and reaching for another cigarette. "I'm not done with them. In fact, I will be very happy to be someone else for a while."

*

After Carmen departed in the brougham, I left as well and walked south on Clark Street. A fine layer of mist hung above the river, alternately hiding and revealing ducks and herons moving about the shoreline. Despite the gathering heat, the city hummed. Carmen had told me that the "Soldier's Fair" had begun the previous day and that people had been arriving for the last week from near and far to attend the event. Halls throughout the city would be dedicated for the next month to displaying and selling everything imaginable as a means of raising money to alleviate the suffering of returning soldiers. Donations of different objects and curiosities had come from around the globe. Chicago had hosted another such fair in 1863, as had many other cities, all to great success.

In little time I found myself standing in front of the Sherman House. It looked the same, yet different too. I went inside. Similar to the theatre the night before, the hotel lobby was filled with people. Also similar to the night before, I slipped into a quiet corner. Such good memories I held of this place. The time I spent here with Marie, before the war. Before everything had changed.

"Can I help you, sir?"

Startled, I turned around. It had been more than three years, but I immediately recognized Daniel, the Sherman House employee who had operated the steam car during that long-ago visit. His hair was shorter and he had grown a mustache, but it was certainly him. When I didn't say anything, he continued, "Are you wanting to buy a ticket for the Fair, sir?"

"What?"

"Because we won't be set up for that until tomorrow. But then you can come to the booth over there," he pointed across the lobby, "and get yourself a ticket. You won't have to pay either, being a soldier and all."

"Yes," I nodded. "Thank you. That is good to know."

"Anything else I can help you with? Would you like me to show you the Gentlemen's Conversation Parlor? Be plenty there happy to buy you a drink."

"No, thank you. I must go. I only wanted to see the inside of the hotel."

Daniel smiled. "It's a fine place. Best in Chicago, in fact!"

After leaving the Sherman House, I went to E.R. Bowen's Military Goods and Gloves, also along Clark Street. Mr. Bowen, a sharp-featured man with thick, black hair pushed back behind his ears, examined the Remington pistol.

"Could use some oil here," he said, "but otherwise it's in pretty good shape. You say you've just returned?"

"Yes, sir."

"You've got a nice piece here. Why you wanna sell it?"

Though tempted to tell him I needed the money to buy a dress, hat, and corset, I instead said only that I needed some money now the war was over. He nodded.

"I can offer fifty dollars."

"Fifty dollars! It's not worth that much!"

Mr. Bowen looked at me surprised. Then he smiled. "Take it or leave it, young man."

"All right, but—"

"Good." He walked to the other end of the counter to withdraw the money from a box. After handing me the money and a receipt, Mr. Bowen stretched out his hand. "You surely deserve this and much more."

I nodded awkwardly and shook his hand. My desire to get out of the blue coat and trousers was increasing by the minute.

For the next couple of hours, I walked around the city. Great masses of people were bunched up at the entrances to Monitor Hall on Randolph Street, Bryan Hall on Clark, and at an enormous, tunnel-shaped structured that took up most of Dearborn Park near the lake. Though the excitement felt infectious, the crowds caused me nervousness as well. The day by now had also grown very warm. Next door to McVicker's Theatre, I went into a business called the Green Room and bought a pale cream ale. After cooling off, I did some shopping, using my money to buy presents for my family. Tobacco for Papa, hats for Mama and Marie, a novel for children called *Ellen's Idol* for Jennie. The effort was such fun that I continued. The Trickles, the Parkers, and Adam too all deserved something from the proceeds of the pistol.

*

That night, Owl arrived home to find two well-dressed ladies waiting for him. "I declare, Jennie Edwards!" he shouted. "Will you never cease to surprise me?"

Carmen had outdone herself on my behalf. In addition to two dresses, boots, gloves, and all the rest, she'd also gone to a business supplying wigs. There she'd bought a false bun for me to hide the fact of my short hair. As I had looked at everything that afternoon, Carmen thought my hesitation reflected a change of mind.

"You don't have to wear these, Jennie. I could buy you a new suit instead."

"No, no, I like them, truly. It's just that...it will feel odd." I fingered the soft material of the dress. "But I cannot answer any more of their questions."

Carmen nodded. "People are curious, Jen, that is all. And grateful. If they knew you were a woman, they would have even more questions."

"I know, and I don't blame them. But I have nothing to tell them."

After Owl poured drinks for all of us and took a seat, he asked me how the new clothes felt.

I sipped the sherry. The dress and all the rest were very fine but also very constricting. The skirt seemed to weigh a hundred pounds, the boots pinched my feet. With the corset, I now had to carefully consider every breath. How did women ever *do* anything dressed like this?

"As for my hair," I added, touching the bun, "I rather like having a bird's nest back there to keep my neck warm." Owl laughed. "You think I'm joking, but right after Carmen attached it, a sparrow flew in the window thinking it had found a home." He laughed more.

"In any case, you look very pretty," he said, then looked at me seriously. "I am so glad you're returned, Jennie. I'm a bit at a loss for words, but that's only from my utter relief and delight that you have survived."

I nodded, uncomfortable. "It is I who am at a loss for words."

"Oh?"

"Your show. The magic. It was not to be believed. Just as you predicted."

Both of them smiled. "Tell us what you liked best, Jennie," said Carmen.

"I liked it all. You were both just perfect in every way. Still, making Carmen float in the air was the most spectacular thing I have ever seen."

"Do you want to know how it was done?"

I took another sip of sherry. "I already know how it was done."

"Oh?"

"Magic, of course."

Owl raised his drink. "Magic, indeed."

He began explaining a new conjure he was devising for their show. This particular conjure had been performed in France in the 1840s but was so complicated it had rarely been done since. Before he could say more, Temple arrived announcing supper. In the dining room, there was more food laid out than I'd seen in years. Oysters on the half shell, braised carrots, a tomato and cucumber salad, salmon, a bowl of glistening cranberries, and a plate of roasted potatoes filled the table.

"Why is there so much?" I asked, stunned.

Owl steered me to a chair. "To celebrate your homecoming, my dear!"

THREE

ON THE AFTERNOON of June the first, the Soldier's Fair opened. Carmen, Owl, and I took the brougham to the Sherman House and bought our tickets. The gold and silver badge that read, "Northwest Sanitary Fair, Chicago, 1865," pinned easily to my dress. Outside again, Owl examined *The Voice of the Fair*. This newspaper described all the halls and events to be seen. After some discussion, we decided to head for Bryan Hall, where the "Curiosity Department" included such items as a 200-year-old elk antler, a $100 loaf of bread, and various items from the late Confederate States of America.

At the entrance, dozens of people clustered like a school of fish waiting for the doors to open. An older man bumped into me and apologized.

"So sorry, miss," he said, attempting to back up but having little success.

"It's all right," I said, "but this bloody crowd—I mean, thank you, I'm fine."

"Never seen such a lively bunch," he continued. "I only hope they're as lively spending their money." As we moved forward a few paces, I asked what was available to buy. "Anything and everything," he smiled. "We've been collecting items from all over the world. Machinery, looms, reapers, even something called a "carbon oil stove." I hope your husband brought lots of money with him!"

"Yes," I agreed. "I hope so too."

"All the proceeds from the Fair," the man explained, "will go toward purchasing goods for the returning soldiers, the maintenance of twenty soldiers' homes, the development of pension agencies, and the care of the permanently disabled." He looked as proud as a new father. "I'm on the organizing committee, but truly, none of this would have happened without Mrs. Livermore and Mrs. Hosmer. Those ladies surely worked me into the ground!" When the doors opened and the crowd began to loosen, the man nodded kindly. "Don't forget to buy, miss! The soldiers deserve everything we can give them!"

Inside Bryan Hall, flags of enormous size hung from the walls. Tables and stalls filled the huge space and in the very middle stood the "Temple of Relics," an enormous, octagon-shaped stage surrounded by Romanesque columns. Inside the temple, we found all manner of strange objects, including a group of ostrich eggs, the tusk of a walrus, a tapestry designed by Queen Elizabeth, and buffalo skin shoes. The $100 loaf of black bread had originally been purchased by a soldier at Gettysburg for five cents; the 200-year-old elk antler amazed everyone, including one particularly silly woman.

"I didn't know they lived that long," she said, running a finger along the antler. "After all, they're just animals, aren't they?" The man standing behind the table glanced my way.

"They're actually very special animals," I said, in a quiet voice. The woman turned around. "You see, there's a plant that only the elk can eat, which causes some of them to live for many decades. Occasionally, one may even live a few centuries. Here, see how smooth it is along the top fork? This indicates a very old animal."

She looked back at the antler, nodding thoughtfully. "What is the plant?"

I chuckled. "It's a funny plant called a mugwort. It can be very poisonous to people but isn't to elk because of a special fluid in their stomachs."

"How do you know so much about this?" the woman asked.

As I was about to answer the woman's husband appeared and told his wife to come see the six-thousand-year-old eye of a fish found in South America. The woman thanked me and said she would tell all of her friends about the mugwort and its powers.

"Oh, do," I said, enthusiastically. "Just make sure they don't try it!"

"Oh, Jennie," said Carmen after the woman had gone.

"I know. But I couldn't help myself."

She smiled and walked over to where Owl was looking at some letters. The man behind the table with the elk antler stared at me.

"None of that was true, was it?"

I shrugged. "There are a lot of plants in the world. Maybe one somewhere could make an elk live for two centuries."

"You sounded very convincing."

"I've had a lot of experience with this kind of thing."

He frowned. "What kind of thing?"

"Telling lies."

The man's face turned red. He was saved from having to respond to this by an elderly gentleman who wanted to know where the ostrich eggs had come from. I slipped away and caught up with Carmen and Owl. We continued on our circuit around the temple. A plaster model of Mr. Lincoln's hand and a pair of Confederate swords both held our attention for some minutes. Next to these lay a simple tree branch. It looked out of place and uninteresting.

"What is it?" I asked Owl, who had bent over to read the placard next to the branch.

"It's from an oak tree at Vicksburg. The very tree under which the terms of the city's surrender were signed."

As I leaned forward to look more closely, someone behind us dropped a tray of glasses. Suddenly, I felt the same kind of dizziness I'd experienced at Owl and Carmen's party. My vision grew blurry. When it cleared, I saw hills and armies and the

Confederate line at the top of a very steep slope. I grabbed the table.

"Jennie? Are you unwell?" Owl's voice sounded far away. He took hold of my arm and I heard Carmen call for a doctor.

"No, I'm fine," I muttered. "It's just a bit warm in here is all."

Someone produced a chair and I sat down. Owl left and returned with a glass of water. A few people had gathered around us but I kept looking at the floor. I didn't want to see Vicksburg or Franklin or any battlefield. After a few minutes, Carmen said we should go home. Owl agreed.

"No," I said. "I'm fine, truly. It's just these clothes, I'm not used to them."

I drank the water and stood up. The hall had returned to being a hall and there were no hills or regiments at the top of them. I felt tired, but insisted we continue on our circuit.

The last stall housed the oddest sight so far: a wax model of a man dressed in women's clothing. The sign beneath the image read, "Jefferson Davis, Fallen President of the Rotten Confederacy."

"I don't understand," I said to my friends.

"When they finally captured Davis in Georgia," Carmen explained, "he was said to be wearing his wife's clothing as a disguise."

Suddenly, a man popped up from behind the Davis statue scaring us all half to death. Attired in a red and yellow shirt with a high, ruffled collar, he clucked happily.

"Madame Tussand's of London!"

"Beg your pardon?" asked Owl.

"Madame Tussand's of London!" he repeated, waving a billowing sleeve. "They created this masterpiece, and all from only one small photograph!" The man petted Jefferson Davis' arm. "Imagine! A man dressed in women's clothing! It is not to be believed!"

*

For the rest of that day and the next, we toured the city and everything to do with the Fair. In addition to the many halls devoted to various exhibitions, there were also outdoor displays. Along Randolph Street at an open field, a great crowd had gathered. Inside a paddock, a mammoth, pure white ox stood sleepily in the shade of a tree. "General Grant," we were told, was a veteran of sanitary fairs, having already attended events in Boston and New York and raising thousands of dollars toward the welfare of returning soldiers. As we stood watching the general, several caretakers arrived. They began washing his ivory fur, an activity which seemed wholly uninteresting to the ox.

Inside Monitor Hall at the east end of Randolph were the "aquatic specialties," including a model world of coastal landscapes where a reenactment took place regularly of the famous clash between the *Monitor* and the *Merrimac*. While many stood wide-eyed watching the tiny vessels belching smoke, I walked to a quieter area of the display. Two sparrows had found a perfect bird bath in one of the miniature coves and were more delightful to watch than the warring ships.

Our last stop was Union Hall. Carmen and Owl became intrigued at a table of sewing and knitting machines, and I wandered away from them toward the sound of a meowing kitten. The yellow and orange creature scampered around a wire cage, batting at the air and chasing its tail. While I tickled its chin, the woman in the stall explained it had come from Fort Sumter. Born under the rebel banner, she explained, the kitten had since taken the oath of allegiance to the United States.

"Will you have her, miss?" she asked me. "Eleven dollars and you'll top the highest bidder!"

"I don't think my old dog would like that much."

"Too bad. I hate to see her in this cage."

"How did she get to Chicago?"

The woman brightened. "Oh, that would be Captain Whittle of the 72nd Board of Trade regiment. He presented her to the Fair though I'm uncertain how he came by her."

My heart skipped a beat. "Captain Whittle, you say?"

"Yes. Do you know the gentleman?"

"Yes. That is, I used to."

Whittle, a lieutenant in Company B, had been badly wounded during the second charge at Vicksburg. He'd gone home to Chicago for convalescence then much to everyone's surprise had returned to the regiment. I rarely saw him in Vicksburg but knew he'd been a popular officer. "Tell me, is the regiment back then?" I asked the woman.

"Oh, no, but how I wish they were! My son writes that they are still in Union Springs, Alabama. They hope to be mustered out soon."

"Yes," I said, beginning to feel weak again. "I'm sure they do."

"I go to the Board of Trade offices nearly every day," the woman continued, "hoping to hear news of their homecoming." She stopped. "Did you say your husband is with the regiment?"

"No, I, um…where are the Board of Trade offices?"

"On La Salle Street, just south of the courthouse. There's a sign out front, so you can't miss them."

*

The Chicago Board of Trade had formed in 1848. Twenty-five businessmen, most of them grain merchants, had seen the need to bring order to the chaotic marketing situation that took place every year in the city. During the winter, prices for grain stayed high; at harvest time, when farmers arrived at the lakeshore by the hundreds, they dropped dramatically. Some individuals, unable to get fair compensation, dumped their corn and wheat into Lake Michigan rather than haul their crops home. The Board of Trade organized people and markets and quickly grew to 150 members, becoming an integral part of civic life in Chicago. During the second year of the war, it had organized three regiments, one of which included the 72nd Illinois.

The next morning, I told Carmen and Owl that I planned to visit the Board of Trade's offices. I explained about the woman with the kitten and how I hoped to learn more about the regiment. Owl nodded.

"I'm meeting Mr. McVicker later but I can accompany you after

291

that," he said.

"That's all right. I thought I'd walk over this morning."

"You can't go by yourself, Jennie." He thought. "Unless you're going dressed as a boy?"

The idea that I couldn't go somewhere by myself, or simply because I wanted to, seemed so peculiar that it took my mind a moment to consider the possibilities. Go to the offices as a young man and cope with the questions and well wishes of all I met, or wear my new clothes and wait for Owl. I chose the latter.

Later that afternoon, at the Board of Trade building a man with short hair that stood up at all angles greeted us. Without inquiring as to our mission, he quickly swept Owl and me inside.

"Come in, come in! We've been expecting you!" He waved an arm about the room. "My apologies for the disarray. Between the end of the war, the Fair, and the ladies leaving, we are up to our ears in work. Obviously, we are so grateful you've come!"

"What's that?" asked Owl.

"You and your wife, of course," the man nodded toward me, "will be handsomely compensated. The Board is flourishing and we have great need of bookkeepers. With your great references, we feel quite fortunate indeed!" The man fairly beamed.

"I'm sorry," said Owl, "but I think you have us mistaken for other people. We aren't married and we aren't here for a job."

The man continued smiling. "Sorry?"

"We've come to inquire after news of the Board of Trade regiments," I said. "We don't wish to keep you, but we're wondering if there's any news of the 72nd Illinois?"

It took the man a moment, but at last he seemed to understand. "I'm sorry, we don't have any more recent news than that the regiment remains in Alabama. Of course, everyone happily awaits their return. We are planning a most spectacular welcome home at Bryan Hall! I don't know if you know much about the 72nd, but they are a most illustrious regiment. They've been in several notable engagements—"

"Yes," I said, interrupting, "I do know."

The man nodded. Then he went to a table and searched through some papers. He returned with a stack of sheets.

"We did receive this recently. It's a roster of the regiment with each soldier's name and his particulars." The man cleared his throat. "This will be printed in the *Tribune* soon. We haven't done so sooner because of the Fair. The mood is too good, and well, we want people to feel hopeful."

I reached for the roster. It didn't take long to find the names.

Biddle, Joseph; Chicago; date of muster-July 30, 1862; Killed at Franklin, Tenn, November 30, 1864.

Johnson, Kit; Chicago; date of muster-August 7, 1862; On duty, Union Springs, Alabama.

Morgan, Christopher; Evanston; date of muster-July 30, 1862; Killed at Franklin, Tenn, November 30, 1864.

Shottenkerk, Archibald; Chicago, date of muster-August 2, 1862; Died at Clifton, Tenn, January 5, 1865, of wounds.

I closed my eyes. Owl asked the man for a chair for me. After a moment, I opened my eyes again and search for the final name.

Taylor, Robert; Kewanee; date of muster-August 1, 1862; Killed at Franklin, Tenn, November 30, 1864.

"Thank you for your time," I said, handing the papers back as the roaring in my ears grew louder. The man nodded gravely.

"I am so sorry, miss. The war has taken so much from all of us."

"Yes," I managed. "It has."

*

Early the next morning I got up and went downstairs. The smell of freshly baked biscuits filled the house and Temple was busy frying eggs and bacon and slicing up pieces of fruit. She pointed to a chair.

"The Mister and Carmen ain't up yet," she said, "but I started cooking anyway."

"Just coffee, Temple. That is, my stomach doesn't feel so good this morning."

"You too skinny, miss," she said, scooping up two eggs and putting them on a plate with several strips of bacon and two biscuits. "Can't see that when you wearing a dress, but shore 'nuff can in them trousers."

"Temple—"

"No, you just set there, get some coffee in you and then try eating. If you really can't, then fine, I feed it to the dog out back. But I think you be able to." I nodded and sat down.

Owl and I hadn't talked about the roster or finding his name listed among the dead. We'd told Carmen only that there was little news though the Board planned a great celebration when the regiment did return. I'd slept very little and now couldn't imagine how I'd finish off this plate of food.

All of the boys were gone except me and Kit. As I thought about them, the kitchen around me turned watery and shapeless; soldiers began gathering around Temple. I lay my head down on the table.

"Miss?" I looked up. "You all right?"

"I'm fine. It's just so hot in here."

Temple soaked a cloth in a bowl of cool water and placed it against my forehead. She put her other hand on my shoulder. "Carmen told me what you done, miss," she said, quietly. "How you left home to go fight for the niggers."

I put my hand on the towel. "That's not why I left home, Temple. I wish it were."

"Carmen told me the places you been," she continued, "and everything you done. And you just a little girl too!" She sat down in the chair across from me. "Well, old Temple been around a long but I ain't never heard of no girl going for a soldier! No, ma'am, I ain't never heard of such a thing. But the good Lord, he musta been watching over you. And will be all the days from here on. Don't matter now if you set around the rest of your life, lazy as an old cat. He look down at you and say, "Well done, good and faithful servant."

I stared at the plate of food. Every time I put on my trousers and blouse and coat, it was the same: people saying or believing things that weren't true. How could I ever tell them what was true? How could I ever explain my reasons for leaving home, which had nothing to do with something as noble as freeing black men and women from bondage? I simply couldn't, especially not to someone who had already decided something for themselves. I nibbled on a biscuit.

"Thank you," I said, miserable.

Temple smiled. "You don't thank *me*, miss. I live my whole life and there still never be enough time to say thank *you*!"

FOUR

IT WAS STILL early enough that there weren't many people on the
streets. I headed south across the river, then east on Lake Street to
the train station. After purchasing my ticket for Kewanee for the
next day, I boarded the horse car. Leaving the city center behind,
the prairie opened wide. Indian grass, big bluestem, and switch
grass all swayed quietly in the early morning breezes. The heads
and tails of deer could be seen bounding away through this blanket
of vegetation, while hawks, catching wind currents, circled high
above.

At the entrance to Camp Douglas, I stepped off the horse car.
The perimeter fence and high arch looked exactly the same as it
had three years ago; the only noticeable difference with the camp
was how quiet it seemed. Two young guards, fresh as daisies in
their clean, crisp uniforms, nodded at me. I continued north a few
blocks then turned west and quickly found myself in front of
"Biddle's Blacksmith." A clapboard home, white with yellow trim,
stood next to the smith, and as I looked at it, now quite uncertain if
I should have come, a boy, not much past fifteen, appeared. I told
him I was looking for Katherine Biddle.

He nodded. "Katie's inside," he said, wiping both hands on his apron. "Can I tell her who's asking?"

I cleared my throat. "I'm Robert Taylor. A friend of her brother."

The boy's eyes grew big, and he told me to follow him. As we entered the yard, I looked back toward the south. Great, cotton clouds filled the sky, and the air around us suddenly felt heavy.

"It's been a piece since it rained," the boy said, following my gaze, "but that's sure to change today."

I waited in the hallway while he went upstairs to get his cousin. Though it would have been unthinkable to come here dressed as a woman, I still felt nervous. This visit wouldn't make Katherine Biddle feel any better, but I had to give her Biddle's things. I also was curious. We had corresponded for many months, and her letters, when I couldn't read Marie's, had helped me feel less alone. I should at least thank her.

Footsteps on the stairs caused me to look up. The cousin scampered down and went back outside. In the next instant, Katherine Biddle stood in front of me. If she was surprised, she didn't show it. She took my hand in both of hers, telling me I was very welcome and bidding me to come into the parlor. I suddenly couldn't speak. Her resemblance to her brother took my breath away. Her hair was long, of course, but curly and dark like Biddle's. She also had the same big, blue eyes. Katherine's voice was deep too; it might have been my friend speaking.

"Please sit," she said, pointing to the sofa. "I will go tell Sally to make us tea. You will have time for tea, of course?"

I looked at her and nodded, my knees shaking. Suddenly, I felt desperately hot in my frock coat. Katherine disappeared for a few minutes then returned with a tray, teapot, and two cups.

"I do apologize, Miss Biddle," I said, as she sat beside me, "for coming unannounced. It's just I have only arrived in town."

"Please do not concern yourself, Mr. Taylor. And do call me Katherine, or Katie if you prefer. After our correspondence, I feel as if I know you and I'm very glad you have come. Unfortunately, my parents are gone to the Fair today. They shall be sorry to have missed you." She poured the tea. "Tell me, is the regiment returned?"

"No. They are still in Alabama it seems."

"Oh." She added sugar to both cups. "How do you come to be here then?"

"That is a very long story, I'm afraid."

She handed me the tea. "Well, you have come some distance to tell me a long story, haven't you?"

"Truthfully? I'm not sure why I've come. I—I feel a bit queer at the moment." Katie nodded. The low rumble of thunder could now be heard and the soft patter of raindrops began hitting the window. "But I did want to see you. I assume you know about the battle at Franklin. About your brother."

"Yes, we know. Shortly after the new year, Captain Williams wrote to us." She seemed about to say more, but then took a sip of tea. "Truly, I can't quite believe it, even now, after so many months. Even after so many lives have been lost, it still seems unlikely that this would have come to pass upon our family too. I suppose that seems rather odd."

"No, it doesn't seem odd. Both of my brothers were killed as well, early in the war. I still can't believe that fully either." I took a deep breath. "I don't really know how to say some things, Katie, but I must say something. Your brother was my very best friend. I don't know how I would have survived without him. Of all the soldiers I knew, he was the best, for many reasons that aren't easily explained. He was good, and kind. I am so sorry for what has happened."

She looked away, tears in her eyes. "He was my best friend too."

I opened up my bag and pulled out the letters. "These are his things. He asked me to keep them just before the battle. I expect he knew he might not make it." Katie looked at the letters. "I am sorry," I said again, "but I didn't want to just send everything in the mail."

"No, of course not. Thank you, I am grateful."

As the rain picked up, a group of frogs began croaking outside the window. The wind grew louder, and the cool breeze coming through the open window felt welcome and refreshing. Absently, Katie refilled our cups. We sat there a long time not speaking. Suddenly, she looked my way.

"Please forgive how abrupt this will sound, but...did my brother know?"

My heart skipped. "Know what?"

"About you?"

I looked out the window. My mind flashed over the more than two years I had known Biddle. We had rarely been apart; I slept next to him, ate with him, laughed and talked with him, and finally, very nearly died with him. It didn't surprise me that Katie understood who I was; it seemed most women I'd met the last three years did. "I don't think so," I said, at last, "but I don't know for sure. Why? Did he write something to you?"

"Not specifically. But he talked about you a lot. How much he cared for you, how much he worried about you. That you seemed lonely in your heart and had no family beyond your father who seemed to have some problems." Katie's cheeks colored. "I am sorry, I have said too much."

I shrugged, embarrassed. "It is fine."

"Some time ago," she continued, "I began to have a funny feeling. That is, my brother seemed so, well...so *close* to you. The likeness he sent of the two of you before the regiment left Vicksburg... Well, perhaps I was just jealous. But then you seemed so nice in your letters, and clearly cared for him too, so I thought I shouldn't worry. As time went by, I decided maybe things weren't exactly as they seemed."

I thought. "Are you telling me that you thought I might be a woman?"

"I don't know what I thought. No, I don't think I thought that, though of course the newspapers had had a few stories of such soldiers. It did sound to me like Joseph cared for you a great deal, perhaps more than he should have, but that's as far as my thinking could go. Like I said, you seemed nice and I enjoyed getting your letters."

I shook my head. "It wasn't like that. I did love him, but only like a brother. If he knew, he never said."

She nodded. "I believe he did, but we'll never know now."

I told Katie then that she should call me Jennie. "That is my real name after all."

"Jennie," Katie smiled. "You know, my brother wasn't a very gregarious person. He had friends, of course, but he could also be quite shy. Yet, when he found someone he liked, that person had a friend for life. I believe you were one of those people."

My stomach hurt. "I should go. I've taken enough of your time. And the rain is letting up."

"Of course. I am grateful you have come."

We both stood, a bit awkward and maybe relieved the conversation was over. As she walked me to the door, I was struck again by the resemblance to her brother. I asked Katie if she'd mind if I wrote to her now the war was over.

"Not at all. I would like that very much." She shook my hand. "Take care of yourself, Jennie."

"Thank you." I kept hold of her hand. "You take care as well."

PART FIVE

ONE

April 10, 1855, Toulon, Illinois

AT FIRST, Jothan wasn't going to let me play. The new game, townball, he explained, couldn't include girls. It required running and hitting the ball hard with a stick and sliding on the ground into the bases. Girls weren't strong enough, Jothan said, and it was no good me going on about it. I looked at my oldest brother like he was crazy.

"What's gotten into you, Jothan Edwards? I can too play this and any other game if I want."

He shook his head. "No, Jen, not anymore. You're getting too old to be playing with us."

"Since when?"

"Since now. Since things have changed. You're ten now and a young lady, and young ladies don't play boys' games."

I stared at him. Jothan's eyes flickered and then I knew what this was all about. The trouble could be explained in two words: Marie Parker. The new, pretty girl who had just moved to Toulon with her parents had created great excitement among all the boys. In addition to being pretty, Marie was funny and nice apparently and everyone wanted to know her. For my money, she wasn't that interesting. She was hopeless at most games, including even the simple ones like kick the can or red rover, and she didn't know a thing about fishing. Still, no one seemed to care much what I thought. I crossed my arms.

"You listen, Jothan Edwards. I'm playing today and that is the end of it. If you keep talking like this, I'm going to tell Papa I saw you taking tobacco from his box."

My brother colored. "Jen—"

"I will also tell him that you borrowed his pipe the other day when he went to Galesburg."

"That's snitching, Jennie."

"It's not snitching because I never promised I wouldn't tell. I don't *want* to tell him but you're being a pill and forcing me to." He looked at me unhappily. "Well?"

"I'm only trying to be a good big brother, Jen. You can't always play with boys and do things that boys do. You might get hurt."

"Playing this game? I don't think so. I'm stronger than most everyone here."

"I don't just mean this game." He sighed. Jothan rarely, if ever, won any of our arguments. "All right, you can play, but I don't like it."

"You're not going to like losing either!" I shouted, running over to our friend Adam, who had wanted me on his team.

Since no one had played townball before, there was a lot of discussion before we actually began. The idea was simple enough: hit the ball with the stick as hard as you could, then run around and touch all the bases before the other team retrieved the ball and tagged you with it. After determining the size of the playing area, where all the bases would go, and who would be the first "striker" and who the first "thrower," we began.

Harry Trickle, Washington's nephew, threw the first ball to Adam, who began as our team's striker. Twice Adam swung and missed, but on the third try, the stick connected with the ball and sent it high over the heads of Jothan's team. Still, a particularly speedy boy named Phillip scooped up the ball and tossed it to

Gardiner forcing Adam to stop at the second base. Two more boys on my team took their turns as strikers before I got my chance. By now, Adam had "come home," scoring one point and looking very happy.

Hitting the ball, I found, wasn't as easy as it looked.

I missed the first two throws from Harry, swinging so hard the second time that the stick nearly flew out of my hand. We each were given five chances and when I missed the third ball, Adam walked over.

"It ain't that hard, Jen," he said. "Keep your eye on the ball as it comes."

I glared at him. "That's what I'm doing, Adam!"

He nodded. "Good. You can do it."

When I looked back out at the other team, I saw Jothan saying something to another boy. Suddenly, I felt hopping mad. I disliked Marie Parker more than ever. With an eagle's eye, I watched the next ball come toward me and swung the stick with all my strength. Crack! The ball sailed into the air. It went higher and higher, far above the head of boy at the other end of the field, until I couldn't see it anymore.

"Run, Jen, run!" Adam shouted, jumping up and down.

We played townball the rest of the afternoon and all agreed it was the best game ever. As my brothers and I walked home, Jothan apologized.

"I'm sorry, Jen. I didn't mean all I said earlier. You should always play with us."

"It's all right, Jothan. I forgive you."

He still looked sad, but I knew it wasn't about the game. It was all about Marie. He hadn't yet worked up the courage to even talk to her, and this clearly bothered him. But I couldn't help with that. All I could do was hope that he'd figure out she wasn't worth all this fuss. In the meantime, I had a plan to get even. Grasshoppers in Marie's pencil box should do the trick.

*

I woke up as the train arrived at the Kewanee station. The air inside the car was stifling and had been the entire trip from Chicago. Several ladies around me fanned themselves, while their gentlemen companions, having furtively loosened their collars during the ride, now began arranging their dress again. Before leaving Chicago, I had purchased a plain pair of trousers and a dress coat, which I wore now, leaving my worn blue coat and the clothes Sarah Hawkins had given me with Owl. In this ordinary costume, no one recognized me for a soldier, but I also wasn't as hot as I would have been in a dress and all that wearing a dress entailed. The women's clothes Carmen had bought me lay folded up in my bag.

After boarding the stage, I arrived in Toulon in the late afternoon. An incoming tide of gray darkened the sky to the south and soon raindrops were tapping upon the carriage roof. As we reached Main Street, a full-on downpour commenced. Debarking the stage, I ducked under the roof of the post office to wait out the storm. Five minutes passed, then ten. Rivulets formed in the street as cascades of water tumbled off the roof. After a half-hour, I found a soggy cigar in my haversack and began chewing on it. Then a cheery voice behind me made me jump.

"Hall-oo!"

I turned to find Mr. Griffin, the postmaster, standing in the doorway. He smiled, but his crinkled forehead and uncertain look told me he saw only a stranger. I put the cigar away and took a deep breath.

"Hello, Mr. Griffin."

The postmaster adjusted his spectacles. "Do I know you, young man?"

"Yes, sir," I nodded, removing my hat. "You do."

*

By the time the rain stopped an hour later, Mr. Griffin had recovered. After telling him who I was, I'd had to help him into a chair and pour us both tea from water he'd just boiled. When at last he could speak, he said simply, "What happened, Jennie?"

I left the post office and headed toward Trickle's. The summer rainstorm had emptied the streets. There were no wagons or horses in front of any of the businesses. The general store was dark and quiet. After a moment standing outside, I pushed open the door and walked in.

My eyes took a moment to adjust. The wooden floors smelled of the familiar pine scent, and mixed with the dry, scratchy odors of grains and beans, the bitter animal smell of leather boots, and the delicate essence of silk and muslin fabrics. Barrels of pickles and crates of onions were where they'd always been, while a new glass cabinet on the counter now housed watches, pipes, and frames for likenesses. The area around the stove looked cleaner than I remembered. A sign on the back wall read, "All Persons Welcome at the Stove, those with Muddy Shoes Excepted."

I sat down. Where was Washington Trickle? If he'd closed up for the day, he'd forgotten to lock the door. And if the store wasn't closed, why wasn't he there? Anybody could just walk and steal everything. Somebody *would* likely do that very thing any minute. I'd never known Washington to be so careless, but then maybe things had changed. Maybe he'd changed. Maybe—

I stood up. What if Washington was dead? It could have happened; people died all the time, now more than ever. But, surely Marie would have told me if that had happened. Yet, it had been many months since her last letter. For that matter, maybe she was dead too. And Mama and Papa, maybe even Jen-Jen. I stumbled toward the door. I had to get out of the store and find out who was still alive.

Suddenly, the front door opened. Washington Trickle walked in carrying a lamp, mumbling. "Don't forget to lock up, she says, but I *didn't* forget. Old woman!" He headed for the counter and only stopped when he saw me standing there. He raised the lamp higher. "What's that? Who's there?"

I couldn't speak, so tremendous was my relief. Washington looked exactly how I remembered him. His moon face might have been a little rounder, and his beard looked uncharacteristically tidy, though it still held a pencil and one rolled-up piece of paper. He also looked a little more ample about the waist.

"Can I help you, young man?" Washington asked, his surpise giving way to curiosity.

I found my voice, though it came out barely above a whisper. "Mr. Trickle, it's me."

"What's that?" He took a step forward.

"It's me, Jennie. I know it doesn't look like me, and I've been gone an awful long time, but it surely is your friend. Jennie."

Washington frowned. He looked at me for a very long time then his eyes grew big. He turned around. Setting the lamp down on the counter, his shoulders began to shake. I heard the pencil fallout of his beard and onto the floor. When I went over and put a hand on his shoulder, the trembling increased.

"We thought you quite gone, Jennie," Washington sobbed. "Quite gone indeed."

*

The shock for Mrs. Trickle was even greater. She turned so pale that I feared she might faint. It took some minutes to convince her the person before her with short hair, trousers, and a man's dress coat really was the Eliza Jane she had always known and not a ghost. When this simple, as well as complicated, fact was confirmed, the crying began along with many cries of "It's not to be believed!" By the time the older woman had gathered herself, I felt completely worn out.

Rosetta had just finished make a beef and oyster pie and we all sat down to supper as if I'd never been away. She attempted to tell me three years' worth of town news in one hour, while her husband brought out several catalogs of all the new items he'd begun carrying in the store. After finishing his pie, Washington collected some things to show me. The most interesting was a new-fangled camera, a big black box with a round hole containing a glass lens. After Washington had explained how now anyone could take photographs and showed me how the whole contraption worked, Rosetta cut in.

"No more show and tell, Washington Trickle! We've been

talking a leg off a centipede! Let's let Jennie talk awhile."

I had just taken another bite of pie. "About what?"

"Whaddya mean, "About what?" shouted Washington. "About everything!"

Rosetta nodded. "The letters from you stopped some time ago, Jennie. Of course, we assumed the worst. Then when Marie received THE letter from your captain, we knew it was true."

I swallowed. "What letter?"

Washington took a deep breath. "The letter telling us that you'd died in Tennessee. Or, rather, that Private Robert Taylor had died. Marie had been sending letters all winter without any word from you. Early in the year one of those letters reached the captain. He immediately sent one back to Marie explaining the battle and his deep condolences."

I sat back in my chair. "And Mama and Papa? They think this too?"

"Just your father," said Rosetta. "Julia still thinks you're in Chicago. No one has had the heart to tell her the truth. Or, what we believed to be the truth."

"I must go to Marie," I said, standing up. "She mustn't think I'm dead a minute longer. I'll see Papa tomorrow, but I must go to Marie now." I headed for the door and Rosetta scampered after me.

"Jennie, are you sure you're ready? Do you know what you'll say?"

"No, I don't know at all, but she has to know I'm not dead."

Rosetta caught up with me and held onto one of my arms. "Oh, Jennie, you don't know how glad I am you're returned! It's like the heavens have just opened up and the angels carried you back to us. Me and Mr. Trickle...well, you know you're like a daughter to us, so this is the happiest day we've had in a long while." She let go, then kissed me on the cheek. "Go on now then! Go tell that sweet girl, Marie, the news that will make her just as glad!"

*

The rain had passed and the summer evening returned bright and fresh. A few people had emerged from their homes and were moving about the streets. I walked with a dream-like feeling through my town, passing the courthouse and the Waxwing Theatre and the homes of people I had known all my life. No one paid me any mind and soon I stood on Greenwood Street.

I remained behind an elm tree and watched the Parker's home. Off to one side of the house, a little girl was jumping around. She wore a light blue dress and had dark, curly hair that fell below her shoulder. Even from across the street, I could hear Jen-Jen talking a mile a minute. The words blurred together but occasionally there would be a shriek followed by "Look, Mama, look!" My heart pounded wildly. Maybe I wasn't ready to see Marie; certainly I *didn't* know what I was going to say. Apart from my own self, all seemed perfectly normal. Up in the sky, pigeons formed a "V" pattern heading north; two women a block down Greenwood walked arm in arm; a small dog barked excitedly from a nearby porch. When the sun began slipping beneath the western horizon, I knew I could delay no longer.

Making my way across Greenwood, I went through the gate and walked toward the side of the house. At the corner of the building, behind a tall rose bush, I stopped again. I could see Marie sitting in a chair and Jen-Jen standing at the edge of the small pond the Parkers had built years before. Marie's mother had planted lilies and ferns around the water and had created a wonderfully cool place to be in the summer. I watched my niece pushing several wooden boats around the water, calling out to various captains and sailors to heave to and turn the ships around. As the armada began to come together, I heard Marie's voice.

"Baby, it's almost time to go in. Maybe you should bring the ships in to port."

"But it's still daytime, Mama."

"Yes, but it's getting darker. They can all sail again tomorrow."

I expected a protest, but instead Jen-Jen shouted, "All ships, into the harbor!" Then she told her mother it might take a minute for some captains weren't as good of sailors as the other captains.

Marie chuckled. "That's fine, my dear."

While Jennie worked to get the ships into a quiet part of the pond, she suddenly said, "I'm glad you're not sad anymore, Mama."

"I haven't been sad, Jen-Jen."

"Yes, you have. But I don't think you're sad now." She looked up. "You're not, are you?"

A pause. "No, baby, I'm not."

"That's good."

The creaking sound of a door opening preceded the arrival of Mrs. Parker on the back porch. She announced that apple-cinnamon cake was just out of the oven. At this, Jennie squealed and raced up the steps into the house. After a moment, Mrs. Parker, said, "Marie?"

"I'll be there in a minute, Mother."

"Very well, but don't be long."

After the door closed behind Mrs. Parker, I steadied myself and took a deep breath. Everything had changed in the time I'd been away and soon that would be clear to Marie and my parents and probably most of Toulon. I didn't care a fig what most people thought, but I cared tremendously what Marie thought. Yet, there was nothing for it but just to move forward and see what happened.

*

Knowing it was myself walking into her garden, I somehow expected Marie to know as well and run immediately up to me with a warm embrace and a happy smile. However, since she *didn't* know it was me, nothing of the kind happened. Marie simply looked up, a bit surprised, then stood and smoothed out her skirt and walked over to me.

"Yes? Can I help you?"

Marie wore a rose-colored day dress, dotted with a design of small, pink flowers and trimmed in burgundy lace. Her strawberry-blond hair was down and longer and straighter, with several light, silver streaks catching the fading sun. Though the silver hairs and faint lines around her eyes made her appear older than her twenty-six years, she looked just as lovely as I'd remembered. I suddenly couldn't speak and after a few seconds, she nodded and glanced around.

"I expect you're here about the gardening. As you can see, we don't need much, just some tidying up around the bushes and over there by the arbor. The truth is," she crossed her arms, "we've never really cleaned up from last fall. If you want to talk to my father, I can fetch him, but that's really about all there is to it." When I still didn't respond, Marie looked at me again. She tilted her head. "I'm sorry, you are here about the garden work, aren't you? Mrs. Trickle said—" She stopped.

At that moment it felt like everything, birdsong and the clattering wheels of wagons and people talking on the street, all went silent. I took off my hat and ran my fingers through my hair. Now I wished I hadn't gotten it cut so short, but at the time, just a week ago in Cairo, it had seemed necessary. Sweat was now running down the side of my face. Marie was staring intently at me, as if trying to remember something she once knew.

"I'm so sorry, Marie," I said, quietly. "Sorry for the shock this will cause. Sorry for, well, for everything."

Suddenly, my friend's face drained of all its color. She brought her hands to her mouth. Then she took a step backward. Of course, she must recognize my voice; *that* hadn't changed. Marie's hands began shaking.

"I know this is hard," I continued quickly. "And I probably seem like a ghost, but I'm not a ghost. It really is me, that is…it's Jennie, your friend." At the sound of my name, she collapsed back onto the bench she had just been occupying. A small cry escaped her lips. She closed her eyes.

"It's not true what the captain wrote, Marie," I added. "He thought it was but it wasn't. And I've had no chance to write you myself until just a few weeks ago, but obviously you haven't gotten that letter yet, a letter that would have been easier to believe than me just turning up like Jesus on the third day."

By now, Marie had covered her face with her hands and was weeping. I sat down on the bench beside her and after a moment put my arms around her. The shaking had increased but she hugged me back.

"Oh, Jennie, I had hoped, yes, I had. For a time at least. Even after the letter came. But you had once told me that they wouldn't write unless they knew for sure."

"I know, and I'm so sorry, Marie. But I am home now. Oh, how much I have missed you!"

At that moment, Mrs. Parker opened the back door to see what was keeping her daughter. "Marie?"

We pulled apart then. Marie kissed my cheek and looked at me beaming. She called over her shoulder, "Oh, Mother, the most wonderful thing has happened! Jennie is returned!"

TWO

THE REST of the evening passed quickly and happily. Marie never let go of my hand, while her parents, after several minutes of stunned silence, talked over one another asking me questions. They wanted to know what had happened, where I had been nearly this whole year when there'd been not one letter from me, and if I was all right. None of the questions prompted simple answers and I stammered trying to put together a story that wouldn't sound as awful as the truth. Fortunately, it didn't matter much what I said. I'd just start talking when either Mr. Parker or his wife would break in with another question.

The only one who said nothing was little Jennie. The excitement and Marie crying, even happily, had sent her to her mother's side where she stared at me with eyes like little blue moons. When at last there was a break in all the talking, and Jennie still hadn't moved or spoken, Marie tried to explain that all was well.

"Jen-Jen, this is Papa's sister," she said. "Remember? The one I told you had gone away for a while? Well, she's returned now."

Jennie thought about this. "Does that mean Papa is coming home too?"

Marie's smile collapsed. She looked at me. Suddenly, I felt confused. Was Jothan coming home? Hadn't I just seen him? No, wait, that was a dream. As the tangle in my mind continued, I distracted myself by asking Jennie if she'd ever seen a magic trick. She shook her head.

I kneeled down next to her, pulling a cloth from my pocket and waving it around for all to see. In my other pocket I organized a rubber thumb that Owl had given me into my closed fist. Waving the cloth more, I asked, "Are you watching closely?"

"Yes," she answered in a quiet voice.

"All right then."

I began stuffing the cloth into my left fist and into the thumb which no one could see. After it was tucked inside, I made one last gesture of stuffing and capped the rubber thumb onto my real right thumb. And just like that, the cloth had vanished! Mrs. Parker breathed in sharply and I heard Mr. Parker say, "What?"

I opened both of my hands and wiggled my fingers to distract anyone from possibly noticing the slightly enlarged thumb on my right hand.

Jen-Jen's mouth fell open. All shyness gone, she immediately ran both of her hands over my left hand where the cloth had gone but there was nothing there. After letting her search for a minute, I said, "Wait a minute, maybe..." I rubbed my hands together, then began pulling something out of my once-again clenched fist. After I'd handed her the cloth, she carefully looked it over.

"How did you do that?" she asked at last.

*

It was very late by the time we all went to bed. Jen-Jen had wanted to see more magic tricks and we all ate two pieces each of Mrs. Parker's apple pie. Marie and her parents, like Mrs. Trickle, tried to catch me up on all the news of Toulon, a nearly impossible task though an amusing one to watch as Marie's parents occasionally sparred over details. Mr. Parker asked a few questions about the war, and seemed satisfied with my brief answers. At last, I felt so tired I feared falling asleep in the chair. It was in that dozing moment that I noticed a person standing outside the window. The man wore a hat and looked in at us with a blank expression. No one else seemed to notice the stranger and as quickly as he appeared, then he was gone.

"Oh, Jennie," Mrs. Parker was saying, "our dreams have truly been answered. You, at least, have come home. When your parents return tomorrow, there shall be no end to the celebration."

I set my cup of tea down and noticed my hand was shaking. "Return? Where are they?"

"They left yesterday for Galesburg. Your father had business in town and Julia accompanied him for a change of scene. With Amos there now to manage the farm, they can get away for a day or two. Your mother is so much better."

"Who's Amos?"

Marie looked at me. "He's the man your father hired after the others moved on. Amos was a soldier too, wounded in a battle back East and discharged. Mr. Trickle met him after he'd come out west. Amos had made it to Kewanee, but by then had run out of money, so Mr. Trickle mentioned your father needing help."

I nodded. "I see."

"In any case," Mrs. Parker continued, "you must stay here tonight. It's far too late and you can't go home to a cold house. You can stay in the guest room."

"Jennie can stay with me, Mother," said Marie, gathering up her sleeping daughter. "Of course she can."

After bidding her parents goodnight and putting Jen-Jen to bed, Marie and I went to her room. It was much as I'd remembered it: clean and bright, filled with pretty things like dolls and ceramic figures of animals and people, shelves of books, her desk. On the mantle above the hearth was the photograph taken of her and Jothan on their wedding day. I stared a long while at my brother, thinking about all that had happened since that wonderful, summer day and this day of my homecoming. Next to the photograph was a small box made of dark wood and inlaid with lighter pieces in the shapes of flowers.

"Both Jothan's and your letters are in that box," Marie said, noticing my interest.

"Really?"

"I take them out occasionally to read. Some I've read to Jen-Jen too."

"Marie—"

She took hold of my hand. "Oh, Jennie, is this real? If I'm only dreaming, I suppose I do not mind. Yet, I shall feel very sad to wake up."

"You aren't dreaming, Marie," I said, squeezing her hand. "Though it doesn't feel very real to me either. I have thought about this day for so long."

"Truly?"

"Truly."

At that moment, Mrs. Parker poked her head into the room. "Do you have everything you need, Jennie?"

"Yes, ma'am, thank you."

"Because I could make you some tea, or bring up another piece of pie. Maybe a sandwich?"

I smiled. "Please don't, Mrs. Parker. It seems like all I'm doing these days is eating!"

"Well, you're still as skinny as a corn stalk."

"Jennie is tired, Mother," said Marie. "We must let her sleep."

"I know, dear. It's just that I still can't believe it. I may have to keep looking in on you to make sure I haven't conjured you from my hopes. This has been a most extraordinary evening."

"For me too, Mrs. Parker."

"Sleep well, girls." She closed the door.

"You're more beautiful than I remember, Marie," I said, after Mrs. Parker had left.

My friend laughed. "That is not true! But you're kind to say it."

"It most certainly *is* true."

Marie went to her bureau and pulled out two nightgowns. "I am older, I feel older, and I look older. But it's also true that for tonight at least, my heart is light as a feather." She handed me one of the gowns. "Thank you, Jennie, for coming home."

I felt strange removing my blouse and trousers in front of Marie, but she didn't seem to mind me helping her undress.

Everything was different now, yet she didn't know that, and I was so tired that my nervousness vanished upon getting into the bed. After we lay there awhile and looked at each other, Marie said, "Jen?"

"Hmm?"

"I do wonder how you did it? I mean, after all these years and no one ever knew. How did you do it?"

I thought a moment, then turned on my back. "Oh, that was easy, Marie. I kept my secret the same way magicians keep theirs. By hiding it in plain sight."

*

When I awoke the next morning, Marie was gone. A note on her pillow read:

Good morning, Jen!

You are still here and not a dream and so I am most happy! Forgive MY not being here when you awake, but I promised Father, who has left for Galesburg, that I would deliver some papers to the courthouse for him. It should not take long and I plan to be back by dinner, if not before. Mother and Jen-Jen are around and breakfast will be waiting for you.

Your very happy friend,

Marie

The day had already turned warm by the time I dressed and went downstairs. Windows had been opened, with soft breezes wafting through. The smells of Mrs. Parker's garden, including those of roses and jasmine vines, enveloped me in the cool, dark parlor. A young servant, who gave her name as Clara and said she was new to the Parker household, appeared and asked if I should like coffee and a scone.

"Just coffee, thank you."

She scampered hastily into the kitchen, reappearing quickly with a cup and saucer. "Mrs. Parker and the little one are in the garden, miss," she said, smiling.

I couldn't have looked less like a "miss" if I'd tried, but Clara seemed not to notice. "Thank you," I said again. My eyes felt gritty and too large; my mind muddled from being home again. I hadn't slept much in the bed with Marie, but it had been a pleasant wakefulness.

Jennie saw me first and came racing over, grabbing my free hand and leading me to the pond. The armada had set sail again and seemed to be on a trip of exploration. For now, my niece explained, the captains wanted to explore close to shore, that is, at the edges of the pond. There were big animals and lots of native people and the men hadn't yet left the ships. I listened to the long story and asked a few questions and Jennie seemed pleased by my interest. When at last I was able to sit down with Mrs. Parker, I felt I'd been on a great journey myself.

"'Native people'?" I asked Marie's mother. "How does she know such words?"

Mrs. Parker smiled, then spoke so her granddaughter couldn't hear. "From her books. From talking to people, asking questions. She's been reading for a year now!"

"Reading! At three-years-old? Isn't she a bit young for reading?"

"Obviously not." Mrs. Parker took a sip of coffee. "She's beyond bright, Jen, and a most amazing child. Your brother would be quite proud."

"Nana, look!" came a shout from the pond. "The people are meeting!"

One small boat was now venturing ashore to meet with the Indians, all of whom (as small sticks stuck into the ground) had gathered to greet the newcomers. I doubted this could end well, but maybe in Jen-Jen's world it would.

"She must wonder about her father," I mused.

"She does, but Marie has always told her stories of Jothan. She hasn't wanted anything to be a secret or upsetting."

"Did Marie tell her what happened?"

"No, not exactly. She only said that Jennie's papa had gone away to do something very important, and that he was the best of men, and now couldn't return home. Marie explained that sometimes you can't see people but that they are still with you. That, not surprisingly, was a little hard to understand, but Jen-Jen is a very thoughtful child, not prone to impatience or upset. Of course, she wishes her father were here, but she's wholly devoted to Marie."

"Yes," I nodded, "I can see that."

Mrs. Parker reached over and grabbed my hand. "I don't mean to go on, my dear, but I cried so much last night, tears of joy for your return. Marie wouldn't like me to say this but her heart fairly broke when you left. And then when it seemed you'd died too... Well, my daughter is strong, yet, I have worried so much."

I looked out at the meeting now taking place and the great conversations, all supplied by Jen-Jen, between the explorers and natives. "I'm sorry I went away, Mrs. Parker. At the time, it seemed the right thing to do."

"And now?"

"And now?" I thought. "I am just glad to be home. That's all."

*

That afternoon, Marie and I went to the Trickles to collect my knapsack and the presents I'd brought from Chicago. Washington had closed the shop for dinner and both he and his wife were sitting outside on the porch.

"Sit down, girls," said Mrs. Trickle, "and have some cake. Otherwise, this fat husband of mine will eat it all!"

Washington nodded happily, his mouth full and his moon face rosy. While Rosetta fetched two more plates and cut us generous helpings of pecan sponge cake, Washington swallowed and looked at Marie.

"What do you think of our Jennie being home?" he asked her.

Marie smiled. "To tell the truth, it's still a little hard to believe." She took my hand. "But I am very happy indeed."

Rosetta shook her head as she sat down. "I couldn't believe it either. I woke up this morning thinking it all must have been a dream. But, thank the Lord, it wasn't! Oh, Jennie, it's so good you're home, and we're both so happy you two girls are together again!"

After eating our cake and discussing the weather and such town news as the next show to come to the Waxwing Theatre, Marie and I left the Trickles, deposited some of the gifts at her home, then departed Toulon in the Parker's Tilbury carriage. As their horse Bessie trotted down Greenwood, I asked Marie if she liked working for her father.

"Oh, yes," she nodded, her face lighting up. "I mostly keep the books, the legal record of Father's dealings with people, as well as managing the income and expenses. I do like the preciseness of the work; the numbers, the need for clear statements that accurately reflect what has occurred. I also make copies of Father's letters, file papers for him at the Court House, manage his appointments, take care of his clients until he can see them. He says I am very organized!"

"I can believe that," I said, feeling happy for my friend.

Despite much that seemed familiar to me about Marie, she also had changed during our years apart. Her expression was more serious and faint lines, not unattractive, extended now from her eyes. Light, silver hairs grew scattered about her otherwise strawberry-blonde mane, and she seemed more thoughtful than I'd remembered. I could imagine Marie herself a lawyer, rather than just a lawyer's assistant, and I was sure she was professional but also warm with people in a way that would make them feel at ease.

"But what about all those "disagreeable people" Marie," I teased her, "that you didn't want to know anything about before?"

She smiled and pushed me gently. "Oh, they're still there. Of course, I don't know the details of Father's cases, but the men and women who come seeking his help are not monsters. They are just people having trouble. Sometimes I find myself having an opinion, but I am careful to keep those to myself."

I nodded, taking her hand. "That seems wise, and perhaps a useful skill in other situations too." In the few short hours since being reunited, I'd had the sense she was thinking many more thoughts than she was sharing. This didn't seem strange however; I was doing the same.

"How is my mother, Marie?" I asked, changing the subject. "I confess I am nervous to see her again."

She squeezed my hand. "You needn't be, Jen. Julia is so much better and mostly her old self again. I think it has helped having Amos around. He is a very nice man and very grateful to your parents. I am sure you will like him." She paused. "There is one thing though."

"What?"

Marie sighed. "Julia does know you've been gone to the war, Jennie. She knows you've been dressed as a boy these many years. She knows you've been with a regiment."

"But I thought—"

"I know. For a long while your mother believed you in Chicago working for Owl, as your letters indicated. So, of course, that's what we all thought she believed. Truthfully, I'm not even so sure about that now. In any case, sometime last year she asked me directly if you had gone to the war. I'm not sure what made her think this, probably the fact that you never came home. Not that a trip from Chicago is so simple, but it's not so far either. I had to tell her the truth."

I closed my eyes. "Poor Mama."

"What she *doesn't* know is anything about the letters your father and I received from your regiment after the battle in Franklin. That you had died was simply not something any of us could share. It was wrong but also easier to keep up the pretense that all was well."

"And when I didn't return, what were you all going to say then?"

Marie shrugged. "I don't know, but happily that is no longer a problem."

We were now well out of Toulon, traveling along Indian Creek. I felt glad to be away from town. People I had known my whole life had waved to Marie as she drove the Tilbury and looked at me with blank, though polite, expressions. Of course, they wouldn't recognize the person they saw now, but I also wondered, did everyone know that Jennie Edwards had gone for the war? And if they did know, did they think me perished or simply delayed the many weeks it was taking many soldiers to make it home? I thought about my mother. On the one hand, this news about Mama was good, for she hadn't ever had to believe me dead. On the other, how much she must have suffered. Not only knowing her daughter to be dressed as a man and living with men, but also that her one remaining child was being subjected every day to the very circumstances that had taken her sons from her. My stomach tightened.

"Jennie, I think Julia is stronger now," Marie interrupted my thoughts. "She found herself again while you were away. Still, it hasn't been easy."

Marie watched the road ahead but she looked worried. I leaned over and kissed her on the cheek. "It will all be fine, Marie."

*

As we began descending the track to Jug Run Creek, a large, dark object stood in the middle of road. Even before we got close, I knew it was Ruby. My mule stood very still. Her ears were turned toward us, her head slightly to one side to get a better look at the approaching visitors.

"I'll be," said Marie. "She must have known you were coming."

"Maybe," I said, jumping down from the Tilbury. "Or, more likely, she's just managed to escape."

At the sound of our voices, Ruby started trotting toward us. I did the same. By the time we met, Ruby was galloping, her hooves tossing up half-dollar-sized globs of mud. I wrapped my arms around the thick neck, burying my face in her fur. Ruby licked my neck and hands. Very soon, the velvety muzzle began searching in vain for my braid to chew on.

"A few things have changed, old girl," I whispered. Ruby bobbed her head as if to indicate she understood. Then she found the collar of my coat and began tugging until the top button was pressed tight against my throat.

"I don't think," said Marie, as she pulled up in the Tilbury, "that Ruby ever believed you wouldn't return. Animals know things, don't they?"

"Yes, they do," I managed, a lump in my throat.

As I tried to wiggle out of Ruby's grasp, I saw that behind us another wagon was now coming down the track. As it got closer, I saw my mother wave. Papa called out hello to Marie, then I heard him say, "Ruby's got out again, Julia!"

My parents couldn't see me easily because I stood partially behind Ruby. Mama asked Marie in a surprised voice if she had come to visit. Then she asked about Jen-Jen. Papa hopped out of the wagon and was walking toward my mule when I stepped into view. For a moment, nothing happened. Papa gave a brief nod, and both of my parents had slightly puzzled look, yet their expressions were nothing out of the ordinary. However, when no one said anything, Papa stopped walking and Mama pushed her hat back. The moment had another curious timeless feel. I wanted to speak, but couldn't; I thought I might go to Papa, but I couldn't do that either. In the end, it was Mama that moved us all forward into our time of reunion.

"Eliza Jane!" she said, getting out of the wagon and running my way quickly. She then had her arms around me. "Welcome home, my girl. It is more than time that you returned to us."

I could barely respond with, "Yes, Mama," and felt dizzy in her so familiar scent and embrace. She wept, but her tears were not the same kind of tears that I saw coursing down my father's cheeks. Papa was so pale and his eyes so big that I feared he might faint right there in the track. I wanted to go to him, but I couldn't leave Mama, who had known me gone but never believed me dead. At last, I did get to my father and he hugged me so fiercely and sobbed so tremendously that Mama and Marie both came to help hold him up. This was the difference between knowing too much and knowing too little. I'm not sure how long we all stood there and cried as the world each of us had come to accept suddenly vanished and became something else altogether.

THREE

I RODE with Mama and Papa in the wagon with Ruby tied alongside, while Marie followed in the Tilbury. Soon we came in sight of our home. Everything, the house and spring house, barn and chicken coop, the fields and fences, all looked exactly the same. Smoke rose from the chimney and I could hear Sam howling. I might have believed myself never gone but for the stranger that suddenly appeared and approached our wagon and spoke to my parents.

"Mrs. Edwards, Mr. Edwards, welcome home."

The man I presumed to be Amos was tall and skinny with coal black eyes and straight hair equally dark. He had only one arm; the sleeve of the other pinned to his shirt. He greeted Marie as well and gave me a quick nod before apologizing about Ruby.

Papa waved his arm. "That's fine, Amos, and not unexpected. We all know what a devil Ruby can be."

I jumped down from the wagon. "She ain't no devil," I said, stroking my girl's trumpet ears. "She just has a mind of her own."

Amos looked at me curiously. "Can't argue with you there."

I stretched out my hand. "I'm Jennie, Julia and Graham's daughter."

"Jennie is just this very minute returned from the war, Amos," my mother explained. "Marie has brought her from town and we are returning to the house for a celebration."

Amos' head tilted slightly, his expression puzzled. "Returned from the war?"

"It's a long story."

His face relaxed slightly. "They all are." He took my hand. "Pleased to meet you, Miss Edwards."

"Please call me Jennie. Nobody's used "miss" to address me in a long time."

He nodded, uncomfortable once more. "Jennie then." At that moment, Sam's barking became obvious again. I asked about him. "He's around by the barn," Amos explained. "Drying out. I had to tie him up and he ain't too happy about it."

"Drying out? Why?"

"Got himself crosswise with a skunk he did." Amos looked at my father. "Happened shortly after y'all left yesterday. I heard a squeal by the smokehouse and came over just in time to see the ass—I mean, business—end of a skunk scampering into that thicket of joe-pye weed behind the building. Sam just stood there, drenched in spray and surprised as a bull in a china shop."

Papa sighed. "I don't know why he's surprised. This has happened many times."

"I got my soap out," Amos continued, "and gave him a bath right away and then another this morning, but it's just gonna take some time, I think. Sam's been howling in protest that there be no more baths, but I ain't promised him anything."

We all laughed at the thought of poor Sam. Mama asked Amos to join us for tea and cake, but he declined as there were still many chores to do. Mama and Marie went into the house, while Papa talked with Amos and I led Ruby to the paddock. I noticed right away there was no rope securing the gate. No wonder she'd escaped.

*

While drinking several cups of tea and eating slices of spice loaf my mother had made before they'd gone to Galesburg, I listened happily to the many stories they all had to tell me. That no one asked me any questions about the war felt like a blessing. Marie had been right; my mother did seem much as I remembered her before Jothan and Gardiner had died, though she looked quite different. Her hair now was mostly gray with only some of the copper strands as reminders of the past. Her face was thinner, but her cheeks had color and the almond eyes shone bright. I didn't quite understand how this return had been accomplished, yet the how of it seemed far less important than the fact of it.

My father looked older too and seemed to have developed a slight hunch to his shoulders. His beard was longer, with some flecks of gray, and his hair had thinned noticeably at the temples. Throughout the cake and tea, he alternately cried and talked, always keeping hold of my hand. My parents told us of their trip to Galesburg and how they'd splurged on a room that featured such luxuries as meal service and running water.

Later that afternoon, I tied Ruby to the back of the Tilbury and accompanied Marie home. On Greenwood Street, we found Mrs. Parker and Jen-Jen in the garden drinking lemonade. We joined them in the shade of the cherry tree until the sun began sinking and I knew I must get home. Marie walked with me over to where Ruby stood eating Mrs. Parker's roses.

"It's selfish of me," she said, "but I wish you could stay."

"I wish that too," I agreed, pulling her into an embrace.

"You will come visit often, won't you, Jennie?"

"Of course, I will. In fact, I'll be here so much that you will become quite tired of me."

Marie smiled. "I doubt that."

The ride home was sweet, spring pleasure. Now that it was mid-June, butterfly weed had erupted across the prairie, and each plant's profuse orbs of orange flowers were attracting great, flittering masses of butterflies. The grasses too had shed their winter reticence and stood tall, though not as tall as they would become by late summer. Added to all this were red sparks of Indian paintbrush, yellow blankets of black-eyed Susans, and blue-purple lupine. Ruby felt the abundance too. She frisked along the road, nipping at each bush containing a sparrow, or prancing when a rabbit or lizard zigzagged away from us. My own spirits soared high; I was home!

When Jug Run Creek came into view, I got off Ruby and removed her halter. "We're running the rest of the way, my friend," I told her, to which she gave a vigorous nod. My one leg felt stiff, but the tingling and numbness I'd first experienced in Sarah's home had finally gone away. I kissed Ruby on the muzzle and took off. Trotting, as it happened, proved more what I was capable of and Ruby soon caught up with me after she understood the game. She would have beaten me back to the house by much more, but she kept slowing down to nip at my arm.

*

"Jennie?"

Washington Trickle set the parcel down on the counter in front of me. "Hey! You all right?"

The edges around the storekeeper's round face stayed blurry while I tried to remember what I'd been doing. I'd come into the store and I'd had a piece of paper in my hand. Yes, I'd come to buy things, that was it, and Mr. Trickle had started gathering what Mama needed. While he had done so, I started looking at a catalog. Then my mind had just slipped away as if it had better things to do.

I nodded, slowly. "I'm fine. It's just I got to thinking on something else. Something from a long time ago, I think."

Washington laughed. "You just looked all dreamy there for a minute."

"I feel kinda dreamy," I admitted. "Have done so since I returned." It had been close to a month I'd been home, and though I'd been working with Papa and Amos, as well as Mama, many was the time I found myself just standing or sitting and staring at nothing in particular.

"That don't surprise me, Jen," Washington said. "You've been living a different life up till now. It'll take a piece to get used to the old one again."

"Yeah," I nodded, still fuzzy, "I s'pose."

Washington pulled a piece of paper out of his beard and began writing on it. "You going to see Marie?" he asked. I nodded. "And Adam?"

Now I shook my head. "Every time I go by to see him, it seems he's out."

"Huh," said the storekeeper, handing me the bag of goods for Mama. "That seems odd."

Back outside, my chest felt fluttery and sweat ran down my sides. Inside the store, when Mr. Trickle found me lost in thought, I'd had the strangest feeling that I'd been somewhere with my brothers, but now the notion seemed silly. Still, the lightheadedness remained and I now felt desperate to see Marie.

At the bottom of the steps, I turned quickly and ran full on into none other than Bertha McRae. The jolt of our collision sent her tilting backward. I reached out and grabbed her by the waist and pulled her back toward me. She didn't recognize me right away due to my clothes and hat and also the fact that her spectacles had gone rather askew. After she'd settled them however, her sharp, green cat eyes fixed upon me.

"Well, well," she said at last, with abundant recognition. "Eliza Jane Edwards. I heard you were back." Then she did something that made me believe myself in another dream: she smiled. "Welcome home."

I stared at her. "Thank you, Mrs. McRae. It is—it is good to see you again."

Her smile grew. "I see you're still a liar, Eliza Jane."

My inclination to protest this assessment gave way to a moment's reflection. Several images from the past three years passed through my mind. At last I said, "You've no idea, Mrs. McRae."

The older woman laughed. "I am sure. In any case, it is well that you have returned, my dear. For your mother's and father's sakes."

Before I could reply to this, she was gone, into the general store, the cool darkness within immediately swallowing her.

*

"She's ill," I told Marie.

"Because she said something nice to you?"

"Well... yes. She called me "my dear.""

"Oh, Jennie." Marie looked at Jen-Jen who had fallen asleep on the sofa beside her. "Is that so odd?"

"How can you even ask me that? You know she's hated me since the day I was born."

"That is absurd, and I told you that a long time ago. Mrs. McRae doesn't *hate* anyone, and certainly not you. Maybe she has trouble expressing her feelings sometimes, but that's all."

Marie was too kind, but it would be wrong of me to argue with her simply because my friend was such a good person. I changed the subject. "How is it possible that Jennie can draw like this?" I asked, casting my gaze toward the pieces of paper on the table nearby. In addition to reading, my niece seemed able to sketch far beyond her years. The scene she'd happily presented me with when I'd arrived was of Jug Run Creek. The details in the buildings, Mama's flower boxes, the fields, and even Ruby and Sam standing by the spring house astonished me.

Marie stroked her daughter's hair. "She's a gifted child. Jothan was smart too remember. The drawing only began a couple of months ago. It is surprising in the very best way." She looked at me. "Gardiner's love of art has not died with him, Jen."

The mention of my brothers reminded me of one of the reasons I had come to visit. "Marie, I've been wanting to tell you something."

She smiled and turned toward me expectantly. Marie always looked pretty, but the pale green dress she wore today suited her strawberry hair and fair complexion in an even more pleasing way. I wondered how I could be so lucky to have such a good friend. To show my appreciation, I leaned over and kissed her. To my surprise, Marie kissed me back immediately. Then she leaned back onto the sofa. She put her hands on my face and we kissed with a freedom that had been denied for so many years. I wanted all of her, all at once and since I had no reason to think she didn't want the same, I began unfastening the buttons on the back of her dress. It didn't matter if anyone walked in right now; it didn't even matter that Jen-Jen lay right next to us sleeping soundly. All that mattered was the two of us, finally, after so long, and after so much had happened. As my hand pressed down upon her bosom, however, a funny thing happened.

Marie reached for her cup of tea.

Then she took my hand.

"What is it, Jen? What do you want to tell me?"

I shook my head, confused. Hadn't we just been doing something else? Marie's smile faded. "Are you all right, dear? You look very pale suddenly."

I closed my eyes. "I'm sorry, Marie, I just…well…never mind. Yes, I wanted to tell you something. Or, rather, give you something. That is, something I brought back with me."

"You don't have to give me anything, darling. Your return is all I need, all I have wanted. Besides, you have already given us presents."

"I know, but this is different. Only I'm worried it will make you sad."

"Oh." Her eyes flickered. "That is intriguing, though I don't much feel like being sad right now."

"I know. I don't either."

From my bag, I pulled out Gardiner's journal and the leather bag of dirt and red stones from my brother's graves. Everything looked out of place among the finery of the Parker's living room and the clean, tidy world of a place that had never seen war. Still, I set them on the table and began, telling Marie about going to Pittsburg Landing, showing her the map Adam had sent shortly after the battle, and describing the ease with which I had found the boys and the marker our friend had so carefully created. There was much to tell: of the rolling hills hidden by the deep snows; the blazing, robin's egg-blue skies above; the man Teddy who had taken me in and his pet wildcat; and, of course, the sweetgum grove and the eventually melting winter world that revealed the spring flowers covering the earth. Silent tears rolled down Marie's cheeks as she listened.

I opened the journal to the page where I'd pressed the violets from my brothers' graves. I pushed everything toward Marie.

"I wish it was me instead," I told her. "You know that, don't you? I would have it that way if I could."

Marie looked at me a long while, then at what I had brought. She closed her eyes. "You mustn't ever say that, Jennie."

"But it's true. You should have your husband with you. Jen-Jen should have her father."

"And you should have your brothers and your parents should have their sons. But that's not the way things are, and we must accept that. We mustn't demand that life be different, Jen, or we shall always be too sad."

I nodded. "Yes, I expect that's so."

"Jothan and Gardiner would be very proud of you, dear. You are a good sister and a good friend. Thank you for bringing them home to us." Marie plucked a violet from Gardiner's journal and looked at it. "I have so many questions. How you managed all this and also how you came to be in Tennessee? The last time you wrote you were still in Vicksburg."

I looked away. "Oh. Well, that is a very long story."

"Will you tell me sometime?"

I nodded. "Maybe."

*

A week later, I saw Marie at the post office. She was talking with Mr. Griffin when I arrived carrying a bundle of post. Marie looked happy to see me, but for some reason I suddenly felt awkward. Perhaps it had to do with the letters I carried, one to Sarah Hawkins and the other to Liza, which reflected a secret life I didn't want to share. I hurriedly pushed them across the counter toward Mr. Griffin and walked out.

"Jen?" Marie came after me.

"Hmm?"

"Is everything all right?"

"Sure. Why wouldn't it be?"

She tilted her head. "I don't know. It's just, I haven't seen you in a while." Marie looked down the street. "Do you want to walk a bit? It's still cool and I don't have to be back right away."

The touch of Marie's hand on my arm sent tingles down my back. We *could* walk today. I had worn of my old dresses, so we'd appear nothing so much as two good friends taking a stroll. I nodded and Marie linked her arm in mine. After we'd gone a block, I said that people were looking at me funny.

"What? Who?" Marie looked around.

"Everyone. They try not to, but they do. Even when I wear a dress and look...normal. They have questions, thoughts." I stopped. "They don't approve of what I've done."

"Since when have you cared what people thought?" she asked. "In any case, it's not true, Jen. People do approve, and they are proud of you, even if they don't know how to say that.

"If it makes you feel any better," she continued, "it's the same for the men who are returning. Several have told me as much. People want to know what the war was like, and we also don't want to know. We want to hear of the victory, but feel afraid to hear how we've all lost as well. No one knows how to ask the questions, so most don't. But any silence you hear is not born out of disapproval."

As we approached the steps to the courthouse, Mrs. McRae appeared. She smiled and waved, stopped briefly to discuss the weather, asked after our parents, then said she must get to Trickle's General Store. I'd barely managed two words in the face of all this friendliness.

"See, Jen?" Marie whispered. "You must not worry."

I found my voice. "With Mrs. McRae behaving like that? I think all I can do is worry!"

Marie laughed. "I only mean that all will be well. You're still the same girl we have always loved." We walked in silence until arriving at Greenwood Street. I turned to face Marie, then kissed her on the cheek.

"That's just it, Marie. I'm not the same girl. I wish I were, but I'm not."

Marie squeezed my hand. "I'm sorry, Jen. I know that's true. But you are still my very best friend."

*

When I told Washington Trickle that Adam never seemed to be home when I called, that wasn't entirely true. The first time I visited, Adam's mother, Mary Ward, had stared at me a long while, then said her son was down with the ague. The second time, he'd gone with his father to Kewanee. The third time, she said he was at Trickle's. I felt suspicious, but offered only that I was glad he was able to get around so well. As a child, I'd always liked Mrs. Ward. She often baked big batches of cookies or cakes for her son and daughters to share with their friends. Jothan and Gardiner and I spent a lot of time at their house; our families took picnic lunches together at Indian Creek. She was a good mother and wife and a good friend to my mother. I assumed her brusque manner now had to do with the family's tremendous sadness around Adam losing his leg.

After the third attempt to see my friend, something compelled me to walk around their house and along the back garden fence. That's when I saw Adam *was* home. He sat in a chair beneath their black hawthorn tree, an unopened book on his lap, a pair of crutches on the ground next to him. I stood watching him doze. It had been almost four years since I'd seen him. Adam's hair was long, as was his beard, now a great carpet of hair hiding most of his face. He never noticed me and I returned to the front door.

Mary Ward looked at me warily. "Yes, Jennie?"

I handed her a package. "This is for Adam. You will give it to him when he returns, won't you?"

Her eyes darted behind me and then to the ground. She knew I knew she was lying to me about her son, and I had a terrible urge to tell her that she had a lot to learn about the art of deception. For one thing, it was crucial to believe at least *somewhat* the lie you were telling; otherwise, the truth always showed up on your face. Second, it was very important to never look away, or color, while expressing the lie. Finally, and the most important rule, was to never, ever, tell a lie that could easily be uncovered. In Mary Ward's case, if she was going to insist her son wasn't home, then he better not be sitting in the backyard plain as a jaybird.

"Of course, I will," she said, then added more softly, "I'm sorry, Jennie."

As I walked back down the path to where I'd left Ruby, I wondered if Mary Ward was sorry for lying to me, or for her son having only one leg? Or, maybe she was sorry for the late war and the many who weren't coming home, or maybe sorry for the rest of us who had? Or, perhaps her lament reflected something else altogether? These days, there were so many reasons for a person to be sorry that you just couldn't assume anything.

FOUR

ADAM'S MELANCHOLY from losing his leg was understandable, but he wasn't the only soldier from Toulon missing parts of himself. Caleb Stevenson had returned just a few weeks before, minus one ear and the other one ringing so much that he scratched at it constantly like a dog. Thornton Daily, his mother reported, was still in Mississippi, having lost sight in one eye and suffering terrible headaches. Miles Bern, devastated by what he'd seen, hadn't spoken a word since arriving home.

Then there was Timothy Hardy.

Timothy had left Toulon the same time as most everyone else, in the spring of 1861, only instead of joining the infantry he'd signed up with an artillery unit. Though gunners stayed far behind the front lines, the danger was no less. The great amount of powder they handled meant that one misstep could kill or maim any number of men. Such an unfortunate event had befallen Timothy. As he related to Washington Trickle, one minute he'd been reaching down for the charges, and the next he was lying on his back, one hand gone and other minus its thumb and forefinger. This had transpired only days from the war's end. Tim had been discharged after a stay in the hospital and had returned home without his regiment.

In early July, I rode into town. Before going to Trickle's, I made my way to Ben Carter's establishment. As I wore my trousers, blouse, and straw hat, a visit to the saloon seemed reasonable and certainly something I had done on many occasions in Vicksburg. I ordered a glass of beer from Eldon, the barkeep, and as my eyes adjusted to the dim interior, I noticed Timothy sitting in the far corner. Paying for a second beer, I carried both glasses over.

"Hey, Tim."

Timothy looked up, frowning. "Who are you?"

I took off my hat. "It's Jennie." He continued to blink at me like an owl. "Jennie Edwards. Just thought maybe you could use another." I set the glass down and turned to leave.

"Wait, Jen. Don't go. Sorry. I heard you were back in town. Just didn't recognize you is all."

"I know."

He nodded. "You wanna sit?"

"Sure."

Timothy was a few years older than Jothan, so I had never known him well. Still, we had all played townball together. He was good, fast and strong, but also patient and helpful with the younger boys. He never seemed to care a whole lot about winning either, just liked to play.

"You really went away then?" he asked after a minute.

"Yep."

"Where?"

"Mississippi mostly, Vicksburg. Also Tennessee."

"Regiment?"

"Seventy-second."

Tim looked at me. "And no one ever knew?"

"Don't think so."

He shook his head. "That's something, Jen."

"Maybe. Maybe not." I waved at Eldon for another beer. He brought it over quickly and I passed him some money. Timothy leaned toward me after the man had left.

"Eldon don't know either, do he?" he whispered.

"Aw, I think he knows. Most here do, though when I wear

these clothes..." I shrugged. "Sometimes people are confused." I changed the subject. "Ain't you gonna drink any?" I asked, pointing at the beer I'd brought over.

To my surprise, Timothy's eyes filled with tears. "Can't drink it. I appreciate your buying it, Jen, but I can't do it."

"You drank this other beer though," I said, nodding toward the nearly empty glass.

"Not without spilling a lot of it." The tears rolled down his face. "Thing is, Jen, I got two legs and I got two arms, but I can't do nothing. Not without hands and fingers, I can't. But I walk down the street and you wouldn't think a thing is wrong with me. Truth is though I can't even button my own trousers; my ma's got to do it for me. Ain't that something? Nigh on thirty-years-old I am and my ma is dressing me like a baby."

I looked down at the table. "Oh, Tim."

"I come into town to buy things for Ma, but Mr. Trickle's got to load them up in the wagon. Some smaller boxes I can carry, but not the big ones. I just can't do it."

"You just got to learn to do things all over again," I said. "It won't be easy, but you can do it. You still got three fingers." I tried to smile, but he looked miserable. "I ain't gonna tell you how sorry I am 'cause you already know that's so."

He nodded. "You was there."

"Listen, this ain't the same, but when I was learning conjures, I had to make my fingers do all kinds of strange things. It took a really long time and was a lot of work." I pulled a quarter from my pocket and weaved it through my fingers, eventually making it disappear and reappear.

Timothy wasn't impressed. "You're using your thumb, Jen. You can't do all that with just fingers."

"Sure you can. When the coin vanishes like this," and I slipped the quarter toward the back of my hand with my palm facing him, "it's only the fingers that have put it there. And when it reappears," the quarter moved back to my palm, "same thing. Normally, you wouldn't see this because I'd wave my other hand in front, or make some kind of distraction, but that's how it works."

Tim still looked like I was trying to sell him a swamp. Like what, I could hear him thinking, did a magic trick have to do with him not being able to button his trousers? Of course, I had no answer to that. I only knew that for my part, it was much easier to talk about disappearing coins than vanished fingers.

"It ain't the same," he said, at last.

I put the coin away. "Nah, it ain't."

"You're a good girl, Jen, always were. And Jothan and Gardiner, fine boys. I was powerful sorry when Ma wrote to say they'd been killed." I nodded, quiet. After a minute, Timothy stood up. "Maybe see you around, huh?"

"Yeah, sure." He took a couple of steps. "Hey, Tim?"

"Yeah?"

"You see anything of Adam?"

"Not in a bit. Why?"

"I just wondered how he's doing."

Timothy sighed. "Pretty bad, truth to tell."

"That's what I figured."

"Bye, Jen."

"Bye."

After Timothy left, I sat a long while finishing my beer and then his. At some point, I noticed the soldier sitting at a nearby table. How I'd missed him before, I didn't know. A musket leaned against a nearby chair and his uniform consisted of butternut trousers and a buttonless, blue frock coat. I gave a slight wave, but the man didn't respond. I watched him for several minutes. Finally, he looked around the room, then toward Eldon. The barkeep continued wiping down the counter. The soldier then stood and walked by my table without glancing at me. I wanted to shout at him to get a better uniform; you couldn't wear trousers and coats from different sides, and anyway, what was he doing wearing a frock coat in this heat? But I didn't. I just continued drinking my beer. Eventually I forgot about the soldier as well as my reason for coming into town. There must have been something I was supposed to do, but for the life of me I couldn't recall what it was.

*

The Independence Day celebration in Toulon was to be unlike any the town had ever seen. Planning for an array of activities and displays had begun in May, and no expenses were to be spared. The town mothers had been working nonstop, Marie informed me, the effort all toward healing the wounds of the nation, celebrating a victory all had known to be inevitable, and comforting those who had lost loved ones. The general themes included celebrating the life of Mr. Lincoln, as well as the country's birth. Details remained vague on purpose: Rosetta Trickle indicated this was to not spoil the surprises to come. I knew only that she, Mrs. McRae, Mrs. Parker, and a whole other "cabal of hens," as Mr. Trickle referred to them, were spending long hours on the arrangements and schedule of events. When I thought about it, a feeling of curiosity arose in me, but most of the time I didn't think about it.

Still, a thorough excitement enveloped us as we arrived in town on the big day. Only when Mr. Lincoln had come to visit seven years before had I seen so many people in Toulon. Wagons and carriages cluttered the streets, turning the tracks to powder from horse hooves, boots, and shoes. Notices posted on every street lamp described the many festivities: jugglers and tightrope walkers, photographic wagons, readings at the Waxwing Theatre of the Declaration of Independence and *Uncle Tom's Cabin*, various races and games for children, and finally, a traveling circus that had been persuaded to offer a day's worth of thrills, including a trio of patriotic clowns, the world's fattest man, a woman with a beard, dancing horses, and a family of acrobats. Wheelbarrows of hay sat on several street corners dispensing ice cream; fires in stoves cooking barbecue on Washington Street mushroomed with smoke. To wash everything down, Ben Carter advertised one free "victory drink" at his saloon. The first order of business, however, was the parade. My parents, Amos, and I joined the Parkers and Trickles in front of the Virginia House to wait.

"It's good to see you, Jennie," said Marie.

I smiled. "You look lovely, Marie." My friend wore a dress of pale reds and blues with billowing sleeves and a wide hat that supported little flags she and Jen-Jen had sewn together.

She laughed. "The hat is a bit much, don't you think?"

"Not a bit."

"You look very pretty too." I'd worn the green dress Carmen had bought me and had taken some extra time with my hair.

Jen-Jen then jumped into my arms and began whispering her latest magic trick in my ear. The conjure, only part of which I could hear owing to the whispered voice in which it was spoken, seemed to involve a magic cloth my niece had made and one of her wooden boats. I whispered back that of course I wanted to see this as soon as possible.

"You will, Aunt Jennie," she said, seriously, "as soon as it's all ready."

"Very good," I nodded.

The sounds of the *Battle Cry of Freedom* from the Toulon Sax Band gathered our attention as the procession began to move. Behind them rode Toulon's ten city council members on horses wearing red, white, and blue fabric braided into the animals' tails and manes. Next appeared several young girls and boys, all holding hands and looking very somber. A row of young women followed holding up a banner for the Toulon Literary Society, then others came with similar banners for the Odd Fellows, the Masons, and the Good Temperance Society. The procession grew less cohesive as individuals ducked out of line to hug or shake hands with those of us watching. I could see Mrs. McRae frowning at this disorderliness, but it all seemed well intentioned. After the last of the civic societies had passed, I thought the parade must be done.

"No," Marie smiled, "there's more to come."

Shortly after she spoke, several wagons appeared. I was surprised to see Mrs. Trickle, who I thought had just been with us, sitting in a chair atop the first wagon. She was knitting with great concentration.

"What's this?" I asked.

"Scenes from the war," Marie whispered. "The ladies wanted to depict the conflict theatrically."

Around Mrs. Trickle, four young women sat near her feet. They, too, seemed to be sewing or placing items in empty boxes. One also had a portable desk on her lap and looked to be writing on a piece of paper; a letter, I presumed.

The second wagon held several older men from town, their white beards streaming in the breeze as they huddled around a table.

"Generals strategizing?" I asked.

Marie nodded. "Something like that."

The third wagon contained a wounded soldier tended by a young lady, the peaceful countenance on the young man unlike any I had ever seen on the battlefield. Two more conveyances depicted black-faced actors as slaves, working cotton fields and sitting around campfires. The last wagon had four young boys, two in blue and two in gray, holding smoothbore muskets and playing at battle. The blue uniforms were winning, the gray sinking lower and lower in the bed. Men around me began shouting. "Give 'em hell, boys!" and "We showed 'em!"

As the show finished, Jen-Jen got out of my arms and began tugging on her mother's skirt. Maybe I had held my niece too long, but I now felt quite light-headed. I heard Marie and my parents and others around us discussing moving on to the other activities, but I also could see the parade wasn't finished. Why was everyone leaving? The very last wagon approached and no one seemed to care about it. Real soldiers this time, some wounded and others not, packed the conveyance in numbers I wouldn't have thought possible. They were all mixed up, blue, gray, officers, enlisted. They looked exhausted, dirty, and a couple of them, not long for this life. This was by far the most realistic of all the "theatrical" efforts, so why was no one clapping and cheering for these men?

As I stood watching, one of the soldiers in gray noticed me. He stared, then whispered to another man and pointed my way. Why I would stand out to him in my dress and hat I couldn't imagine, but he continued to nudge his fellow soldier. Puzzled, I glanced down. To my surprise, I found I wasn't wearing a dress at all, but rather my old uniform.

In the next moment, I slumped to the ground.

*

It's the heat, someone declared. A second far-off voice said perhaps I'd been felled by the summer ague. Finally, my mother stated firmly it was because I'd had little to eat that morning and was just too skinny in general. My family and friends stood in a circle looking down at me as if I'd just fallen from the sky. Marie kneeled on the ground beside me, her cool hand on my forehead. Soon, my father and Amos were transporting me to the Parker house to lie down. I protested this extreme action in the face of my simply overheating. No one listened.

After a half-hour in the cool of her home, Marie convinced my parents to return to the celebration while she would stay with me.

"It's only this heat, Julia," my friend said. "And too, Jennie's not used to wearing dresses and they are so uncomfortable. She'll be fine."

Mama nodded. "Of course, you are right."

They left saying they'd be back in a few hours and we'd all return to Jug Run Creek. That was the last thing I remembered before falling fast asleep in Marie's bed.

*

The summer, unconcerned with wars or peace or the fragile or hearty state of any one person, cheerfully gobbled up each new day. July passed, then August. Old timers said they'd never experienced such heat, or such rain. The wheat and corn grew to record heights. Wild plants thrived too. I'd never seen the big bluestem and cord grass so tall, with stalks as thick as my wrist. I cut sheaf after sheaf for Mama's basket making. Though I'd stopped trying to see Adam, I also took some bunches of grass to Mary Ward and left them on the porch.

Toulon similarly pulsed with industry. Now that the war was behind us, it was time to get on with increasing trade and

343

development. John Culbertson, a local mill operator, expanded his business and hired a dozen new workers. A Mr. Nicholas opened a new hardware and stove establishment where he planned to specialize in pots from Egypt. There was even talk of some rich man wanting to open a luxury hotel in Toulon, similar to those in Chicago, as well as the idea of extending the railroad to our humble village. The enthusiasm was infectious. Washington Trickle began expanding his stock, while my father spent most of his evenings reading up on the latest farm equipment. The North had won the war after all. Now was the time to get the country back on the right track!

For my part, I had no interest in Mr. Culbertson's expansion, new hotels, pots from Egypt, or the coming railroad. Our land on Jug Run Creek took up all my family's time. There were the crops to tend, the buildings to repair, and on top of all that, we had much more stock than before. Several more chickens, at least a half-dozen new pigs and two additional cows had all come to us after the deaths of several men in town and the removal of their wives and children to live with family elsewhere. An old brindled cow named Abigail took a liking to me and followed me everywhere. She and Ruby also became close friends. In the evenings, I'd spy them together, Ruby's mouth near Abigail's ear as if imparting some deep secret.

I helped Mama and Amos and Papa as best I could, but as the summer unfolded, a greater part of each day found me staring off into space and doing nothing at all. I read the letters I received from Liza and Sarah over and over and at times I had a peculiar desire to be back in the South. Strange as it had been during those years, being a man and being a soldier, there had been a purpose to my life at least. I hinted as much in one letter to Liza, and she replied in her next with understanding. "The sentiment seems the same for many here, dear Robert. Many of the men coming to my place now are not coming for the expected reasons. They want company, but sometimes little else. They want to talk. I offer them an ear, of course, but I cannot sympathize with the undoing of a system that has kept my people shackled for centuries."

Most nights, I crawled into my bed dreaming of Liza and wishing desperately for her arms around me.

As I grew less helpful around the farm, my parents determined that going into town for supplies would be a better job for me. Yet when I returned twice with nothing and apparently never having even gotten to Trickle's, my mother started accompanying me. Early one morning, as we rode in the wagon together, Mama told me how nice I looked. On this outing I had worn the pale, red dress Carmen had bought me and had also attached my hair bun beneath a light gray hat.

"Thank you, Mama."

She reached over and touched my cheek. "You're a pretty girl, Eliza Jane." When I didn't say anything, she changed the subject and asked if I liked Amos.

"Amos? I guess so. He seems like a hard worker."

"We are lucky to have found him. I don't know how we would have managed without him. And before you returned, of course."

Dust billowed up like clouds around the wagon wheels. Though we had left Jug Run Creek early, I could already feel the heat causing sweat to trickle down my back, inside the infernal corset and the heavy dress material. As I prayed there'd be no fainting today, I knew I wouldn't have worn such ridiculous clothing but for Mama's presence.

"Eliza Jane?"

"Hmm?"

"I want to tell you something, dear, and, well, I'm sorry to have waited so long to do so." She paused. "It's just that, when you left after...that is, after the news came, I wasn't myself. Truthfully, I don't even remember much from that time."

"Mama, you don't have to say anything."

"Yes, my dear, I do. The thing is...I am well...now, so you mustn't worry about me. Of course, once I came back to myself, I knew what you had done. Of course, you would have left. You had wanted to before, and I had stopped you, but only for a time.

There was no need for your father or anyone else to try and protect me." She took a deep breath. "Put simply, Eliza Jane, I am sorry."

I turned to her. "You have nothing to be sorry for, Mama."

"Oh, but I do. I should have paid more attention to the child I still had rather than the two I had lost. I am not sure I *could* have done any different at the time, but I will always *wish* that I had. Do you understand what I'm saying?"

After a moment, I nodded. "I do. I understand because I couldn't have done any different either, though sometimes I wish I had as well."

My mother took my hand. "I am so very glad you're home, my girl. You just don't know."

*

Papa's research into the latest developments in farm equipment resulted in the purchase of something called a "sulky plow." Every spring, we'd walk behind our oxen as they pulled the plows, making sure the rows were straight, and it was dusty, dirty work. However, with this new invention, a person could guide the animals while sitting down. A sketch in Washington Trickle's catalog showed a funny-looking contraption, with a seat installed behind and high above the wheels, resembling something a lady might ride on her way to the courthouse. When the sulky plow arrived, Papa and Amos and I all went into town to pick it up.

The arrival of the new invention precipitated the first real conversation between me and Amos. Though I'd never had cause to think Amos didn't like me, I also sensed his discomfort in my presence. This didn't bother me overmuch as I also felt his genuine affection for my parents. He and Papa had built a small cabin for him to use and while he took all his meals with us, he also spent most of his time alone at the cabin.

One morning, after the plow was all put together, Amos and I were making some final adjustments. He was greasing the moveable parts and I was making sure the seat was secure. After doing this, I looked over at him crouched on the ground and thought I saw my brother Jothan instead. I blinked but the image persisted. When I closed my eyes, a tremendous dizziness rolled over me and I grabbed the seat to keep from falling.

"Jennie?"

I opened my eyes. Amos had stood up and was looking at me. "You all right?"

"Sure," I nodded. "I'm fine."

He looked back at the new plow. "Your father wants to practice using this tomorrow."

"You think it'll work?"

"Sure, it'll work. Most things do. It's just a question of how well." He pushed his straight hair behind his ears, then grabbed a cloth and started wiping down parts of the plow. I watched him.

"Where were you, Amos?" I asked.

He didn't hesitate. "Virginia. 25th New York. In for a bit over a year before they got my arm at South Mountain. Wasn't much of a war for me." He looked up. "You?"

"Mississippi, Tennessee. 72nd Illinois." I thought. "Two years and a bit."

"Lively times?"

"A few. What happened after you lost the arm?"

"Discharged. Home. There wasn't nothing for me there, so I came west."

"No family?"

"Why the questions all of a sudden?"

I shrugged. "No reason."

"People always got a reason."

"Listen, where you're concerned, I got no reasons at all. You do good work for Mama and Papa and they..." I felt my face grow warm, "well, they adore you. That's all I care about. This is just conversation. You can take it or leave it."

He thought. "My ma is dead and my pa, well, he was sober enough to notice me home, I might have stayed. But he wasn't, so I left."

Amos folded the cloth up and set it on the bench nearby. "You know, I didn't even know your folks had a daughter till long after I come here. Happened upon your pa one day down by the river, right after he'd gotten the letter from your regiment saying you'd been killed. I'd seen men sob like that but it had been awhile. I felt mighty bad. Graham kept saying that he would forever hate himself for not fetching you home."

We started walking toward the barn door. Amos collected his hat then we walked out into the sun. "Your pa's a good man, Jennie. I'm awful glad you made it back. I'm awful glad he don't have to hate himself."

"Thanks," I said, feeling awkward. "I'm glad too."

We went over to a section of the paddock fence that Abigail had crumpled with her head scratching. As we began moving the logs back into place, Amos said, "We had a couple of women in our regiment too. One got found out and sent home. The other died at South Mountain. A bunch of us knew she was a woman, but we didn't never say anything. I ain't seen too many soldiers good as her."

In that moment, Marie appeared driving the Tilbury. She waved and smiled and looked as happy as I'd ever seen her. I waved back and went over to the wagon. Marie gave me an enthusiastic embrace, then whispered, "I have something to tell you, Jen!"

"What?" I smiled.

"I'll tell you in a minute." She looked over toward the fence. "Hello, Amos!"

"Mrs. Edwards," he nodded, removing his hat. "It's nice to see you again."

"Yes, you too. Is Jennie making you do all the work around here?"

"Pretty much."

"That's what I thought," she laughed. Marie looked at me. "Can you walk a bit?"

"Of course."

We headed for the creek. "What's your secret?" I asked her.

Marie smiled. "It's not a secret, just some news."

"Well, what's your news?"

"Do you remember how I told you Father was getting busier? How he had so many clients and new cases that he thought he might have to hire an assistant to help him?"

"I do."

"Well, he's hired someone!" Marie looked close to bursting.

"Who?"

"Me!"

I stopped. "But you're already working for him."

"That was just doing accounts and correspondence. Now, I'm going to help him with actual cases! I'll be doing research at the library in Galesburg and taking notes when he meets with people. I may even get to attend some of the trials!"

"That's wonderful, Marie." I said, taking the opportunity to hug her again. "I'm very happy for you."

"I'm happy too. I do pray though that I don't let Father down."

"Let him down? Impossible! There is no one kinder or smarter or anyone who works as hard. Truly, it's a wonder that your father didn't think of this sooner."

Marie kissed me. "Thank you, Jen. Your belief in me means so much, I can't tell you."

We followed the path to the creek and then farther down to the Spoon River. The summer clouds hung like castles in the sky. A few deer grazed along the shore, while swallows did acrobatics above the river. Marie updated me on the latest with Jen-Jen and her mother, as well as the surprising news that Mrs. McRae and the town mothers were working to present medals of honor to all the returning soldiers.

"Of course, she wants to include you as well," said Marie. "And rightly so." I stared out across the river. "Jennie?"

"Yes?"

"I'm sorry, I've been doing all the talking. How are you, dearest?"

"Me? I'm fine. Working a lot, I guess."

"You look tired."

"Do I? I suppose I don't sleep so well anymore." Marie sat

down on the ground and motioned me to join her. "You're going to get quite dirty, Marie."

"I don't care. Sit with me." After I did so, she leaned her head on my shoulder. "I wish you'd come visit more, Jen. Even spend the night sometimes. I like being close to you. Don't you? Maybe you'd sleep better with me there?"

I smiled. "Oh, Marie, I don't think so."

"Why not?"

"Nothing. I'm sorry. Of course, I should come visit more, and I will. It's just that it's busy on the farm these days. And now you'll be busier too."

"I'll never be too busy to see you."

"You're a good friend to me, Marie, better than I deserve."

"That's silly! Promise me you'll come and soon. Jen-Jen misses you too. She says her magic trick is almost ready. Mother is about at her wits end with all the things my daughter is making disappear around the house."

I smiled, but felt bad for not visiting the Parkers more. I leaned over and kissed her, leaving my lips slightly longer on hers than usual.

"I will come by very soon," I promised.

Marie smiled. "Good."

FIVE

THAT NIGHT, I awoke to whispered voices. At first, I thought I was dreaming. Then, when the talking continued, I got out of bed. My parents must be awake for some reason. As the moments passed, however, I realized the voices were coming from my brothers' room. At the knot in our shared wall, I placed my ear and was startled to hear Jothan and Gardiner chatting, as they often did before going to sleep, as they had often done during all the years before the war. One difference though seemed to be that they were actually discussing the war. Jothan said he hoped the conflict didn't last long; he sorely missed Marie and his baby girl. Gardiner agreed. My youngest brother couldn't wait to get home and see the folks and me. I waited for more, but soon only soft snores could be heard through the knot.

The next night, their conversation resumed. Jothan felt worried about me; Gardiner said I was stronger than most girls. I looked through the knot. A nearly full moon cast shadows on my brothers sitting cross-legged on the floor. Gardiner reached for a pot of coffee, pouring the steaming liquid into two cups. I looked away and rubbed my eyes. When I looked back, they were gone.

The next morning, after laying awake all night, I went into the boys' room. Both of the beds had a rumpled look; I must have just missed them. Mama suddenly walked in carrying a bundle of fresh bedding. She seemed surprised to see me.

"I thought I'd make these up just in case we have guests some time." She started working, then noticed me still standing there. "Are you unwell, Eliza Jane? You look quite pale."

I stared at the beds. "I'm fine, Mama."

Later that day, I rode Ruby into town. I went to the post office and also collected some items for Papa from the blacksmith. I briefly considered seeing Marie but then, owing to the lack of sleep, turned Ruby for home. Some distance out of Toulon, my mule suddenly stopped and thrust her ears forward. Someone stood in the track ahead of us. It was a man, walking with a limp, hunched over as if a cold wind blew through his bones. He seemed not to notice us, his gaze focused steadily toward his feet. I encouraged Ruby forward.

"Hello, Adam."

My friend looked up. His face shined with sweat. "Hello, Jennie. It's been a long time."

"Yes, it has. Even longer since you won't see me when I come to visit."

"I ain't been home."

"Oh, yes, you have. I know you have because I've seen you. If you don't want to see me, Adam, fine, but please don't lie to me."

Adam had the grace to look ashamed for a moment. Then his eyes flashed. "Truth is I ain't wanted to see you. Not after what you done."

I jumped down. "And what, may I ask, have I done?"

He snorted. "What *haven't* you done, Jen? Truly, going off like you did, leaving your folks, living like a man. God, how could you?"

"As a matter of fact, it was easy."

"Oh, was it? I'll wager it wasn't easy for Graham and Julia. What if you had ended up dead too? What then? Didja ever think of that?"

"Only every day."

"It ain't right what you done. It just ain't right."

"I see," I said, my heart pounding. "But it was right for you, wasn't it, Adam? And for Timothy Hardy and Miles Bern and all the others?" My voice grew louder. "And, of course, it was perfectly all right for my brothers too, wasn't it?"

Adam colored. "You blame me."

"I do not."

"Yes, you do. And you're right. I shoulda been able to do something. Save at least one of 'em, but I couldn't." Adam looked near to tears. "It just—it just was so messed up, Jen, you don't know."

This was the last straw. "I sure in the hell do know, Adam Ward! Whaddya think I been doing this whole time, taking a holiday in the South? God! Don't ever tell me I don't know because I do know, only too well. Maybe what I did wasn't right, but I did it and I'm not sorry I did it. As for the other, I do *not* blame you. Never did. You can believe that or not, as you like, but it's the truth."

Adam leaned heavily on the cane, saying nothing. Ruby, fidgeting, walked over to a patch of switchgrass to investigate the plant's occupants. "You didn't ever write, Jen. Not once."

"That's not true."

"I mean after you left."

I thought. "You're right, I didn't. And I'm sorry for that, but I hardly wrote to anyone. Ask Marie if you don't believe me."

"But, why?"

"I don't know." This wasn't true, but it seemed an easier answer than trying to explain something to Adam that he was never going to understand.

He nodded slowly, then took off his hat. "First time I been out with this thing."

"You're doing pretty good to get all the way out here."

He shrugged. "Pa said if I didn't start using it, he was gonna toss it in the fire. I didn't want folks staring, so I come out here."

"It works then."

"Guess so. Takes some getting used to. I don't go nowhere fast, that's sure." Adam tried to smile but the grin came out crooked and fragile.

"Maybe not, but that doesn't matter. Important thing is you can get around. And I'll bet it'll get easier."

"Maybe." He replaced his hat. "I best be getting home."

"Yeah, me too."

Adam began hobbling away. After a few steps, he turned around. "Jennie?"

"Yeah?"

"I am sorry for not seeing you. I mean, before. It's just, well, I ain't felt so good lately."

I nodded. "I understand. Good to see you now though."

"Yep. Same here."

*

"You have to go back to your room, Jen. Mama will be worried." Gardiner sat on his bed, looking down at me at me curled up under the blanket.

"It's cold in my room," I said, then started to cry. "I don't have anyone since you and Jothan left."

"But we ain't left."

"Sure you have. You've gone to the war."

My brother didn't reply. Instead, he removed a scarf from his pocket and asked me to do a magic trick.

I shook my head. "No. I don't believe in magic anymore."

He laughed. "Don't believe in magic? But that's dumb. I'm sitting right here talking to you. Can't have more magic than that."

I wrapped the blanket around me tighter. "Just let me sleep here tonight, Gardiner. I don't want to be alone."

"You're not alone, Jen. We're here. And you also have Marie."

I sniffed. "Marie loves Jothan."

"'Course she does. But she loves you too."

"I miss you, Gardiner."

"I know. I miss you too." My brother stroked my head. "I'm

glad your hair is getting longer, Jen."

*

Mama found me the next morning in my brother's bed. I still wore my trousers and blouse from the day before, the material creased and flattened from being slept in.

"Jennie?" She sat down on the bed. "What are you doing here?"

I looked around. "I don't know."

"I heard you get up last night." Mama seemed about to say more, but then didn't. I tried to remember what had happened but quickly gave up. There was nothing in my memory besides the faintest residue of Gardiner talking to me.

"I saw Adam, Mama."

"You did? Where?"

"Out on the East Road. He was walking with his new leg. We talked awhile."

"How is he?"

"All right, I guess. Better."

Mama nodded. "I saw Mary Ward the other week. They are struggling. Between Adam's situation and their lack of money and Elijah working so much in Galesburg. They have lost much."

"He's still alive at least."

"True." Mama looked out the window. "I know this is hard, Jennie. I know how much you miss your brothers. Your father and I, we've both had time to get used to how things are now. It's still difficult, of course. Some mornings I wonder where the strength for another day will come. But it is better for me, and it will be for you too."

"I know, Mama. I'm fine, truly." To prove this, I got out of the bed, went downstairs and washed up, and then went outside to help Amos and Papa. I'd slept better in Gardiner's bed than I had for the past week in my own. Except for not remembering getting there, all seemed fine.

*

The white-hot days of summer at last stepped aside for the orange and gold coolness of autumn. The fall harvest and farm repairs and any number of chores kept me from going to town much. I saw Marie once when we attended a minstrel show together at the Waxwing Theatre, and very briefly Adam when I stopped by his house to bring them a basket of apples. He looked better. He told me he was getting out more with his new leg and felt glad to be doing something. We fumbled for conversation beyond his leg. Neither of us seemed inclined to discuss the late war, yet the goings-on in town seemed wholly uninteresting. For my part, I found it easier to simply not go to Toulon. I didn't have to feel guilty about Marie, and I didn't have to feel uncomfortable around Adam.

As it happened, the person I spent the most time with that fall was Amos. It made sense given we both lived at Jug Run Creek, but I also began to genuinely like him. One evening, we decided to play townball. Jothan had made his own bat years ago and I dug this out of my brother's trunk, along with a couple of balls. Amos amazed me with his ability to hit the ball having only one arm. With just two of us, it wasn't exactly a "game," but we pitched to each other and both played as strikers.

Some evenings, we'd go down to the river. One night, we sat in the cool air on the rock ledge and watched the sun go down. Amos talked a bit about his home in New York, and his ma who had died when he was ten. A much older brother and sister led their own lives in Boston and his father, as he'd already mentioned, was a drunk. He never hit his son, Amos told me, but he just wasn't any kind of a father or provider. Amos managed the house, earning money by working at a nearby livery and tending the few animals they owned. He had just been considering what to do and where to go when the war broke out.

"That kind of decided things for me," he finished. "Only not the way I expected. Still, I got away from my pa and that was a good thing."

I nodded, curious as to what had become of his father, but hesitant to ask. Instead, I shared the story of how Papa had come to the land on Jug Run Creek and how he and Mama had built our home and started the farm. I told Amos about Mr. Lincoln's visit so long ago, and how our president and my father had been in the militia together. Finally, I told him about Owl.

Amos nodded. "I heard you were a magician."

"I'm not really, though maybe I will be some day. I just like learning conjures. And fooling people."

"I'd heard that too. Do one for me now, Jennie."

Amos looked smug making this request, so I was glad I happened to have a deck of cards in my pocket. I cut and shuffled the deck, did a few fancy moves with it, and finally spread the cards in a fan and asked him to take one.

"Look at it and memorize it, then put it back," I instructed. He did so, then I reshuffled the deck and had him do this a second time. "Do you have both cards memorized?" Amos nodded. "All right then."

"What?"

"I am now going to read your mind and tell you which cards you chose." He looked alarmed by this idea, which made me laugh. I then closed my eyes, tossed my head around as if thinking hard, and pressed my fingers to my temples. Finally, I opened my eyes.

"Two of hearts. King of spades."

Amos' expression flattened like a pancake. After a moment, his mouth slowly opened but no words came out. I felt almost guilty: it was such a simple trick, even a child could do it.

"How did you do that?"

I smiled. "Magic, of course. How else?"

He shook his head. "That's something, Jen."

"Don't be too impressed, Amos. I can do much better ones though I'm some out of practice."

"It's true though," he said, thoughtfully.

"What's true?"

"That you're different. That you can do things other people can't."

"I am different, Amos, in more ways than you can guess. But ain't everybody?"

He looked at me. "I 'spect so. But this..." he pointed at the cards. "Well, I can see now how you passed and never got discovered."

I laughed. "You figure that out from a card trick?"

"Will you tell me how you did it, Jen? I mean, about passing?"

"Maybe someday. For now, I don't want to think too much about them times. The thing is done now."

Amos looked down at the swallows flying above the river, dipping in and out of the water and making chittering noises. In a quiet voice, he said, "True. The thing is done. Thank God."

*

The Harvest Dance, held each year in October at the Grange Hall, brought people to town from every corner of the county. Young and old, well-off and poor, farmers and business owners, all gathered to share in the collective gratitude for the season's bounty. Music, dancing, apple bobbing, and tables full of squashes and pickles, corn and breads filled the hall.

Shortly after my family and I arrived, Amos asked me to dance. He seemed not the least bit self-conscious having only one arm to hold me and we stayed on the floor for a few dances. At some point, I noticed Marie standing near the punch table. A tall, robust-looking gentleman had her attention and when he began waving his arms in exaggerated circles, she laughed. Upon finishing my dance with Amos, I walked over. Marie kissed my cheek, then introduced me.

Joshua Harper, a lawyer in Galesburg, who knew Marie's father, gave a slight bow. "It's nice to meet you, Miss Edwards. Marie has told me a lot about you." He was an extremely tidy looking man with not a hair out of place, a coat that appeared spotless, and glasses that shone. He was too clean and my suspicion grew.

I nodded, trying to smile. "My pleasure as well. Though I don't believe Marie has mentioned *you.*"

"Mr. Harper sometimes works on cases with Father," Marie explained. "He's been teaching me how to do research."

"Indeed? Well, that's great. How long have you lived in

Galesburg, Mr. Harper?"

"Just a few years. I removed there from Chicago after my discharge."

"So, you were in the war?"

"Only briefly. My wife died three years ago while I was gone, and I returned shortly thereafter to take care of my children. I suppose I needed a change from the big city and I knew Marie's father from the times he'd come to Chicago. When he told me of an office in Galesburg needing a lawyer, I decided to take it."

"I'm sorry. About your wife, I mean."

He nodded. "Thank you."

"You were an officer then, I gather?"

"Yes."

"That's fortunate. An enlisted man wouldn't have gotten to come home."

He tilted his head. "Ah, yes. Marie told me you also were in the war. If I may say, that's quite unusual. Where exactly where you?"

"Vicksburg mostly. Also Tennessee. I only got home a few months ago."

"I see." He thought. "Your loyalty is admirable, Miss Edwards. I don't believe I've heard of any women serving in the ranks."

"Oh, we were there, Mr. Harper. You just never noticed."

"Yes," he nodded. "Perhaps that's true."

Despite my best efforts to think otherwise, Joshua Harper didn't seem like a bad person. Before anyone could say more, Marie's father appeared. He wanted the younger lawyer to meet someone and with a quick smile to both of us, Mr. Harper was gone. Marie looked at me.

"You look pretty tonight, Jennie."

"I feel ridiculous."

"Ridiculous? Why?"

"I think my days of wearing dresses are mostly behind me." I changed the subject. "How is Jen-Jen? And your work? Guess I haven't been by much recently."

"No, you haven't."

Marie smiled, but I could see her hurt at my continued absence. Still, she happily related all the latest news of her daughter and the cases she was researching, as well as some of the people she was meeting. After not seeing me since our trip to the Waxwing a few weeks before, she had much to tell. I listened with interest, but soon found my gaze wandering. There were so many people in the hall. The spaces around the tables had grown crowded with everyone drinking punch and piling small plates full of pickles, oysters, and sweet cakes. I could see many neighbors that I knew and other people that I didn't. I kept looking back at Marie, then into the crowd. Suddenly, my eyes saw the soldier.

It was the same man from the saloon, the man I'd seen after talking with Timothy, at the beginning of the summer. I knew it was the same person because he wore the butternut trousers and the blue frock. At the moment, he stood in a far corner of the hall. People passed by him, but nobody spoke to him. I thought this strange given the man held a musket in his hands. Surely, the town mothers would prefer there not be muskets at the Harvest Dance.

"Jennie?"

With effort, I looked away from the soldier. "What?"

"What is it, dearest? You've gone quite pale."

I shook my head. "I'm not sure. I thought I just saw someone that I knew. From before, that is."

The floor of the hall began moving up and down beneath my feet. Leaning on the table helped. I took several deep breaths. The floor eventually stopped moving, and my mind slowly cleared.

When I looked up however, Marie and I were no longer inside the Grange Hall. Instead, we stood outside in our coats, a nearly full moon illuminating a few people milling around beneath the lamps. I slumped against the side of the building.

"Jennie!" Marie grabbed my arm.

"What...happened?" I closed my eyes. "How did we get out here?"

Marie's eyes were wide as dollar coins. "You said you wanted to come outside, that you wanted to tell me something. So, we got our coats, and now we're outside."

"Yes, yes...of course. I'm sorry, Marie," I took her hand and held it tightly, "I just felt unwell for a moment."

She studied me. "Let's sit, dear."

Marie lead the way to a nearby bench beneath the expansive sycamore that stood at the corner of the Grange Hall. The tree still hosted its leaves, causing the moonlight to throw a dappled look onto the ground below. As we sat, Marie put her arm around me.

"Oh, Jennie, I am so worried about you. Please tell me what is going on. Your mother tells me that you hardly eat, that you leave the farm and they don't know where you go, that you don't seem to remember conversations." She shook her head. "Maybe I shouldn't ask, but you are my best friend."

"I'm fine, Marie," I said, weakly.

"That's not true, Jennie," she said, her tone more stern. "You are decidedly not fine. I want to help, but you won't talk to me. You won't even come to see me."

"I'm sorry, Marie. It's just, well, it's not so simple anymore. That is, you and me...and me...now...how I feel... It's just that things are different now." If I thought this would elicit sympathy, it didn't.

"I *know* things are different now, Jennie. Every day, I know this. I have a daughter with no father and friends with no sons or brothers. We now live in a town full of people who are shadowy figures at the best of times and hopeless, broken men at the worst. Each morning, I pray for the strength to find something, *anything*, that offers some celebration, and sometimes I don't find it, but you know what? I get up anyway, and I smile anyway, and I go to work, and I care for my daughter, and I help my parents, and between all the responsibilities I tell Adam and you, when you're around, and Tim and all the others that I'm here for each of you." Her voice broke while she caught her breath. "But I'm not sure I have any more for you, Jen. Not if you won't talk to me."

"I can't, Marie."

Marie pulled her arm back and stood up. "Fine then."

I grabbed her hand. "I'm just trying to protect you."

"I don't need any protection, Jennie. Not from you or anyone else. Just because you went off to the war doesn't mean you're the only one who can take care of herself. I've had four terrible long years on my own after all. You left. I'm not saying you were wrong, but you left and I stayed. I stayed right here, and I managed through the loneliness of losing my husband *and* you *and* so many others. It was different to be sure, and I won't ever compare what you experienced with what I have gone through, but please, don't patronize me like that. I can take care of myself."

"I know you can."

"Then why don't you trust me?"

I stood up too. It took all my strength to keep my voice steady. "I love you, Marie."

Her shoulders sagged. "I know that, Jen. I love you too. Of course, I do."

"I don't mean like that, Marie. I don't mean like sisters, or—or friends." My face burned. I took her hands in mine. "I love you, Marie, and I want to love you. That's why I don't come around. I want to be close to you, but it's better if I don't visit."

"Better for whom exactly?" she asked, angrily.

"Marie, don't you understand what I'm telling you?"

"I understand, Jennie. Believe me, I understand more than you think."

"As to all the rest," I said, waving my arm into the night where the Confederate soldiers lurked, "I can't tell you what's going on because I don't *know* what's going. Sometimes, I feel like I'm only an outline of myself, like there's no real person here. I don't know, Marie. Sometimes, I think..." a sob filled my throat, pushing the words back down.

"What, Jen? What do you think?"

"Sometimes, I think I did die, Marie. That all this, coming home, seeing you, my folks, the town, it's all just a dream. Perhaps everything now is just the result of the last things in my mind before I died. And you, my dear, sweet friend," I touched her cheek, "would have been most in my thoughts in those last moments." The night seemed deadly still now. "I'm so sorry, Marie."

"Oh, Jennie." She reached for me, but I walked away, into the night and away from the words that I wish I hadn't been forced to speak.

SIX

THE STREETS of Toulon were empty due to all being at the Harvest Dance. Except for a family of scuttling raccoons and the quick streak of a prairie wolf snatching up what looked to be a rat. I walked alone. This suited me fine. After talking to Marie, I had no words for anyone else. Yet, when I arrived at Trickle's, a man sat smoking on the bench out front. Another dance refugee, I quickly surmised.

"Hey, Jennie," came a familiar voice.

"Hey, Tim."

"Have a seat. Enjoying the dance?"

"Thanks." I sat down. "Not really, truth to tell. Thought I'd get some air."

He nodded. "Yep. Me too."

We sat in silence. Then Tim asked me if I'd like a cigar. The sweet smoke made me light-headed in a pleasant way. Mama had been upset the one time I'd tried smoking at home, so I had opted to leave the habit for the most part. After a few minutes, I asked Tim if he'd seen the family of coons.

"Yep," he nodded, the cigar bobbing up and down. "Put up a terrible fuss a bit ago, the lot of 'em. I think one of the little ones found something good to eat, then a bigger one took it away." He turned toward me. "They ain't much for sharing, are they?"

"Nope."

"I been thinking about you, Jen," he said, changing the subject.

"Me? Why?"

"Just wondering how you're getting on. Being home and all."

I smoked. "It ain't easy sometimes."

"You get problems from anyone?"

"What kind of problems?"

"I dunno. Just folks wondering why you done it. Being a girl and all."

"Nah, no problems. People don't say anything at all for the most part. I'm sure there's talk, but I don't care much."

"Mrs. McRae wondered where you were the other night."

"Mrs. McRae? Why?"

"At the Toulon Literary Society meeting. Didn't you know? The town mothers made medals to present to all the returning soldiers. Even Adam came though I don't think he stayed long enough to get his medal. Anyhow, seemed like she hoped you would be there. Leastwise, she was asking after you. When it was clear you weren't there, she said she'd bring it by your place. But I guess you ain't seen her yet?"

"No," I said, slowly, "I ain't seen her." I thought a moment. "You went though, Tim? I'm glad for that."

He shrugged. "Made my ma happy. There's precious little I can do to make her happy these days."

"Things not much better?"

"Not really, but I keep on. Ain't much else to do, is there?"

After a minute, I asked, "You see Adam much?"

"Some. He's not too good, but he's doing his best."

The glowing form of a barn owl swooped by. It landed on the eave of the building across the street, a radiant being in the black of night. Most folks considered the appearance of an owl a bad sign, but the birds never worried me. We had owls in our barn as well as a couple of pairs that lived in the sycamore trees along Jug Run Creek. Their hooting helped me fall asleep at night, and their hunting kept mice and rats out of our food.

"Hey, Tim?"

"Hmm?"

"Does something ever happen to you where you think you're in one place, and then it turns out you're really in another?"

"What, you mean like getting lost?"

I shook my head. "No, not like getting lost. It's more like, I don't know, just waking up and finding you're in another room from where you went to bed."

He thought. "Nah, can't say that it has. Why?"

"Oh, no reason. Just a funny thought I had."

Timothy dropped the stub of his cigar near his feet and crushed it. "Guess I'd better get back or Ma will start to worry. You coming?"

"Not yet. I'll just finish this."

He patted my shoulder. "Take care, Jen."

"Yep. You too."

*

Some weeks later I went to see Adam. Winter's fast approach meant there'd be fewer trips to Toulon, fewer opportunities to make sure he still fared all right. This particular day, the sun shone, and I felt hopeful. Life for me had been quiet, with no funny forgetful episodes or visions of lost soldiers. I'd even started sleeping better. The last leaves were falling and rustling in breezy knots in the streets as I left the East Road and walked Ruby toward Adam's. Birds formed dark masses overhead, enroute to warmer, winter lands and the blue sky had a tinge of copper to it behind clouds stretching away as far as the eye could see.

No one answered my knock at the front door, so I went around to the back. Adam was sitting in the Wards' garden. I began to shout hello, but then noticed his slumped appearance. Then, too, the shaking shoulders. As I got closer, Adam's hair looked a mess, clumpy and unwashed. He slowly raised his head and I started. In only a few weeks, his face had grown gaunt. His cheeks were ash-colored beneath dark circles supporting red-rimmed eyes. The buttons on his blouse had come off, the material hanging on his frame like a scarecrow. Crutches lay on the ground next to him, but of the artificial leg, there was no sign.

"Jesus, Adam, what's happened? Why are you sitting out here like this?"

He sobbed like a baby. "I've tried, Jen, I have. But it just don't work!"

I got down on my knees next to him. "What doesn't work?" When he didn't answer, I grabbed his arm. "Adam!"

"Nothing! Nothing works, all right? Not that infernal leg over there..." he threw his arm in the direction of the boxwood hedge where I now saw the wooden leg sticking out like a broken-off tree branch, "...not the leg I still have, not my arms, nothing!"

"Not your arms? What the hell are you talking about, Adam?"

"It's just I can't do anything, Jen. I try, but I can't. Can't work, can't carry stuff, can't ride. I'm useless for sure. I even heard Pa say as much to Ma the other night." He sighed. "I'm gonna kill myself, Jen."

"You are doing nothing of the kind, Adam Ward! What's the matter with you? Don't you ever, *ever* say such a thing, do you hear me?" He began whimpering. "You are NOT useless, so stop this! Stop feeling sorry for yourself right now!"

"You don't know, Jen." Adam rubbed his sleeve across his face.

"I do so know, Adam. Life is different now, that's all. And it's just that you gotta find a different way to live. Lots of people got only one leg now and they're figuring it out too. I know it can be done. I ain't saying it'll be easy, but only a coward would give up." I paused. "And I know you ain't a coward."

"I don't know about that. Maybe I am."

"Stop this right now! I don't want to hear you say one more word like that. Even if you think such thoughts, I don't want to hear you speak them, all right?" He looked at me, then sort of nodded. I glanced up at the house. "Where are the folks and your sisters?"

"Gone to Kewanee."

"Huh." I made a note as I stood up to talk to Mary Ward later about just going off and leaving her son in such a fragile state. After walking over the boxwood hedge to retrieve the wooden leg, I said, "We're going out, Adam."

He looked alarmed. "Out? Where?"

"Anywhere you want. But we're going, and now. I'm your friend, though I haven't been a very good friend of late. I let you get too sad and I'm very sorry about that, but it's going to be all right. I'll help you figure this out." He looked away. "No, Adam, no more. You're not alone. This'll be work, but I know you can do it. You're not alone, all right?"

He nodded, crying. "Don't leave me again, Jen."

"Nope, I'm not going to do that."

*

That afternoon, Ruby carried both me and Adam and his leg to Indian Creek. Not so far from town, a necklace of pools fell one into another as the creek carried the water away toward the Spoon River. Many times, in the lives we'd led before the war, my friend and I had fished these pools. This late in the year, after such a dry, hot summer, the water was so low that some areas held little more than enough to wash a face. But the trout were there; we could see them. I didn't know exactly what to do with Adam, so for a long while we simply sat and watched the fish. Adam perked up a little; after awhile he said next time we should bring the poles. At last, I asked him to tell me what the trouble with the leg was. He explained with the quiet resignation of one who believes nothing will ever change.

It wasn't very comfortable, he acknowledged, but that wasn't the main problem. It helped him to stand in one place; the challenge was walking. Adam felt as if he were dragging a log around with him. The thing didn't actually seem to help, he said, unless he wasn't trying to do anything. If he attempted to chop wood, he toppled over; if he tried to walk downstairs, the leg slipped out from underneath him; carrying anything in his arms was out because both hands were needed for the crutches.

I thought for a bit then determined upon a plan. It wouldn't be any kind of miracle, it had only to do with figuring out the right way to do things and then practicing them until he could do them in his sleep.

"You weren't born knowing how to walk," I said. "That took practice too. I will bring a lunch for us tomorrow and we'll work right here. The only thing you gotta do tonight, Adam, is have a bath and put on some decent clothes. We can't have people seeing you like this. Is that a deal?"

After a minute, he nodded. "Thanks, Jen."

*

Helping Adam was good for me too. It was good to have a problem to solve, and it didn't hurt either that it was also someone else's problem. This must have been apparent because my mother and father didn't say anything about me doing fewer chores and spending more of my time away from home.

The main challenge I saw with the way Adam was using his leg was that he wasn't using it. Standing, he rested his weight on the leg; walking, he put everything onto his good leg and yes, dragged the other around like an old log. When I pointed this out, he shrugged.

"I can't feel nothing. I don't trust it, I expect."

At first, I had him put his arm around me and lean into me and the leg. In this fashion, we walked. Along the sandy banks of Indian Creek, up above on the trail through the grasses. The uneven ground made the task harder, but once Adam got the hang of it, and trusted it, his skill was even better. Level ground turned out to be a piece of cake. That first week, all we did was walk. Fortunately, the weather held off and the snowfalls were light. Even so, the snow presented further challenge, but with his confidence restored, Adam managed. When the weather got too bad, we worked at his home. By my paying attention to her son, Mary Ward seemed to have warmed again to me. She made us cakes and tea and lavished praise upon Adam, some of which made him distinctly uncomfortable. I simply felt pleased that my friend felt better.

After walking became easier, we started practicing chores. Chopping wood and carrying things were mostly a question of good balance. Now that Adam could rely more on the wooden leg, he could get by with just using one crutch, leaving the other arm free to hold a bucket or a small package or a few pieces of wood. We worked on these just a few steps at a time. Once it felt familiar and more comfortable, I directed Adam up and down three or four stairs and even over a small fence in the garden, just to see if he could manage an obstacle. The more he did, the better he got. He didn't say much, and getting him to smile was like wrangling a muddy pig; it would almost happen and then his eyes would grow cloudy again. One afternoon, however, I showed up and Adam's hair had been trimmed and his beard shaved. Without the beard, Adam's face appeared even thinner, but at least he now looked more like the boy I remembered.

One afternoon, as the snow fell, Adam and I went to Trickle's. It had taken all my powers of persuasion to get him to go, but the fact that the weather was nasty and that no one would likely be there had helped. Washington Trickle gave Adam a big hug, then boomed that he thought the young man must have gotten married since he hadn't seen him in so long. Adam colored like a tomato.

"I ain't got married, Mr. Trickle," he said, turning redder. "No one would have me now."

"Nonsense!" the storekeeper shouted. "Any number of fine young ladies would be proud to have such an honorable, brave young fellow. Now, you two go sit by the stove while I make some fresh coffee. Ain't no one here but me and the cats. Them felines ain't left the stove since this morning."

I hadn't been in Trickle's in some weeks either. It felt good to warm up by the stove and pet the cats that were more melted puddles of fur than living, wild animals.

"They ain't got much to worry about, do they?" asked Adam, after Mr. Trickle had poured us coffee then left to catch up on chores while the store was quiet. He took a careful sip of his drink.

"I dreamed about them last night."

"The cats?"

"No. Your brothers."

"Oh." I looked at my cup. "It's all right, Adam."

"You ever dream about them, Jen?"

"Sure, sometimes."

"The world just don't seem right without them in it."

"No, it don't. But it's the way it is." When he opened his mouth to say more, I added, "You got to stop thinking about it, Adam."

At that moment, the appearance of Mrs. Bertha McRae saved us from having to continue a conversation that would end up making us both sad. Snow covered her cape and hat and she stood at the steps to the stove area, a puddle forming at her feet.

"Eliza Jane," she nodded. "Adam."

"Mrs. McRae," we said in unison like school children. Then I added, "You've braved the weather, ma'am."

"I have indeed. I saw you two walking this way, so I put on my coat and came as quick as I could."

Adam looked at me. "But why?" he asked.

"Because you two are as slippery as a couple of eels, that's why," she said, sternly. As we continued to look puzzled, Mrs. McRae smiled and asked if she might sit. I felt a dizzy spell coming on from experiencing the kindness of the woman, while Adam nodded at her and reached for a nearby chair, tipping off one of the cats in the process.

"Would you like some coffee?" I asked.

"Yes, I would, thank you." She removed her hat and gratefully accepted the steaming cup. "You look to be very well, Adam, and doing fine with your new leg."

He colored again and looked down. "Thank you, ma'am. Jennie has been helping me."

Mrs. McRae nodded. "I know she has. I don't mean to interrupt, but I have these for you both and it is past time that I delivered them. My apologies for not having come to your homes to do so before now." She sipped the coffee. For the first time in my life, I saw Mrs. McRae look uncertain. "I wanted to, but then I didn't," she finished, flatly.

With that, she handed us each a small box tied with a ribbon. Inside each was a large copper medallion, heavy, as big around as my palm and as thick as my little finger. On one side an eagle with outstretched wings had been engraved; on the opposite were two crossed swords and the dates, "1861–1865."

"We'd hoped to have more inscribed," Mrs. McRae explained, "like perhaps your names, or a part of a poem, but then we couldn't all come to a decision, so it remains simple."

I moved my hand up and down feeling the weight of the medal. Then I looked at her. "Thank you, Mrs. McRae. This is kind."

She looked stern, but her eyes were soft. "You've always done exactly what you wanted, Eliza Jane. Some day that will surely get you into trouble. Truthfully, I never thought you would amount to anything beyond a troublemaker." Mrs. McRae looked at Adam. "Either of you for that matter. But how wrong I've been." Adam continued to blush and kept his eyes lowered. I felt sure I should say something, but couldn't think of what. Fortunately, Mrs. McRae had now finished her coffee and stood up. "Several people told me neither of you would consent to a public presentation, so on behalf of the town, thank you. For your service to this country and to Toulon."

By now, Adam was curling up like a bug and seemed wholly disinclined to respond to Mrs. McRae. I began a less than elegant thank you to the town mothers and everyone else, but in fact, the older woman had already turned and was heading back toward the front of the store. All that remained of the visit were the two medallions and a trail of wet boot prints on the store floor.

*

Adam may have implored me not to leave him, but he didn't hold himself to any such promise. The day after we saw Mrs. McRae, the first of the winter storms arrived and left more than a foot of snow on the ground. It took a few days of cleaning up and organizing animals and stores on the farm before I was next able to go to

Adam's. When I got there, Mary Ward greeted me at the door with the news that her son had left.

"Left?" I asked, assuming he must have just gone to town. "Where?"

"To my brother's. To Nebraska."

"Nebraska! But why? What's happened?"

"Nothing's happened, Jennie, except he finally decided to leave." The woman was pale. "He packed a bag, took some money from his father, and caught the stage for Kewanee. From there, he was going on the cars to my brother's in Greenville."

"But it's winter! How can he just leave? I thought things were better."

"Well, you thought wrong! Things aren't better, Jennie. Or, maybe they are. Either way, I wouldn't know. My son doesn't talk to me." She began to cry. "He doesn't talk to any of us."

"Well, we must bring him back! Adam needs to be here. Where he can be with family and friends."

"No. I don't know what Adam needs but it's not our help. You have done a lot for him, and I do thank you. I'm sorry too that I haven't always been so kind to you. It's just, well, I just thought things would be so different." Mary Ward wiped her eyes. "In any case, perhaps a change will do him good. My brother is lately widowed, he had no children, and he could use some help at his place."

I didn't know what to say. Adam's mother turned away toward a table in their hall. From one corner, she grabbed a small envelope and the medallion Mrs. McRae had given Adam. "He asked that I give these to you if you came by." She placed both in my hands and began closing the door. "I'm sorry, Jennie."

SEVEN

THE STAGE was just leaving from in front of Trickle's when I got there. With some money borrowed from Washington, I climbed on board. As soon as we were away from Toulon, I read Adam's brief note:

> *Dear Jen,*
> *Thank you for all you've done for me—you're a good friend. Please tell Mrs. McRae I cannot accept the medallion as I don't deserve it. I will miss you, yet I must leave now.*
> *Your friend,*
> *Adam*

The cars had left Kewanee just an hour before I arrived. The next train would not depart for another week. I walked through the town thinking maybe Adam had changed his mind. Everyone I met heard the same question: had they seen a young man with blond hair and a wooden leg? Most shook their heads. A few thought so but couldn't remember where. One lady said yes, certainly she had, and sent me into a saloon where I found a dark-haired man with no legs at all and a wheeled chair parked next to him. Finally, an old-timer gave me a grim smile. "Son, we got a lotta one-legged men around here now."

After searching all over, I returned to the saloon and ordered a beer. The man without legs looked pretty far gone, from drink and despair, it seemed. I asked the barkeeper when the next stage left for Toulon. I was in luck, he said, as it would be arriving soon from Galesburg and was scheduled to leave in a half-hour. I bought a ticket from him and finished the beer. Before leaving, I walked over and put the last of Washington's money on the table in front of the crippled man.

At the depot, I didn't have long to wait. Despite the weather, the stage arrived promptly and departed promptly. The funny thing however was that even though I stepped into the conveyance, I had no memory of stepping back out. The next thing I knew I was sitting at the supper table with my parents and Amos. Their plates of fried chicken and potatoes seemed to be mostly eaten; mine very little. Everyone was looking at me. Mama said something. I replied, my voice sounding far away. She nodded, smiling. Amos and Papa continued eating. For the next several minutes, I managed to tread through the unknown of another gap in my memory. Eventually, I determined that more than two days had passed since I'd gone to Kewanee.

*

After Adam left, I found it even harder to concentrate. I couldn't sleep, had trouble managing chores, and found myself staring into space for long stretches at a time. About the only thing I could do was be a lookout. Despite the weather, I spent most of my time at the rock ledge above the Spoon River, which was the best place to watch for Confederates. They were sneaky, hunkering down below in the bushes, creeping this way and that. Still, they couldn't get past me. At night, I'd report what I'd seen to my brothers. They always nodded and said I was a good sister, but they looked worried too. Jothan said I didn't need to look out every day. He said there wasn't any fight left in the Rebs. I didn't argue, but Jothan didn't know Rebs like I did; he hadn't been in the war as long as I had.

One afternoon, it was snowing too much to go anywhere. I was in the barn brushing Ruby and Abigail (I'd never met a cow that liked to be brushed but this one sure did) when I fairly jumped upon hearing my name. I turned around. Marie stood just inside the door. Her blue cape and hood had turned white from a layer of snowflakes. She gave a slight shake and pushed the hood back.

"Hello, Jennie."

I set the comb down and walked over to her. Once again, it had been weeks since we'd seen each other. I should have apologized. Instead, I put my hands in my pockets. "You look well, Marie."

"So do you."

I attempted a smile. "That's not true, but you're kind to say so."

"Jennie, we need to talk. I'm sorry I wasn't at home the other day when you came by. Mother had hoped you'd wait, but I expect you had other things to do?" I nodded as if I knew what she was talking about. "In any case, can we talk now? Maybe somewhere private?"

I looked around the barn. Papa and Amos were outside fixing something somewhere. "This is private."

"And cold!"

"We can go in the house then."

Mama was in the kitchen. She'd already seen Marie, having directed her to the barn to find me, but she now said again how glad she was to see her daughter-in-law and hoped Marie would come back soon with Jen-Jen. Of course, Marie said she would and very soon too. Then Mama was gone. I motioned my friend to sit.

"Would you like some coffee?" I asked.

"No," she shook her head, then, "I mean, yes, that would be nice."

The coffee pot was still warm, so I poured us two cups. Marie warmed her hands around the mug, then said, "Jennie, I want to talk about our conversation at the dance. I assume that's what you wanted to talk about when you came to see me the other day."

My face grew warm. "I'm sorry, Marie. About that evening, I

mean. I don't know what I was thinking. I must have had too much to drink."

She looked puzzled. "You didn't have anything to drink."

I took a sip of coffee and noticed my hand shaking. "Look, Marie, I shouldn't have said anything. I'm sorry I told you what I did. I would never hurt you."

"You didn't hurt me, dear. And you know of course that I care about you very much. That is, well, I must have similar feelings too, mustn't I?" I very much doubted Marie had the same feelings for me, or ever had the kinds of thoughts I had. She took my hand. "Jennie, we will always be friends."

I was wavering in and out of myself. One second, I knew my place as her friend; in the next, I felt a tremendous desire to show her just what I meant. It seemed that on so many occasions, I had done everything right, yet, it didn't seem to matter. I had done all I could for Adam, and he'd left anyway. I had done all my brothers had asked of me, and they'd gone as well. Then there was Biddle. So, in the end, what did it all mean? Right or wrong, proper or not? I scooted my chair closer to Marie and took both her hands in mine.

"But that's just it, Marie, I don't *want* to be just friends." I kissed her fingers. "I want much more than that, my dear. I want...well, I want to hold you and kiss you and be with you all the time."

Marie's expression grew tight. "I find that very hard to believe, Jennie Edwards! Since you've been home, I've seen you only a handful of times. Explain to me, please, how your infrequent visits could even come close to reflecting this desire you claim to want to be with me all the time!"

I had no good answer to this, so I leaned forward and kissed her. We had kissed so many times, but this was clearly different. For me, it was perfect; for Marie, I couldn't tell. She didn't push me away, at least not immediately. Maybe, I thought, it was enough to have just one brief moment together. That's all anyone had anyway, just the briefest of moments together. Even many years together could feel as mere seconds once the people inside those years were gone.

"Marie," I whispered, leaving my lips very close to hers. "I love you. You must know what I mean when I say that."

She pulled back from me. "It's impossible, Jennie. I'm sorry."

"Nothing's impossible, Marie."

"Some things are, Jennie, and you know it. Please don't make this harder than it is."

"Why is it hard? Doesn't it make you happy to know how much I love you? Doesn't it make you happy to know there is someone who adores you more than anything? Who wants to be with you every day and night?"

I tried to kiss her again, but she pushed me away. "Stop it, Jen. This won't do. It just won't."

"Marie—"

"No, I mean it. You must stop with this fantasy. It simply can't be. Surely, you must see that?"

"I see nothing of the kind. I know that what seems impossible is often possible. I *know* that, Marie."

"But this is not a magic trick, my dear. It's not even as simple as pretending you're a man, which I know wasn't simple at all." She started to cry and I gathered her into an embrace. I felt shabby in my old coat and trousers, but Marie hugged me tightly and I kissed her hair. "Oh, Jennie, I adore you too, I do. But, I'm not like you. I'm not—"

"Marie—"

"—brave like you. You do what you want and care nothing for what other people think. But, I'm not like that. I do care what other people think, I want to be liked, well regarded. I *must* be accepted. For Jen-Jen's sake also. Please try to understand. It's different for you, easier, I think."

"Easy?" I asked. "Does my life look easy to you?"

"You know what I mean."

"No, Marie, I don't know what you mean," I said, feeling impatient. "Nothing about my life feels easy these days, but some things are simple. How I feel about you is simple."

Marie sat back in the chair. She stared at me now, her eyes hard. "Well, what would you propose then? That we get married? That we move into a little cottage somewhere? That we start having a passel of children?"

"You're making fun of me."

"I'm trying to shake you out of your reverie."

"And I'm trying to tell you it isn't a reverie!"

Marie sighed, but she also looked resolved. She sat up straighter in the chair and smoothed out her dress. "I'm sorry you feel that way, Jennie, but you must respect my wishes on this issue. What you propose is never going to happen. Never. Is that clear?"

Though I heard the words, they suddenly didn't seem very important. Behind Marie, through the window, a shadow had appeared. It could have been either of my parents, or Amos, but I knew the dark outline belonged to none of them. My fears that a Confederate soldier had made it from the river to our house were born out, as the person leaned further into the center of the window. I could feel the dizziness coming on. Marie noticed the change too. Her stern countenance softened as I began tilting to one side.

"Jennie?"

I was bone tired. My brother had been wrong; it wasn't the Rebs who had no fight left in them, it was me. "They've found us, Marie," I mumbled, moving my feet apart on the floor to steady myself further. When she looked puzzled, I pointed at the window. She turned around in the chair. Marie seemed to think about something, then stood and went to the window. "Don't go over there!" I shouted. After a moment, she returned to the chair.

"There's no one there, dear."

I started shaking, but I could see she was right. No one was there *now*. "I thought I saw someone."

"Jennie," Marie's voice trembled, "you *must* tell me what's going on with you."

My entire body began shaking. After several deep breaths, I said, "Sometimes I see people, Marie, people that aren't alive.

They're soldiers, usually Confederates. They come and they go. I've seen them at your house too...and during the Independence Day parade. One was also at the Harvest Dance." Marie stared at me, her eyes wide. Strangely enough, the effect of telling her helped clear my mind. "It's a bit like I'm dreaming, though I'm awake and anyway, it's more real than a dream."

She turned back briefly to look toward the window. "And these soldiers, do they talk to you?"

"No," I said, then added slowly, "but the boys do."

"The boys?"

"Jothan and Gardiner." There was a sharp breath from Marie. I began to feel blurry again. "In their room. At night. I hear them talking in their room. Sometimes, I just listen. Sometimes I go over and join them. Oh, Marie, Jothan misses you so much. He is so proud that you are now a woman of business. That perhaps soon you'll even be a lawyer yourself."

By this time, all the blood had drained from Marie's face. She opened her mouth but no words came out. I continued. "There's something else too, Marie. Sometimes, I—I disappear."

"Disappear?" The word was barely a whisper.

I nodded. "Like at the dance. We were inside and then we were outside. I don't remember that at all. The other week, too, when I went to Kewanee to find Adam, I don't remember coming home. Here, sometimes I go to sleep in my bed, but wake up somewhere else. In the boys' room, or down at the river...just...other places."

In the next minute, Marie was holding me fiercely. I buried my head in her shoulder and felt deeply of her and breathed her smell into me and, for the first time, I knew full well that I was soon going to be somewhere else. Even if I didn't remember anything, even if I never came back, I knew I'd be all right if Marie stayed with me, and I believed with all my heart that she would. She was speaking to me, my name and other words, but the sounds kept getting farther and farther away. Then there was nothing.

*

Mama was staring at me. "You have to eat, Eliza Jane."

I looked around. "What?"

My mother poured more coffee into our cups. "Eat your breakfast, my girl. It's getting cold."

"Where's Marie?"

"Marie?" Mama stood up. "I expect she's at home."

"But—but we were just—I mean…"

My mother went to the stove and took another biscuit from the warming bowl. She returned and put it on my plate. "You were what?"

I picked up the biscuit and studied it. "Oh, nothing."

"Eat up, Jennie. We have much to do today. Amos and your father are out fetching Ruby and Abigail who escaped again last night. I thought you might help me in the spring house." I nodded absently. It seemed silly to bother organizing our supplies for the winter when the Confederate Army would just steal everything anyway. Mama put her hands on her hips. "Well? Aren't you going to eat anything?"

"I'm not hungry."

"And you ate nothing last night either."

"I'm rationing myself."

"You're going to make yourself sick."

"I'm fine, Mama."

"You are not fine, Eliza Jane." Mama sat down again. "Your father and I are worried. So is Marie. She wants you to go see her."

"I can't see Marie anymore," I whimpered. "She doesn't love me."

"What? Of course she loves you."

"No, she doesn't."

Mama sighed. "Oh, Jennie, what can I do for you?"

"It's no good, Mama, I'm done. I've tried and it's come to nothing and now I'm done. I'm sorry."

Tears filled my mother's eyes. Then she walked behind me and began stroking my hair, now down below my shoulder. "Listen, Jen, next week is the Thanksgiving holiday. You know the Parkers are coming here. Amos too. We have a nice meal planned. I know this is a hard time, but let us try to be grateful for what we still have. Please, Jen. Can we do that?"

After a moment, I nodded. "Yes, Mama, we can do that."

*

After a few days, I began to feel, once more, myself again. The day before the holiday, I helped Papa butcher one of our hogs; later that afternoon, Amos and I dug up potatoes and collected wild onions. We also harvested bunches of late-flowering blue salvia and goldenrod for the supper table. Mama seemed pleased and the smells of baking pies and cakes filled our home. On Thanksgiving morning, the sun appeared bright in a clear sky, covering the snowy landscape in a golden glow. All the animals frisked about in the cold air. Ruby and Abigail romped in the far field with a doe and last spring's fawn. Sam traded off barking at them and a rabbit he'd cornered in the woodpile.

The day was beautiful, full of promise, and the supper would be pleasant. I would be glad to see Marie, and we could start over. I had no idea how our conversation had ended the other week, but if she still wanted to see me, it must not have been too bad. I helped Mama that morning baking bread and boiling a pudding, then went up to my room to change. I sat on my bed, admiring the dresses Carmen had bought me. Suddenly, I missed my friends and Chicago very much. A letter had arrived from Owl a few weeks before and now that I was well again, I knew I must write back to him. This thought made me happy, but as I began taking off my blouse I heard the voices.

I immediately knelt down by the knot in the wall. I'd never heard my brothers during the day, but there they were, Jothan reading, Gardiner drawing. This time, however, they weren't alone. Several others either sat or stood in the room. Someone seemed to be telling a joke; another asked if anyone wanted to play bluff. Camping gear had been strewn around, on shelves and tables, covering every inch of floor. As I watched and listened, another sound grew louder in the distance. Drums. The long roll. Fast as a shot, I ran into the hall and opened the door to my brothers' room.

It was empty.

The beds looked tidy, the night tables empty. Only a single blue coat hung on a nail right above where the knot in the wall was. Someone shouted downstairs: Mama shooing Sam out of the house. Carefully, I stepped into the room.

Everything around me disintegrated. The floors, the walls, the beds, all of it turned into a blackened, dusty landscape. The stuff of soldiers lay everywhere: torn papers, books and letters, broken watches, fragments of clothing, twisted cups and pans. In the middle of it all burned a small, fading fire. Around the fire huddled not only my brothers, but also my friends: Biddle, Bean, Christmas. I could not believe my good fortunate in having found everyone together. I waved happily. Then I said hello.

At the sound of my voice, everything vanished and I stood once again in my brothers' empty room. Suddenly, the floor tilted wildly. The room spun in sickening circles. A lone drum played. I turned and staggered down the stairs and out of the house.

Sometime later, I awoke. My face felt hot and leathery, my body cold. A hand was gripping my shoulder lifting me up. I struggled. I could hear the water and knew I was at the Spoon River. I also knew that the Southern soldiers had found me. One of them spoke.

"Jennie! Jennie! Wake up!"

I opened my eyes. Amos leaned over me, his face wrinkled with worry. "C'mon, Jen! Your folks are wondering where you've been, and the Parkers are soon to arrive!"

I threw my arms across my face. "I can't do it, Adam. I mean, Amos. They'll be back any minute. We've got to go!" I tried to sit up.

"What? Who'll be back?"

"Them! The Secesh! You know how they are! They're out there waiting." I started to cry. "Just waiting."

At first, Amos didn't say anything. Then he said, quietly, "It's all right, Jen, they're gone. You don't have to worry."

I grabbed him by the collar and pulled him close to me. "You saw them then?"

"Sure, I saw them. But they're gone now." I lay back again, relieved. Amos was a good man. It was good he was around for he loved my parents and when I was gone, he would take care of them. "Let's go back to the house, Jen."

I shook my head. "I can't, Amos. I'm disappearing again. I won't be here much longer." Amos' expression again grew so worried that I wondered if he'd spoken too soon about the Confederates being gone. "Maybe they're not gone..." I began.

"They're gone," he said, firmly, then, "Let's get you sitting up so you can see."

Amos helped prop me up against a rock and then sat down next to me. I realized we were on the ledge above the river and for a full ten minutes I scanned the far shore, but Amos was right, they were gone. I leaned into him, relaxing. He wrapped his coat and arm around me. It was starting to snow lightly. A few hearty birds scuffled in the bushes nearby. Slowly, the world started fitting back together again. There was nothing around me that looked like a battlefield; there were no dead people pretending to be alive. I began to cry. Amos handed me a handkerchief.

"I'm sorry, Amos," I said, blowing my nose after a few minutes. "I don't feel much like myself these days."

"You don't have to be sorry, Jen. The war messed us all up. It was months before I stopped dreaming about it."

"Sometimes I don't know what's a dream and what's real."

He nodded. "Listen, Jen, you're a good person. You're just going through a bad spell is all. Happened to me too, and I seen it happen to a bunch of others also. But I got through it and you will too. C'mon now. Your mama's made a big supper and she'll be cross if we're late." Amos stood and helped me up.

We walked up the trail away from Jug Run Creek and back toward the house. Just at the rise where the trail emerged onto the area by the springhouse, I stopped. The Parkers had already arrived. The Tilbury was parked outside the house, and Papa and Mr. Parker had unhitched Bessie and were leading the mare to the barn. They were talking gaily and looking in the other direction so they didn't see Amos and me. My glance then went to the house. It was already growing darker on this fall day and the windows glowed from the lamps inside. I could see Marie and Mama and Mrs. Parker moving back and forth by the windows, carrying plates heaped with food and other pans and trays.

Amos started walking again, but I hesitated. When he stopped and looked back at me, I resumed, but in that brief pause I had made a decision. In Owl's recent letter, he had invited me back to Chicago. I knew in this moment that I would go, that I *must* go. I understood now why Adam had left Toulon and why Amos had left his home as well. Chicago had Owl and Carmen and magic and the possibility for me to be yet another person. Who that woman would be wasn't at all clear, but the thought of finding her brought me a comfort I had not felt in a very long time.

PART SIX

ONE

September 10, 1866, Chicago, Illinois

CARMEN AND TEMPLE clapped loudly. "Bravo, Jennie! Bravo!" The noise made Oscar the rabbit kick at the air. Pulling the little animal closer to my chest, I felt him immediately begin nuzzling under my chin. "That was perfect, Jen!" Carmen added.

"Opening the bag took longer than it should have," I said, dissatisfied.

Carmen shook her head. "Not from the audience's perspective. In one moment, you are reaching into what all believe to be an box. In the next, you are holding a rabbit in your hand."

"And the bag is not apparent to those sitting at the outer edges of the house?"

"No. Your hands are well-placed. No one can see into the box."

I set Oscar on the table. He sniffed and looked around, then stood for his obligatory bow. We all laughed and Temple said, "That boy has no shame!"

"It's so simple," I said, placing the box on the floor and watching Oscar hop around.

Carmen smiled. "They all are once you know how they're done."

The rabbit-in-the-box trick Owl had performed so many years ago was an excellent illusion for me to practice. It required few props, needing only a table, a box, a bag, and a rabbit, but the conjure also required dexterity so that it provided some challenge. A small bag attached to the lid of the box held Oscar behind the table. The box on the table is then demonstrated to be empty. The lid is subsequently lifted and placed in front of the box, while Oscar, inside the bag, has descended into the box. The lid can then be shown to be unconnected to anything, such as a bag containing a rabbit. At this point, the magician may provide some patter, or ask the audience a question, anything that will prolong people's interest and raise their anticipation. Finally, after lifting the lid and reaching inside the box, the magical rabbit is produced.

Temple returned to the kitchen to fetch the raspberry scones she had made along with a pot of tea. The late-summer afternoon had grown warm, but was mercifully cooler from the previous months of summer. I ate a scone while Carmen asked me about my most recent letter from Marie.

"She says she will come in October."

"For opening night?"

I nodded. "There is a trial in Galesburg the week before, but then her work should be less."

"I am glad, Jennie. It will be good to see her."

"Yes," I agreed, feeling the familiar longing for my friend. "It will."

Carmen sipped her tea. After a moment, she lit one of her thin cigarettes then asked if I had given any more thought to Owl's recent proposal to include me in their show. The week before he had requested my participation, even suggesting I do some conjures of my own. I had thought the idea absurd for several reasons and had said so right then. When I didn't answer right away now, Carmen added, "You are better now, Jennie."

I thought. "I still see them though."

"Not as often."

"That's true, but it's unpredictable. What if something were to happen onstage?"

Carmen shrugged. "If something happens, then something happens. It is no more or less than that. Yet, I do not believe that will occur, and neither does Owl. In any case, you shall not do anything you do not want to do. It is only an offer."

"And a generous one," I said, taking a second scone. "You both are too good to me, Carmen."

She laughed. "You are loved, dear girl!" Then she nodded at the scone. "Temple will be glad to see you eating a second."

"Yes, but I am getting fat."

"Fat like a sparrow in winter is fat."

Suddenly, I noticed the clock on the wall. "Uh-oh, I'm supposed to meet Katie at three at the Sherman House!" It was now a quarter to three.

Carmen chuckled and stood up. "Then you had better start running."

*

I had been in Chicago for nearly nine months. Shortly after the new year and after I'd woken up one morning along the Spoon River nearly frozen to death and with no memory of getting there, I told my family of my desire to return to the big city. Mama and Papa agreed a change of scene would be good for me and the following week Marie accompanied me east on the cars. My friend remained with me for a month before returning to Toulon. From that February day on, Temple had assumed the responsibility for "bringing me back to myself" as she put it. The cook said she'd seen this condition before and knew what to do. She brewed special teas and made special foods and instructed that I rest and be subjected to no concerns whatsoever. Eating during these weeks felt like a task for which I had no interest. However, after a period of time had passed where Temple had allowed me to only minimally participate in meals, she began requiring I do more to nourish myself. It seemed to help. I started to regain my strength, and the visions of soldiers arrived less frequently.

As the summer began, I saw my friend Kit for the first time

since that horrible night in Franklin a year and a half before. It had been sometime shortly after my arrival that I had told Carmen about Kit, that he and I were the only ones left from our mess, and that I assumed he must have returned to Chicago. She immediately said I must get in touch with him.

"He doesn't know who I really am, Carmen," I said, shaking my head. "It would be too hard. Maybe for both of us, but certainly for him."

Carmen looked thoughtful. "I think you must write him, Jennie. As you said, you are the only two that remain. My guess is that he will be needing you."

"And when he learns that I am a woman?" I asked. "No, I cannot imagine such a meeting going very well."

"You may be surprised, my dear."

I felt most decided I should not see Kit. Then I experienced a tremendous vision one morning where I watched an entire regiment marching down Clark Street before forming a battle line just below Carmen and Owl's home on Michigan Avenue. It had taken more than an hour for the street to clear in my mind and refill with the residents of Chicago. After that, I sat down and wrote the letter to Kit. As I had no idea where he was exactly, I sent it care of the Board of Trade. Within a month, a surprising reply came:

Dear Taylor,

My friend. Your letter was a miracle to my eyes. I broke down and cried upon receiving it, much to the alarm of my mother. You see, I believed fully that the world had emptied of all those I loved best and these many months I have felt so alone. But now you are returned, and living in Chicago! Well, I cannot believe my good fortune.

As to your other news, yes, I am surprised, but perhaps not as much as you may think. We all thought there was something a bit different about you, but no one cared too much and certainly not me! You were always a good friend to me, no matter what mistakes I made, and I always felt glad for your friendship. Besides, after living through the war, something I never expected to come to pass at all, nothing surprises me anymore. After reading your letter, I also remembered an article I'd read in the Vicksburg newspaper about a girl soldier who'd been discovered and drummed out of the army immediately. Seems you were a lot smarter than her. At all rates, you're still just Taylor to me.

He had signed his letter "Kendall" and added "(my real name)."

Kit hoped we could meet up someday and after some weeks we decided to do so at Camp Douglas. Though prepared for an awkwardness to now exist between us, I was pleased to find the exact opposite. Three hours passed quickly during which time we shared how the war had ended for both of us, me recuperating in Franklin and Kit continuing on with the regiment all the way south to the salt waters of Mobile Bay, Alabama. Since that first meeting, I'd seen Kit several more times.

I'd also gotten in touch with Katherine Biddle, meeting up with her a few times for tea when her busy schedule permitted it. At first, it felt difficult to be with her. The resemblance to Biddle was so strong, and her mannerisms and voice so jarringly similar to her brother's. But eventually, Katie felt more like her own person to me, with drive and ambition, as well as a confidence in her own abilities, that seemed markedly different from what I remembered of my friend.

In the first year after the war's end, Katie had increased her devotion to the cause of women's suffrage. Along with her mother, she now wrote articles for Pastor and Mrs. Livermore's *New Covenant* newspaper, speaking out on such topics as the importance of education for girls and women, managing family and work, and the true capabilities of the fairer sex. She covered the entire city by foot and horsecar, posting fliers of upcoming meetings, speaking with businesses about hiring women, and giving lectures on the need for suffrage and independence. Just hearing about everything she did made me tired. Yet, one could not help be impressed. Still, Katie had waved away my praise.

"The cause is all to me," she had said one afternoon in the spring, "yet I also work so hard merely to keep busy. Otherwise, elings I do not wish to feel will find me."

To my surprise, I arrived first at the hotel. I hadn't bothered h fresh clothes, throwing on only a tie and a jacket and running omb through my hair before donning my bowler. The waiter sat me at a table next to the fountain, a refreshingly cool location. As I waited for Katie, I considered that more than a year had passed since my return from the war. The months had gone by with the speed of a locomotive, even as they'd also dragged interminably. How, I wondered, was it possible time could unfold slowly and quickly at the same time?

"I declare, Jennie Edwards!" Katie Biddle smiled, hands on her hips, and suddenly standing before me. "I never know when meeting you whether I'll find a man or a woman!"

I stood up, kissed Katie's hand, then pulled out a chair for her. "I often don't know myself."

She sat down. "That must be nice."

After the waiter took our order for a pot of green tea and two servings of almond cake with raisins, I nodded. "It has its advantages. As well as disadvantages. Like anything, I suppose."

Katie agreed, then asked, "Have you heard from Marie?"

One thing I'd quickly learned about Katherine Biddle was her total disinterest in small conversation. She did not care to discuss the weather, the price of any type of goods, the social activities of the wealthy and well-known (unless they were important to the movement), or anything to do with fashion. She *was* interested in people and ideas, relationships, and the social-political world. Biddle had once told me that his sister was the smartest person he knew; she read voraciously, asked endless questions, and never forgot a fact or a face. At the time, I'd considered his praise to be simply brotherly devotion; now I knew it all to be quite true.

"Yes," I nodded. "I received a letter just a few days ago."

"And?"

"She and Jen-Jen are well, as are my parents. Marie continues working for her father. She is busy but she sounds happy."

The waiter returned with our tea and cake. He poured two cups quickly, then vanished.

"And how is your apprenticeship coming?" Katie asked, taking a bite of cake.

"Well. It is good to have something to do. If I am thinking about magic, I am not thinking about other things." I paused. "Now, Owl wants me to join them onstage. To do a few conjures of my own, it seems."

"I know."

"You do?"

"Yes. I saw Owl and Carmen recently at Mrs. Allenton's home. She was hosting a fundraiser for the Soldier's Homes, and Mother and I both attended. Owl says you are better than you think and that he would like to see you perform."

"I'm not ready for that."

"You will be though." Katie placed her hand on mine. "You are good, Jennie."

"Thank you. We shall see." I changed the subject. "And what of you? How are your parents?"

As we ate our cake, Katie described her father's business thriving in the post-war economy, and the steady supply of orders which gave him little time to brood over his only son's death. Mrs. Biddle found refuge in her suffrage and sanitary work, pouring the care she had been saving for one boy onto the hundreds of young men who had returned. There were also Katie's cousins, two orphaned boys who had been living with them for some years.

"And you, my friend?" I asked, after she'd supplied so much information about everything but herself.

She shrugged. "I am my mother and father's daughter."

"Meaning?"

Katie put down her fork. "Jennie, I want to talk to you about something. I've been to see Kit."

"Oh?" Sometime around the Independence Day holiday, I had taken Kit to meet the Biddles. We were both, he and I, the family's last connection to their son and brother, and it seemed they should all know Kit as well as me. He was nervous, but in fact, the meeting was easier than the first one I'd had with our friend's parents. Although Mr. and Mrs. Biddle had welcomed me into their family, the manner in which I changed dress and personas made them noticeably uncomfortable. Kit, by contrast, was simply himself: a young man, who wasn't going to suddenly arrive in a dress or reveal a previous life held together by secrets and half-truths. "How is he?" I asked.

"He is well. He's obtained the job of typesetter at the *Tribune* and is very happy about it. There's much to learn and it keeps him busy.

"The thing is, Jennie," she continued, "I was telling Kit about a new organization that has recently formed. It's called the "Grand Army of the Republic." Have you heard of it?" I shook my head. "It began here in Illinois just this past spring and membership is open to all returning soldiers. Any person who served with honor in the late war shall be admitted. Its mission is to provide assistance and friendship to all veterans." Katie finished her cake and pushed the plate aside. "You must join this organization, Jennie."

"Me? Why?"

"What do you mean, "Why?" Are you not a veteran?"

I looked around, hoping the people at the nearby tables couldn't hear our conversation. "I don't know, Katie. Surely such an organization is reserved for men. What I did might not apply."

"What you did most certainly does apply! You gave everything you had to this country. You joined, without any help from anyone, I might add, then you fought and very nearly died in service to the Union. Just like every other man wearing a uniform."

I ate my last bite of cake. What Katie said was true, but what she didn't know was how much I wished it wasn't true. I had no desire to bring attention to my service, or to benefit from it, especially when so many others had not survived. Still, I knew Katherine Biddle well enough by now to know that once she became convinced of the worth of an idea, she would not drop it even if, as in this case, I might ask her to.

"Perhaps you're right," I said, weakly. "I will consider it."

"Good. You may not think I understand, Jennie, but I do. I, too, would like very much to forgot about this awful war that has stolen so much from all of us. But I feel just as strongly that it must *not* be forgotten. That those who have died must not be forgotten and that the people who didn't, especially women like you, must also *not* be forgotten.

*

After leaving Katie and the Sherman House, I walked west on Randolph Street to the river. From there, I zigzagged my way north toward Haddock Street where I could see Wolf Point across the water. This protrusion of land, around which the north branch of the Chicago River edged to meet the south branch, had been the birthplace of the city. It was here that the first white people had settled. It was here that they built three taverns and bridges and the very first hotel known as the Sauganash. In the early 1830s, there had been only twelve houses in the village, a fact hard to believe given that just thirty years later, many-storied buildings, railroads, and canals, as well as horse cars, telegraph systems, packed streets, and people stacked upon more people now made the city beat like an over-excited heart. Wolf Point at present housed a lumber yard and the depot for the Galena and Chicago Union Railroad. As I watched the rail cars coming and going and all the other traffic around the yard and nearby streets, it seemed surely true that the landscape would never again hear the howl of wolves.

Crossing over the river, I soon found myself at the *Chicago Tribune*. To my delight, I found Kit sitting on a bench outside the newspaper office, smoking a cigar and reading the paper. In recent weeks, my friend had grown a mustache and chin beard. These, along with the gray flecks that dotted the facial hair, made him appear older than his twenty years.

"Taylor!" he stood upon hearing me call his name. "What are you doing here?"

"Looking for you of course!"

He frowned. "Me? Why?"

"Why not? I had tea with Katie and now I'm headed home. She

told me about your new job. Congratulations."

Kit held up his ink-stained hands and grinned happily. "Thanks! It's a good job and Mama is pleased." He motioned for me to sit down. "And you? Katie told *me* that you're going to be in Owl's show."

"I haven't decided that."

He thought. "Katie has though and that's practically the same thing."

"True."

Kit looked at me. "Still, you must, I think. Carmen has come to the newspaper recently to pay for advertisements for the show. She says you're very good."

I shrugged. "The work keeps my mind occupied."

He nodded. "Yes. That's a good thing."

"Tell me about your job," I said, changing the subject.

For the next half-hour, I heard all about typesetting machines, newspaper deadlines, and the stories behind the stories. Kit's boss was great, the pay was great, and he'd even met a girl he liked, the sister of a co-worker who brought her brother lunch every day.

"Can't imagine she'd see anything in a lump like me," he said. "But it's nice to think about all the same. And Davey says that Mattie never used to bring him lunch. I've been thinking of calling on them at home, but haven't had the nerve to do it yet."

I punched him. "Well, you best get on it, my friend. You're only getting older and uglier!"

Kit shoved me. "That's true!"

I stood up. "Well, I best get going."

"Yeah, me too. Mr. Penny gives me one hour for lunch." He suddenly looked somber. "I don't want to be late or do anything to mess this up."

"Mess what up?"

"I don't know...this job...whatever." He put his hands in his pockets. "The truth is, Taylor, sometimes I feel so afraid. At night mostly, but sometimes during the day too. I don't even know what I'm afraid of half the time." Kit paused. "My heart starts racing, sweat rolls down my back, sometimes my vision goes blurry." He'd gone pale just thinking of these things.

"I know," I said, after a moment. "Same thing happens to me."

"It does?" I nodded, wondering if I should tell Kit about the soldiers and other strange things I saw. But then I decided I against it. The fewer people who knew about them, the better.

"Sometimes, I'll be walking home after work," he continued, "and I'll suddenly think that maybe my house won't be there when I get home. Maybe it will have burned down, or been blown away in a windstorm. Or maybe I just won't remember where it is. And what if my house *is* there, but Mama isn't? What if she's been killed or captured? It could happen, couldn't it? Terrible things happen, don't they, Taylor? Both of us know that." Kit's eyes had gone wild and his lower lip trembled.

"Listen, Kit," I said, firmly. "It's true that anything *can* happen, but none of what you just mentioned is *going* to happen. Your home will not burn or vanish mysteriously, and your mother cares about you very much and she will not leave you. I'm here as well. If you get worried when you start heading home, just come get me at Owl's. It's not that far and I'm always there. We can walk back to your place together, all right?" He nodded, tears in his eyes. I hugged him. "It will be all right, my friend."

Kit held onto me. "Goddammit, Taylor, I'm glad you're here."

TWO

SEVERAL NIGHTS LATER, with Owl and Carmen out for the evening, I sat reading letters. Three had come that day, one each from Marie, Sarah, and Liza. Though I had received a few letters from Sarah and Liza since my return, their communications were still few and far between. Though neither woman complained, the strain of regular life permeated the pages. Liza seemed the most optimistic. Business remained good for her, though not as good as during the occupation. Still, she was luckier than many. "What I sell," she wrote, "will always be in demand."

Sarah shared that her one remaining brother had at last returned home and also that a portion of the Federal troops still remained in Franklin. By contrast, most of her family's servants had left, leaving Ravenswood without workers. "Those who should not be here have stayed," she finished, "and those who should have stayed are now gone." Sarah also wondered if I still did magic tricks. She had been practicing the one I had shown her with the cup and bandana and upon showing it to her sisters they had been most impressed.

Marie wrote of her work, daughter, and our parents. All seemed well; Papa was planning to order another new device for the farm, something called a portable steam thresher, and Mama kept busy with various groups in Toulon and spending time with her granddaughter. Amos, for his part, seemed to be seeing one of the young ladies in town, while nobody had heard much from Adam, though Mary Ward indicated her son was doing well. Marie finished the letter with,

You are never far from my thoughts, Jennie. I so look forward to our meeting in just a few weeks.

I folded up the letter and returned it to its envelope. Yes, I thought, so do I.

*

When Owl and Carmen returned later that night, Owl went straight to his study without a word.

"What's with him?" I asked as Temple went to the kitchen to put on water for tea.

"Owl has been distracted most of the evening," Carmen smiled. "But it's good. He is near to finishing work on his new conjure."

I nodded. Both Owl and Carmen had been working on this for months. The mysterious conjure that had been born in France in the 1840s and rarely performed since was to be the great attraction for opening night in just a few weeks. Owl had refused to say anything about it.

Temple returned with the tea. "Should I take one to Mister?" she asked.

"No," Carmen shook her head. "It would only grow cold. Sit and have some tea yourself, Temple. It is nearly ten. You can surely stop working now."

The old woman snorted. "I been sitting too much already. Just doing my stitching while Jennie reads the newspaper." Temple did sit, however, and poured tea for all of us.

"I see." Carmen looked at me. "That explains the sour look."

"What sour look?"

"The one you were wearing when we arrived." She lit a

cigarette. "What is it?"

I looked out the window. "Nothing."

"Jennie." I handed her the *Chicago Tribune* and pointed to the middle of the front page. Carmen took the paper. "The Port Huron and Chicago Railroad—"

"No, the article just below that."

She read. "Woman's Rights—A Woman with a Wife." Carmen looked up and I nodded. The article had come from the *New Bedford Mercury*, a newspaper in Massachusettes. My friend settled back in her chair and began to read out loud.

"About a year ago a daughter of Major Daniel Perry, who is somewhat deranged, disappeared, and, wandering off, was at last lodged in the Sullivan County, New York, alms house as a vagrant. Here she met another monomaniac, by the name of Lucy Slater, and the two becoming very much attached to each other, decided to become man and wife. They left the alms house last summer, and returned to Abington, where they have lived in the bonds of wedlock, as supposed by the neighbors—Lucy, *alias* James Slater, wearing male attire up to the present time."

Carmen looked at me, then set the newspaper on the table. "You're not bothered by this, are you?"

I shrugged, then noticed a funny smell in the room. "Is something burning?"

Temple looked alarmed, but Carmen shook her head. "It is only Owl and the conjure."

"It's nothing really," I said, returning to Carmen's question. "I have only been thinking that before the war I was the most ordinary of girls. Now I am anything but."

Carmen smiled. "I have known you for many years, Jennie. You've never been ordinary, not even as a young girl."

"Perhaps not. Yet, it mattered less then."

"And it does now?"

"I don't know. Maybe. The world expects one thing of me; I believe I am giving it quite another. For myself, I am not so concerned, but for others, my friends, it may not be so simple."

At that moment, Owl swooped into the room. "It is done!" he shouted. "The conjure has finally worked and we will be ready for opening night! I may now enjoy my first fitful sleep in weeks!" He skipped over to the sideboard and poured us all brandys. After distributing them around, he lifted his glass high into the air. "To the future!"

"To the future!" we echoed.

Just as I was about to press Owl about the conjure, he sat down and asked, "Have you given any more thought to my suggestion?"

"No."

He took a sip. "You are more than ready, Jen. You are graceful and confident and you know many conjures. You can also patter better than almost anyone I know."

"I've had a lot of experience making things up." I changed the subject. "Tell me about your new conjure."

Owl ignored this. "Then can you think of one reason not to join us onstage?"

"Actually, I can think of several."

"You're being modest."

I laughed. "No one's accused me of that before!"

Owl set his drink down and leaned forward. "Jennie, I am quite serious. This shall be our best show ever and we want you to be part of it. You can choose what you want to do, and we can put you on right before the intermission. That way, your work will linger with the audience before the second part. I know you will impress them!"

"You flatter me, Owl. I'm not as good as you believe."

"You're better, my dear."

"Truthfully, I've never heard of any magician wanting to share his stage."

"Would you feel better if I told you my reasons were perfectly selfish?"

"Probably, though I'm not sure I'd believe you."

"You are talented, my dear, and you are unlike anyone else. It would not hurt my reputation to be the person who presents you to the world. I love magic before I love anything else. I know you do too. Why shouldn't we work together?"

They all looked at me. After a moment, I said, "All right, yes, a part of me would like to do it. Yet, another part is terrified. What if something goes wrong? What if the visions return?"

Owl shook his head. "There will always be uncertainty. That is part of the allure! Yet, I would never ask this of you if I didn't think you could do it."

"Who would I be up there?"

"You would simply be you."

"But—"

"A man or a woman, it doesn't matter. You know it's not the real world, and the clothes are unimportant. The people will think only about the magic you perform. That is one thing you can be certain of."

Temple and Carmen had remained quiet through all this, but now they were nodding their heads encouragingly. It still did not seem like a wholly good idea to me, but I *was* curious. I had certainly done more improbable things in my life. Too, I loved my friends. They had done so much for me and this seemed terribly important to them.

"Fine," I said, throwing up my arms in surrender. "You've worn me down. I'll do it!"

*

Now that I'd committed to Owl, my days filled with planning and practice. I pondered all the conjures I knew, then imagined doing them in front of an audience. Some seemed better suited for the stage, yet this didn't make my decisions easier for I loved them all.

One evening, I asked Temple what conjures she liked best. She sat down in the chair opposite me and thought.

"I think the ones where there's someone else in them."

"Someone else?"

"Um. Someone from the audience. Don't matter who Mister or Carmen pick out, no one ever refuses, and ooh, how some of 'em love getting up there! One time, Mister did that conjure with the heavy and light box. You know the one, where a child comes up and lifts up a box sitting on the floor? Then a man goes up and can't lift it at all?" I nodded. "This big man, and I do mean, BIG, went up and he couldn't move that box for nothing. Got all beet red in the face, but he still went back to his seat smiling."

"People love Owl, even when he makes a fool of them."

"They shall love you too, Miss Jennie."

"I don't know why I'm doing this."

"Maybe just to show you can."

*

At long last, the day of Marie's arrival came. Her train was due at 3:30, but at 2:30 I was still deciding what to wear. On the bed I'd spread out one of the dresses Carmen had bought me, as well as my frock, white blouse, and trousers. When Carmen walked in, I asked her opinion.

"I think you should wear whatever is comfortable."

I sat down. "I'm nervous to see her, Carmen."

"You must tell her how you feel, my dear."

"I have told her. She doesn't feel the same."

Carmen wrinkled her nose. "I'm not sure I believe that. I've seen you two together. While that was awhile ago now, I doubt the affection has changed much."

"I think I better wear the dress."

"You must not worry, dear girl. All will be well."

*

The sun sinking in the western sky cast a golden light upon the disembarking passengers. The Chicago, Burlington, and Quincy line had been almost an hour late. According to a depot man, the delay had been caused by a herd of sheep crossing the tracks near the south branch of the Chicago River.

"Oh, Jennie!" Marie said, embracing me tightly. "I am so glad to see you!"

I felt dizzy to smell and touch her, and powerfully aware that the romantic desire for my friend had not ebbed in the months we spent apart. Words got jammed in my throat as I hugged her back.

At last I managed, "And I am so glad to see you, Marie."

Owl's driver sat waiting with the brougham on Michigan Avenue. Marie had brought only one small trunk and this was easily placed on the back of the conveyance. When Tucker opened the door for us, Marie hesitated.

"The evening is so lovely, Jen. Might we walk instead? The Sherman House is not so far."

I agreed, though Tucker looked uneasy. I assured him we would be fine and he could simply deliver Mrs. Edwards' trunk to the Sherman House and then return home. Though unhappy about this development, the man did as requested. After he'd pulled away, Marie linked her arm through mine and we started walking west on Lake Street.

All around us, the thoroughfare hummed. The city's residents, revitalized in the cool evening air, shouted and laughed and moved along like so many ants. Carriage wheels clattered, while the screeching sounds of children, dogs, and the occasional pig added to the mayhem. At the storefront for Scott, Keen, & Co. Clothing, we stopped and looked at the window display. Boasting shipments received directly from Paris, the business sold everything from ladies dresses and cloak trimmings to fans, corsets, fringes, and buttons.

"It is so good to be back in the city," said Marie. "I have been gone too long." She moved her gaze from the window display to me. "You look well, Jen. Much improved from the last time I saw you."

I nodded. "That wouldn't be hard considering. And you, Marie," I couldn't help kissing her, "look just beautiful."

She smiled and leaned into me. "Oh, I have missed you, dear."

That evening, during our supper of turtle soup and goose with turnips in the Sherman House dining room, Marie caught me up on news of home. A few new families had moved to town; Papa was trying to convince others to go in with him on the purchase of the portable threshing machine; many continued to push for a railway line to the village; and the selling of flesh pots from Egypt so far seemed to be a success. Also, the Toulon Literary Society had grown in membership, much to the delight of Mrs. McRae who continued on as president, and Mary and Ethan Ward were thinking of removing to Nebraska to be near their son.

Yet, the most surprising news of all was that Washington Trickle had shaved his beard.

"*What?*"

"It's true," Marie nodded, her eyes sparkling. "Kept his mustache though."

"Where will he keep his pencils and paper though?"

She laughed. "Behind his ear, of course, like everyone else!"

"But why did he do it?"

Marie shrugged. "Washington said Rosetta had told him he was just like an old dog, unable to learn any new tricks. This was not a new complaint, but for some reason this time her words really affected him. The very next day he went to the barber."

"And Rosetta?"

"Collapsed immediately. After regaining her wits, which took some time I was told, she said she hadn't seen her husband's face in thirty-five years."

I studied Marie for a moment to see if she was pulling my leg. When it was clear she wasn't, we both began to laugh. Then we couldn't stop. At some point, the waiter hurried over to see if we were quite well. We assured him we were and very soon he returned with our dessert, vanilla and orange ice cream topped with toasted almonds.

"How is Mama?" I asked.

"She is well. She misses you, of course, but she understands. Too, Julia believes you will return soon." Marie considered her ice cream.

"But?"

"It seems to me that Chicago suits you, Jennie. I have wondered if you *would* come home." Before I could answer, she added, "There are good reasons to stay of course."

I nodded. "Are you still enjoying your work?"

Marie's eyes lit up. "Oh, yes. Most days I am so busy, the hours fairly fly. Going here and there, reading studies, making notes, doing every sort of job for Father. I am pleased that he finds my efforts so useful. He told me recently that I am "utterly reliable." Isn't that nice?"

I laughed. "Yes, and true, certainly."

She smiled too and then grew serious. "You know, Jen, it has taken a long time, but I believe I am finally happy again. I even think Jothan would be happy knowing of my work and interest now in what always fascinated him." She shook her head. "Do you think that could be true?"

"I am certain of it."

"Sometimes I even dream about becoming a lawyer myself. It is impossible, of course, but I enjoy thinking about it."

I took my last bite of ice cream. "Nothing is impossible, Marie."

She looked thoughtful. "Do you really believe that?"

"You know I do."

After supper, we had coffee in the ladies parlor, then stood on the balcony overlooking the hotel's entrance on Clark Street. A lamplighter made his way down Clark, each of his charges suddenly aglow like new moons. Despite the approaching darkness, there seemed to be more activity outside than there had been earlier. As we watched the comings and goings, I linked my arm through hers.

"We might do many things while you're here, Marie. Museums, opera, there's also a flower and musical festival at the First Baptist Church. Tell me what you'd like!"

She smiled. "I don't much care what we do, Jen. In fact, we could do nothing at all and I should be very satisfied."

THREE

THE NEXT DAY, after picking up a tuxedo I'd had made for the show, I met Marie and Katherine Biddle at the Sherman House for lunch. My two friends embraced as if they'd been chums all their lives. We ordered a substantial meal of lamb cutlets with baked potatoes and boiled turnips. Katie said she was starving, having been in the city all day, organizing the next suffragist meeting and gathering more sponsors for the *New Covenant*.

"But listen to me going on!" Katie said, interrupting her own narrative and looking pointedly at Marie. "Jennie has told me about your work, but I would very much like to hear more."

"Oh," Marie suddenly looked shy. "There's not so much to tell."

"I don't believe that! It is most important that women fully understand the legal system, and you are now one of those women. This is critical to our gaining equality and the vote. Please, tell me of your cases."

Marie smiled at me. I had told her of Katie's forthrightness and unabashed interest in anything she felt might help the cause. I had also surmised correctly that Marie's work would be an important topic of discussion today. "They are not my cases," she said, amused. "I merely assist my father."

Katie waved an arm. "Yes, but you are learning."

Marie thought. "Some things I cannot tell, but Father is involved in a situation right now very important for all women, I believe."

Marie explained Mr. Parker's present engagement to represent a woman who sought sole custody of her two children. The husband had accused his wife of madness and being unfit to mother the young boy and girl, and the woman claimed having suffered abuse of various forms from her husband. The man's accusations appeared to have no basis in truth, while hers had been more than amply documented by any number of neighbors and friends. Still, the law did not always support women in such circumstances, especially when the man in question was also a respected member of the community.

"While I'm here in Chicago," continued Marie, "I'll be doing research for Father. There have been other cases where the woman was favored with positive outcomes, and those are the ones we must study. The case is to come before the judge in early November."

Katie nodded. "Does your father defend many women?"

"His clientele is about two-thirds men and one-third women. It is often much harder for women to pay and so they are reluctant, or unable, to come to him. Of course, he will always work with someone regarding price, but the shame of having no means can be a great deterrent to seeking help in the first place."

Marie and Katie continued their discussion of the law and women, while I ate my food and happily thought of little beyond the fact that life seemed so much better these days. Marie was right; Chicago did suit me. I missed Mama and Papa, but at the moment I couldn't imagine going home. I hadn't dreamed of my brothers in months, and the last vision, the regiment marching down Clark Street, had occurred early in the summer. I felt more like myself, even as that self floated in outward appearance between being a man or a woman, a fact which did seem odd if I thought too much about it.

Suddenly, I noticed both Marie and Katie looking at me.

"What?" I asked, startled.

"I was just asking," Katie smiled, "if you agreed that Marie should remove to Chicago. She could accomplish more for her father living here, I should think."

"Of course, I agree. I would like nothing better."

"You are both kind," smiled Marie. "I do love the city. We shall see. Toulon is a more salubrious place for Jen-Jen, though I know she would find Chicago exciting."

"Perhaps you could live here part of the year then," suggested Katie. "Maybe the cooler part?"

Marie laughed. "I shall consider it!"

*

After saying good-bye to Katie, Marie and I walked to Lake Park. A breeze blowing off the water helped counter the late-summer heat. Near the station for the Baltimore and Ohio Railroad, we sat on a bench beneath an expansive magnolia tree. The steamboat *Sunset* eased by on Lake Michigan. Passengers lined the railings like rows of dolls. Their voices carried above the curling waves, eventually depositing words and parts of sentences in the air around us. We attempted to turn the wind-blown fragments, "The man is a—," "Who could believe—," and "If only—," into complete stories. By the time *Sunset* was north of the Chicago River, the voices could no longer be heard. After sitting quietly for a few minutes, I asked Marie what she'd done that morning.

She looked chagrined. "You will think me quite spoiled, Jen, but I slept until almost nine-thirty! Only a knock on the door—the maid coming to clean—finally roused me."

"Yes, but how often do you do that? It is quite acceptable when you're on holiday."

"Perhaps, but I am not totally on holiday. Thus, I attempted to make up for my idleness by going to the library and starting my work. I will return tomorrow as well." She looked at me. "I assume you'll be busy with Owl."

"Yes, that is true."

Marie took my hand. "I am so glad you are doing this, Jennie.

411

It's very brave and I'm very proud of you!"

I kissed her hand. "Thank you. I believe I am glad too. As well as terrified."

"That seems perfectly normal."

We began walking back on Lake Street. I confided to Marie that I felt the best I had in some months, due in no small part to her arrival, but also because of my improving health. Marie said she could see this and that nothing made her happier. Though I didn't share the continuation of my feelings for her, I realized that I could be satisfied with her friendship. The most important thing was that she remain in my life.

We turned onto State Street and looked at the window displays of various businesses. At a millinery shop, we marveled at the hats of many colors and designs, then moved on toward a bookstore and haberdashery. Beyond these businesses, an alley extended into the canyon of buildings and away from State. For some reason, I stopped and looked down the alley. A group of men were there working in a long ditch. Their heads stuck up like little balls, the sounds of shovels striking rock sending pinging echoes up and down the long space. Clods of dirt spattered into the air; a man at one end shouted something.

I suddenly felt unable to move. High on the building walls above the alley, the setting sun cast an amber light. The temperature had now dropped noticeably. I could see my breath. "Ready!" a man in the ditch yelled. Another, sitting on his haunches above, began sliding down into the pit.

The last thing I remembered was grabbing my musket and running. Just as I reached the works, my hat flew off my head. Cracks of gunfire filled the air. Darkness fell. The only light now came from the orange and yellow bursts of the machines of war.

*

"Jennie?"

The voice seemed very far away. At first, I ignored it. The voice was calling someone else; Robert Taylor, not Jennie, was my name. But the voice persisted, so at last I opened my eyes.

Marie sat in a chair in front of me. She wore her nightgown and her sleeping jacket and her hair was down. The oil lamp behind her gave off a buttery glow. My friend looked pale and her eyes were red. As pieces of memory slowly braided themselves back together in my mind—the alley, the men, the melting away of the present for the past—I knew I must have done something terrible for Marie to look so worried. Something I would not be able to remember no matter how hard I tried.

"What happened?" I asked, my throat dry. When she didn't say anything, but continued to stare at me with a look I'd never seen before, I said, "You must tell me, Marie!"

"Oh, Jennie!" Marie touched my face, then leaned down and rested her head in my lap.

"The last I knew I was..." What? The strange, nightmarish images, of running and darkness and the screams and crying of the men in the trench, did not lend themselves to easy description. I shook my head. "How long have I been away?"

Marie raised her head. "It's after two in the morning, Jen. You've been sitting in that chair for more than six hours. You haven't moved an inch, or spoken. You've only sat there, staring out the window. Finally—I don't know when—you lay your head back and went to sleep." She began to cry. "Truly, I didn't know if you would ever return."

I closed my eyes. "I'm so sorry, Marie."

"You jumped into the ditch with those men, Jennie," she continued. I nodded, not sure now that I wanted to hear what happened. "You pushed through the lot of them getting to the man who had slipped and fallen in. They all were so surprised that they immediately stopped working. You were shouting." She stopped.

"What? What was I shouting?"

Marie paused. "Biddle. You kept shouting for Biddle."

"And then?"

"And then," she paused, "there was a loud noise from the street. Something—a barrel, I think—fell off the back of a carriage and rolled into the alley toward the ditch. It was very loud, and strange. It rolling like that, not stopping. You looked up and at that moment, you fainted. Those men helped me bring you here. They were kind, Jennie, and they knew."

"Knew what?"

"That you'd been in the war. Several had been soldiers, and they said they'd seen this before. Some had had the same experiences. One man said that only recently has he been able to work in the ditch without breaking into a cold sweat."

Leaning my head back on the chair, I let silent tears roll down my face. Marie got up to get us some water. When she returned, she helped me up to the sofa where we could sit together.

"I will never be well, Marie," I said, at last.

"Don't say that, Jen. These things take time."

"I won't live long enough for the time it would take."

"Please, Jennie. You know how much I love you. I will help you. I'll always be here for you."

"I know, and I believe you mean that. But that doesn't change the truth."

"Please don't shut me out anymore, Jen. I have sat here for hours, hoping and praying that you would return to me, but being quite uncertain that you would. I have wept and I have thought. I don't know what is happening, to you or the many other boys I know who are so broken-hearted and lost. Oh, Jennie," she took my hands in hers, "I do love you, so very much. I don't want to live without you. I don't really know, how this can work, or even if it's right, but I do love you." She kissed my hands.

I looked at her. "What are you saying, Marie?"

"I'm still not as brave as you. Yet, I have thought about many things these last months. Life is short. I don't know the answers, Jennie. I just know what I know, even if that hasn't been easy for me to admit."

"I don't know the answers either, Marie. I just know how happy I feel when I'm with you."

Marie smiled for the first time since I'd woken up. She rubbed my hand. "I think you must rest now, my dear."

"Yes," I smiled too. "I am exhausted." I went to the sink and washed my face, while Marie went to the bed. I then got undressed and crawled in next to her. "Hold me, Marie."

She put her arms out and I curled around her body like a child. "I will hold you, Jen, and I will not let go."

*

Despite only a few hours of real sleep, I awoke later that morning refreshed and terribly in love. Marie could not be coaxed awake, though when I kissed her several times, she opened her eyes and smiled.

"You must go, Jen," she mumbled. "This is your big day."

"I love you, Marie."

"And I love you."

Gathering up my tuxedo, I went directly to McVicker's Theatre guessing, correctly, that Owl and Carmen would already be there. They immediately expressed concern. Marie had managed to send them a note that I was not feeling well and would be staying with her, but she hadn't elaborated. I said I was fine and would explain later, which, after some convincing, seemed to satisfy.

We worked on last minute details. Like so many times before, my experience returning to the past faded in the light of the present. Owl's show was sold out, and had been for more than a week. I spent an hour practicing my set, but I, too, couldn't have been more prepared. Though what had happened the previous night, in other circumstances, might have made me lose my nerve, this time I found myself thinking about it very little. Instead, I thought of Marie. I was the luckiest person in the world, it was now just that simple.

That evening, Marie appeared briefly backstage to wish me luck and to say that all our friends had arrived: the Biddle family, Mr. and Mrs. Allenton, Temple, Kit Johnson and Mrs. Johnson, and even Oliver Timmons, who I had not seen since that day on the street when I'd first dressed as a boy.

"Break a leg, Jen," she smiled, brushing at my coat. "You will be fabulous."

"You look stunning, Marie." The soft pink gown with high collar and billowing sleeves made her look like one of the rich women I sometimes observed in their grand carriages around Chicago.

She laughed. "I am glad you like it." Then she kissed me on the cheek and was gone.

From behind the curtain backstage, I peered out and watched the theatre go dark. Nothing happened for some seconds. Gaslights glowed along the walls of the theatre, but the stage remained dark and empty. The audience began to fidget. A few people coughed. Then a light appeared and settled right smack in the middle section of theatre goers. There sat Owl! Pretending to read the program, he seemed nothing more than one of his own fans. Even though I knew he was planning this, I still didn't know how he would manage, given his most recognizable person, to slip into the row without anyone noticing. But he had and the crowd loved it. A second light then shone down a few rows behind Owl. There sat Carmen, who pretended at nothing. She smiled beautifully at those around her and the entire theatre erupted in one loud cheer. The show had begun!

*

Owl had never been better. Carmen had never been better. Together, they worked as one, each so attuned to the other that I could imagine them as simply one being. Anything that touched their hands was very likely to disappear. Anything that disappeared was sure to turn up somewhere surprising. They joked with each other; they joked with the audience. All manner of colors and shapes filled the stage, while the animals, Constance and Oscar, brought their own charm to the show. Carmen and Owl had worked so very hard these last months, the effect of which was that the show now seemed like no work at all.

Right before Owl was to present me, my confidence faltered. Surely the audience would not want to see the antics of some amateur magician after the extraordinary show they'd watched so far. Yet, I was wrong. People were so devoted to my friends that anything they asked of them would be accepted with complete confidence. Owl introduced me as only his "esteemed colleague." We had discussed for some days what sort of name I should take for the stage, but I had been oddly uninspired on the topic. Owl said not to worry, something would come to me for the next engagement, and perhaps for this first time I should remain nameless to enhance the mystery. The applause that greeted me sent the nervousness in my stomach away and my voice didn't falter or shake as I began my own relationship with those who loved magic as much as we did.

The conjures I did were simple, but fun. Pulling a long, colored scarf from my mouth, placing several eggs into my hat and making them disappear, and causing my wand to vanish beneath a crumpled newspaper (then finding it again in my coat pocket), all proved popular. Too soon arrived the time for the conjure we had planned together, by far the most ambitious one I had ever attempted.

Owl explained that the final presentation before intermission would be a feat of escapism. "First though," he boomed, "we must have two strong volunteers."

I went out into the audience. One eager young man in the center section raised his hand and looked hopeful as I approached. I nodded at him and he climbed bulkily over four people to get to the aisle. The second volunteer was an older, but solidly built, gentleman, who also seemed delighted at the prospect of participating.

Owl's two assistants had wheeled onto the stage four, six-foot panels, each draped with a black curtain. Three were arranged like the walls of a small room, while the fourth sat off to the side for the moment. Inside the room was a chair and one small table where a hat, a black piece of fabric and two stuffed animals sat. Three piles of rope lay next to the table. While I took off my coat, donned the black hat, and sat down in the chair, Owl addressed the volunteers.

"Gentlemen, if you would please help me to restrain my

esteemed colleague, I would be most appreciative." He directed the younger man to tie my right leg to the chair, while the other man worked on my left. With the third piece of rope, the younger tied my hands together in front of me. Finally, the older gentleman, under Owl's instruction, removed my hat, placed the black fabric over my head, secured it behind my head with a knot, and lastly, replaced the hat. A final check was made of all the ropes. Then the three men stepped out of the room. Owl slid the final panel into the opening, closing me off from view.

After just a few seconds, the audience watched the hat sail out onto the stage! Then came the stuffed rabbit! Then the stuffed plump, green duck! Owl wheeled back the panel. I remained tied up and blindfolded. The audience gasped. Owl moved a second chair into the room and asked the older man to sit in it. Owl blindfolded him. He asked the man to place one of his hands on my arm and the other on my forehead. Again, the panel was returned to hide us from view. When it was rolled away a few seconds later, my hat had moved onto the man's head and I was still tied up but once again wearing my coat.

As clapping and cheers shook the theatre, Owl untied me and removed the blindfold. He thanked our volunteers, who looked as if they had just awoken from a funny dream. We all took several bows.

*

After an intermission where I basked in the praise of my friends, I returned with Marie and the others to the audience. When the time arrived for the finale, Owl stood very seriously in front of the stage's black curtain. He spoke to us of how much we had to be grateful for. That we now as a country had enjoyed more than a year without war.

"As we mourn those lost," he continued, "we know that sometimes we must live without knowing; accept without understanding. My work for you is about making possible what seems impossible. To believe in magic is to have faith, ladies and gentlemen."

With that, Owl moved to the side of the stage. The curtain was raised. The stage was bare except for a small table where sat a scraggly tree in a pot. Next to the pot was what appeared to be a bottle of spirits. Owl then borrowed a purple handkerchief from an obliging lady in the front row. He rubbed the cloth between his hands into a smaller and smaller ball until it disappeared. Next, he poured a small amount of the spirits into a vial. Then he set the vial on fire. Placing the flame beneath the tiny leaves of the tree, Owl allowed the vapors to just reach the foliage. I leaned forward in my seat, uncertain what I was supposed to be seeing. But then I did see.

The tree was growing.

Owl moved the blue-orange flame beneath the plant. The leaves responded. They spread out, twisted around, grew up and out, and eventually, after many seconds, fell upon the table. In the blink of an eye, the leaves were replaced by bright, snow-white blossoms. Owl stepped back and waved his wand over the tree. The flowers now vanished. Round oranges appeared in their place. As people all around me gasped, the oranges grew larger and larger.

When at last the oranges stopped growing, Owl plucked one from the tree. He studied it. He seemed to be thinking hard about something. Then Owl walked down the steps into the audience and found our row. Reaching across Kit and Marie who sat closest to the aisle, he handed the fruit to me. It was a real orange.

Owl returned to the marvelous orange tree, plucked off more oranges, and handed them to others in the audience. People began peeling and eating the fruit. I turned to Marie, who looked pale but was smiling. I handed her the orange and we both started to cry. Back onstage, one last orange hung on the tree below the very top branch. Owl waved his wand and the orange split wide open. Inside lay the lady's purple handkerchief!

As if all this wasn't enough, the most extraordinary thing happened next. Two butterflies appeared out of nowhere and flitted through the air. The creatures took the corners of the purple cloth and spread the material out above the tree. Then the butterflies hovered for many seconds. Owl smiled and blew a kiss to the audience as the curtain fell in front of him.

ABOUT THE AUTHOR

BETSY L. HOWELL is a writer and wildlife biologist living on Washington State's Olympic Peninsula. In 1999, she began transcribing the journals of her great, great, grandfather, James Darsie Heath, who served with the 72nd Illinois Infantry from 1862–1865. After taking two trips to retrace this man's travels, she wrote *Acoustic Shadows*, a memoir about the generational effects of war, and also became interested in the women who disguised themselves as men in order to serve their country. Howell has also published articles on natural history and travel in *American Forests*, *Earth Island Journal*, *South Loop Review*, *Clackamas Literary Review*, *Apple Valley Review*, and *Women in Natural Resources*. She lives in Port Townsend, Washington.

Made in the USA
Middletown, DE
03 September 2018